WANDERINGS OVER THE WORLD

A CHESTERTON READER

Cluny Classics

Wanderings over the World

A CHESTERTON READER:

The Napoleon of Notting Hill
The Man Who Was Thursday
The Ballad of the White Horse

G. K. Chesterton

Cluny Classics

Cluny Media edition, 2019

This book is a reprint of the 1904 John Lane edition of *The Napoleon of Notting Hill*; the 1908 Dodd, Mead, and Company edition of *The Man Who Was Thursday*; and the 1911 Methuen & Co., Ltd., edition of *The Ballad of the White Horse*.

For more information regarding this title
or any other Cluny Media publication,
please write to info@clunymedia.com, or to
Cluny Media, P.O. Box 1664, Providence, RI, 02901

VISIT US ONLINE AT WWW.CLUNYMEDIA.COM

ISBN: 978-1949899962

Cover design by Clarke & Clarke
Cover image: John Atkinson Grimshaw,
Boar Lane, Leeds, by Lamplight,
1881, oil on canvas
Courtesy of Wikimedia Commons

Contents

THE NAPOLEON OF NOTTING HILL

To Hilaire Belloc

For every tiny town or place
God made the stars especially;
Babies look up with owlish face
And see them tangled in a tree:
You saw a moon from Sussex Downs,
A Sussex moon, untravelled still,
I saw a moon that was the town's,

The largest lamp on Campden Hill.
Yea; Heaven is everywhere at home
The big blue cap that always fits,
And so it is (be calm; they come
To goal at last, my wandering wits),
So is it with the heroic thing;
This shall not end for the world's end,
And though the sullen engines swing,
Be you not much afraid, my friend.

This did not end by Nelson's urn
Where an immortal England sits—
Nor where your tall young men in turn
Drank death like wine at Austerlitz.

And when the pedants bade us mark
What cold mechanic happenings
Must come; our souls said in the dark,
"Belike; but there are likelier things."

Likelier across these flats afar
These sulky levels smooth and free
The drums shall crash a waltz of war
And Death shall dance with Liberty;
Likelier the barricades shall blare
Slaughter below and smoke above,
And death and hate and hell declare
That men have found a thing to love.

Far from your sunny uplands set
I saw the dream; the streets I trod
The lit straight streets shot out and met
The starry streets that point to God.
This legend of an epic hour
A child I dreamed, and dream it still,
Under the great grey water-tower
That strikes the stars on Campden Hill.

G. K. C.

Book I

CHAPTER I

Introductory Remarks on the Art of Prophecy

The human race, to which so many of my readers belong, has been playing at children's games from the beginning, and will probably do it till the end, which is a nuisance for the few people who grow up. And one of the games to which it is most attached is called "Keep tomorrow dark," and which is also named (by the rustics in Shropshire, I have no doubt) "Cheat the Prophet." The players listen very carefully and respectfully to all that the clever men have to say about what is to happen in the next generation. The players then wait until all the clever men are dead, and bury them nicely. They then go and do something else. That is all. For a race of simple tastes, however, it is great fun.

For human beings, being children, have the childish wilfulness and the childish secrecy. And they never have from the beginning of the world done what the wise men have seen to be inevitable. They stoned the false prophets, it is said; but they could have stoned true prophets with a greater and juster enjoyment. Individually, men may present a more or less rational appearance, eating, sleeping, and scheming. But humanity as a whole is changeful, mystical, fickle, delightful. Men are men, but Man is a woman.

But in the beginning of the twentieth century the game of Cheat the Prophet was made far more difficult than it had ever been before. The reason was, that there were so many prophets and so many prophecies, that it was difficult to elude all their ingenuities. When a man did something free and frantic and entirely his own, a horrible thought struck him afterwards; it might have been predicted. Whenever a duke climbed a lamp-post, when a dean got drunk, he could not be really happy, he could not be certain that he was not fulfilling some prophecy. In the beginning of the twentieth century you could not see the ground for clever men. They were so common that a stupid man was quite exceptional, and when they found him, they followed him in crowds down the street and treasured him up and gave him some high post in the State. And all these clever men were at work giving accounts of what would happen in the next age, all quite clear, all quite keen-sighted and ruthless, and all quite different. And it seemed that the good old game of hoodwinking your ancestors could not really be managed this time, because the ancestors neglected meat and sleep and practical politics, so that they might meditate day and night on what their descendants would be likely to do.

But the way the prophets of the twentieth century went to work was this. They took something or other that was certainly going on in their time, and then said that it would go on more and more until something extraordinary happened. And very often they added that in some odd place that extraordinary thing had happened, and that it showed the signs of the times.

Thus, for instance, there were Mr. H. G. Wells and others, who thought that science would take charge of the future; and just as the motor-car was quicker than the coach, so some lovely thing would be quicker than the motor-car; and so on for ever. And there arose from their ashes Dr. Quilp, who said that a man could be sent on his machine so fast round the world that he could keep up a long, chatty conversation in some old-world village by saying a word of a sentence each time he came round. And it was said that the experiment had been tried on an apoplectic old major, who was sent round the world so fast that there seemed to be (to the inhabitants of some other star) a continuous band round the earth of white whiskers, red complexion and tweeds—a thing like the ring of Saturn.

Then there was the opposite school. There was Mr. Edward Carpenter, who thought we should in a very short time return to

Nature, and live simply and slowly as the animals do. And Edward Carpenter was followed by James Pickie, D.D. (of Pocohontas College), who said that men were immensely improved by grazing, or taking their food slowly and continuously, after the manner of cows. And he said that he had, with the most encouraging results, turned city men out on all fours in a field covered with veal cutlets. Then Tolstoy and the Humanitarians said that the world was growing more merciful, and therefore no one would ever desire to kill. And Mr. Mick not only became a vegetarian, but at length declared vegetarianism doomed ("shedding," as he called it finely, "the green blood of the silent animals"), and predicted that men in a better age would live on nothing but salt. And then came the pamphlet from Oregon (where the thing was tried), the pamphlet called "Why should Salt suffer?" and there was more trouble.

And on the other hand, some people were predicting that the lines of kinship would become narrower and sterner. There was Mr. Cecil Rhodes, who thought that the one thing of the future was the British Empire, and that there would be a gulf between those who were of the Empire and those who were not, between the Chinaman in Hong Kong and the Chinaman outside, between the Spaniard on the Rock of Gibraltar and the Spaniard off it, similar to the gulf between man and the lower animals. And in the same way his impetuous friend, Dr. Zoppi ("the Paul of Anglo-Saxonism"), carried it yet further, and held that, as a result of this view, cannibalism should be held to mean eating a member of the Empire, not eating one of the subject peoples, who should, he said, be killed without needless pain. His horror at the idea of eating a man in British Guiana showed how they misunderstood his stoicism who thought him devoid of feeling. He was, however, in a hard position; as it was said that he had attempted the experiment, and, living in London, had to subsist entirely on Italian organ-grinders. And his end was terrible, for just when he had begun, Sir Paul Swiller read his great paper at the Royal Society, proving that the savages were not only quite right in eating their enemies, but right on moral and hygienic grounds, since it was true that the qualities of the enemy, when eaten, passed into the eater. The notion that the nature of an Italian organ-man was irrevocably growing and burgeoning inside him was almost more than the kindly old professor could bear.

There was Mr. Benjamin Kidd, who said that the growing note of our race would be the care for and knowledge of the future. His idea was developed more powerfully by William Borker, who wrote that passage which every schoolboy knows by heart, about men in future ages weeping by the graves of their descendants, and tourists being shown over the scene of the historic battle which was to take place some centuries afterwards.

And Mr. Stead, too, was prominent, who thought that England would in the twentieth century be united to America; and his young lieutenant, Graham Podge, who included the states of France, Germany, and Russia in the American Union, the State of Russia being abbreviated to Ra.

There was Mr. Sidney Webb, also, who said that the future would see a continuously increasing order and neatness in the life of the people, and his poor friend Fipps, who went mad and ran about the country with an axe, hacking branches off the trees whenever there were not the same number on both sides.

All these clever men were prophesying with every variety of ingenuity what would happen soon, and they all did it in the same way, by taking something they saw "going strong," as the saying is, and carrying it as far as ever their imagination could stretch. This, they said, was the true and simple way of anticipating the future. "Just as," said Dr. Pellkins, in a fine passage, "just as when we see a pig in a litter larger than the other pigs, we know that by an unalterable law of the Inscrutable it will some day be larger than an elephant—just as we know, when we see weeds and dandelions growing more and more thickly in a garden, that they must, in spite of all our efforts, grow taller than the chimney-pots and swallow the house from sight, so we know and reverently acknowledge, that when any power in human politics has shown for any period of time any considerable activity, it will go on until it reaches to the sky."

And it did certainly appear that the prophets had put the people (engaged in the old game of Cheat the Prophet) in a quite unprecedented difficulty. It seemed really hard to do anything without fulfilling some of their prophecies.

But there was, nevertheless, in the eyes of labourers in the streets, of peasants in the fields, of sailors and children, and especially women, a strange look that kept the wise men in a perfect fever of doubt. They could not fathom the motionless mirth in their eyes. They still had something up their sleeve; they were still playing the game of Cheat the Prophet.

Then the wise men grew like wild things, and swayed hither and thither, crying, "What can it be? What can it be? What will London be like a century hence? Is there anything we have not thought of? Houses upside down—more hygienic, perhaps? Men walking on hands—make feet flexible, don't you know? Moon… motor-cars…no heads…." And so they swayed and wondered until they died and were buried nicely.

Then the people went and did what they liked. Let me no longer conceal the painful truth. The people had cheated the prophets of the twentieth century. When the curtain goes up on this story, eighty years after the present date, London is almost exactly like what it is now.

CHAPTER II

The Man in Green

Very few words are needed to explain why London, a hundred years hence, will be very like it is now, or rather, since I must slip into a prophetic past, why London, when my story opens, was very like it was in those enviable days when I was still alive.

The reason can be stated in one sentence. The people had absolutely lost faith in revolutions. All revolutions are doctrinal—such as the French one, or the one that introduced Christianity. For it stands to common sense that you cannot upset all existing things, customs, and compromises, unless you believe in something outside them, something positive and divine. Now, England, during this century, lost all belief in this. It believed in a thing called Evolution. And it said,

"All theoretic changes have ended in blood and ennui. If we change, we must change slowly and safely, as the animals do. Nature's revolutions are the only successful ones. There has been no conservative reaction in favour of tails."

And some things did change. Things that were not much thought of dropped out of sight. Things that had not often happened did not happen at all. Thus, for instance, the actual physical force ruling the country, the soldiers and police, grew smaller and smaller, and at last vanished almost to a point. The people combined could have swept the few policemen away in ten minutes: they did not, because they did not believe it would do them the least good. They had lost faith in revolutions.

Democracy was dead; for no one minded the governing class governing. England was now practically a despotism, but not an hereditary one. Some one in the official class was made King. No one cared how: no one cared who. He was merely an universal secretary.

In this manner it happened that everything in London was very quiet. That vague and somewhat depressed reliance upon things happening as they have always happened, which is with all Londoners a mood, had become an assumed condition. There was really no reason for any man doing anything but the thing he had done the day before.

There was therefore no reason whatever why the three young men who had always walked up to their Government office together should not walk up to it together on this particular wintry and cloudy morning. Everything in that age had become mechanical, and Government clerks especially. All those clerks assembled regularly at their posts. Three of those clerks always walked into town together. All the neighbourhood knew them: two of them were tall and one short. And on this particular morning the short clerk was only a few seconds late to join the other two as they passed his gate: he could have overtaken them in three strides; he could have called after them easily. But he did not.

For some reason that will never be understood until all souls are judged (if they are ever judged; the idea was at this time classed with fetish worship) he did not join his two companions, but walked steadily behind them. The day was dull, their dress was dull, everything was dull; but in some odd impulse he walked through street after street, through district after district, looking at the backs of the two men, who would have swung round at the sound of his voice.

Now, there is a law written in the darkest of the Books of Life, and it is this: If you look at a thing nine hundred and ninety-nine times, you are perfectly safe; if you look at it the thousandth time, you are in frightful danger of seeing it for the first time.

So the short Government official looked at the coat-tails of the tall Government officials, and through street after street, and round corner after corner, saw only coat-tails, coat-tails, and again coat-tails—when, he did not in the least know why, something happened to his eyes.

Two black dragons were walking backwards in front of him. Two black dragons were looking at him with evil eyes. The dragons were walking backwards it was true, but they kept their eyes fixed on him none the less. The eyes which he saw were, in truth, only the two buttons at the back of a frock-coat: perhaps some traditional memory of their meaningless character gave this half-witted prominence to their gaze. The slit between the tails was the nose-line of the monster: whenever the tails flapped in the winter wind the dragons licked their lips. It was only a momentary fancy, but the small clerk found it imbedded in his soul ever afterwards. He never could again think of men in frock-coats except as dragons walking backwards. He explained afterwards, quite tactfully and nicely, to his two official friends, that (while feeling an inexpressible regard for each of them) he could not seriously regard the face of either of them as anything but a kind of tail. It was, he admitted, a handsome tail—a tail elevated in the air. But if, he said, any true friend of theirs wished to see their faces, to look into the eyes of their soul, that friend must be allowed to walk reverently round behind them, so as to see them from the rear. There he would see the two black dragons with the blind eyes.

But when first the two black dragons sprang out of the fog upon the small clerk, they had merely the effect of all miracles—they changed the universe. He discovered the fact that all romantics know—that adventures happen on dull days, and not on sunny ones. When the chord of monotony is stretched most tight, then it breaks with a sound like song. He had scarcely noticed the weather before, but with the four dead eyes glaring at him he looked round and realised the strange dead day.

The morning was wintry and dim, not misty, but darkened with that shadow of cloud or snow which steeps everything in a green or copper twilight. The light there is on such a day seems not so much to come from the clear heavens as to be a phosphorescence clinging to the shapes themselves. The load of heaven and the clouds is like a load of waters, and the men move like fishes, feeling that they are on the floor of a sea. Everything in a London street completes the fantasy; the carriages and cabs themselves resemble deep-sea creatures with eyes of flame. He had been startled at first to meet two dragons. Now he found he was among deep-sea dragons possessing the deep sea.

The two young men in front were like the small young man himself, well-dressed. The lines of their frock-coats and silk hats had that luxuriant severity which makes the modern fop, hideous as he is, a favourite exercise of the modern draughtsman; that element which Mr. Max Beerbohm has admirably expressed in speaking of "certain congruities of dark cloth and the rigid perfection of linen."

They walked with the gait of an affected snail, and they spoke at the longest intervals, dropping a sentence at about every sixth lamp-post.

They crawled on past the lamp-posts; their mien was so immovable that a fanciful description might almost say, that the lamp-posts crawled past the men, as in a dream. Then the small man suddenly ran after them and said—

"I want to get my hair cut. I say, do you know a little shop anywhere where they cut your hair properly? I keep on having my hair cut, but it keeps on growing again."

One of the tall men looked at him with the air of a pained naturalist.

"Why, here is a little place," cried the small man, with a sort of imbecile cheerfulness, as the bright bulging window of a fashionable toilet-saloon glowed abruptly out of the foggy twilight. "Do you know, I often find hair-dressers when I walk about London. I'll lunch with you at Cicconani's. You know, I'm awfully fond of hair-dressers' shops. They're miles better than those nasty butchers'." And he disappeared into the doorway.

The man called James continued to gaze after him, a monocle screwed into his eye.

"What the devil do you make of that fellow?" he asked his companion, a pale young man with a high nose.

The pale young man reflected conscientiously for some minutes, and then said—

"Had a knock on his head when he was a kid, I should think."

"No, I don't think it's that," replied the Honourable James Barker.

"I've sometimes fancied he was a sort of artist, Lambert."

"Bosh!" cried Mr. Lambert, briefly.

"I admit I can't make him out," resumed Barker, abstractedly; "he never opens his mouth without saying something so indescribably half-witted that to call him a fool seems the very feeblest attempt at characterisation. But there's another thing about him that's rather funny. Do you know that he has the one collection of Japanese lacquer in Europe? Have you ever seen his books? All Greek poets and mediaeval French and that sort of thing. Have you ever been in his rooms? It's like being inside an amethyst. And he moves about in all that and talks like—like a turnip."

"Well, damn all books. Your blue books as well," said the ingenuous Mr. Lambert, with a friendly simplicity. "You ought to understand such things. What do you make of him?"

"He's beyond me," returned Barker. "But if you asked me for my opinion, I should say he was a man with a taste for nonsense, as they call it—artistic fooling, and all that kind of thing. And I seriously believe that he has talked nonsense so much that he has half bewildered his own mind and doesn't know the difference between sanity and insanity. He has gone round the mental world, so to speak, and found the place where the East and the West are one, and extreme idiocy is as good as sense. But I can't explain these psychological games."

"You can't explain them to me," replied Mr. Wilfrid Lambert, with candour.

As they passed up the long streets towards their restaurant the copper twilight cleared slowly to a pale yellow, and by the time they reached it they stood discernible in a tolerable winter daylight. The

Honourable James Barker, one of the most powerful officials in the English Government (by this time a rigidly official one), was a lean and elegant young man, with a blank handsome face and bleak blue eyes. He had a great amount of intellectual capacity, of that peculiar kind which raises a man from throne to throne and lets him die loaded with honours without having either amused or enlightened the mind of a single man. Wilfrid Lambert, the youth with the nose which appeared to impoverish the rest of his face, had also contributed little to the enlargement of the human spirit, but he had the honourable excuse of being a fool.

Lambert would have been called a silly man; Barker, with all his cleverness, might have been called a stupid man. But mere silliness and stupidity sank into insignificance in the presence of the awful and mysterious treasures of foolishness apparently stored up in the small figure that stood waiting for them outside Cicconani's. The little man, whose name was Auberon Quin, had an appearance compounded of a baby and an owl. His round head, round eyes, seemed to have been designed by nature playfully with a pair of compasses. His flat dark hair and preposterously long frockcoat gave him something of the look of a child's "Noah." When he entered a room of strangers, they mistook him for a small boy, and wanted to take him on their knees, until he spoke, when they perceived that a boy would have been more intelligent.

"I have been waiting quite a long time," said Quin, mildly. "It's awfully funny I should see you coming up the street at last."

"Why?" asked Lambert, staring. "You told us to come here yourself."

"My mother used to tell people to come to places," said the sage.

They were about to turn into the restaurant with a resigned air, when their eyes were caught by something in the street. The weather, though cold and blank, was now quite clear, and across the dull brown of the wood pavement and between the dull grey terraces was moving something not to be seen for miles round— not to be seen perhaps at that time in England—a man dressed in bright colours. A small crowd hung on the man's heels.

He was a tall stately man, clad in a military uniform of brilliant green, splashed with great silver facings. From the shoulder swung a short green furred cloak, somewhat like that of a Hussar, the lining of which gleamed every now and then with a kind of tawny crimson. His breast glittered with medals; round his neck was the red ribbon and star of some foreign order; and a long straight sword, with a blazing hilt, trailed and clattered along the pavement. At this time the pacific and utilitarian development of Europe had relegated all such customs to the Museums. The only remaining force, the small but well-organised police, were attired in a sombre and hygienic manner. But even those who remembered the last Life Guards and Lancers who disappeared in 1912 must have known at a glance that this was not, and never had been, an English uniform; and this conviction would have been heightened by the yellow aquiline face, like Dante carved in bronze, which rose, crowned with white hair, out of the green military collar, a keen and distinguished, but not an English face.

The magnificence with which the green-clad gentleman walked down the centre of the road would be something difficult to express in human language. For it was an ingrained simplicity and arrogance, something in the mere carriage of the head and body, which made ordinary moderns in the street stare after him; but it had comparatively little to do with actual conscious gestures or expression. In the matter of these merely temporary movements, the man appeared to be rather worried and inquisitive, but he was inquisitive with the inquisitiveness of a despot and worried as with the responsibilities of a god. The men who lounged and wondered behind him followed partly with an astonishment at his brilliant uniform, that is to say, partly because of that instinct which makes us all follow one who looks like a madman, but far more because of that instinct which makes all men follow (and worship) any one who chooses to behave like a king. He had to so sublime an extent that great quality of royalty—an almost imbecile unconsciousness of everybody, that people went after him as they do after kings—to see what would be the first thing or person he would take notice of. And all the time, as we have said, in spite of his quiet splendour, there was an air about him as if he were looking for somebody; an expression of inquiry.

Suddenly that expression of inquiry vanished, none could tell why, and was replaced by an expression of contentment. Amid the rapt attention of the mob of idlers, the magnificent green gentleman deflected himself from his direct course down the centre of the road and walked to one side of it. He came to a halt opposite to a large poster of Colman's Mustard erected on a wooden hoarding. His spectators almost held their breath.

He took from a small pocket in his uniform a little penknife; with this he made a slash at the stretched paper. Completing the rest of the operation with his fingers, he tore off a strip or rag of paper, yellow in colour and wholly irregular in outline. Then for the first time the great being addressed his adoring onlookers—

"Can any one," he said, with a pleasing foreign accent, "lend me a pin?"

Mr. Lambert, who happened to be nearest, and who carried innumerable pins for the purpose of attaching innumerable buttonholes, lent him one, which was received with extravagant but dignified bows, and hyperboles of thanks.

The gentleman in green, then, with every appearance of being gratified, and even puffed up, pinned the piece of yellow paper to the green silk and silver-lace adornments of his breast. Then he turned his eyes round again, searching and unsatisfied.

"Anything else I can do, sir?" asked Lambert, with the absurd politeness of the Englishman when once embarrassed.

"Red," said the stranger, vaguely, "red."

"I beg your pardon?"

"I beg yours also, Señor," said the stranger, bowing. "I was wondering whether any of you had any red about you."

"Any red about us?—well really—no, I don't think I have—I used to carry a red bandanna once, but—"

"Barker," asked Auberon Quin, suddenly, "where's your red cockatoo? Where's your red cockatoo?"

"What do you mean?" asked Barker, desperately. "What cockatoo? You've never seen me with any cockatoo!"

"I know," said Auberon, vaguely mollified. "Where's it been all the time?"

Barker swung round, not without resentment.

"I am sorry, sir," he said, shortly but civilly, "none of us seem to have anything red to lend you. But why, if one may ask—"

"I thank you, Señor, it is nothing. I can, since there is nothing else, fulfil my own requirements."

And standing for a second of thought with the penknife in his hand, he stabbed his left palm. The blood fell with so full a stream that it struck the stones without dripping. The foreigner pulled out his handkerchief and tore a piece from it with his teeth. The rag was immediately soaked in scarlet.

"Since you are so generous, Señor," he said, "another pin, perhaps."

Lambert held one out, with eyes protruding like a frog's.

The red linen was pinned beside the yellow paper, and the foreigner took off his hat.

"I have to thank you all, gentlemen," he said; and wrapping the remainder of the handkerchief round his bleeding hand, he resumed his walk with an overwhelming stateliness.

While all the rest paused, in some disorder, little Mr. Auberon Quin ran after the stranger and stopped him, with hat in hand. Considerably to everybody's astonishment, he addressed him in the purest Spanish—

"Señor," he said in that language, "pardon a hospitality, perhaps indiscreet, towards one who appears to be a distinguished, but a solitary guest in London. Will you do me and my friends, with whom you have held some conversation, the honour of lunching with us at the adjoining restaurant?"

The man in the green uniform had turned a fiery colour of pleasure at the mere sound of his own language, and he accepted the invitation with that profusion of bows which so often shows, in the case of the Southern races, the falsehood of the notion that ceremony has nothing to do with feeling.

"Señor," he said, "your language is my own; but all my love for my people shall not lead me to deny to yours the possession of so chivalrous an entertainer. Let me say that the tongue is Spanish but the heart English." And he passed with the rest into Cicconani's.

"Now, perhaps," said Barker, over the fish and sherry, intensely polite, but burning with curiosity, "perhaps it would be rude of me to ask why you did that?"

"Did what, Señor?" asked the guest, who spoke English quite well, though in a manner indefinably American.

"Well," said the Englishman, in some confusion, "I mean tore a strip off a hoarding and...er...cut yourself...and...."

"To tell you that, Señor," answered the other, with a certain sad pride, "involves merely telling you who I am. I am Juan del Fuego, President of Nicaragua."

The manner with which the President of Nicaragua leant back and drank his sherry showed that to him this explanation covered all the facts observed and a great deal more. Barker's brow, however, was still a little clouded.

"And the yellow paper," he began, with anxious friendliness, "and the red rag...."

"The yellow paper and the red rag," said Fuego, with indescribable grandeur, "are the colours of Nicaragua."

"But Nicaragua..." began Barker, with great hesitation, "Nicaragua is no longer a...."

"Nicaragua has been conquered like Athens. Nicaragua has been annexed like Jerusalem," cried the old man, with amazing fire. "The Yankee and the German and the brute powers of modernity have trampled it with the hoofs of oxen. But Nicaragua is not dead. Nicaragua is an idea."

Auberon Quin suggested timidly, "A brilliant idea."

"Yes," said the foreigner, snatching at the word. "You are right, generous Englishman. An idea *brilliant*, a burning thought. Señor, you asked me why, in my desire to see the colours of my country, I snatched at paper and blood. Can you not understand the ancient sanctity of colours? The Church has her symbolic colours. And think of what colours mean to us—think of the position of one like myself, who can see nothing but those two colours, nothing but the red and the yellow. To me all shapes are equal, all common and noble things are in a democracy of combination. Wherever there is a field of marigolds and the red cloak of an old woman, there is Nicaragua. Wherever there is a field of poppies and a yellow patch of sand, there is Nicaragua. Wherever there is a lemon and a red sunset, there is my country. Wherever I see a red pillar-box and a yellow sunset, there my heart beats. Blood and a splash of mustard can be my heraldry. If there be yellow mud and red mud in the same ditch, it is better to me than white stars."

"And if," said Quin, with equal enthusiasm, "there should happen to be yellow wine and red wine at the same lunch, you could not confine yourself to sherry. Let me order some Burgundy, and complete, as it were, a sort of Nicaraguan heraldry in your inside."

Barker was fiddling with his knife, and was evidently making up his mind to say something, with the intense nervousness of the amiable Englishman.

"I am to understand, then," he said at last, with a cough, "that you, ahem, were the President of Nicaragua when it made its—er—one must, of course, agree—its quite heroic resistance to—er—"

The ex-President of Nicaragua waved his hand.

"You need not hesitate in speaking to me," he said. "I'm quite fully aware that the whole tendency of the world of today is against Nicaragua and against me. I shall not consider it any diminution of your evident courtesy if you say what you think of the misfortunes that have laid my republic in ruins."

Barker looked immeasurably relieved and gratified.

"You are most generous, President," he said, with some hesitation over the title, "and I will take advantage of your generosity to express the doubts which, I must confess, we moderns have about such things as—er—the Nicaraguan independence."

"So your sympathies are," said Del Fuego, quite calmly, "with the big nation which—"

"Pardon me, pardon me, President," said Barker, warmly; "my sympathies are with no nation. You misunderstand, I think, the modern intellect. We do not disapprove of the fire and extravagance of such commonwealths as yours only to become more extravagant on a larger scale. We do not condemn Nicaragua because we think Britain ought to be more Nicaraguan. We do not discourage small nationalities because we wish large nationalities to have all their smallness, all their uniformity of outlook, all their exaggeration of spirit. If I differ with the greatest respect from your Nicaraguan enthusiasm, it is not because a nation or ten nations were against you; it is because civilisation was against you. We moderns believe in a great cosmopolitan civilisation, one which shall include all the talents of all the absorbed peoples—"

"The Señor will forgive me," said the President. "May I ask the Señor how, under ordinary circumstances, he catches a wild horse?"

"I never catch a wild horse," replied Barker, with dignity.

"Precisely," said the other; "and there ends your absorption of the talents. That is what I complain of your cosmopolitanism. When you say you want all peoples to unite, you really mean that you want all peoples to unite to learn the tricks of your people. If the Bedouin Arab does not know how to read, some English missionary or schoolmaster must be sent to teach him to read, but no one ever says, 'This schoolmaster does not know how to ride on a camel; let us pay a Bedouin to teach him.' You say your civilisation will include all talents. Will it? Do you really mean to say that at the moment when the Esquimaux has learnt to vote for a County Council, you will have learnt to spear a walrus? I recur to the example I gave. In Nicaragua we had a way of catching wild horses—by lassooing the fore feet—which was supposed to be the best in South America. If you are going to include all the talents, go and do it. If not, permit me to say what I have always said, that something went from the world when Nicaragua was civilised."

"Something, perhaps," replied Barker, "but that something a mere barbarian dexterity. I do not know that I could chip flints as well as a primeval man, but I know that civilisation can make these knives which are better, and I trust to civilisation."

"You have good authority," answered the Nicaraguan. "Many clever men like you have trusted to civilisation. Many clever Babylonians, many clever Egyptians, many clever men at the end of Rome. Can you tell me, in a world that is flagrant with the failures of civilisation, what there is particularly immortal about yours?"

"I think you do not quite understand, President, what ours is," answered Barker. "You judge it rather as if England was still a poor and pugnacious island; you have been long out of Europe. Many things have happened."

"And what," asked the other, "would you call the summary of those things?"

"The summary of those things," answered Barker, with great animation, "is that we are rid of the superstitions, and in becoming so we have not merely become rid of the superstitions which have been most frequently and most enthusiastically so described. The superstition of big nationalities is bad, but the superstition of small nationalities is worse. The superstition of reverencing our own country is bad, but the superstition of reverencing other people's countries is worse. It is so everywhere, and in a hundred ways. The superstition of monarchy is bad, and the superstition of aristocracy is bad, but the superstition of democracy is the worst of all."

The old gentleman opened his eyes with some surprise.

"Are you, then," he said, "no longer a democracy in England?"

Barker laughed.

"The situation invites paradox," he said. "We are, in a sense, the purest democracy. We have become a despotism. Have you not noticed how continually in history democracy becomes despotism? People call it the decay of democracy. It is simply its fulfilment. Why take the trouble to number and register and enfranchise all the innumerable John Robinsons, when you can take one John Robinson with the same intellect or lack of intellect as all the rest, and have done with it? The old idealistic republicans used to found democracy on the idea that all men were equally intelligent. Believe me, the sane and enduring democracy is founded on the fact that all men are equally idiotic. Why should we not choose out of them one as much as another. All that we want for Government is a man not criminal and insane, who can rapidly look over some petitions and sign some proclamations. To think what time was wasted in arguing about the House of Lords, Tories saying it ought to be preserved because it was clever, and Radicals saying it ought to be destroyed because it was stupid, and all the time no one saw that it was right because it was stupid, because that chance mob of ordinary men thrown there by accident of blood, were a great democratic protest against the Lower House, against the eternal insolence of the aristocracy of talents. We have established now in England, the thing towards which all systems have dimly groped, the dull popular despotism without illusions. We want one man at the head of our State, not because he is brilliant or virtuous, but because he is one man and not a chattering crowd. To avoid the possible chance of hereditary diseases or such things, we have abandoned hereditary monarchy. The King of England is chosen like a juryman upon an official rotation list. Beyond that the whole system is quietly despotic, and we have not found it raise a murmur."

"Do you really mean," asked the President, incredulously, "that you choose any ordinary man that comes to hand and make him despot—that you trust to the chance of some alphabetical list...."

"And why not?" cried Barker. "Did not half the historical nations trust to the chance of the eldest sons of eldest sons, and did not half of them get on tolerably well? To have a perfect system is impossible; to have a system is indispensable. All hereditary monarchies were a matter of luck: so are alphabetical monarchies. Can you find a deep philosophical meaning in the difference between the Stuarts and the Hanoverians? Believe me, I will undertake to find a deep philosophical meaning in the contrast between the dark tragedy of the A's, and the solid success of the B's."

"And you risk it?" asked the other. "Though the man may be a tyrant or a cynic or a criminal."

"We risk it," answered Barker, with a perfect placidity. "Suppose he is a tyrant—he is still a check on a hundred tyrants. Suppose he is a cynic, it is to his interest to govern well. Suppose he is a criminal—by removing poverty and substituting power, we put a check on his criminality. In short, by substituting despotism we have put a total check on one criminal and a partial check on all the rest."

The Nicaraguan old gentleman leaned over with a queer expression in his eyes.

"My church, sir," he said, "has taught me to respect faith. I do not wish to speak with any disrespect of yours, however fantastic. But do you really mean that you will trust to the ordinary man, the man who may happen to come next, as a good despot?"

"I do," said Barker, simply. "He may not be a good man. But he will be a good despot. For when he comes to a mere business routine of government he will endeavour to do ordinary justice. Do we not assume the same thing in a jury?"

The old President smiled.

"I don't know," he said, "that I have any particular objection in detail to your excellent scheme of Government. My only objection is a quite personal one. It is, that if I were asked whether I would belong to it, I should ask first of all, if I was not permitted, as an alternative, to be a toad in a ditch. That is all. You cannot argue with the choice of the soul."

"Of the soul," said Barker, knitting his brows, "I cannot pretend to say anything, but speaking in the interests of the public—"

Mr. Auberon Quin rose suddenly to his feet.

"If you'll excuse me, gentlemen," he said, "I will step out for a moment into the air."

"I'm so sorry, Auberon," said Lambert, good-naturedly; "do you feel bad?"

"Not bad exactly," said Auberon, with self-restraint; "rather good, if anything. Strangely and richly good. The fact is, I want to reflect a little on those beautiful words that have just been uttered.

'Speaking,' yes, that was the phrase, 'speaking in the interests of the public.' One cannot get the honey from such things without being alone for a little."

"Is he really off his chump, do you think?" asked Lambert.

The old President looked after him with queerly vigilant eyes.

"He is a man, I think," he said, "who cares for nothing but a joke. He is a dangerous man."

Lambert laughed in the act of lifting some maccaroni to his mouth.

"Dangerous!" he said. "You don't know little Quin, sir!"

"Every man is dangerous," said the old man without moving, "who cares only for one thing. I was once dangerous myself."

And with a pleasant smile he finished his coffee and rose, bowing profoundly, passed out into the fog, which had again grown dense and sombre. Three days afterwards they heard that he had died quietly in lodgings in Soho.

Drowned somewhere else in the dark sea of fog was a little figure shaking and quaking, with what might at first sight have seemed terror or ague: but which was really that strange malady, a lonely laughter.

He was repeating over and over to himself with a rich accent—"But speaking in the interests of the public...."

CHAPTER III

The Hill of Humour

"In a little square garden of yellow roses, beside the sea," said Auberon Quin, "there was a Nonconformist minister who had never been to Wimbledon. His family did not understand his sorrow or the strange look in his eyes. But one day they repented their neglect, for they heard that a body had been found on the shore, battered, but wearing patent leather boots. As it happened, it turned out not to be the minister at all. But in the dead man's pocket there was a return ticket to Maidstone."

There was a short pause as Quin and his friends Barker and Lambert went swinging on through the slushy grass of Kensington Gardens. Then Auberon resumed.

"That story," he said reverently, "is the test of humour."

They walked on further and faster, wading through higher grass as they began to climb a slope.

"I perceive," continued Auberon, "that you have passed the test, and consider the anecdote excruciatingly funny; since you say nothing. Only coarse humour is received with pot-house applause. The great anecdote is received in silence, like a benediction. You felt pretty benedicted, didn't you, Barker?"

"I saw the point," said Barker, somewhat loftily.

"Do you know," said Quin, with a sort of idiot gaiety, "I have lots of stories as good as that. Listen to this one."

And he slightly cleared his throat.

"Dr. Polycarp was, as you all know, an unusually sallow

bimetallist. 'There,' people of wide experience would say, 'There goes the sallowest bimetallist in Cheshire.' Once this was said so that he overheard it: it was said by an actuary, under a sunset of mauve and grey. Polycarp turned upon him. 'Sallow!' he cried fiercely, 'sallow! *Quis tulerit Gracchos de seditione querentes.*' It was said that no actuary ever made game of Dr. Polycarp again."

Barker nodded with a simple sagacity. Lambert only grunted.

"Here is another," continued the insatiable Quin. "In a hollow of the grey-green hills of rainy Ireland, lived an old, old woman, whose uncle was always Cambridge at the Boat Race. But in her grey-green hollows, she knew nothing of this: she didn't know that there was a Boat Race. Also she did not know that she had an uncle. She had heard of nobody at all, except of George the First, of whom she had heard (I know not why), and in whose historical memory she put her simple trust. And by and by in God's good time, it was discovered that this uncle of hers was not really her uncle, and they came and told her so. She smiled through her tears, and said only, 'Virtue is its own reward.'"

Again there was a silence, and then Lambert said—

"It seems a bit mysterious."

"Mysterious!" cried the other. "The true humour is mysterious. Do you not realise the chief incident of the nineteenth and twentieth centuries?"

"And what's that?" asked Lambert, shortly.

"It is very simple," replied the other. "Hitherto it was the ruin of a joke that people did not see it. Now it is the sublime victory of a joke that people do not see it. Humour, my friends, is the one sanctity remaining to mankind. It is the one thing you are thoroughly afraid of. Look at that tree."

His interlocutors looked vaguely towards a beech that leant out towards them from the ridge of the hill.

"If," said Mr. Quin, "I were to say that you did not see the great truths of science exhibited by that tree, though they stared any man of intellect in the face, what would you think or say? You would merely regard me as a pedant with some unimportant theory about vegetable cells. If I were to say that you did not see in that tree the vile mismanagement of local politics, you would dismiss me as a Socialist crank with some particular fad about public parks. If I were to say that you were guilty of the supreme blasphemy of looking at that tree and not seeing in it a new religion, a special revelation of God, you would simply say I was a mystic, and think no more about me. But if"—and he lifted a pontifical hand—"if I say that you cannot see the humour of that tree, and that I see the humour of it—my God! you will roll about at my feet."

He paused a moment, and then resumed.

"Yes; a sense of humour, a weird and delicate sense of humour, is the new religion of mankind! It is towards that men will strain themselves with the asceticism of saints. Exercises, spiritual exercises, will be set in it. It will be asked, 'Can you see the humour of this iron railing?' or 'Can you see the humour of this field of corn? Can you see the humour of the stars? Can you see the humour of the sunsets?' How often I have laughed myself to sleep over a violet sunset."

"Quite so," said Mr. Barker, with an intelligent embarrassment.

"Let me tell you another story. How often it happens that the M.P.'s for Essex are less punctual than one would suppose. The least punctual Essex M.P., perhaps, was James Wilson, who said, in the very act of plucking a poppy—"

Lambert suddenly faced round and struck his stick into the ground in a defiant attitude.

"Auberon," he said, "chuck it. I won't stand it. It's all bosh."

Both men stared at him, for there was something very explosive about the words, as if they had been corked up painfully for a long time.

"You have," began Quin, "no—"

"I don't care a curse," said Lambert, violently, "whether I have 'a delicate sense of humour' or not. I won't stand it. It's all a confounded fraud. There's no joke in those infernal tales at all. You know there isn't as well as I do."

"Well," replied Quin, slowly, "it is true that I, with my rather gradual mental processes, did not see any joke in them. But the finer sense of Barker perceived it."

Barker turned a fierce red, but continued to stare at the horizon.

"You ass," said Lambert; "why can't you be like other people? Why can't you say something really funny, or hold your tongue? The man who sits on his hat in a pantomime is a long sight funnier than you are."

Quin regarded him steadily. They had reached the top of the ridge and the wind struck their faces.

"Lambert," said Auberon, "you are a great and good man, though I'm hanged if you look it. You are more. You are a great revolutionist or deliverer of the world, and I look forward to seeing you carved in marble between Luther and Danton, if possible in your present attitude, the hat slightly on one side. I said as I came up the hill that the new humour was the last of the religions. You have made it the last of the superstitions. But let me give you a very serious warning. Be careful how you ask me to do anything *outré*, to imitate the man in the pantomime, and to sit on my hat. Because I am a man whose soul has been emptied of all pleasures but folly. And for twopence I'd do it."

"Do it, then," said Lambert, swinging his stick impatiently. "It would be funnier than the bosh you and Barker talk."

Quin, standing on the top of the hill, stretched his hand out towards the main avenue of Kensington Gardens.

"Two hundred yards away," he said, "are all your fashionable acquaintances with nothing on earth to do but to stare at each other and at us. We are standing upon an elevation under the open sky, a peak as it were of fantasy, a Sinai of humour. We are in a great pulpit or platform, lit up with sunlight, and half London can see us. Be careful how you suggest things to me. For there is in me a madness which goes beyond martyrdom, the madness of an utterly idle man."

"I don't know what you are talking about," said Lambert, contemptuously. "I only know I'd rather you stood on your silly head, than talked so much."

"Auberon! for goodness' sake…" cried Barker, springing forward; but he was too late. Faces from all the benches and avenues were turned in their direction. Groups stopped and small crowds collected; and the sharp sunlight picked out the whole scene in blue, green and black, like a picture in a child's toy-book. And on the top of the small hill Mr. Auberon Quin stood with considerable athletic neatness upon his head, and waved his patent-leather boots in the air.

"For God's sake, Quin, get up, and don't be an idiot," cried Barker, wringing his hands; "we shall have the whole town here."

"Yes, get up, get up, man," said Lambert, amused and annoyed. "I was only fooling; get up."

Auberon did so with a bound, and flinging his hat higher than the trees, proceeded to hop about on one leg with a serious expression.

Barker stamped wildly.

"Oh, let's get home, Barker, and leave him," said Lambert; "some of your proper and correct police will look after him. Here they come!"

Two grave-looking men in quiet uniforms came up the hill towards them.

One held a paper in his hand.

"There he is, officer," said Lambert, cheerfully; "we ain't responsible for him."

The officer looked at the capering Mr. Quin with a quiet eye.

"We have not come, gentlemen," he said, "about what I think you are alluding to. We have come from head-quarters to announce the selection of His Majesty the King. It is the rule, inherited from the old *régime*, that the news should be brought to the new Sovereign immediately, wherever he is; so we have followed you across Kensington Gardens."

Barker's eyes were blazing in his pale face. He was consumed with ambition throughout his life. With a certain dull magnanimity of the intellect he had really believed in the chance method of selecting despots. But this sudden suggestion, that the selection might have fallen upon him, unnerved him with pleasure.

"Which of us," he began, and the respectful official interrupted him.

"Not you, sir, I am sorry to say. If I may be permitted to say so, we know your services to the Government, and should be very thankful if it were. The choice has fallen...."

"God bless my soul!" said Lambert, jumping back two paces. "Not me. Don't say I'm autocrat of all the Russias."

"No, sir," said the officer, with a slight cough and a glance towards Auberon, who was at that moment putting his head between his legs and making a noise like a cow; "the gentleman whom we have to congratulate seems at the moment—er—er—occupied."

"Not Quin!" shrieked Barker, rushing up to him; "it can't be. Auberon, for God's sake pull yourself together. You've been made King!"

With his head still upside down between his legs, Mr. Quin answered modestly—

"I am not worthy. I cannot reasonably claim to equal the great men who have previously swayed the sceptre of Britain. Perhaps the only peculiarity that I can claim is that I am probably the first monarch that ever spoke out his soul to the people of England with his head and body in this position. This may in some sense give me, to quote a poem that I wrote in my youth—

> A nobler office on the earth
> Than valour, power of brain, or birth
> Could give the warrior kings of old.
> The intellect clarified by this posture—"

Lambert and Barker made a kind of rush at him.

"Don't you understand?" cried Lambert. "It's not a joke. They've really made you King. By gosh! they must have rum taste."

"The great Bishops of the Middle Ages," said Quin, kicking his legs in the air, as he was dragged up more or less upside down, "were in the habit of refusing the honour of election three times and then accepting it. A mere matter of detail separates me from those great men. I will accept the post three times and refuse it afterwards. Oh! I will toil for you, my faithful people! You shall have a banquet of humour."

By this time he had been landed the right way up, and the two men were still trying in vain to impress him with the gravity of the situation.

"Did you not tell me, Wilfrid Lambert," he said, "that I should be of more public value if I adopted a more popular form of humour? And when should a popular form of humour be more firmly riveted upon me than now, when I have become the darling of a whole people? Officer," he continued, addressing the startled messenger, "are there no ceremonies to celebrate my entry into the city?"

"Ceremonies," began the official, with embarrassment, "have been more or less neglected for some little time, and—"

Auberon Quin began gradually to take off his coat.

"All ceremony," he said, "consists in the reversal of the obvious. Thus men, when they wish to be priests or judges, dress up like women. Kindly help me on with this coat." And he held it out.

"But, your Majesty," said the officer, after a moment's bewilderment and manipulation, "you're putting it on with the tails in front."

"The reversal of the obvious," said the King, calmly, "is as near as we can come to ritual with our imperfect apparatus. Lead on."

The rest of that afternoon and evening was to Barker and Lambert a nightmare, which they could not properly realise or recall. The King, with his coat on the wrong way, went towards the streets that were awaiting him, and the old Kensington Palace which was the Royal residence. As he passed small groups of men, the groups turned into crowds, and gave forth sounds which seemed strange in welcoming an autocrat. Barker walked behind, his brain reeling, and, as the crowds grew thicker and thicker, the sounds became more and more unusual. And when he had reached the great market-place opposite the church, Barker knew that he had reached it, though he was roods behind, because a cry went up such as had never before greeted any of the kings of the earth.

Book II

CHAPTER I

The Charter of the Cities

L ambert was standing bewildered outside the door of the King's apartments amid the scurry of astonishment and ridicule. He was just passing out into the street, in a dazed manner, when James Barker dashed by him.

"Where are you going?" he asked.

"To stop all this foolery, of course," replied Barker; and he disappeared into the room.

He entered it headlong, slamming the door, and slapping his incomparable silk hat on the table. His mouth opened, but before he could speak, the King said—

"Your hat, if you please."

Fidgeting with his fingers, and scarcely knowing what he was doing, the young politician held it out.

The King placed it on his own chair, and sat on it.

"A quaint old custom," he explained, smiling above the ruins. "When the King receives the representatives of the House of Barker, the hat of the latter is immediately destroyed in this manner. It represents the absolute finality of the act of homage expressed in the removal of it. It declares that never until that hat shall once more appear upon your head (a contingency which I firmly believe to be remote) shall the House of Barker rebel against the Crown of England."

Barker stood with clenched fist, and shaking lip.

"Your jokes," he began, "and my property—" and then exploded with an oath, and stopped again.

"Continue, continue," said the King, waving his hands.

"What does it all mean?" cried the other, with a gesture of passionate rationality. "Are you mad?"

"Not in the least," replied the King, pleasantly. "Madmen are always serious; they go mad from lack of humour. You are looking serious yourself, James."

"Why can't you keep it to your own private life?" expostulated the other. "You've got plenty of money, and plenty of houses now to play the fool in, but in the interests of the public—"

"Epigrammatic," said the King, shaking his finger sadly at him. "None of your daring scintillations here. As to why I don't do it in private, I rather fail to understand your question. The answer is of comparative limpidity. I don't do it in private, because it is funnier to do it in public. You appear to think that it would be amusing to be dignified in the banquet hall and in the street, and at my own fireside (I could procure a fireside) to keep the company in a roar. But that is what every one does. Every one is grave in public, and funny in private. My sense of humour suggests the reversal of this; it suggests that one should be funny in public, and solemn in private. I desire to make the State functions, parliaments, coronations, and so on, one roaring old-fashioned pantomime. But, on the other hand, I shut myself up alone in a small store-room for two hours a day, where I am so dignified that I come out quite ill."

By this time Barker was walking up and down the room, his frock coat flapping like the black wings of a bird.

"Well, you will ruin the country, that's all," he said shortly.

"It seems to me," said Auberon, "that the tradition of ten centuries is being broken, and the House of Barker is rebelling against the Crown of England. It would be with regret (for I admire your appearance) that I should be obliged forcibly to decorate your head with the remains of this hat, but—"

"What I can't understand," said Barker flinging up his fingers with a feverish American movement, "is why you don't care about anything else but your games."

The King stopped sharply in the act of lifting the silken remnants, dropped them, and walked up to Barker, looking at him steadily.

"I made a kind of vow," he said, "that I would not talk seriously, which always means answering silly questions. But the strong man will always be gentle with politicians.

'The shape my scornful looks deride
Required a God to form';

if I may so theologically express myself. And for some reason I cannot in the least understand, I feel impelled to answer that question of yours, and to answer it as if there were really such a thing in the world as a serious subject. You ask me why I don't care for anything else. Can you tell me, in the name of all the gods you don't believe in, why I should care for anything else?"

"Don't you realise common public necessities?" cried Barker. "Is it possible that a man of your intelligence does not know that it is every one's interest—"

"Don't you believe in Zoroaster? Is it possible that you neglect Mumbo-Jumbo?" returned the King, with startling animation. "Does a man of your intelligence come to me with these damned early Victorian ethics? If, on studying my features and manner, you detect any particular resemblance to the Prince Consort, I assure you you are mistaken. Did Herbert Spencer ever convince you—did he ever convince anybody—did he ever for one mad moment convince himself—that it must be to the interest of the individual to feel a public spirit? Do you believe that, if you rule your department badly, you stand any more chance, or one half of the chance, of being guillotined, that an angler stands of being pulled into the river by a strong pike? Herbert Spencer refrained from theft for the same reason that he refrained from wearing feathers in his hair, because he was an English gentleman with different tastes. I am an English gentleman with different tastes. He liked philosophy. I like art. He liked writing ten books on the nature of human society.

I like to see the Lord Chamberlain walking in front of me with a piece of paper pinned to his coat-tails. It is my humour. Are you answered? At any rate, I have said my last serious word today, and my last serious word I trust for the remainder of my life in this Paradise of Fools. The remainder of my conversation with you today, which I trust will be long and stimulating, I propose to conduct in a new language of my own by means of rapid and symbolic movements of the left leg." And he began to pirouette slowly round the room with a preoccupied expression.

Barker ran round the room after him, bombarding him with demands and entreaties. But he received no response except in the new language. He came out banging the door again, and sick like a man coming on shore.

As he strode along the streets he found himself suddenly opposite Cicconani's restaurant, and for some reason there rose up before him the green fantastic figure of the Spanish General, standing, as he had seen him last, at the door, with the words on his lips, "You cannot argue with the choice of the soul."

The King came out from his dancing with the air of a man of business legitimately tired. He put on an overcoat, lit a cigar, and went out into the purple night.

"I will go," he said, "and mingle with the people."

He passed swiftly up a street in the neighbourhood of Notting Hill, when suddenly he felt a hard object driven into his waistcoat. He paused, put up his single eye-glass, and beheld a boy with a wooden sword and a paper cocked hat, wearing that expression of awed satisfaction with which a child contemplates his work when he has hit some one very hard. The King gazed thoughtfully for some time at his assailant, and slowly took a note-book from his breast-pocket.

"I have a few notes," he said, "for my dying speech;" and he turned over the leaves. "Dying speech for political assassination; ditto, if by former friend—h'm, h'm. Dying speech for death at hands of injured husband (repentant). Dying speech for same (cynical). I am not quite sure which meets the present...."

"I'm the King of the Castle," said the boy, truculently, and very pleased with nothing in particular.

The King was a kind-hearted man, and very fond of children, like all people who are fond of the ridiculous.

"Infant," he said, "I'm glad you are so stalwart a defender of your old inviolate Notting Hill. Look up nightly to that peak, my child, where it lifts itself among the stars so ancient, so lonely, so unutterably Notting. So long as you are ready to die for the sacred mountain, even if it were ringed with all the armies of Bayswater—"

The King stopped suddenly, and his eyes shone.

"Perhaps," he said, "perhaps the noblest of all my conceptions. A revival of the arrogance of the old mediæval cities applied to our glorious suburbs. Clapham with a city guard. Wimbledon with a city wall. Surbiton tolling a bell to raise its citizens. West Hampstead going into battle with its own banner. It shall be done. I, the King, have said it." And, hastily presenting the boy with half a crown, remarking, "For the war-chest of Notting Hill," he ran violently home at such a rate of speed that crowds followed him for miles. On reaching his study, he ordered a cup of coffee, and plunged into profound meditation upon the project. At length he called his favourite Equerry, Captain Bowler, for whom he had a deep affection, founded principally upon the shape of his whiskers.

"Bowler," he said, "isn't there some society of historical research, or something of which I am an honorary member?"

"Yes, sir," said Captain Bowler, rubbing his nose, "you are a member of 'The Encouragers of Egyptian Renaissance,' and 'The Teutonic Tombs Club,' and 'The Society for the Recovery of London Antiquities,' and—"

"That is admirable," said the King. "The London Antiquities does my trick. Go to the Society for the Recovery of London Antiquities and speak to their secretary, and their sub-secretary, and their president, and their vice-president, saying, 'The King of England is proud, but the honorary member of the Society for the Recovery of London Antiquities is prouder than kings. I should like to tell you of certain discoveries I have made touching the neglected traditions of the London boroughs. The revelations may cause some excitement, stirring burning memories and touching old wounds in Shepherd's Bush and Bayswater, in Pimlico and South Kensington. The King hesitates, but the honorary member is firm. I approach you invoking the vows of my initiation, the Sacred Seven Cats, the Poker of Perfection, and the Ordeal of the Indescribable Instant (forgive me if I mix you up with the Clanna-Gael or some other club I belong to), and ask you to permit me to read a paper at your next meeting on the 'Wars of the London Boroughs." Say all this to the Society, Bowler. Remember it very carefully, for it is most important, and I have forgotten it altogether, and send me another cup of coffee and some of the cigars that we keep for vulgar and successful people. I am going to write my paper."

The Society for the Recovery of London Antiquities met a month after in a corrugated iron hall on the outskirts of one of the southern suburbs of London. A large number of people had collected there under the coarse and flaring gas-jets when the King arrived, perspiring and genial. On taking off his great-coat, he was perceived to be in evening dress, wearing the Garter. His appearance at the small table, adorned only with a glass of water, was received with respectful cheering.

The chairman (Mr. Huggins) said that he was sure that they had all been pleased to listen to such distinguished lecturers as they had heard for some time past (hear, hear). Mr. Burton (hear, hear), Mr. Cambridge, Professor King (loud and continued cheers), our old friend Peter Jessop, Sir William White (loud laughter), and other eminent men, had done honour to their little venture (cheers). But there were other circumstances which lent a certain unique quality to the present occasion (hear, hear). So far as his recollection went, and in connection with the Society for the Recovery of London Antiquities it went very far (loud cheers), he did not remember that any of their lecturers had borne the title of King. He would therefore call upon King Auberon briefly to address the meeting.

The King began by saying that this speech might be regarded as the first declaration of his new policy for the nation. "At this supreme hour of my life I feel that to no one but the members of the Society for the Recovery of London Antiquities can I open my heart (cheers). If the world turns upon my policy, and the storms of popular hostility begin to rise (no, no), I feel that it is here, with my brave Recoverers around me, that I can best meet them, sword in hand" (loud cheers).

His Majesty then went on to explain that, now old age was creeping upon him, he proposed to devote his remaining strength to bringing about a keener sense of local patriotism in the various municipalities of London. How few of them knew the legends of their own boroughs! How many there were who had never heard of the true origin of the Wink of Wandsworth! What a large proportion of the younger generation in

Chelsea neglected to perform the old Chelsea Chuff! Pimlico no longer pumped the Pimlies. Battersea had forgotten the name of Blick.

There was a short silence, and then a voice said "Shame!"

The King continued: "Being called, however unworthily, to this high estate, I have resolved that, so far as possible, this neglect shall cease. I desire no military glory. I lay claim to no constitutional equality with Justinian or Alfred. If I can go down to history as the man who saved from extinction a few old English customs, if our descendants can say it was through this man, humble as he was, that the Ten Turnips are still eaten in Fulham, and the Putney parish councillor still shaves one half of his head, I shall look my great fathers reverently but not fearfully in the face when I go down to the last house of Kings."

The King paused, visibly affected, but collecting himself, resumed once more.

"I trust that to very few of you, at least, I need dwell on the sublime origins of these legends. The very names of your boroughs bear witness to them. So long as Hammersmith is called Hammersmith, its people will live in the shadow of that primal hero, the

Blacksmith, who led the democracy of the Broadway into battle till he drove the chivalry of Kensington before him and over-threw them at that place which in honour of the best blood of the defeated aristocracy is still called Kensington Gore. Men of Hammersmith will not fail to remember that the very name of Kensington originated from the lips of their hero. For at the great banquet of reconciliation held after the war, when the disdainful oligarchs declined to join in the songs of the men of the Broadway (which are to this day of a rude and popular character), the great Republican leader, with his rough humour, said the words which are written in gold upon his monument, 'Little birds that can sing and won't sing, must be made to sing.' So that the Eastern Knights were called Cansings or Kensings ever afterwards. But you also have great memories, O men of Kensington! You showed that you could sing, and sing great war-songs. Even after the dark day of Kensington Gore, history will not forget those three Knights who guarded your disordered retreat from Hyde Park (so called from your hiding there), those three Knights after whom Knightsbridge is named. Nor will it forget the day of your re-emergence, purged in the fire of calamity, cleansed of your oligarchic corruptions, when, sword in hand, you drove the Empire of Hammersmith back mile by mile, swept it past its own Broadway, and broke it at last in a battle so long and bloody that the birds of prey have left their name upon it. Men have called it, with austere irony, the Ravenscourt. I shall not, I trust, wound the patriotism of Bayswa-ter, or the lonelier pride of Brompton, or that of any other historic township, by taking these two special examples. I select them, not because they are more glorious than the rest, but partly from per-sonal association (I am myself descended from one of the three heroes of Knightsbridge), and partly from the consciousness that I am an amateur antiquarian, and cannot presume to deal with times and places more remote and more mysterious. It is not for me to settle the question between two such men as Professor Hugg and Sir William Whisky as to whether Notting Hill means Nutting Hill (in allusion to the rich woods which no longer cover it), or whether it is a corruption of Nothing-ill, referring to its reputation among the ancients as an Earthly Paradise. When a Podkins and a Jossy confess themselves doubtful about the boundaries of West Kensington (said to have been traced in the blood of Oxen), I need not be ashamed to confess a similar doubt. I will ask you to excuse me from further history, and to assist me with your encouragement in dealing with the problem which faces us today. Is this ancient spirit of the London townships to die out? Are our omnibus conductors and policemen to lose altogether that light which we see so often in their eyes, the dreamy light of

'Old unhappy far-off things
And battles long ago'

—to quote the words of a little-known poet who was a friend of my youth? I have resolved, as I have said, so far as possible, to preserve the eyes of policemen and omnibus conductors in their present dreamy state. For what is a state without dreams? And the remedy I propose is as follows:

"Tomorrow morning at twenty-five minutes past ten, if Heaven spares my life, I purpose to issue a Proclamation. It has been the work of my life, and is about half finished. With the assistance of a whisky and soda, I shall conclude the other half tonight, and my people will receive it tomorrow. All these boroughs where you were born, and hope to lay your bones, shall be reinstated in their ancient magnificence—Hammersmith, Kensington, Bayswater, Chelsea, Battersea, Clapham, Balham, and a hundred others. Each shall immediately build a city wall with gates to be closed at sunset. Each shall have a city guard, armed to the teeth. Each shall have a banner, a coat-of-arms, and, if convenient, a gathering cry. I will not enter into the details now, my heart is too full. They will be found in the proclamation itself. You will all, however, be subject to enrolment in the local city guards, to be summoned together by a thing called the Tocsin, the meaning of which I am studying in my researches into history. Personally, I believe a tocsin to be some kind of highly paid official. If, therefore, any of you happen to have such a thing as a halberd in the house, I should advise you to practise with it in the garden."

Here the King buried his face in his handkerchief and hurriedly left the platform, overcome by emotions.

The members of the Society for the Recovery of London Antiquities rose in an indescribable state of vagueness. Some were purple with indignation; an intellectual few were purple with laughter; the great majority found their minds a blank. There remains a tradition that one pale face with burning blue eyes remained fixed upon the lecturer, and after the lecture a red-haired boy ran out of the room.

CHAPTER II

The Council of the Provosts

The King got up early next morning and came down three steps at a time like a schoolboy. Having eaten his breakfast hurriedly, but with an appetite, he summoned one of the highest officials of the Palace, and presented him with a shilling. "Go and buy me," he said, "a shilling paint-box, which you will get, unless the mists of time mislead me, in a shop at the corner of the second and dirtier street that leads out of Rochester Row. I have already requested the Master of the Buckhounds to provide me with cardboard. It seemed to me (I know not why) that it fell within his department."

The King was happy all that morning with his cardboard and his paint-box. He was engaged in designing the uniforms and coats-of-arms for the various municipalities of London. They gave him deep and no inconsiderable thought. He felt the responsibility.

"I cannot think," he said, "why people should think the names of places in the country more poetical than those in London. Shallow romanticists go away in trains and stop in places called Hugmy-in-the-Hole, or Bumps-on-the-Puddle. And all the time they could, if they liked, go and live at a place with the dim, divine name of St. John's Wood. I have never been to St. John's Wood. I dare not. I should be afraid of the innumerable night of fir trees, afraid to come upon a blood-red cup and the beating of the wings of the Eagle. But all these things can be imagined by remaining reverently in the Harrow train."

And he thoughtfully retouched his design for the head-dress of the halberdier of St. John's Wood, a design in black and red, compounded of a pine tree and the plumage of an eagle. Then he turned to another card. "Let us think of milder matters," he said. "Lavender Hill! Could any of your glebes and combes and all the rest of it produce so fragrant an idea? Think of a mountain of lavender lifting itself in purple poignancy into the silver skies and filling men's nostrils with a new breath of life—a purple hill of incense. It is true that upon my few excursions of discovery on a halfpenny tram I have failed to hit the precise spot. But it must be there; some poet called it by its name. There is at least warrant enough for the solemn purple plumes (following the botanical formation of lavender) which I have required people to wear in the neighbourhood of Clapham Junction. It is so everywhere, after all. I have never been actually to Southfields, but I suppose a scheme of lemons and olives represent their austral instincts. I have never visited Parson's Green, or seen either the Green or the Parson, but surely the pale-green shovel-hats I have designed must be more or less in the spirit. I must work in the dark and let my instincts guide me. The great love I bear to my people will certainly save me from distressing their noble spirit or violating their great traditions."

As he was reflecting in this vein, the door was flung open, and an official announced Mr. Barker and Mr. Lambert.

Mr. Barker and Mr. Lambert were not particularly surprised to find the King sitting on the floor amid a litter of water-colour sketches. They were not particularly surprised because the last time they had called on him they had found him sitting on the floor, surrounded by a litter of children's bricks, and the time before surrounded by a litter of wholly unsuccessful attempts to make paper darts. But the trend of the royal infant's remarks, uttered from amid this infantile chaos, was not quite the same affair. For some time they let him babble on, conscious that his remarks meant nothing. And then a horrible thought began to steal over the mind of James Barker. He began to think that the King's remarks did not mean nothing.

"In God's name, Auberon," he suddenly volleyed out, startling the quiet hall, "you don't mean that you are really going to have these city guards and city walls and things?"

"I am, indeed," said the infant, in a quiet voice. "Why shouldn't I have them? I have modelled them precisely on your political principles. Do you know what I've done, Barker? I've behaved like a true Barkerian. I've…but perhaps it won't interest you, the account of my Barkerian conduct."

"Oh, go on, go on," cried Barker.

"The account of my Barkerian conduct," said Auberon, calmly, "seems not only to interest, but to alarm you. Yet it is very simple. It merely consists in choosing all the provosts under any new scheme by the same principle by which you have caused the central despot to be appointed. Each provost, of each city, under my charter, is to be appointed by rotation. Sleep, therefore, my Barker, a rosy sleep."

Barker's wild eyes flared.

"But, in God's name, don't you see, Quin, that the thing is quite different? In the centre it doesn't matter so much, just because the whole object of despotism is to get some sort of unity. But if any damned parish can go to any damned man—"

"I see your difficulty," said King Auberon, calmly. "You feel that your talents may be neglected. Listen!" And he rose with immense magnificence. "I solemnly give to my liege subject, James Barker, my special and splendid favour, the right to override the obvious text of the Charter of the Cities, and to be, in his own right, Lord High Provost of South Kensington. And now, my dear James, you are all right. Good day."

"But—" began Barker.

"The audience is at an end, Provost," said the King, smiling.

How far his confidence was justified, it would require a somewhat complicated description to explain. "The Great Proclamation of the Charter of the Free Cities" appeared in due course that morning, and was posted by bill-stickers all over the front of the Palace, the King assisting them with animated directions, and standing in the middle of the road, with his head on one side, contemplating the result. It was also carried up and down the main thoroughfares by sandwichmen, and the King was, with difficulty, restrained from going out in that capacity himself, being, in fact, found by the Groom of the Stole and Captain Bowler, struggling between two boards. His excitement had positively to be quieted like that of a child.

The reception which the Charter of the Cities met at the hands of the public may mildly be described as mixed. In one sense it was popular enough. In many happy homes that remarkable legal document was read aloud on winter evenings amid uproarious appreciation, when everything had been learnt by heart from that quaint but immortal old classic, Mr. W. W. Jacobs. But when it was discovered that the King had every intention of seriously requiring the provisions to be carried out, of insisting that the grotesque cities, with their tocsins and city guards, should really come into existence, things were thrown into a far angrier confusion. Londoners had no particular objection to the King making a fool of himself, but they became indignant when it became evident that he wished to make fools of them; and protests began to come in.

The Lord High Provost of the Good and Valiant City of West Kensington wrote a respectful letter to the King, explaining that upon State occasions it would, of course, be his duty to observe what formalities the King thought proper, but that it was really awkward for a decent householder not to be allowed to go out and put a post-card in a pillar-box without being escorted by five heralds, who announced, with formal cries and blasts of a trumpet, that the Lord High Provost desired to catch the post.

The Lord High Provost of North Kensington, who was a prosperous draper, wrote a curt business note, like a man complaining of a railway company, stating that definite inconvenience had been caused him by the presence of the halberdiers, whom he had to take with him everywhere. When attempting to catch an omnibus to the City, he had found that while room could have been found for himself, the halberdiers had a difficulty in getting in to the vehicle—believe him, theirs faithfully.

The Lord High Provost of Shepherd's Bush said his wife did not like men hanging round the kitchen.

The King was always delighted to listen to these grievances, delivering lenient and kingly answers, but as he always insisted, as the absolute *sine qua non*, that verbal complaints should be presented to him with the fullest pomp of trumpets, plumes, and halberds, only a few resolute spirits were prepared to run the gauntlet of the little boys in the street.

Among these, however, was prominent the abrupt and business-like gentleman who ruled North Kensington. And he had, before long, occasion to interview the King about a matter wider and even more urgent than the problem of the halberdiers and the omnibus. This was the great question which then and for long afterwards brought a stir to the blood and a flush to the cheek of all the speculative builders and house agents from Shepherd's Bush to the Marble Arch, and from Westbourne Grove to High Street, Kensington. I refer to the great affair of the improvements in Notting Hill. The scheme was conducted chiefly by Mr. Buck, the abrupt North Kensington magnate, and by Mr. Wilson, the Provost of Bayswater. A great thoroughfare was to be driven through three boroughs, through West Kensington, North Kensington and Notting Hill, opening at one end into Hammersmith Broadway, and at the other into Westbourne Grove. The negotiations, buyings, sellings, bullying and bribing took ten years, and by the end of it Buck, who had conducted them almost single-handed, had proved himself a man of the strongest type of material energy and material diplomacy. And just as his splendid patience and more splendid impatience had finally brought him victory, when workmen were already demolishing houses and walls along the great line from Hammersmith, a sudden obstacle appeared that had neither been reckoned with nor dreamed of, a small and strange obstacle, which, like a speck of grit in a great machine, jarred the whole vast scheme and brought it to a stand-still, and Mr. Buck, the draper, getting with great impatience into his robes of office and summoning with indescribable disgust his halberdiers, hurried over to speak to the King.

Ten years had not tired the King of his joke. There were still new faces to be seen looking out from the symbolic head-gears he had designed, gazing at him from amid the pastoral ribbons of Shepherd's Bush or from under the sombre hoods of the Black-friars Road. And the interview which was promised him with the Provost of North Kensington he anticipated with a particular pleasure, for "he never really enjoyed," he said, "the full richness of the mediaeval garments unless the people compelled to wear them were very angry and business-like."

Mr. Buck was both. At the King's command the door of the audience-chamber was thrown open and a herald appeared in the purple colours of Mr. Buck's commonwealth emblazoned with the Great Eagle which the King had attributed to North Kensington, in vague reminiscence of Russia, for he always insisted on regarding North Kensington as some kind of semi-arctic neighbourhood. The herald announced that the Provost of that city desired audience of the King.

"From North Kensington?" said the King, rising graciously. "What news does he bring from that land of high hills and fair women? He is welcome."

The herald advanced into the room, and was immediately followed by twelve guards clad in purple, who were followed by an attendant bearing the banner of the Eagle, who was followed by another attendant bearing the keys of the city upon a cushion, who was followed by Mr. Buck in a great hurry. When the King saw his strong animal face and steady eyes, he knew that he was in the presence of a great man of business, and consciously braced himself.

"Well, well," he said, cheerily coming down two or three steps from a dais, and striking his hands lightly together, "I am glad to see you. Never mind, never mind. Ceremony is not everything."

"I don't understand your Majesty," said the Provost, stolidly.

"Never mind, never mind," said the King, gaily. "A knowledge of Courts is by no means an unmixed merit; you will do it next time, no doubt."

The man of business looked at him sulkily from under his black brows and said again without show of civility—

"I don't follow you."

"Well, well," replied the King, good-naturedly, "if you ask me I don't mind telling you, not because I myself attach any importance to these forms in comparison with the Honest Heart. But it is usual—it is usual—that is all, for a man when entering the presence of Royalty to lie down on his back on the floor and elevating his feet towards heaven (as the source of Royal power) to say three times 'Monarchical institutions improve the manners.' But there, there—such pomp is far less truly dignified than your simple kindliness."

The Provost's face was red with anger, and he maintained silence.

"And now," said the King, lightly, and with the exasperating air of a man softening a snub; "what delightful weather we are having! You must find your official robes warm, my Lord. I designed them for your own snow-bound land."

"They're as hot as hell," said Buck, briefly. "I came here on business."

"Right," said the King, nodding a great number of times with quite unmeaning solemnity; "right, right, right. Business, as the sad glad old Persian said, is business. Be punctual. Rise early. Point the pen to the shoulder. Point the pen to the shoulder, for you know not whence you come nor why. Point the pen to the shoulder, for you know not when you go nor where."

The Provost pulled a number of papers from his pocket and savagely flapped them open.

"Your Majesty may have heard," he began, sarcastically, "of Hammersmith and a thing called a road. We have been at work ten years buying property and getting compulsory powers and fixing compensation and squaring vested interests, and now at the very end, the thing is stopped by a fool. Old Prout, who was Provost of Notting Hill, was a business man, and we dealt with him quite satisfactorily. But he's dead, and the cursed lot has fallen on a young man named Wayne, who's up to some game that's perfectly incomprehensible to me. We offer him a better price than any one ever dreamt of, but he won't let the road go through. And his Council seems to be backing him up. It's midsummer madness."

The King, who was rather inattentively engaged in drawing the Provost's nose with his finger on the window-pane, heard the last two words.

"What a perfect phrase that is!" he said. "'Midsummer madness'!"

"The chief point is," continued Buck, doggedly, "that the only part that is really in question is one dirty little street—Pump Street—a street with nothing in it but a public-house and a penny toy-shop, and that sort of thing. All the respectable people of Notting Hill have accepted our compensation. But the ineffable Wayne sticks out over Pump Street. Says he's Provost of Notting Hill. He's only Provost of Pump Street."

"A good thought," replied Auberon. "I like the idea of a Provost of Pump Street. Why not let him alone?"

"And drop the whole scheme!" cried out Buck, with a burst of brutal spirit. "I'll be damned if we do. No. I'm for sending in workmen to pull down without more ado."

"Strike for the purple Eagle!" cried the King, hot with historical associations.

"I'll tell you what it is," said Buck, losing his temper altogether. "If your Majesty would spend less time in insulting respectable people with your silly coats-of-arms, and more time over the business of the nation—"

The King's brow wrinkled thoughtfully.

"The situation is not bad," he said; "the haughty burgher defying the King in his own Palace. The burgher's head should be thrown back and the right arm extended; the left may be lifted towards Heaven, but that I leave to your private religious sentiment. I have sunk back in this chair, stricken with baffled fury. Now again, please."

Buck's mouth opened like a dog's, but before he could speak another herald appeared at the door.

"The Lord High Provost of Bayswater," he said, "desires an audience."

"Admit him," said Auberon. "This is a jolly day."

The halberdiers of Bayswater wore a prevailing uniform of green, and the banner which was borne after them was emblazoned with a green bay-wreath on a silver ground, which the King, in the course of his researches into a bottle of champagne, had discovered to be the quaint old punning cognisance of the city of Bayswater.

"It is a fit symbol," said the King, "your immortal bay-wreath. Fulham may seek for wealth, and Kensington for art, but when did the men of Bayswater care for anything but glory?"

Immediately behind the banner, and almost completely hidden by it, came the Provost of the city, clad in splendid robes of green and silver with white fur and crowned with bay. He was an anxious little man with red whiskers, originally the owner of a small sweet-stuff shop.

"Our cousin of Bayswater," said the King, with delight; "what can we get for you?" The King was heard also distinctly to mutter, "Cold beef, cold 'am, cold chicken," his voice dying into silence.

"I came to see your Majesty," said the Provost of Bayswater, whose name was Wilson, "about that Pump Street affair."

"I have just been explaining the situation to his Majesty," said Buck, curtly, but recovering his civility. "I am not sure, however, whether his Majesty knows how much the matter affects you also."

"It affects both of us, yer see, yer Majesty, as this scheme was started for the benefit of the 'ole neighbourhood. So Mr. Buck and me we put our 'eads together—"

The King clasped his hands.

"Perfect!" he cried in ecstacy. "Your heads together! I can see it! Can't you do it now? Oh, do do it now!"

A smothered sound of amusement appeared to come from the halberdiers, but Mr. Wilson looked merely bewildered, and Mr. Buck merely diabolical.

"I suppose," he began bitterly, but the King stopped him with a gesture of listening.

"Hush," he said, "I think I hear some one else coming. I seem to hear another herald, a herald whose boots creak."

As he spoke another voice cried from the doorway—

"The Lord High Provost of South Kensington desires an audience."

"The Lord High Provost of South Kensington!" cried the King. "Why, that is my old friend James Barker! What does he want, I wonder? If the tender memories of friendship have not grown misty, I fancy he wants something for himself, probably money. How are you, James?"

Mr. James Barker, whose guard was attired in a splendid blue, and whose blue banner bore three gold birds singing, rushed, in his blue and gold robes, into the room. Despite the absurdity of all the dresses, it was worth noticing that he carried his better than the rest, though he loathed it as much as any of them. He was a gentleman, and a very handsome man, and could not help unconsciously wearing even his preposterous robe as it should be worn. He spoke quickly, but with the slight initial hesitation he always showed in addressing the King, due to suppressing an impulse to address his old acquaintance in the old way.

"Your Majesty—pray forgive my intrusion. It is about this man in Pump Street. I see you have Buck here, so you have probably heard what is necessary. I—"

The King swept his eyes anxiously round the room, which now blazed with the trappings of three cities.

"There is one thing necessary," he said.

"Yes, your Majesty," said Mr. Wilson of Bayswater, a little eagerly.

"What does yer Majesty think necessary?"

"A little yellow," said the King, firmly. "Send for the Provost of West Kensington."

Amid some materialistic protests he was sent for, and arrived with his yellow halberdiers in his saffron robes, wiping his forehead with a handkerchief. After all, placed as he was, he had a good deal to say on the matter.

"Welcome, West Kensington," said the King. "I have long wished to see you touching that matter of the Hammersmith land to the south of the Rowton House. Will you hold it feudally from the Provost of Hammersmith? You have only to do him homage by putting his left arm in his overcoat and then marching home in state."

"No, your Majesty; I'd rather not," said the Provost of West Kensington, who was a pale young man with a fair moustache and whiskers, who kept a successful dairy.

The King struck him heartily on the shoulder.

"The fierce old West Kensington blood," he said; "they are not wise who ask it to do homage."

Then he glanced again round the room. It was full of a roaring sunset of colour, and he enjoyed the sight, possible to so few artists—the sight of his own dreams moving and blazing before him. In the foreground the yellow of the West Kensington liveries outlined itself against the dark blue draperies of South Kensington. The crests of these again brightened suddenly into green as the almost woodland colours of Bayswater rose behind them. And over and behind all, the great purple plumes of North Kensington showed almost funereal and black.

"There is something lacking," said the King—"something lacking. What can—ah, there it is! There it is!"

In the doorway had appeared a new figure, a herald in flaming red. He cried in a loud but unemotional voice—

"The Lord High Provost of Notting Hill desires an audience."

BOOK I

CHAPTER III

Enter a Lunatic

The King of the Fairies, who was, it is to be presumed, the godfather of King Auberon, must have been very favourable on this particular day to his fantastic godchild, for with the entrance of the guard of the Provost of Notting Hill there was a certain more or less inexplicable addition to his delight. The wretched navvies and sandwich-men who carried the colours of Bayswater or South Kensington, engaged merely for the day to satisfy the Royal hobby, slouched into the room with a comparatively hang-dog air, and a great part of the King's intellectual pleasure consisted in the contrast between the arrogance of their swords and feathers and the meek misery of their faces. But these Notting Hill halberdiers in their red tunics belted with gold had the air rather of an absurd gravity. They seemed, so to speak, to be taking part in the joke. They marched and wheeled into position with an almost startling dignity and discipline.

They carried a yellow banner with a great red lion, named by the King as the Notting Hill emblem, after a small public-house in the neighbourhood, which he once frequented.

Between the two lines of his followers there advanced towards the King a tall, red-haired young man, with high features and bold blue eyes. He would have been called handsome, but that a certain indefinable air of his nose being too big for his face, and his feet for his legs, gave him a look of awkwardness and extreme youth. His robes were red, according to the King's heraldry, and, alone among the Provosts, he was girt with a great sword. This was Adam Wayne, the intractable Provost of Notting Hill.

The King flung himself back in his chair, and rubbed his hands.

"What a day, what a day!" he said to himself. "Now there'll be a row. I'd no idea it would be such fun as it is. These Provosts are so very indignant, so very reasonable, so very right. This fellow, by the look in his eyes, is even more indignant than the rest. No sign in those large blue eyes, at any rate, of ever having heard of a joke. He'll remonstrate with the others, and they'll remonstrate with him, and they'll all make themselves sumptuously happy remonstrating with me."

"Welcome, my Lord," he said aloud. "What news from the Hill of a Hundred Legends? What have you for the ear of your King? I know that troubles have arisen between you and these others, our cousins, but these troubles it shall be our pride to compose. And I doubt not, and cannot doubt, that your love for me is not less tender, no less ardent, than theirs."

Mr. Buck made a bitter face, and James Barker's nostrils curled;

Wilson began to giggle faintly, and the Provost of West Kensington followed in a smothered way. But the big blue eyes of Adam Wayne never changed, and he called out in an odd, boyish voice down the hall—

"I bring homage to my King. I bring him the only thing I have—my sword."

And with a great gesture he flung it down on the ground, and knelt on one knee behind it.

There was a dead silence.

"I beg your pardon," said the King, blankly.

"You speak well, sire," said Adam Wayne, "as you ever speak, when you say that my love is not less than the love of these. Small would it be if it were not more. For I am the heir of your scheme— the child of the great Charter. I stand here for the rights the Charter gave me, and I swear, by your sacred crown, that where I stand, I stand fast."

The eyes of all five men stood out of their heads.

Then Buck said, in his jolly, jarring voice: "Is the whole world mad?"

The King sprang to his feet, and his eyes blazed.

"Yes," he cried, in a voice of exultation, "the whole world is mad, but Adam Wayne and me. It is true as death what I told you long ago, James Barker, seriousness sends men mad. You are mad, because you care for politics, as mad as a man who collects tram tickets. Buck is mad, because he cares for money, as mad as a man who lives on opium. Wilson is mad, because he thinks himself right, as mad as a man who thinks himself God Almighty. The Provost of West Kensington is mad, because he thinks he is respectable, as mad as a man who thinks he is a chicken. All men are mad but the humorist, who cares for nothing and possesses everything. I thought that there was only one humorist in England. Fools!—dolts!—open your cows' eyes; there are two! In Notting Hill—in that unpromising elevation—there has been born an artist! You thought to spoil my joke, and bully me out of it, by becoming more and more modern, more and more practical, more and more bustling and rational. Oh, what a feast it was to answer you by becoming more and more august, more and more gracious, more and more ancient and mellow! But this lad has seen how to bowl me out. He has answered me back, vaunt for vaunt, rhetoric for rhetoric. He has lifted the only shield I cannot break, the shield of an impenetrable pomposity. Listen to him. You have come, my Lord, about Pump Street?"

"About the city of Notting Hill," answered Wayne, proudly, "of which Pump Street is a living and rejoicing part."

"Not a very large part," said Barker, contemptuously.

"That which is large enough for the rich to covet," said Wayne, drawing up his head, "is large enough for the poor to defend."

The King slapped both his legs, and waved his feet for a second in the air.

"Every respectable person in Notting Hill," cut in Buck, with his cold, coarse voice, "is for us and against you. I have plenty of friends in Notting Hill."

"Your friends are those who have taken your gold for other men's hearthstones, my Lord Buck," said Provost Wayne. "I can well believe they are your friends."

"They've never sold dirty toys, anyhow," said Buck, laughing shortly.

"They've sold dirtier things," said Wayne, calmly: "they have sold themselves."

"It's no good, my Buckling," said the King, rolling about on his chair. "You can't cope with this chivalrous eloquence. You can't cope with an artist. You can't cope with the humorist of Notting Hill. Oh, *Nunc dimittis*—that I have lived to see this day! Provost Wayne, you stand firm?"

"Let them wait and see," said Wayne. "If I stood firm before, do you think I shall weaken now that I have seen the face of the King? For I fight for something greater, if greater there can be, than the hearthstones of my people and the Lordship of the Lion. I fight for your royal vision, for the great dream you dreamt of the League of the Free Cities. You have given me this liberty. If I had been a beggar and you had flung me a coin, if I had been a peasant in a dance and you had flung me a favour, do you think I would have let it be taken by any ruffians on the road? This leadership and liberty of Notting Hill is a gift from your Majesty, and if it is taken from me, by God! it shall be taken in battle, and the noise of that battle shall be heard in the flats of Chelsea and in the studios of St. John's Wood."

"It is too much—it is too much," said the King. "Nature is weak. I must speak to you, brother artist, without further disguise. Let me ask you a solemn question. Adam Wayne, Lord High Provost of Notting Hill, don't you think it splendid?"

"Splendid!" cried Adam Wayne. "It has the splendour of God."

"Bowled out again," said the King. "You will keep up the pose. Funnily, of course, it is serious. But seriously, isn't it funny?"

"What?" asked Wayne, with the eyes of a baby.

"Hang it all, don't play any more. The whole business—the Charter of the Cities. Isn't it immense?"

"Immense is no unworthy word for that glorious design."

"Oh, hang you! But, of course, I see. You want me to clear the room of these reasonable sows. You want the two humorists alone together. Leave us, gentlemen."

Buck threw a sour look at Barker, and at a sullen signal the whole pageant of blue and green, of red, gold, and purple, rolled out of the room, leaving only two in the great hall, the King sitting in his seat on the dais, and the red-clad figure still kneeling on the floor before his fallen sword.

The King bounded down the steps and smacked Provost Wayne on the back.

"Before the stars were made," he cried, "we were made for each other. It is too beautiful. Think of the valiant independence of Pump Street. That is the real thing. It is the deification of the ludicrous."

The kneeling figure sprang to his feet with a fierce stagger.

"Ludicrous!" he cried, with a fiery face.

"Oh, come, come," said the King, impatiently, "you needn't keep it up with me. The augurs must wink sometimes from sheer fatigue of the eyelids. Let us enjoy this for half an hour, not as actors, but as dramatic critics. Isn't it a joke?"

Adam Wayne looked down like a boy, and answered in a constrained voice—

"I do not understand your Majesty. I cannot believe that while I fight for your royal charter your Majesty deserts me for these dogs of the gold hunt."

"Oh, damn your... But what's this? What the devil's this?"

The King stared into the young Provost's face, and in the twilight of the room began to see that his face was quite white and his lip shaking.

"What in God's name is the matter?" cried Auberon, holding his wrist.

Wayne flung back his face, and the tears were shining on it.

"I am only a boy," he said, "but it's true. I would paint the Red Lion on my shield if I had only my blood."

King Auberon dropped the hand and stood without stirring, thunderstruck.

"My God in Heaven!" he said; "is it possible that there is within the four seas of Britain a man who takes Notting Hill seriously?"

"And my God in Heaven!" said Wayne passionately; "is it possible that there is within the four seas of Britain a man who does not take it seriously?"

The King said nothing, but merely went back up the steps of the daïs, like a man dazed. He fell back in his chair again and kicked his heels.

"If this sort of thing is to go on," he said weakly, "I shall begin to doubt the superiority of art to life. In Heaven's name, do not play with me. Do you really mean that you are—God help me!—a Notting Hill patriot; that you are—?"

Wayne made a violent gesture, and the King soothed him wildly.

"All right—all right—I see you are; but let me take it in. You do really propose to fight these modern improvers with their boards and inspectors and surveyors and all the rest of it?"

"Are they so terrible?" asked Wayne, scornfully.

The King continued to stare at him as if he were a human curiosity.

"And I suppose," he said, "that you think that the dentists and small tradesmen and maiden ladies who inhabit Notting Hill, will rally with war-hymns to your standard?"

"If they have blood they will," said the Provost.

"And I suppose," said the King, with his head back among the cushions, "that it never crossed your mind that"—his voice seemed to lose itself luxuriantly—"never crossed your mind that any one ever thought that the idea of a Notting Hill idealism was—er—slightly—slightly ridiculous?"

"Of course they think so," said Wayne. "What was the meaning of mocking the prophets?"

"Where," asked the King, leaning forward—"where in Heaven's name did you get this miraculously inane idea?"

"You have been my tutor, Sire," said the Provost, "in all that is high and honourable."

"Eh?" said the King.

"It was your Majesty who first stirred my dim patriotism into flame. Ten years ago, when I was a boy (I am only nineteen), I was playing on the slope of Pump Street, with a wooden sword and a paper helmet, dreaming of great wars. In an angry trance I struck out with my sword, and stood petrified, for I saw that I had struck you, Sire, my King, as you wandered in a noble secrecy, watching over your people's welfare. But I need have had no fear. Then was I taught to understand Kingliness. You neither shrank nor frowned. You summoned no guards. You invoked no punishments. But in august and burning words, which are written in my soul, never to be erased, you told me ever to turn my sword against the enemies of my inviolate city. Like a priest pointing to the altar, you pointed to the hill of Notting. 'So long,' you said, 'as you are ready to die for the sacred mountain, even if it were ringed with all the armies of Bayswater.' I have not forgotten the words, and I have reason now to remember them, for the hour is come and the crown of your prophecy. The sacred hill is ringed with the armies of Bayswater, and I am ready to die."

The King was lying back in his chair, a kind of wreck.

"Oh, Lord, Lord, Lord," he murmured, "what a life! What a life! All my work! I seem to have done it all. So you're the red-haired boy that hit me in the waistcoat. What have I done? God, what have I done? I thought I would have a joke, and I have created a passion. I tried to compose a burlesque, and it seems to be turning halfway through into an epic. What is to be done with such a world? In the Lord's name, wasn't the joke broad and bold enough? I abandoned my subtle humour to amuse you, and I seem to have brought tears to your eyes. What's to be done with people when you write a pantomime for them—call the sausages classic festoons, and the policeman cut in two a tragedy of public duty? But why am I talking? Why am I asking questions of a nice young gentleman who is totally mad? What is the good of it? What is the good of anything? Oh, Lord! Oh, Lord!"

Suddenly he pulled himself upright.

"Don't you really think the sacred Notting Hill at all absurd?"

"Absurd?" asked Wayne, blankly. "Why should I?"

The King stared back equally blankly.

"I beg your pardon," he said.

"Notting Hill," said the Provost, simply, "is a rise or high ground of the common earth, on which men have built houses to live, in which they are born, fall in love, pray, marry, and die. Why should I think it absurd?"

The King smiled.

"Because, my Leonidas—" he began, then suddenly, he knew not how, found his mind was a total blank. After all, why was it absurd? Why was it absurd? He felt as if the floor of his mind had given way. He felt as all men feel when their first principles are hit hard with a question. Barker always felt so when the King said, "Why trouble about politics?"

The King's thoughts were in a kind of rout; he could not collect them.

"It is generally felt to be a little funny," he said vaguely.

"I suppose," said Adam, turning on him with a fierce suddenness—"I suppose you fancy crucifixion was a serious affair?"

"Well, I—" began Auberon—"I admit I have generally thought it had its graver side."

"Then you are wrong," said Wayne, with incredible violence. "Crucifixion is comic. It is exquisitely diverting. It was an absurd and obscene kind of impaling reserved for people who were made to be laughed at—for slaves and provincials, for dentists and small tradesmen, as you would say. I have seen the grotesque gallows-shape, which the little Roman gutter-boys scribbled on walls as a vulgar joke, blazing on the pinnacles of the temples of the world. And shall I turn back?"

The King made no answer.

Adam went on, his voice ringing in the roof.

"This laughter with which men tyrannise is not the great power you think it. Peter was crucified, and crucified head downwards. What could be funnier than the idea of a respectable old

Apostle upside down? What could be more in the style of your modern humour? But what was the good of it? Upside down or right side up, Peter was Peter to mankind. Upside down he stills hangs over Europe, and millions move and breathe only in the life of his Church."

King Auberon got up absently.

"There is something in what you say," he said. "You seem to have been thinking, young man."

"Only feeling, sire," answered the Provost. "I was born, like other men, in a spot of the earth which I loved because I had played boys' games there, and fallen in love, and talked with my friends through nights that were nights of the gods. And I feel the riddle. These little gardens where we told our loves. These streets where we brought out our dead. Why should they be commonplace? Why should they be absurd? Why should it be grotesque to say that a pillar-box is poetic when for a year I could not see a red pillar-box against the yellow evening in a certain street without being wracked with something of which God keeps the secret, but which is stronger than sorrow or joy? Why should any one be able to raise a laugh by saying 'the Cause of Notting Hill'?—Notting Hill where thousands of immortal spirits blaze with alternate hope and fear."

Auberon was flicking dust off his sleeve with quite a new seriousness on his face, distinct from the owlish solemnity which was the pose of his humour.

"It is very difficult," he said at last. "It is a damned difficult thing. I see what you mean; I agree with you even up to a point— or I should like to agree with you, if I were young enough to be a prophet and poet. I feel a truth in everything you say until you come to the words 'Notting Hill.' And then I regret to say that the old Adam awakes roaring with laughter and makes short work of the new Adam, whose name is Wayne."

For the first time Provost Wayne was silent, and stood gazing dreamily at the floor. Evening was closing in, and the room had grown darker.

"I know," he said, in a strange, almost sleepy voice, "there is truth in what you say, too. It is hard not to laugh at the common names—I only say we should not. I have thought of a remedy; but such thoughts are rather terrible."

"What thoughts?" asked Auberon.

The Provost of Notting Hill seemed to have fallen into a kind of trance; in his eyes was an elvish light.

"I know of a magic wand, but it is a wand that only one or two may rightly use, and only seldom. It is a fairy wand of great fear, stronger than those who use it—often frightful, often wicked to use. But whatever is touched with it is never again wholly common; whatever is touched with it takes a magic from outside the world. If I touch, with this fairy wand, the railways and the roads of Notting Hill, men will love them, and be afraid of them for ever."

"What the devil are you talking about?" asked the King.

"It has made mean landscapes magnificent, and hovels outlast cathedrals," went on the madman. "Why should it not make lamp-posts fairer than Greek lamps; and an omnibus-ride like a painted ship? The touch of it is the finger of a strange perfection."

"What is your wand?" cried the King, impatiently.

"There it is," said Wayne; and pointed to the floor, where his sword lay flat and shining.

"The sword!" cried the King; and sprang up straight on the dais.

"Yes, yes," cried Wayne, hoarsely. "The things touched by that are not vulgar; the things touched by that—"

King Auberon made a gesture of horror.

"You will shed blood for that!" he cried. "For a cursed point of view—"

"Oh, you kings, you kings!" cried out Adam, in a burst of scorn. "How humane you are, how tender, how considerate! You will make war for a frontier, or the imports of a foreign harbour; you will shed blood for the precise duty on lace, or the salute to an admiral. But for the things that make life itself worthy or miserable—how humane you are! I say here, and I know well what I speak of, there were never any necessary wars but the religious wars. There were never any just wars but the religious wars. There were never any humane wars but the religious wars. For these men were fighting for something that claimed, at least, to be the happiness of a man, the virtue of a man. A Crusader thought, at least, that Islam hurt the soul of every man, king or tinker, that it could really capture. I think Buck and Barker and these rich vultures hurt the soul of every man, hurt every inch of the ground, hurt every brick of the houses, that they can really capture. Do you think I have no right to fight for Notting Hill, you whose English Government has so often fought for tomfooleries? If, as your rich friends say, there are no gods, and the skies are dark above us, what should a man fight for, but the place where he had the Eden of childhood and the short heaven of first love? If no temples and no scriptures are sacred, what is sacred if a man's own youth is not sacred?"

The King walked a little restlessly up and down the dais.

"It is hard," he said, biting his lips, "to assent to a view so desperate—so responsible...."

As he spoke, the door of the audience chamber fell ajar, and through the aperture came, like the sudden chatter of a bird, the high, nasal, but well-bred voice of Barker.

"I said to him quite plainly—the public interests—"

Auberon turned on Wayne with violence.

"What the devil is all this? What am I saying? What are you saying? Have you hypnotised me? Curse your uncanny blue eyes! Let me go. Give me back my sense of humour. Give it me back—give it me back, I say!"

"I solemnly assure you," said Wayne, uneasily, with a gesture, as if feeling all over himself, "that I haven't got it."

The King fell back in his chair, and went into a roar of Rabelaisian laughter.

"I don't think you have," he cried.

Book III

CHAPTER I

The Mental Condition of Adam Wayne

A little while after the King's accession a small book of poems appeared, called "Hymns on the Hill." They were not good poems, nor was the book successful, but it attracted a certain amount of attention from one particular school of critics. The King himself, who was a member of the school, reviewed it in his capacity of literary critic to "Straight from the Stables," a sporting journal. They were known as the Hammock School, because it had been calculated malignantly by an enemy that no less than thirteen of their delicate criticisms had begun with the words, "I read this book in a hammock: half asleep in the sleepy sunlight, I…"; after that there were important differences. Under these conditions they liked everything, but especially everything silly. "Next to authentic goodness in a book," they said—"next to authentic goodness in a book (and that, alas! we never find) we desire a rich badness." Thus it happened that their praise (as indicating the presence of a rich badness) was not universally sought after, and authors became a little disquieted when they found the eye of the Hammock School fixed upon them with peculiar favour.

The peculiarity of "Hymns on the Hill" was the celebration of the poetry of London as distinct from the poetry of the country. This sentiment or affectation was, of course, not uncommon in the twentieth century, nor was it, although sometimes exaggerated, and sometimes artificial, by any means without a great truth at its root, for there is one respect in which a town must be more poetical than the country, since it is closer to the spirit of man; for London, if it be not one of the masterpieces of man, is at least one of his sins. A street is really more poetical than a meadow, because a street has a secret. A street is going somewhere, and a meadow nowhere. But, in the case of the book called "Hymns on the Hill," there was another peculiarity, which the King pointed out with great acumen in his review. He was naturally interested in the matter, for he had himself published a volume of lyrics about London under his pseudonym of "Daisy Daydream."

This difference, as the King pointed out, consisted in the fact that, while mere artificers like "Daisy Daydream" (on whose elaborate style the King, over his signature of "Thunderbolt," was perhaps somewhat too severe) thought to praise London by comparing it to the country—using nature, that is, as a background from which all poetical images had to be drawn—the more robust author of "Hymns on the Hill" praised the country, or nature, by comparing it to the town, and used the town itself as a background. "Take," said the critic, "the typically feminine lines, 'To the Inventor of The Hansom Cab'—

> 'Poet, whose cunning carved this amorous shell,
> Where twain may dwell.'"

"Surely," wrote the King, "no one but a woman could have written those lines. A woman has always a weakness for nature; with her art is only beautiful as an echo or shadow of it. She is praising the hansom cab by theme and theory, but her soul is still a child by the sea, picking up shells. She can never be utterly of the town, as a man can; indeed, do we not speak (with sacred propriety) of 'a man about town'? Who ever spoke of a woman about town? However much, physically, 'about town' a woman may be, she still models herself on nature; she tries to carry nature with her; she bids grasses to grow on her head, and furry beasts to bite her about the throat. In the heart of a dim city, she models her hat on a flaring cottage garden of flowers. We, with our nobler civic sentiment, model ours on a chimney pot; the ensign of civilisation. And rather than be without birds, she will commit massacre, that she may turn her head into a tree, with dead birds to sing on it."

This kind of thing went on for several pages, and then the critic remembered his subject, and returned to it.

> "Poet, whose cunning carved this amorous shell,
> Where twain may dwell."

"The peculiarity of these fine though feminine lines," continued "Thunderbolt," "is, as we have said, that they praise the hansom cab by comparing it to the shell, to a natural thing. Now, hear the author of 'Hymns on the Hill,' and how he deals with the same subject. In his fine nocturne, entitled 'The Last Omnibus' he relieves the rich and poignant melancholy of the theme by a sudden sense of rushing at the end—

> 'The wind round the old street corner
> Swung sudden and quick as a cab.'

"Here the distinction is obvious. 'Daisy Daydream' thinks it a great compliment to a hansom cab to be compared to one of the spiral chambers of the sea. And the author of 'Hymns on the Hill' thinks it a great compliment to the immortal whirlwind to be compared to a hackney coach. He surely is the real admirer of London. We have no space to speak of all his perfect applications of the idea; of the poem in which, for instance, a lady's eyes are compared, not to stars, but to two perfect street-lamps guiding the wanderer. We have no space to speak of the fine lyric, recalling the Elizabethan spirit, in which the poet, instead of saying that the rose and the lily contend in her complexion, says, with a purer modernism, that the red omnibus of Hammersmith and the white omnibus of Fulham fight there for the mastery. How perfect the image of two contending omnibuses!"

Here, somewhat abruptly, the review concluded, probably because the King had to send off his copy at that moment, as he was in some want of money. But the King was a very good critic, whatever he may have been as King, and he had, to a considerable extent, hit the right nail on the head. "Hymns on the Hill" was not at all like the poems originally published in praise of the poetry of London. And the reason was that it was really written by a man who had seen nothing else but London, and who regarded it, therefore, as the universe. It was written by a raw, red-headed lad of seventeen, named Adam Wayne, who had been born in Notting Hill. An accident in his seventh year prevented his being taken away to the seaside, and thus his whole life had been passed in his own Pump Street, and in its neighbourhood. And the consequence was, that he saw the street-lamps as things quite as eternal as the stars; the two fires were mingled. He saw the houses as things enduring, like the mountains, and so he wrote about them as one would write about mountains. Nature puts on a disguise when she speaks to every man; to this man she put on the disguise of Notting Hill. Nature would mean to a poet born in the Cumberland hills, a stormy sky-line and sudden rocks. Nature would mean to a poet born in the Essex flats, a waste of splendid waters and splendid sunsets. So nature meant to this man Wayne a line of violet roofs and lemon lamps, the chiaroscuro of the town. He did not think it clever or funny to praise the shadows and colours of the town; he had seen no other shadows or colours, and so he praised them—because they were shadows and colours. He saw all this because he was a poet, though in practice a bad poet. It is too often forgotten that just as a bad man is nevertheless a man, so a bad poet is nevertheless a poet.

Mr. Wayne's little volume of verse was a complete failure; and he submitted to the decision of fate with a quite rational humility, went back to his work, which was that of a draper's assistant, and wrote no more. He still retained his feeling about the town of Notting Hill, because he could not possibly have any other feeling, because it was the back and base of his brain. But he does not seem to have made any particular attempt to express it or insist upon it. He was a genuine natural mystic, one of those who live on the border of fairyland. But he was perhaps the first to realise how often the boundary of fairyland runs through a crowded city. Twenty feet from him (for he was very short-sighted) the red and white and yellow suns of the gas-lights thronged and melted into each other like an orchard of fiery trees, the beginning of the woods of elf-land.

But, oddly enough, it was because he was a small poet that he came to his strange and isolated triumph. It was because he was a failure in literature that he became a portent in English history. He was one of those to whom nature has given the desire without the power of artistic expression. He had been a dumb poet from his cradle. He might have been so to his grave, and carried unuttered into the darkness a treasure of new and sensational song. But he was born under the lucky star of a single coincidence. He happened to be at the head of his dingy municipality at the time of the King's jest, at the time when all municipalities were suddenly commanded to break out into banners and flowers. Out of the long procession of the silent poets, who have been passing since the beginning of the world, this one man found himself in the midst of an heraldic vision, in which he could act and speak and live lyrically. While the author and the victims alike treated the whole matter as a silly public charade, this one man, by taking it seriously, sprang suddenly into a throne of artistic omnipotence. Armour, music, standards, watch-fires, the noise of drums, all the theatrical properties were thrown before him. This one poor rhymster, having burnt his own rhymes, began to live that life of open air and acted poetry of which all the poets of the earth have dreamed in vain; the life for which the *Iliad* is only a cheap substitute.

Upwards from his abstracted childhood, Adam Wayne had grown strongly and silently in a certain quality or capacity which is in modern cities almost entirely artificial, but which can be natural, and was primarily almost brutally natural in him, the quality or capacity of patriotism. It exists, like other virtues and vices, in a certain undiluted reality. It is not confused with all kinds of other things. A child speaking of his country or his village may make every mistake in Mandeville or tell every lie in Munchausen, but in his statement there will be no psychological lies any more than there can be in a good song. Adam Wayne, as a boy, had for his dull streets in Notting Hill the ultimate and ancient sentiment that went out to Athens or Jerusalem. He knew the secret of the passion, those secrets which make real old national songs sound so strange to our civilisation. He knew that real patriotism tends to sing about sorrows and forlorn hopes much more than about victory. He knew that in proper names themselves is half the poetry of all national poems. Above all, he knew the supreme psychological fact about patriotism, as certain in connection with it as that a fine shame comes to all lovers, the fact that the patriot never under any circumstances boasts of the largeness of his country, but always, and of necessity, boasts of the smallness of it.

All this he knew, not because he was a philosopher or a genius, but because he was a child. Any one who cares to walk up a side slum like Pump Street, can see a little Adam claiming to be king of a paving-stone. And he will always be proudest if the stone is almost too narrow for him to keep his feet inside it.

It was while he was in such a dream of defensive battle, marking out some strip of street or fortress of steps as the limit of his haughty claim, that the King had met him, and, with a few words flung in mockery, ratified for ever the strange boundaries of his soul. Thenceforward the fanciful idea of the defence of Notting Hill in war became to him a thing as solid as eating or drinking or lighting a pipe. He disposed his meals for it, altered his plans for it, lay awake in the night and went over it again. Two or three shops were to him an arsenal; an area was to him a moat; corners of balconies and turns of stone steps were points for the location of a culverin or an archer. It is almost impossible to convey to any ordinary imagination the degree to which he had transmitted the leaden London landscape to a romantic gold. The process began almost in babyhood, and became habitual like a literal madness. It was felt most keenly at night, when London is really herself, when her lights shine in the dark like the eyes of innumerable cats, and the outline of the dark houses has the bold simplicity of blue hills. But for him the night revealed instead of concealing, and he read all the blank hours of morning and afternoon, by a contradictory phrase, in the light of that darkness. To this man, at any rate, the inconceivable had happened. The artificial city had become to him nature, and he felt the curbstones and gas-lamps as things as ancient as the sky.

One instance may suffice. Walking along Pump Street with a friend, he said, as he gazed dreamily at the iron fence of a little front garden,

"How those railings stir one's blood!"

His friend, who was also a great intellectual admirer, looked at them painfully, but without any particular emotion. He was so troubled about it that he went back quite a large number of times on quiet evenings and stared at the railings, waiting for something to happen to his blood, but without success. At last he took refuge in asking Wayne himself. He discovered that the ecstacy lay in the one point he had never noticed about the railings even after his six visits—the fact that they were, like the great majority of others—in London, shaped at the top after the manner of a spear. As a child, Wayne had half unconsciously compared them with the spears in pictures of Lancelot and St. George, and had grown up under the shadow of the graphic association. Now, whenever he looked at them, they were simply the serried weapons that made a hedge of steel round the sacred homes of Notting Hill. He could not have cleansed his mind of that meaning even if he tried. It was not a fanciful comparison, or anything like it. It would not have been true to say that the familiar railings reminded him of spears; it would have been far truer to say that the familiar spears occasionally reminded him of railings.

A couple of days after his interview with the King, Adam Wayne was pacing like a caged lion in front of five shops that occupied the upper end of the disputed street. They were a grocer's, a chemist's, a barber's, an old curiosity shop and a toy-shop that sold also newspapers. It was these five shops which his childish fastidiousness had first selected as the essentials of the Notting Hill campaign, the citadel of the city. If Notting Hill was the heart of the universe, and Pump Street was the heart of Notting Hill, this was the heart of Pump Street. The fact that they were all small and side by side realised that feeling for a formidable comfort and compactness which, as we have said, was the heart of his patriotism, and of all patriotism. The grocer (who had a wine and spirit licence) was included because he could provision the garrison; the old curiosity shop because it contained enough swords, pistols, partisans, cross-bows, and blunderbusses to arm a whole irregular regiment; the toy and paper shop because Wayne thought a free press an essential centre for the soul of Pump Street; the chemist's to cope with outbreaks of disease among the besieged; and the barber's because it was in the middle of all the rest, and the barber's son was an intimate friend and spiritual affinity.

It was a cloudless October evening settling down through purple into pure silver around the roofs and chimneys of the steep little street, which looked black and sharp and dramatic. In the deep shadows the gas-lit shop fronts gleamed like five fires in a row, and before them, darkly outlined like a ghost against some purgatorial furnaces, passed to and fro the tall bird-like figure and eagle nose of Adam Wayne.

He swung his stick restlessly, and seemed fitfully talking to himself.

"There are, after all, enigmas," he said "even to the man who has faith. There are doubts that remain even after the true philosophy is completed in every rung and rivet. And here is one of them. Is the normal human need, the normal human condition, higher or lower than those special states of the soul which call out a doubtful and dangerous glory? those special powers of knowledge or sacrifice which are made possible only by the existence of evil? Which should come first to our affections, the enduring sanities of peace or the half-maniacal virtues of battle? Which should come first, the man great in the daily round or the man great in emergency? Which should come first, to return to the enigma before me, the grocer or the chemist? Which is more certainly the stay of the city, the swift chivalrous chemist or the benignant all-providing grocer? In such ultimate spiritual doubts it is only possible to choose a side by the higher instincts, and to abide the issue. In any case, I have made my choice. May I be pardoned if I choose wrongly, but I choose the grocer."

"Good morning, sir," said the grocer, who was a middle-aged man, partially bald, with harsh red whiskers and beard, and forehead lined with all the cares of the small tradesman. "What can I do for you, sir?"

Wayne removed his hat on entering the shop, with a ceremonious gesture, which, slight as it was, made the tradesman eye him with the beginnings of wonder.

"I come, sir," he said soberly, "to appeal to your patriotism."

"Why, sir," said the grocer, "that sounds like the times when I was a boy and we used to have elections."

"You will have them again," said Wayne, firmly, "and far greater things. Listen, Mr. Mead. I know the temptations which a grocer has to a too cosmopolitan philosophy. I can imagine what it must be to sit all day as you do surrounded with wares from all the ends of the earth, from strange seas that we have never sailed and strange forests that we could not even picture. No Eastern king ever had such argosies or such cargoes coming from the sunrise and the sunset, and Solomon in all his glory was not enriched like one of you. India is at your elbow," he cried, lifting his voice and pointing his stick at a drawer of rice, the grocer making a movement of some alarm, "China is before you, Demerara is behind you, America is above your head, and at this very moment, like some old Spanish admiral, you hold Tunis in your hands."

Mr. Mead dropped the box of dates which he was just lifting, and then picked it up again vaguely.

Wayne went on with a heightened colour, but a lowered voice—

"I know, I say, the temptations of so international, so universal a vision of wealth. I know that it must be your danger not to fall like many tradesmen into too dusty and mechanical a narrowness, but rather to be too broad, to be too general, too liberal. If a narrow nationalism be the danger of the pastry-cook, who makes his own wares under his own heavens, no less is cosmopolitanism the danger of the grocer. But I come to you in the name of that patriotism which no wanderings or enlightenments should ever wholly extinguish, and I ask you to remember Notting Hill. For, after all, in this cosmopolitan magnificence, she has played no small part. Your dates may come from the tall palms of Barbary, your sugar from the strange islands of the tropics, your tea from the secret villages of the Empire of the Dragon. That this room might be furnished, forests may have been spoiled under the Southern Cross, and leviathans speared under the Polar Star. But you yourself—surely no inconsiderable treasure—you yourself, the brain that wields these vast interests—you yourself, at least, have grown to strength and wisdom between these grey houses and under this rainy sky. This city which made you, and thus made your fortunes, is threatened with war. Come forth and tell to the ends of the earth this lesson. Oil is from the North and fruits from the South; rices are from India and spices from Ceylon; sheep are from New Zealand and men from Notting Hill."

The grocer sat for some little while, with dim eyes and his mouth open, looking rather like a fish. Then he scratched the back of his head, and said nothing. Then he said—

"Anything out of the shop, sir?"

Wayne looked round in a dazed way. Seeing a pile of tins of pine-apple chunks, he waved his stick generally towards them.

"Yes," he said; "I'll take those."

"All those, sir?" said the grocer, with greatly increased interest.

"Yes, yes; all those," replied Wayne, still a little bewildered, like a man splashed with cold water.

"Very good, sir; thank you, sir," said the grocer with animation. "You may count upon my patriotism, sir."

"I count upon it already," said Wayne, and passed out into the gathering night.

The grocer put the box of dates back in its place.

"What a nice fellow he is!" he said. "It's odd how often they are nice. Much nicer than those as are all right."

Meanwhile Adam Wayne stood outside the glowing chemist's shop, unmistakably wavering.

"What a weakness it is!" he muttered. "I have never got rid of it from childhood—the fear of this magic shop. The grocer is rich, he is romantic, he is poetical in the truest sense, but he is not—no, he is not supernatural. But the chemist! All the other shops stand in Notting Hill, but this stands in Elf-land. Look at those great burning bowls of colour. It must be from them that God paints the sunsets. It is superhuman, and the superhuman is all the more uncanny when it is beneficent. That is the root of the fear of God. I am afraid. But I must be a man and enter."

He was a man, and entered. A short, dark young man was behind the counter with spectacles, and greeted him with a bright but entirely business-like smile.

"A fine evening, sir," he said.

"Fine indeed, strange Father," said Adam, stretching his hands somewhat forward. "It is on such clear and mellow nights that your shop is most itself. Then they appear most perfect, those moons of green and gold and crimson, which from afar oft guide the pilgrim of pain and sickness to this house of merciful witchcraft."

"Can I get you anything?" asked the chemist.

"Let me see," said Wayne, in a friendly but vague manner. "Let me have some Sal Volatile."

"Eightpence, tenpence, or one and sixpence a bottle?" said the young man, genially.

"One and six—one and six," replied Wayne, with a wild submissiveness. "I come to ask you, Mr. Bowles, a terrible question."

He paused and collected himself.

"It is necessary," he muttered—"it is necessary to be tactful, and to suit the appeal to each profession in turn."

"I come," he resumed aloud, "to ask you a question which goes to the roots of your miraculous toils. Mr. Bowles, shall all this witchery cease?" And he waved his stick around the shop.

Meeting with no answer, he continued with animation—

"In Notting Hill we have felt to its core the elfish mystery of your profession. And now Notting Hill itself is threatened."

"Anything more, sir?" asked the chemist.

"Oh," said Wayne, somewhat disturbed—"oh, what is it chemists sell? Quinine, I think. Thank you. Shall it be destroyed? I have met these men of Bayswater and North Kensington—Mr. Bowles, they are materialists. They see no witchery in your work, even when it is wrought within their own borders. They think the chemist is commonplace. They think him human."

The chemist appeared to pause, only a moment, to take in the insult, and immediately said—

"And the next article, please?"

"Alum," said the Provost, wildly. "I resume. It is in this sacred town alone that your priesthood is reverenced. Therefore, when you fight for us you fight not only for yourself, but for everything you typify. You fight not only for Notting Hill, but for Fairyland, for as surely as Buck and Barker and such men hold sway, the sense of Fairyland in some strange manner diminishes."

"Anything more, sir?" asked Mr. Bowles, with unbroken cheerfulness.

"Oh yes, jujubes—Gregory powder—magnesia. The danger is imminent. In all this matter I have felt that I fought not merely for my own city (though to that I owe all my blood), but for all places in which these great ideas could prevail. I am fighting not merely for Notting Hill, but for Bayswater itself; for North Kensington itself. For if the gold-hunters prevail, these also will lose all their ancient sentiments and all the mystery of their national soul. I know I can count upon you."

"Oh yes, sir," said the chemist, with great animation; "we are always glad to oblige a good customer."

Adam Wayne went out of the shop with a deep sense of fulfilment of soul.

"It is so fortunate," he said, "to have tact, to be able to play upon the peculiar talents and specialities, the cosmopolitanism of the grocer and the world-old necromancy of the chemist. Where should I be without tact?"

CHAPTER II

The Remarkable Mr. Turnbull

Afterter two more interviews with shopmen, however, the patriot's confidence in his own psychological diplomacy began
vaguely to wane. Despite the care with which he considered the
peculiar rationale and the peculiar glory of each separate shop,
there seemed to be something unresponsive about the shopmen. Whether it was a dark resentment against the uninitiate
for peeping into their masonic magnificence, he could not quite
conjecture.

His conversation with the man who kept the shop of curiosities
had begun encouragingly. The man who kept the shop of curiosities had, indeed, enchanted him with a phrase. He was standing
drearily at the door of his shop, a wrinkled man with a grey pointed
beard, evidently a gentleman who had come down in the world.

"And how does your commerce go, you strange guardian of the
past?" said Wayne, affably.

"Well, sir, not very well," replied the man, with that patient
voice of his class which is one of the most heart-breaking things in
the world. "Things are terribly quiet."

Wayne's eyes shone suddenly.

"A great saying," he said, "worthy of a man whose merchandise
is human history. Terribly quiet; that is in two words the spirit of
this age, as I have felt it from my cradle. I sometimes wondered
how many other people felt the oppression of this union between
quietude and terror. I see blank well-ordered streets and men in

black moving about inoffensively, sullenly. It goes on day after day, day after day, and nothing happens; but to me it is like a dream from which I might wake screaming. To me the straightness of our life is the straightness of a thin cord stretched tight. Its stillness is terrible. It might snap with a noise like thunder. And you who sit, amid the debris of the great wars, you who sit, as it were, upon a battlefield, you know that war was less terrible than this evil peace; you know that the idle lads who carried those swords under Francis or Elizabeth, the rude Squire or Baron who swung that mace about in Picardy or Northumberland battles, may have been terribly noisy, but were not like us, terribly quiet."

Whether it was a faint embarrassment of conscience as to the original source and date of the weapons referred to, or merely an engrained depression, the guardian of the past looked, if anything, a little more worried.

"But I do not think," continued Wayne, "that this horrible silence of modernity will last, though I think for the present it will increase. What a farce is this modern liberality! Freedom of speech means practically, in our modern civilisation, that we must only talk about unimportant things. We must not talk about religion, for that is illiberal; we must not talk about bread and cheese, for that is talking shop; we must not talk about death, for that is depressing; we must not talk about birth, for that is indelicate. It cannot last. Something must break this strange indifference, this strange dreamy egoism, this strange loneliness of millions in a crowd. Something must break it. Why should it not be you and I? Can you do nothing else but guard relics?"

The shopman wore a gradually clearing expression, which would have led those unsympathetic with the cause of the Red Lion to think that the last sentence was the only one to which he had attached any meaning.

"I am rather old to go into a new business," he said, "and I don't quite know what to be, either."

"Why not," said Wayne, gently having reached the crisis of his delicate persuasion—"why not be a colonel?"

It was at this point, in all probability, that the interview began to yield more disappointing results. The man appeared inclined at first to regard the suggestion of becoming a colonel as outside the sphere of immediate and relevant discussion. A long exposition of the inevitable war of independence, coupled with the purchase of a doubtful sixteenth-century sword for an exaggerated price, seemed to resettle matters. Wayne left the shop, however, somewhat infected with the melancholy of its owner.

That melancholy was completed at the barber's.

"Shaving, sir?" inquired that artist from inside his shop.

"War!" replied Wayne, standing on the threshold.

"I beg your pardon," said the other, sharply.

"War!" said Wayne, warmly. "But not for anything inconsistent with the beautiful and the civilised arts. War for beauty. War for society. War for peace. A great chance is offered you of repelling that slander which, in defiance of the lives of so many artists, attributes poltroonery to those who beautify and polish the surface of our lives. Why should not hairdressers be heroes? Why should not—"

"Now, you get out," said the barber, irascibly. "We don't want any of your sort here. You get out."

And he came forward with the desperate annoyance of a mild person when enraged.

Adam Wayne laid his hand for a moment on the sword, then dropped it.

"Notting Hill," he said, "will need her bolder sons," and he turned gloomily to the toy-shop.

It was one of those queer little shops so constantly seen in the side streets of London, which must be called toy-shops only because toys upon the whole predominate; for the remainder of goods seem to consist of almost everything else in the world—tobacco, exercise-books, sweet-stuff, novelettes, halfpenny paper clips, halfpenny pencil sharpeners, bootlaces, and cheap fireworks. It also sold newspapers, and a row of dirty-looking posters hung along the front of it.

"I am afraid," said Wayne, as he entered, "that I am not getting on with these tradesmen as I should. Is it that I have neglected to rise to the full meaning of their work? Is there some secret buried in each of these shops which no mere poet can discover?"

He stepped to the counter with a depression which he rapidly conquered as he addressed the man on the other side of it—a man of short stature, and hair prematurely white, and the look of a large baby.

"Sir," said Wayne, "I am going from house to house in this street of ours, seeking to stir up some sense of the danger which now threatens our city. Nowhere have I felt my duty so difficult as here. For the toy-shop keeper has to do with all that remains to us of Eden before the first wars began. You sit here meditating continually upon the wants of that wonderful time when every staircase leads to the stars, and every garden-path to the other end of nowhere. Is it thoughtlessly, do you think, that I strike the dark old drum of peril in the paradise of children? But consider a moment; do not condemn me hastily. Even that paradise itself contains the rumour or beginning of that danger, just as the Eden that was made for perfection contained the terrible tree. For judge childhood, even by your own arsenal of its pleasures. You keep bricks; you make yourself thus, doubtless, the witness of the constructive instinct older than the destructive. You keep dolls; you make yourself the priest of that divine idolatry. You keep Noah's Arks; you perpetuate the memory of the salvation of all life as a precious, an irreplaceable thing. But do you keep only, sir, the symbols of this prehistoric sanity, this childish rationality of the earth? Do you not keep more terrible things? What are those boxes, seemingly of lead soldiers, that I see in that glass case? Are they not witnesses to that terror and beauty, that desire for a lovely death, which could not be excluded even from the immortality of Eden? Do not despise the lead soldiers, Mr. Turnbull."

"I don't," said Mr. Turnbull, of the toy-shop, shortly, but with great emphasis.

"I am glad to hear it," replied Wayne. "I confess that I feared for my military schemes the awful innocence of your profession.

How, I thought to myself, will this man, used only to the wooden swords that give pleasure, think of the steel swords that give pain? But I am at least partly reassured. Your tone suggests to me that I have at least the entry of a gate of your fairyland—the gate through which the soldiers enter, for it cannot be denied—I ought, sir, no longer to deny, that it is of soldiers that I come to speak. Let your gentle employment make you merciful towards the troubles of the world. Let your own silvery experience tone down our sanguine sorrows. For there is war in Notting Hill."

The little toy-shop keeper sprang up suddenly, slapping his fat hands like two fans on the counter.

"War?" he cried. "Not really, sir? Is it true? Oh, what a joke! Oh, what a sight for sore eyes!"

Wayne was almost taken aback by this outburst.

"I am delighted," he stammered. "I had no notion—"

He sprang out of the way just in time to avoid Mr. Turnbull, who took a flying leap over the counter and dashed to the front of the shop.

"You look here, sir," he said; "you just look here."

He came back with two of the torn posters in his hand which were flapping outside his shop.

"Look at those, sir," he said, and flung them down on the counter.

Wayne bent over them, and read on one—

LAST FIGHTING.

REDUCTION OF THE CENTRAL DERVISH CITY.

REMARKABLE, ETC.

On the other he read—

LAST SMALL REPUBLIC ANNEXED.

NICARAGUAN CAPITAL SURRENDERS

AFTER A MONTH'S FIGHTING.

GREAT SLAUGHTER.

Wayne bent over them again, evidently puzzled; then he looked at the dates. They were both dated in August fifteen years before.

"Why do you keep these old things?" he said, startled entirely out of his absurd tact of mysticism. "Why do you hang them outside your shop?"

"Because," said the other, simply, "they are the records of the last war. You mentioned war just now. It happens to be my hobby."

Wayne lifted his large blue eyes with an infantile wonder.

"Come with me," said Turnbull, shortly, and led him into a parlour at the back of the shop.

In the centre of the parlour stood a large deal table. On it were set rows and rows of the tin and lead soldiers which were part of the shopkeeper's stock. The visitor would have thought nothing of it if it had not been for a certain odd grouping of them, which did not seem either entirely commercial or entirely haphazard.

"You are acquainted, no doubt," said Turnbull, turning his big eyes upon Wayne—"you are acquainted, no doubt, with the arrangement of the American and Nicaraguan troops in the last battle," and he waved his hand towards the table.

"I am afraid not," said Wayne. "I—"

"Ah! you were at that time occupied too much, perhaps, with the Dervish affair. You will find it in this corner." And he pointed to a part of the floor where there was another arrangement of children's soldiers grouped here and there.

"You seem," said Wayne, "to be interested in military matters."

"I am interested in nothing else," answered the toy-shop keeper, simply.

Wayne appeared convulsed with a singular, suppressed excitement.

"In that case," he said, "I may approach you with an unusual degree of confidence. Touching the matter of the defence of Notting Hill, I—"

"Defence of Notting Hill? Yes, sir. This way, sir," said Turnbull, with great perturbation. "Just step into this side room," and he led Wayne into another apartment, in which the table was entirely covered with an arrangement of children's bricks. A second glance at it told Wayne that the bricks were arranged in the form of a precise and perfect plan of Notting Hill. "Sir," said Turnbull, impressively, "you have, by a kind of accident, hit upon the whole secret of my life. As a boy, I grew up among the last wars of the world, when Nicaragua was taken and the dervishes wiped out. And I adopted it as a hobby, sir, as you might adopt astronomy or bird-stuffing. I had no ill-will to any one, but I was interested in war as a science, as a game. And suddenly I was bowled out. The big Powers of the world, having swallowed up all the small ones, came to that confounded agreement, and there was no more war. There was nothing more for me to do but to do what I do now—to read the old campaigns in dirty old newspapers, and to work them out with tin soldiers. One other thing had occurred to me. I thought it an amusing fancy to make a plan of how this district or ours ought to be defended if it were ever attacked. It seems to interest you too."

"If it were ever attacked," repeated Wayne, awed into an almost mechanical enunciation. "Mr. Turnbull, it is attacked. Thank Heaven, I am bringing to at least one human being the news that is at bottom the only good news to any son of Adam. Your life has not been useless. Your work has not been play. Now, when the hair is already grey on your head, Turnbull, you shall have your youth. God has not destroyed, He has only deferred it. Let us sit down here, and you shall explain to me this military map of Notting Hill. For you and I have to defend Notting Hill together."

Mr. Turnbull looked at the other for a moment, then hesitated, and then sat down beside the bricks and the stranger. He did not rise again for seven hours, when the dawn broke.

The headquarters of Provost Adam Wayne and his Commander-in-Chief consisted of a small and somewhat unsuccessful milk-shop at the corner of Pump Street. The blank white morning had only just begun to break over the blank London buildings when Wayne and Turnbull were to be found seated in the cheerless and unswept shop. Wayne had something feminine in his character; he belonged to that class of persons who forget their meals when anything interesting is in hand. He had had nothing for sixteen hours but hurried glasses of milk, and, with a glass standing empty beside him, he was writing and sketching and dotting and crossing out with inconceivable rapidity with a pencil and a piece of paper. Turnbull was of that more masculine type in which a sense of responsibility increases the appetite, and with his sketch-map beside him he was dealing strenuously with a pile of sandwiches in a paper packet, and a tankard of ale from the tavern opposite, whose shutters had just been taken down. Neither of them spoke, and there was no sound in the living stillness except the scratching of Wayne's pencil and the squealing of an aimless-looking cat. At length Wayne broke the silence by saying—

"Seventeen pounds eight shillings and ninepence."

Turnbull nodded and put his head in the tankard.

"That," said Wayne, "is not counting the five pounds you took yesterday. What did you do with it?"

"Ah, that is rather interesting!" replied Turnbull, with his mouth full. "I used that five pounds in a kindly and philanthropic act."

Wayne was gazing with mystification in his queer and innocent eyes.

"I used that five pounds," continued the other, "in giving no less than forty little London boys rides in hansom cabs."

"Are you insane?" asked the Provost.

"It is only my light touch," returned Turnbull. "These hansom-cab rides will raise the tone—raise the tone, my dear fellow—of our London youths, widen their horizon, brace their nervous system, make them acquainted with the various public monuments of our great city. Education, Wayne, education. How many excellent thinkers have pointed out that political reform is useless until we produce a cultured populace. So that twenty years hence, when these boys are grown up—"

"Mad!" said Wayne, laying down his pencil. "And five pounds gone!"

"You are in error," explained Turnbull. "You grave creatures can never be brought to understand how much quicker work really goes with the assistance of nonsense and good meals. Stripped of its decorative beauties, my statement was strictly accurate. Last night I gave forty half-crowns to forty little boys, and sent them all over London to take hansom cabs. I told them in every case to tell the cabman to bring them to this spot. In half an hour from now the declaration of war will be posted up. At the same time the cabs will have begun to come in, you will have ordered out the guard, the little boys will drive up in state, we shall commandeer the horses for cavalry, use the cabs for barricade, and give the men the choice between serving in our ranks and detention in our basements and cellars. The little boys we can use as scouts. The main thing is that we start the war with an advantage unknown in all the other armies—horses. And now," he said, finishing his beer, "I will go and drill the troops."

And he walked out of the milk-shop, leaving the Provost staring.

A minute or two afterwards, the Provost laughed. He only laughed once or twice in his life, and then he did it in a queer way as if it were an art he had not mastered. Even he saw something funny in the preposterous coup of the half-crowns and the little boys. He did not see the monstrous absurdity of the whole policy and the whole war. He enjoyed it seriously as a crusade, that is, he enjoyed it far more than any joke can be enjoyed. Turnbull enjoyed it partly as a joke, even more perhaps as a reversion from the things he hated—modernity and monotony and civilisation. To break up the vast machinery of modern life and use the fragments as engines of war, to make the barricade of omnibuses and points of vantage of chimney-pots, was to him a game worth infinite risk and trouble. He had that rational and deliberate preference which will always to the end trouble the peace of the world, the rational and deliberate preference for a short life and a merry one.

CHAPTER III

The Experiment of Mr. Buck

An earnest and eloquent petition was sent up to the King signed with the names of Wilson, Barker, Buck, Swindon, and others. It urged that at the forthcoming conference to be held in his Majesty's presence touching the final disposition of the property in Pump Street, it might be held not inconsistent with political decorum and with the unutterable respect they entertained for his Majesty if they appeared in ordinary morning dress, without the costume decreed for them as Provosts. So it happened that the company appeared at that council in frock-coats and that the King himself limited his love of ceremony to appearing (after his not unusual manner), in evening dress with one order—in this case not the Garter, but the button of the Club of Old Clipper's Best Pals, a decoration obtained (with difficulty) from a halfpenny boy's paper. Thus also it happened that the only spot of colour in the room was Adam Wayne, who entered in great dignity with the great red robes and the great sword.

"We have met," said Auberon, "to decide the most arduous of modern problems. May we be successful." And he sat down gravely.

Buck turned his chair a little, and flung one leg over the other.

"Your Majesty," he said, quite good-humouredly, "there is only one thing I can't understand, and that is why this affair is not settled in five minutes. Here's a small property which is worth a thousand to us and is not worth a hundred to any one else. We offer the thousand. It's not business-like, I know, for we ought to get it for less, and it's not reasonable and it's not fair on us, but I'm damned if I can see why it's difficult."

"The difficulty may be very simply stated," said Wayne. "You may offer a million and it will be very difficult for you to get Pump Street."

"But look here, Mr. Wayne," cried Barker, striking in with a kind of cold excitement. "Just look here. You've no right to take up a position like that. You've a right to stand out for a bigger price, but you aren't doing that. You're refusing what you and every sane man knows to be a splendid offer simply from malice or spite—it must be malice or spite. And that kind of thing is really criminal; it's against the public good. The King's Government would be justified in forcing you."

With his lean fingers spread on the table, he stared anxiously at Wayne's face, which did not move.

"In forcing you…it would," he repeated.

"It shall," said Buck, shortly, turning to the table with a jerk. "We have done our best to be decent."

Wayne lifted his large eyes slowly.

"Was it my Lord Buck," he inquired, "who said that the King of England 'shall' do something?"

Buck flushed and said testily—

"I mean it must—it ought to. As I say, we've done our best to be generous; I defy any one to deny it. As it is, Mr. Wayne, I don't want to say a word that's uncivil. I hope it's not uncivil to say that you can be, and ought to be, in gaol. It is criminal to stop public works for a whim. A man might as well burn ten thousand onions in his front garden or bring up his children to run naked in the street, as do what you say you have a right to do. People have been compelled to sell before now. The King could compel you, and I hope he will."

"Until he does," said Wayne, calmly, "the power and government of this great nation is on my side and not yours, and I defy you to defy it."

"In what sense," cried Barker, with his feverish eyes and hands, "is the Government on your side?"

With one ringing movement Wayne unrolled a great parchment on the table. It was decorated down the sides with wild water-colour sketches of vestrymen in crowns and wreaths.

"The Charter of the Cities," he began.

Buck exploded in a brutal oath and laughed.

"That tomfool's joke. Haven't we had enough—"

"And there you sit," cried Wayne, springing erect and with a voice like a trumpet, "with no argument but to insult the King before his face."

Buck rose also with blazing eyes.

"I am hard to bully," he began—and the slow tones of the King struck in with incomparable gravity—

"My Lord Buck, I must ask you to remember that your King is present. It is not often that he needs to protect himself among his subjects."

Barker turned to him with frantic gestures.

"For God's sake don't back up the madman now," he implored. "Have your joke another time. Oh, for Heaven's sake—"

"My Lord Provost of South Kensington," said King Auberon, steadily, "I do not follow your remarks, which are uttered with a rapidity unusual at Court. Nor do your well-meant efforts to convey the rest with your fingers materially assist me. I say that my Lord Provost of North Kensington, to whom I spoke, ought not in the presence of his Sovereign to speak disrespectfully of his Sovereign's ordinances. Do you disagree?"

Barker turned restlessly in his chair, and Buck cursed without speaking. The King went on in a comfortable voice—

"My Lord Provost of Notting Hill, proceed."

Wayne turned his blue eyes on the King, and to every one's surprise there was a look in them not of triumph, but of a certain childish distress.

"I am sorry, your Majesty," he said; "I fear I was more than equally to blame with the Lord Provost of North Kensington. We were debating somewhat eagerly, and we both rose to our feet. I did so first, I am ashamed to say. The Provost of North Kensington is, therefore, comparatively innocent. I beseech your Majesty to address your rebuke chiefly, at least, to me. Mr. Buck is not innocent, for he did no doubt, in the heat of the moment, speak disrespectfully. But the rest of the discussion he seems to me to have conducted with great good temper."

Buck looked genuinely pleased, for business men are all simple-minded, and have therefore that degree of communion with fanatics. The King, for some reason, looked, for the first time in his life, ashamed.

"This very kind speech of the Provost of Notting Hill," began Buck, pleasantly, "seems to me to show that we have at least got on to a friendly footing. Now come, Mr. Wayne. Five hundred pounds have been offered to you for a property you admit not to be worth a hundred. Well, I am a rich man and I won't be outdone in generosity. Let us say fifteen hundred pounds, and have done with it. And let us shake hands;" and he rose, glowing and laughing.

"Fifteen hundred pounds," whispered Mr. Wilson of Bayswater; "can we do fifteen hundred pounds?"

"I'll stand the racket," said Buck, heartily. "Mr. Wayne is a gentleman and has spoken up for me. So I suppose the negotiations are at an end."

Wayne bowed.

"They are indeed at an end. I am sorry I cannot sell you the property."

"What?" cried Mr. Barker, starting to his feet.

"Mr. Buck has spoken correctly," said the King.

"I have, I have," cried Buck, springing up also; "I said—"

"Mr. Buck has spoken correctly," said the King; "the negotiations are at an end."

All the men at the table rose to their feet; Wayne alone rose without excitement.

"Have I, then," he said, "your Majesty's permission to depart? I have given my last answer."

"You have it," said Auberon, smiling, but not lifting his eyes from the table. And amid a dead silence the Provost of Notting Hill passed out of the room.

"Well?" said Wilson, turning round to Barker—"well?"

Barker shook his head desperately.

"The man ought to be in an asylum," he said. "But one thing is clear—we need not bother further about him. The man can be treated as mad."

"Of course," said Buck, turning to him with sombre decisiveness.

"You're perfectly right, Barker. He is a good enough fellow, but he can be treated as mad. Let's put it in simple form. Go and tell any twelve men in any town, go and tell any doctor in any town, that there is a man offered fifteen hundred pounds for a thing he could sell commonly for four hundred, and that when asked for a reason for not accepting it he pleads the inviolate sanctity of Notting Hill and calls it the Holy Mountain. What would they say? What more can we have on our side than the common sense of everybody? On what else do all laws rest? I'll tell you, Barker, what's better than any further discussion. Let's send in workmen on the spot to pull down Pump Street. And if old Wayne says a word, arrest him as a lunatic. That's all."

Barker's eyes kindled.

"I always regarded you, Buck, if you don't mind my saying so, as a very strong man. I'll follow you."

"So, of course, will I," said Wilson.

Buck rose again impulsively.

"Your Majesty," he said, glowing with popularity, "I beseech your Majesty to consider favourably the proposal to which we have committed ourselves. Your Majesty's leniency, our own offers, have fallen in vain on that extraordinary man. He may be right. He may be God. He may be the devil. But we think it, for practical purposes, more probable that he is off his head. Unless that assumption were acted on, all human affairs would go to pieces. We act on it, and we propose to start operations in Notting Hill at once."

The King leaned back in his chair.

"The Charter of the Cities..." he said with a rich intonation.

But Buck, being finally serious, was also cautious, and did not again make the mistake of disrespect.

"Your Majesty," he said, bowing, "I am not here to say a word against anything your Majesty has said or done. You are a far better educated man than I, and no doubt there were reasons, upon intellectual grounds, for those proceedings. But may I ask you and appeal to your common good-nature for a sincere answer? When you drew up the Charter of the Cities, did you contemplate the rise of a man like Adam Wayne? Did you expect that the Charter—whether it was an experiment, or a scheme of decoration, or a joke—could ever really come to this—to stopping a vast scheme of ordinary business, to shutting up a road, to spoiling the chances of cabs, omnibuses, railway stations, to disorganising half a city, to risking a kind of civil war? Whatever were your objects, were they that?"

Barker and Wilson looked at him admiringly; the King more admiringly still.

"Provost Buck," said Auberon, "you speak in public uncommonly well. I give you your point with the magnanimity of an artist. My scheme did not include the appearance of Mr. Wayne. Alas! Would that my poetic power had been great enough."

"I thank your Majesty," said Buck, courteously, but quickly. "Your Majesty's statements are always clear and studied; therefore I may draw a deduction. As the scheme, whatever it was, on which you set your heart did not include the appearance of Mr. Wayne, it will survive his removal. Why not let us clear away this particular Pump Street, which does interfere with our plans, and which does not, by your Majesty's own statement, interfere with yours."

"Caught out!" said the King, enthusiastically and quite impersonally, as if he were watching a cricket match.

"This man Wayne," continued Buck, "would be shut up by any doctors in England. But we only ask to have it put before them. Meanwhile no one's interests, not even in all probability his own, can be really damaged by going on with the improvements in Notting Hill. Not our interests, of course, for it has been the hard and quiet work of ten years. Not the interests of Notting Hill, for nearly all its educated inhabitants desire the change. Not the interests of your Majesty, for you say, with characteristic sense, that you never contemplated the rise of the lunatic at all. Not, as I say, his own interests, for the man has a kind heart and many talents, and a couple of good doctors would probably put him righter than all the free cities and sacred mountains in creation. I therefore assume, if I may use so bold a word, that your Majesty will not offer any obstacle to our proceeding with the improvements."

And Mr. Buck sat down amid subdued but excited applause among the allies.

"Mr. Buck," said the King, "I beg your pardon, for a number of beautiful and sacred thoughts, in which you were generally classified as a fool. But there is another thing to be considered. Suppose you send in your workmen, and Mr. Wayne does a thing regrettable indeed, but of which, I am sorry to say, I think him quite capable— knocks their teeth out?"

"I have thought of that, your Majesty," said Mr. Buck, easily, "and I think it can simply be guarded against. Let us send in a strong guard of, say, a hundred men—a hundred of the North Kensington Halberdiers" (he smiled grimly), "of whom your Majesty is so fond. Or say a hundred and fifty. The whole population of Pump Street, I fancy, is only about a hundred."

"Still they might stand together and lick you," said the King, dubiously.

"Then say two hundred," said Buck, gaily.

"It might happen," said the King, restlessly, "that one Notting Hiller fought better than two North Kensingtons."

"It might," said Buck, coolly; "then say two hundred and fifty."

The King bit his lip.

"And if they are beaten too?" he said viciously.

"Your Majesty," said Buck, and leaned back easily in his chair, "suppose they are. If anything be clear, it is clear that all fighting matters are mere matters of arithmetic. Here we have a hundred and fifty, say, of Notting Hill soldiers. Or say two hundred. If one of them can fight two of us—we can send in, not four hundred, but six hundred, and smash him. That is all. It is out of all immediate probability that one of them could fight four of us. So what I say is this. Run no risks. Finish it at once. Send in eight hundred men and smash him—smash him almost without seeing him. And go on with the improvements."

And Mr. Buck pulled out a bandanna and blew his nose.

"Do you know, Mr. Buck," said the King, staring gloomily at the table, "the admirable clearness of your reason produces in my mind a sentiment which I trust I shall not offend you by describing as an aspiration to punch your head. You irritate me sublimely. What can it be in me? Is it the relic of a moral sense?"

"But your Majesty," said Barker, eagerly and suavely, "does not refuse our proposals?"

"My dear Barker, your proposals are as damnable as your manners. I want to have nothing to do with them. Suppose I stopped them altogether. What would happen?"

Barker answered in a very low voice—

"Revolution."

The King glanced quickly at the men round the table. They were all looking down silently: their brows were red.

He rose with a startling suddenness, and an unusual pallor.

"Gentlemen," he said, "you have overruled me. Therefore I can speak plainly. I think Adam Wayne, who is as mad as a hatter, worth more than a million of you. But you have the force, and, I admit, the common sense, and he is lost. Take your eight hundred halberdiers and smash him. It would be more sportsmanlike to take two hundred."

"More sportsmanlike," said Buck, grimly, "but a great deal less humane. We are not artists, and streets purple with gore do not catch our eye in the right way."

"It is pitiful," said Auberon. "With five or six times their number, there will be no fight at all."

"I hope not," said Buck, rising and adjusting his gloves. "We desire no fight, your Majesty. We are peaceable business men."

"Well," said the King, wearily, "the conference is at an end at last."

And he went out of the room before any one else could stir.

Forty workmen, a hundred Bayswater Halberdiers, two hundred from South, and three from North Kensington, assembled at the foot of Holland Walk and marched up it, under the general direction of Barker, who looked flushed and happy in full dress. At the end of the procession a small and sulky figure lingered like an urchin. It was the King.

"Barker," he said at length, appealingly, "you are an old friend of mine—you understand my hobbies as I understand yours. Why can't you let it alone? I hoped that such fun might come out of this Wayne business. Why can't you let it alone? It doesn't really so much matter to you—what's a road or so? For me it's the one joke that may save me from pessimism. Take fewer men and give me an hour's fun. Really and truly, James, if you collected coins or humming-birds, and I could buy one with the price of your road, I would buy it. I collect incidents—those rare, those precious things. Let me have one. Pay a few pounds for it. Give these Notting Hillers a chance. Let them alone."

"Auberon," said Barker, kindly, forgetting all royal titles in a rare moment of sincerity, "I do feel what you mean. I have had moments when these hobbies have hit me. I have had moments when I have sympathised with your humours. I have had moments, though you may not easily believe it, when I have sympathised with the madness of Adam Wayne. But the world, Auberon, the real world, is not run on these hobbies. It goes on great brutal wheels of facts—wheels on which you are the butterfly; and Wayne is the fly on the wheel."

Auberon's eyes looked frankly at the other's.

"Thank you, James; what you say is true. It is only a parenthetical consolation to me to compare the intelligence of flies somewhat favourably with the intelligence of wheels. But it is the nature of flies to die soon, and the nature of wheels to go on for ever. Go on with the wheel. Good-bye, old man."

And James Barker went on, laughing, with a high colour, slapping his bamboo on his leg.

The King watched the tail of the retreating regiment with a look of genuine depression, which made him seem more like a baby than ever. Then he swung round and struck his hands together.

"In a world without humour," he said, "the only thing to do is to eat. And how perfect an exception! How can these people strike dignified attitudes, and pretend that things matter, when the total ludicrousness of life is proved by the very method by which it is supported? A man strikes the lyre, and says, 'Life is real, life is earnest,' and then goes into a room and stuffs alien substances into a hole in his head. I think Nature was indeed a little broad in her humour in these matters. But we all fall back on the pantomime, as I have in this municipal affair. Nature has her farces, like the act of eating or the shape of the kangaroo, for the more brutal appetite. She keeps her stars and mountains for those who can appreciate something more subtly ridiculous." He turned to his equerry. "But, as I said 'eating,' let us have a picnic like two nice little children. Just run and bring me a table and a dozen courses or so, and plenty of champagne, and under these swinging boughs, Bowler, we will return to Nature."

It took about an hour to erect in Holland Lane the monarch's simple repast, during which time he walked up and down and whistled, but still with an unaffected air of gloom. He had really been done out of a pleasure he had promised himself, and had that empty and sickened feeling which a child has when disappointed of a pantomime. When he and the equerry had sat down, however, and consumed a fair amount of dry champagne, his spirits began mildly to revive.

"Things take too long in this world," he said. "I detest all this Barkerian business about evolution and the gradual modification of things. I wish the world had been made in six days, and knocked to pieces again in six more. And I wish I had done it. The joke's good enough in a broad way, sun and moon and the image of God, and all that, but they keep it up so damnably long. Did you ever long for a miracle, Bowler?"

"No, sir," said Bowler, who was an evolutionist, and had been carefully brought up.

"Then I have," answered the King. "I have walked along a street with the best cigar in the cosmos in my mouth, and more Burgundy inside me than you ever saw in your life, and longed that the lamp-post would turn into an elephant to save me from the hell of blank existence. Take my word for it, my evolutionary Bowler, don't you believe people when they tell you that people sought for a sign, and believed in miracles because they were ignorant. They did it because they were wise, filthily, vilely wise—too wise to eat or sleep or put on their boots with patience. This seems delightfully like a new theory of the origin of Christianity, which would itself be a thing of no mean absurdity. Take some more wine."

The wind blew round them as they sat at their little table, with its white cloth and bright wine-cups, and flung the tree-tops of Holland Park against each other, but the sun was in that strong temper which turns green into gold. The King pushed away his plate, lit a cigar slowly, and went on—

"Yesterday I thought that something next door to a really entertaining miracle might happen to me before I went to amuse the worms. To see that red-haired maniac waving a great sword, and making speeches to his incomparable followers, would have been a glimpse of that Land of Youth from which the Fates shut us out. I had planned some quite delightful things. A Congress of Knightsbridge with a treaty, and myself in the chair, and perhaps a Roman triumph, with jolly old Barker led in chains. And now these wretched prigs have gone and stamped out the exquisite Mr. Wayne altogether, and I suppose they will put him in a private asylum somewhere in their damned humane way. Think of the treasures daily poured out to his unappreciative keeper! I wonder whether they would let me be his keeper. But life is a vale. Never forget at any moment of your existence to regard it in the light of a vale. This graceful habit, if not acquired in youth—"

The King stopped, with his cigar lifted, for there had slid into his eyes the startled look of a man listening. He did not move for a few moments; then he turned his head sharply towards the high, thin, and lath-like paling which fenced certain long gardens and similar spaces from the lane. From behind it there was coming a curious scrambling and scraping noise, as of a desperate thing imprisoned in this box of thin wood. The King threw away his cigar, and jumped on to the table.

From this position he saw a pair of hands hanging with a hungry clutch on the top of the fence. Then the hands quivered with a convulsive effort, and a head shot up between them—the head of one of the Bayswater Town Council, his eyes and whiskers wild with fear. He swung himself over, and fell on the other side on his face, and groaned openly and without ceasing. The next moment the thin, taut wood of the fence was struck as by a bullet, so that it reverberated like a drum, and over it came tearing and cursing, with torn clothes and broken nails and bleeding faces, twenty men at one rush. The King sprang five feet clear off the table on to the ground. The moment after the table was flung over, sending bottles and glasses flying, and the debris was literally swept along the ground by that stream of men pouring past, and Bowler was borne along with them, as the King said in his famous newspaper article, "like a captured bride." The great fence swung and split under the load of climbers that still scaled and cleared it. Tremendous gaps were torn in it by this living artillery; and through them the King could see more and more frantic faces, as in a dream, and more and more men running. They were as miscellaneous as if some one had taken the lid off a human dustbin. Some were untouched, some were slashed and battered and bloody, some were splendidly dressed, some tattered and half naked, some were in the fantastic garb of the burlesque cities, some in the dullest modern dress. The King stared at all of them, but none of them looked at the King. Suddenly he stepped forward.

"Barker," he said, "what is all this?"

"Beaten," said the politician—"beaten all to hell!" And he plunged past with nostrils shaking like a horse's, and more and more men plunged after him.

Almost as he spoke, the last standing strip of fence bowed and snapped, flinging, as from a catapult, a new figure upon the road. He wore the flaming red of the halberdiers of Notting Hill, and on his weapon there was blood, and in his face victory. In another moment masses of red glowed through the gaps of the fence, and the pursuers, with their halberds, came pouring down the lane. Pursued and pursuers alike swept by the little figure with the owlish eyes, who had not taken his hands out of his pockets.

The King had still little beyond the confused sense of a man caught in a torrent—the feeling of men eddying by. Then something happened which he was never able afterwards to describe, and which we cannot describe for him. Suddenly in the dark entrance, between the broken gates of a garden, there appeared framed a flaming figure.

Adam Wayne, the conqueror, with his face flung back, and his mane like a lion's, stood with his great sword point upwards, the red raiment of his office flapping round him like the red wings of an archangel. And the King saw, he knew not how, something new and overwhelming. The great green trees and the great red robes swung together in the wind. The sword seemed made for the sunlight. The preposterous masquerade, born of his own mockery, towered over him and embraced the world. This was the normal, this was sanity, this was nature; and he himself, with his rationality and his detachment and his black frock-coat, he was the exception and the accident—a blot of black upon a world of crimson and gold.

Book IV

CHAPTER I

The Battle of the Lamps

M r. Buck, who, though retired, frequently went down to his big drapery stores in Kensington High Street, was locking up those premises, being the last to leave. It was a wonderful evening of green and gold, but that did not trouble him very much. If you had pointed it out, he would have agreed seriously, for the rich always desire to be artistic.

He stepped out into the cool air, buttoning up his light yellow coat, and blowing great clouds from his cigar, when a figure dashed up to him in another yellow overcoat, but unbuttoned and flying behind him.

"Hullo, Barker!" said the draper. "Any of our summer articles? You're too late. Factory Acts, Barker. Humanity and progress, my boy."

"Oh, don't chatter," cried Barker, stamping. "We've been beaten."

"Beaten—by what?" asked Buck, mystified.

"By Wayne."

Buck looked at Barker's fierce white face for the first time, as it gleamed in the lamplight.

"Come and have a drink," he said.

They adjourned to a cushioned and glaring buffet, and Buck established himself slowly and lazily in a seat, and pulled out his cigar-case.

"Have a smoke," he said.

Barker was still standing, and on the fret, but after a moment's hesitation, he sat down as if he might spring up again the next minute. They ordered drinks in silence.

"How did it happen?" asked Buck, turning his big bold eyes on him.

"How the devil do I know?" cried Barker. "It happened like—like a dream. How can two hundred men beat six hundred? How can they?"

"Well," said Buck, coolly, "how did they? You ought to know."

"I don't know; I can't describe," said the other, drumming on the table. "It seemed like this. We were six hundred, and marched with those damned poleaxes of Auberon's—the only weapons we've got. We marched two abreast. We went up Holland Walk, between the high palings which seemed to me to go straight as an arrow for Pump Street. I was near the tail of the line, and it was a long one. When the end of it was still between the high palings, the head of the line was already crossing Holland Park Avenue. Then the head plunged into the network of narrow streets on the other side, and the tail and myself came out on the great crossing. When we also had reached the northern side and turned up a small street that points, crookedly as it were, towards Pump Street, the whole thing felt different. The streets dodged and bent so much that the head of our line seemed lost altogether: it might as well have been in North America. And all this time we hadn't seen a soul."

Buck, who was idly dabbing the ash of his cigar on the ashtray, began to move it deliberately over the table, making feathery grey lines, a kind of map.

"But though the little streets were all deserted (which got a trifle on my nerves), as we got deeper and deeper into them, a thing began to happen that I couldn't understand. Sometimes a long way ahead—three turns or corners ahead, as it were—there broke suddenly a sort of noise, clattering, and confused cries, and then stopped. Then, when it happened, something, I can't describe it—a kind of shake or stagger went down the line, as if the line were a live thing, whose head had been struck, or had been an electric cord.

None of us knew why we were moving, but we moved and jostled. Then we recovered, and went on through the little dirty streets, round corners, and up twisted ways. The little crooked streets began to give me a feeling I can't explain—as if it were a dream. I felt as if things had lost their reason, and we should never get out of the maze. Odd to hear me talk like that, isn't it? The streets were quite well-known streets, all down on the map. But the fact remains. I wasn't afraid of something happening. I was afraid of nothing ever happening—nothing ever happening for all God's eternity."

He drained his glass and called for more whisky. He drank it, and went on.

"And then something did happen. Buck, it's the solemn truth, that nothing has ever happened to you in your life. Nothing had ever happened to me in my life."

"Nothing ever happened!" said Buck, staring. "What do you mean?"

"Nothing has ever happened," repeated Barker, with a morbid obstinacy.

"You don't know what a thing happening means? You sit in your office expecting customers, and customers come; you walk in the street expecting friends, and friends meet you; you want a drink, and get it; you feel inclined for a bet, and make it. You expect either to win or lose, and you do either one or the other. But things happening!" and he shuddered ungovernably.

"Go on," said Buck, shortly. "Get on."

"As we walked wearily round the corners, something happened. When something happens, it happens first, and you see it afterwards. It happens of itself, and you have nothing to do with it. It proves a dreadful thing—that there are other things besides one's self. I can only put it in this way. We went round one turning, two turnings, three turnings, four turnings, five. Then I lifted myself slowly up from the gutter where I had been shot half senseless, and was beaten down again by living men crashing on top of me, and the world was full of roaring, and big men rolling about like nine-pins."

Buck looked at his map with knitted brows.

"Was that Portobello Road?" he asked.

"Yes," said Barker—"yes; Portobello Road. I saw it afterwards; but, my God, what a place it was! Buck, have you ever stood and let a six foot of man lash and lash at your head with six feet of pole with six pounds of steel at the end? Because, when you have had that experience, as Walt Whitman says, 'you re-examine philosophies and religions.'"

"I have no doubt," said Buck. "If that was Portobello Road, don't you see what happened?"

"I know what happened exceedingly well. I was knocked down four times; an experience which, as I say, has an effect on the mental attitude. And another thing happened, too. I knocked down two men. After the fourth fall (there was not much bloodshed—more brutal rushing and throwing—for nobody could use their weapons), after the fourth fall, I say, I got up like a devil, and I tore a poleaxe out of a man's hand and struck where I saw the scarlet of Wayne's fellows, struck again and again. Two of them went over, bleeding on the stones, thank God; and I laughed and found myself sprawling in the gutter again, and got up again, and struck again, and broke my halberd to pieces. I hurt a man's head, though."

Buck set down his glass with a bang, and spat out curses through his thick moustache.

"What is the matter?" asked Barker, stopping, for the man had been calm up to now, and now his agitation was far more violent than his own.

"The matter?" said Buck, bitterly; "don't you see how these maniacs have got us? Why should two idiots, one a clown and the other a screaming lunatic, make sane men so different from themselves? Look here, Barker; I will give you a picture. A very well-bred young man of this century is dancing about in a frock-coat. He has in his hands a nonsensical seventeenth-century halberd, with which he is trying to kill men in a street in Notting Hill. Damn it! Don't you see how they've got us? Never mind how you felt—that is how you looked. The King would put his cursed head on one side and call it exquisite. The Provost of Notting Hill would put his cursed nose in the air and call it heroic. But in Heaven's name what would you have called it—two days before?"

Barker bit his lip.

"You haven't been through it, Buck," he said. "You don't understand fighting—the atmosphere."

"I don't deny the atmosphere," said Buck, striking the table. "I only say it's their atmosphere. It's Adam Wayne's atmosphere. It's the atmosphere which you and I thought had vanished from an educated world for ever."

"Well, it hasn't," said Barker; "and if you have any lingering doubts, lend me a poleaxe, and I'll show you."

There was a long silence, and then Buck turned to his neighbour and spoke in that good-tempered tone that comes of a power of looking facts in the face—the tone in which he concluded great bargains.

"Barker," he said, "you are right. This old thing—this fighting, has come back. It has come back suddenly and taken us by surprise. So it is first blood to Adam Wayne. But, unless reason and arithmetic and everything else have gone crazy, it must be next and last blood to us. But when an issue has really arisen, there is only one thing to do—to study that issue as such and win in it. Barker, since it is fighting, we must understand fighting. I must understand fighting as coolly and completely as I understand drapery; you must understand fighting as coolly and completely as you understand politics. Now, look at the facts. I stick without hesitation to my original formula. Fighting, when we have the stronger force, is only a matter of arithmetic. It must be. You asked me just now how two hundred men could defeat six hundred. I can tell you. Two hundred men can defeat six hundred when the six hundred behave like fools. When they forget the very conditions they are fighting in; when they fight in a swamp as if it were a mountain; when they fight in a forest as if it were a plain; when they fight in streets without remembering the object of streets."

"What is the object of streets?" asked Barker.

"What is the object of supper?" cried Buck, furiously. "Isn't it obvious? This military science is mere common sense. The object of a street is to lead from one place to another; therefore all streets join; therefore street fighting is quite a peculiar thing. You advanced into that hive of streets as if you were advancing into an open plain where you could see everything. Instead of that, you were advancing into the bowels of a fortress, with streets pointing at you, streets turning on you, streets jumping out at you, and all in the hands of the enemy. Do you know what Portobello Road is? It is the only point on your journey where two side streets run up opposite each other. Wayne massed his men on the two sides, and when he had let enough of your line go past, cut it in two like a worm. Don't you see what would have saved you?"

Barker shook his head.

"Can't your 'atmosphere' help you?" asked Buck, bitterly. "Must I attempt explanations in the romantic manner? Suppose that, as you were fighting blindly with the red Notting Hillers who imprisoned you on both sides, you had heard a shout from behind them. Suppose, oh, romantic Barker, that behind the red tunics you had seen the blue and gold of South Kensington taking them in the rear, surrounding them in their turn and hurling them on to your halberds."

"If the thing had been possible," began Barker, cursing.

"The thing would have been as possible," said Buck, simply, "as simple as arithmetic. There are a certain number of street entries that lead to Pump Street. There are not nine hundred; there are not nine million. They do not grow in the night. They do not increase like mushrooms. It must be possible, with such an overwhelming force as we have, to advance by all of them at once. In every one of the arteries, or approaches, we can put almost as many men as Wayne can put into the field altogether. Once do that, and we have him to demonstration. It is like a proposition of Euclid."

"You think that is certain?" said Barker, anxious, but dominated delightfully.

"I'll tell you what I think," said Buck, getting up jovially. "I think Adam Wayne made an uncommonly spirited little fight; and I think I am confoundedly sorry for him."

"Buck, you are a great man!" cried Barker, rising also. "You've knocked me sensible again. I am ashamed to say it, but I was getting romantic. Of course, what you say is adamantine sense. Fighting, being physical, must be mathematical. We were beaten because we were neither mathematical nor physical nor anything else—because we deserved to be beaten. Hold all the approaches, and with our force we must have him. When shall we open the next campaign?"

"Now," said Buck, and walked out of the bar.

"Now!" cried Barker, following him eagerly. "Do you mean now? It is so late."

Buck turned on him, stamping.

"Do you think fighting is under the Factory Acts?" he said, and he called a cab. "Notting Hill Gate Station," he said; and the two drove off.

A genuine reputation can sometimes be made in an hour. Buck, in the next sixty or eighty minutes, showed himself a really great man of action. His cab carried him like a thunderbolt from the King to Wilson, from Wilson to Swindon, from Swindon to Barker again; if his course was jagged, it had the jaggedness of the lightning. Only two things he carried with him—his inevitable cigar and the map of North Kensington and Notting Hill. There were, as he again and again pointed out, with every variety of persuasion and violence, only nine possible ways of approaching Pump Street within a quarter of a mile round it; three out of Westbourne Grove, two out of Ladbroke Grove, and four out of Notting Hill High Street. And he had detachments of two hundred each, stationed at every one of the entrances before the last green of that strange sunset had sunk out of the black sky.

The sky was particularly black, and on this alone was one false protest raised against the triumphant optimism of the Provost of

North Kensington. He overruled it with his infectious common sense.

"There is no such thing," he said, "as night in London. You have only to follow the line of street lamps. Look, here is the map. Two hundred purple North Kensington soldiers under myself march up Ossington Street, two hundred more under Captain Bruce, of the North Kensington Guard, up Clanricarde Gardens.[†] Two hundred yellow West Kensingtons under Provost Swindon attack from Pembridge Road. Two hundred more of my men from the eastern streets, leading away from Queen's Road. Two detachments of yellows enter by two roads from Westbourne Grove. Lastly, two hundred green Bayswaters come down from the North through Chepstow Place, and two hundred more under Provost Wilson himself, through the upper part of Pembridge Road. Gentlemen, it is mate in two moves. The enemy must either mass in Pump Street and be cut to pieces; or they must retreat past the Gaslight & Coke Co., and rush on my four hundred; or they must retreat past St. Luke's Church, and rush on the six hundred from the West. Unless we are all mad, it's plain. Come on. To your quarters and await Captain Brace's signal to advance. Then you have only to walk up a line of gas-lamps and smash this nonsense by pure mathematics. Tomorrow we shall all be civilians again."

His optimism glowed like a great fire in the night, and ran round the terrible ring in which Wayne was now held helpless. The fight was already over. One man's energy for one hour had saved the city from war.

For the next ten minutes Buck walked up and down silently beside the motionless clump of his two hundred. He had not changed his appearance in any way, except to sling across his yellow overcoat a case with a revolver in it. So that his light-clad modern figure showed up oddly beside the pompous purple uniforms of his halberdiers, which darkly but richly coloured the black night.

[†]   Clanricarde Gardens at this time was no longer a cul-de-sac, but was connected by Pump Street to Pembridge Square. See map.

At length a shrill trumpet rang from some way up the street; it was the signal of advance. Buck briefly gave the word, and the whole purple line, with its dimly shining steel, moved up the side alley. Before it was a slope of street, long, straight, and shining in the dark. It was a sword pointed at Pump Street, the heart at which nine other swords were pointed that night.

A quarter of an hour's silent marching brought them almost within earshot of any tumult in the doomed citadel. But still there was no sound and no sign of the enemy. This time, at any rate, they knew that they were closing in on it mechanically, and they marched on under the lamplight and the dark without any of that eerie sense of ignorance which Barker had felt when entering the hostile country by one avenue alone.

"Halt—point arms!" cried Buck, suddenly, and as he spoke there came a clatter of feet tumbling along the stones. But the halberds were levelled in vain. The figure that rushed up was a messenger from the contingent of the North.

"Victory, Mr. Buck!" he cried, panting; "they are ousted. Provost Wilson of Bayswater has taken Pump Street."

Buck ran forward in his excitement.

"Then, which way are they retreating? It must be either by St. Luke's to meet Swindon, or by the Gas Company to meet us. Run like mad to Swindon, and see that the yellows are holding the St. Luke's Road. We will hold this, never fear. We have them in an iron trap. Run!"

As the messenger dashed away into the darkness, the great guard of North Kensington swung on with the certainty of a machine. Yet scarcely a hundred yards further their halberd-points again fell in line gleaming in the gaslight; for again a clatter of feet was heard on the stones, and again it proved to be only the messenger.

"Mr. Provost," he said, "the yellow West Kensingtons have been holding the road by St. Luke's for twenty minutes since the capture of Pump Street. Pump Street is not two hundred yards away; they cannot be retreating down that road."

"Then they are retreating down this," said Provost Buck, with a final cheerfulness, "and by good fortune down a well-lighted road, though it twists about. Forward!"

As they moved along the last three hundred yards of their journey, Buck fell, for the first time in his life, perhaps, into a kind of philosophical reverie, for men of his type are always made kindly, and as it were melancholy, by success.

"I am sorry for poor old Wayne, I really am," he thought. "He spoke up splendidly for me at that Council. And he blacked old Barker's eye with considerable spirit. But I don't see what a man can expect when he fights against arithmetic, to say nothing of civilisation. And what a wonderful hoax all this military genius is! I suspect I've just discovered what Cromwell discovered, that a sensible tradesman is the best general, and that a man who can buy men and sell men can lead and kill them. The thing's simply like adding up a column in a ledger. If Wayne has two hundred men, he can't put two hundred men in nine places at once. If they're ousted from Pump Street they're flying somewhere. If they're not flying past the church they're flying past the Works. And so we have them. We business men should have no chance at all except that cleverer people than we get bees in their bonnets that prevent them from reasoning properly—so we reason alone. And so I, who am comparatively stupid, see things as God sees them, as a vast machine. My God, what's this?" and he clapped his hands to his eyes and staggered back.

Then through the darkness he cried in a dreadful voice—

"Did I blaspheme God? I am struck blind."

"What?" wailed another voice behind him, the voice of a certain Wilfred Jarvis of North Kensington.

"Blind!" cried Buck; "blind!"

"I'm blind too!" cried Jarvis, in an agony.

"Fools, all of you," said a gross voice behind them; "we're all blind. The lamps have gone out."

"The lamps! But why? where?" cried Buck, turning furiously in the darkness. "How are we to get on? How are we to chase the enemy? Where have they gone?"

"The enemy went—" said the rough voice behind, and then stopped doubtfully.

"Where?" shouted Buck, stamping like a madman.

"They went," said the gruff voice, "past the Gas Works, and they've used their chance."

"Great God!" thundered Buck, and snatched at his revolver; "do you mean they've turned out—"

But almost before he had spoken the words, he was hurled like a stone from catapult into the midst of his own men.

"Notting Hill! Notting Hill!" cried frightful voices out of the darkness, and they seemed to come from all sides, for the men of North Kensington, unacquainted with the road, had lost all their bearings in the black world of blindness.

"Notting Hill! Notting Hill!" cried the invisible people, and the invaders were hewn down horribly with black steel, with steel that gave no glint against any light.

Buck, though badly maimed with the blow of a halberd, kept an angry but splendid sanity. He groped madly for the wall and found it. Struggling with crawling fingers along it, he found a side opening and retreated into it with the remnants of his men. Their adventures during that prodigious night are not to be described. They did not know whether they were going towards or away from the enemy. Not knowing where they themselves were, or where their opponents were, it was mere irony to ask where was the rest of their army. For a thing had descended upon them which London does not know—darkness, which was before the stars were made, and they were as much lost in it as if they had been made before the stars. Every now and then, as those frightful hours wore on, they buffeted in the darkness against living men, who struck at them and at whom they struck, with an idiot fury.

When at last the grey dawn came, they found they had wandered back to the edge of the Uxbridge Road. They found that in those horrible eyeless encounters, the North Kensingtons and the Bayswaters and the West Kensingtons had again and again met and butchered each other, and they heard that Adam Wayne was barricaded in Pump Street.

CHAPTER II

The Correspondent of the Court Journal

Journalism had become, like most other such things in England under the cautious government and philosophy represented by James Barker, somewhat sleepy and much diminished in importance. This was partly due to the disappearance of party government and public speaking, partly to the compromise or dead-lock which had made foreign wars impossible, but mostly, of course, to the temper of the whole nation which was that of a people in a kind of back-water. Perhaps the most well known of the remaining newspapers was the *Court Journal*, which was published in a dusty but genteel-looking office just out of Kensington High Street. For when all the papers of a people have been for years growing more and more dim and decorous and optimistic, the dimmest and most decorous and most optimistic is very likely to win. In the journalistic competition which was still going on at the beginning of the twentieth century, the final victor was the *Court Journal*.

For some mysterious reason the King had a great affection for hanging about in the Court Journal office, smoking a morning cigarette and looking over files. Like all ingrainedly idle men, he was very fond of lounging and chatting in places where other people were doing work. But one would have thought that, even in the prosaic England of his day, he might have found a more bustling centre.

On this particular morning, however, he came out of Kensington Palace with a more alert step and a busier air than usual.

He wore an extravagantly long frock-coat, a pale-green waistcoat, a very full and *dégagé* black tie, and curious yellow gloves. This was his uniform as Colonel of a regiment of his own creation, the 1st Decadents Green. It was a beautiful sight to see him drilling them. He walked quickly across the Park and the High Street, lighting his cigarette as he went, and flung open the door of the *Court Journal* office.

"You've heard the news, Pally—you've heard the news?" he said.

The Editor's name was Hoskins, but the King called him Pally, which was an abbreviation of Paladium of our Liberties.

"Well, your Majesty," said Hoskins, slowly (he was a worried, gentlemanly looking person, with a wandering brown beard)— "well, your Majesty, I have heard rather curious things, but I—"

"You'll hear more of them," said the King, dancing a few steps of a kind of negro shuffle. "You'll hear more of them, my blood-and-thunder tribune. Do you know what I am going to do for you?"

"No, your Majesty," replied the Paladium, vaguely.

"I'm going to put your paper on strong, dashing, enterprising lines," said the King. "Now, where are your posters of last night's defeat?"

"I did not propose, your Majesty," said the Editor, "to have any posters exactly—"

"Paper, paper!" cried the King, wildly; "bring me paper as big as a house. I'll do you posters. Stop, I must take my coat off." He began removing that garment with an air of set intensity, flung it playfully at Mr. Hoskins' head, entirely enveloping him, and looked at himself in the glass. "The coat off," he said, "and the hat on. That looks like a sub-editor. It is indeed the very essence of sub-editing.

Well," he continued, turning round abruptly, "come along with that paper."

The Paladium had only just extricated himself reverently from the folds of the King's frock-coat, and said bewildered—

"I am afraid, your Majesty—"

"Oh, you've got no enterprise," said Auberon. "What's that roll in the corner? Wall-paper? Decorations for your private residence? Art in the home, Pally? Fling it over here, and I'll paint such posters on the back of it that when you put it up in your drawing-room you'll paste the original pattern against the wall." And the King unrolled the wall-paper, spreading it over the whole floor. "Now give me the scissors," he cried, and took them himself before the other could stir.

He slit the paper into about five pieces, each nearly as big as a door. Then he took a big blue pencil, and went down on his knees on the dusty oil-cloth and began to write on them, in huge letters—

FROM THE FRONT.

GENERAL BUCK DEFEATED.

DARKNESS, DANGER, AND DEATH.

WAYNE SAID TO BE IN PUMP STREET.

FEELING IN THE CITY.

He contemplated it for some time, with his head on one side, and got up, with a sigh.

"Not quite intense enough," he said—"not alarming. I want the *Court Journal* to be feared as well as loved. Let's try something more hard-hitting." And he went down on his knees again. After sucking the blue pencil for some time, he began writing again busily. "How will this do?" he said—

WAYNE'S WONDERFUL VICTORY.

"I suppose," he said, looking up appealingly, and sucking the pencil—"I suppose we couldn't say 'wictory'—'Wayne's wonderful wictory'? No, no. Refinement, Pally, refinement. I have it."

WAYNE WINS.

ASTOUNDING FIGHT IN THE DARK.

The gas-lamps in their courses fought against Buck.

"(Nothing like our fine old English translation.) What else can we say? Well, anything to annoy old Buck;" and he added, thoughtfully, in smaller letters—

RUMOURED COURT-MARTIAL ON GENERAL BUCK.

"Those will do for the present," he said, and turned them both face downwards. "Paste, please."

The Paladium, with an air of great terror, brought the paste out of an inner room.

The King slabbed it on with the enjoyment of a child messing with treacle. Then taking one of his huge compositions fluttering in each hand, he ran outside, and began pasting them up in prominent positions over the front of the office.

"And now," said Auberon, entering again with undiminished vivacity—"now for the leading article."

He picked up another of the large strips of wall-paper, and, laying it across a desk, pulled out a fountain-pen and began writing with feverish intensity, reading clauses and fragments aloud to himself, and rolling them on his tongue like wine, to see if they had the pure journalistic flavour.

"The news of the disaster to our forces in Notting Hill, awful as it is—awful as it is—(no, distressing as it is), may do some good if it draws attention to the what's-his-name inefficiency (scandalous inefficiency, of course) of the Government's preparations. In our present state of information, it would be premature (what a jolly word!)—it would be premature to cast any reflections upon the conduct of General Buck, whose services upon so many stricken fields (ha, ha!), and whose honourable scars and laurels, give him a right to have judgment upon him at least suspended. But there is one matter on which we must speak plainly. We have been silent on it too long, from feelings, perhaps of mistaken caution, perhaps of mistaken loyalty.

This situation would never have arisen but for what we can only call the indefensible conduct of the King. It pains us to say such things, but, speaking as we do in the public interests (I plagiarise from Barker's famous epigram), we shall not shrink because of the distress we may cause to any individual, even the most exalted. At this crucial moment of our country, the voice of the People demands with a single tongue, 'Where is the King?' What is he doing while his subjects tear each other in pieces in the streets of a great city? Are his amusements and his dissipations (of which we cannot pretend to be ignorant) so engrossing that he can spare no thought for a perishing nation? It is with a deep sense of our responsibility that we warn that exalted person that neither his great position nor his incomparable talents will save him in the hour of delirium from the fate of all those who, in the madness of luxury or tyranny, have met the English people in the rare day of its wrath."

"I am now," said the King, "going to write an account of the battle by an eye-witness." And he picked up a fourth sheet of wall-paper. Almost at the same moment Buck strode quickly into the office. He had a bandage round his head.

"I was told," he said, with his usual gruff civility, "that your Majesty was here."

"And of all things on earth," cried the King, with delight, "here is an eye-witness! An eye-witness who, I regret to observe, has at present only one eye to witness with. Can you write us the special article, Buck? Have you a rich style?"

Buck, with a self-restraint which almost approached politeness, took no notice whatever of the King's maddening geniality.

"I took the liberty, your Majesty," he said shortly, "of asking Mr. Barker to come here also."

As he spoke, indeed, Barker came swinging into the office, with his usual air of hurry.

"What is happening now?" asked Buck, turning to him with a kind of relief.

"Fighting still going on," said Barker. "The four hundred from West Kensington were hardly touched last night. They hardly got near the place. Poor Wilson's Bayswater men got cut about, though. They fought confoundedly well. They took Pump Street once. What mad things do happen in the world. To think that of all of us it should be little Wilson with the red whiskers who came out best."

The King made a note on his paper—

"*Romantic Conduct of Mr. Wilson.*"

"Yes," said Buck; "it makes one a bit less proud of one's h's."

The King suddenly folded or crumpled up the paper, and put it in his pocket.

"I have an idea," he said. "I will be an eye-witness. I will write you such letters from the Front as will be more gorgeous than the real thing. Give me my coat, Paladium. I entered this room a mere King of England. I leave it, Special War Correspondent of the *Court Journal*. It is useless to stop me, Pally; it is vain to cling to my knees, Buck; it is hopeless, Barker, to weep upon my neck. 'When duty calls'—the remainder of the sentiment escapes me. You will receive my first article this evening by the eight-o'clock post."

And, running out of the office, he jumped upon a blue Bayswater omnibus that went swinging by.

"Well," said Barker, gloomily, "well."

"Barker," said Buck, "business may be lower than politics, but war is, as I discovered last night, a long sight more like business. You politicians are such ingrained demagogues that even when you have a despotism you think of nothing but public opinion. So you learn to tack and run, and are afraid of the first breeze. Now we stick to a thing and get it. And our mistakes help us. Look here! At this moment we've beaten Wayne."

"Beaten Wayne," repeated Barker.

"Why the dickens not?" cried the other, flinging out his hands. "Look here. I said last night that we had them by holding the nine entrances. Well, I was wrong. We should have had them but for a singular event—the lamps went out. But for that it was certain. Has it occurred to you, my brilliant Barker, that another singular event has happened since that singular event of the lamps going out?"

"What event?" asked Barker.

"By an astounding coincidence, the sun has risen," cried out Buck, with a savage air of patience. "Why the hell aren't we holding all those approaches now, and passing in on them again? It should have been done at sunrise. The confounded doctor wouldn't let me go out. You were in command."

Barker smiled grimly.

"It is a gratification to me, my dear Buck, to be able to say that we anticipated your suggestions precisely. We went as early as possible to reconnoitre the nine entrances. Unfortunately, while we were fighting each other in the dark, like a lot of drunken navvies, Mr. Wayne's friends were working very hard indeed. Three hundred yards from Pump Street, at every one of those entrances, there is a barricade nearly as high as the houses. They were finishing the last, in Pembridge Road, when we arrived. Our mistakes," he cried bitterly, and flung his cigarette on the ground. "It is not we who learn from them."

There was a silence for a few moments, and Barker lay back wearily in a chair. The office clock ticked exactly in the stillness.

At length Barker said suddenly—

"Buck, does it ever cross your mind what this is all about? The Hammersmith to Maida Vale thoroughfare was an uncommonly good speculation. You and I hoped a great deal from it. But is it worth it? It will cost us thousands to crush this ridiculous riot. Suppose we let it alone?"

"And be thrashed in public by a red-haired madman whom any two doctors would lock up?" cried out Buck, starting to his feet. "What do you propose to do, Mr. Barker? To apologise to the admirable Mr. Wayne? To kneel to the Charter of the Cities? To clasp to your bosom the flag of the Red Lion? To kiss in succession every sacred lamp-post that saved Notting Hill? No, by God! My men fought jolly well—they were beaten by a trick. And they'll fight again."

"Buck," said Barker, "I always admired you. And you were quite right in what you said the other day."

"In what?"

"In saying," said Barker, rising quietly, "that we had all got into Adam Wayne's atmosphere and out of our own. My friend, the whole territorial kingdom of Adam Wayne extends to about nine streets, with barricades at the end of them. But the spiritual kingdom of Adam Wayne extends, God knows where—it extends to this office, at any rate. The red-haired madman whom any two doctors would lock up is filling this room with his roaring, unreasonable soul. And it was the red-haired madman who said the last word you spoke."

Buck walked to the window without replying. "You understand, of course," he said at last, "I do not dream of giving in."

The King, meanwhile, was rattling along on the top of his blue omnibus. The traffic of London as a whole had not, of course, been greatly disturbed by these events, for the affair was treated as a Notting Hill riot, and that area was marked off as if it had been in the hands of a gang of recognised rioters. The blue omnibuses simply went round as they would have done if a road were being mended, and the omnibus on which the correspondent of the *Court Journal* was sitting swept round the corner of Queen's Road, Bayswater.

The King was alone on the top of the vehicle, and was enjoying the speed at which it was going.

"Forward, my beauty, my Arab," he said, patting the omnibus encouragingly, "fleetest of all thy bounding tribe. Are thy relations with thy driver, I wonder, those of the Bedouin and his steed? Does he sleep side by side with thee—"

His meditations were broken by a sudden and jarring stoppage. Looking over the edge, he saw that the heads of the horses were being held by men in the uniform of Wayne's army, and heard the voice of an officer calling out orders. King Auberon descended from the omnibus with dignity. The guard or picket of red halberdiers who had stopped the vehicle did not number more than twenty, and they were under the command of a short, dark, clever-looking young man, conspicuous among the rest as being clad in an ordinary frock-coat, but girt round the waist with a red sash and a long seventeenth-century sword. A shiny silk hat and spectacles completed the outfit in a pleasing manner.

"To whom have I the honour of speaking?" said the King, endeavouring to look like Charles I, in spite of personal difficulties.

The dark man in spectacles lifted his hat with equal gravity.

"My name is Bowles," he said. "I am a chemist. I am also a captain of O Company of the army of Notting Hill. I am distressed at having to incommode you by stopping the omnibus, but this area is covered by our proclamation, and we intercept all traffic. May I ask to whom I have the honour—Why, good gracious, I beg your Majesty's pardon. I am quite overwhelmed at finding myself concerned with the King."

Auberon put up his hand with indescribable grandeur.

"Not with the King," he said; "with the special war correspondent of the *Court Journal*."

"I beg your Majesty's pardon," began Mr. Bowles, doubtfully.

"Do you call me Majesty? I repeat," said Auberon, firmly, "I am a representative of the press. I have chosen, with a deep sense of responsibility, the name of Pinker. I should desire a veil to be drawn over the past."

"Very well, sir," said Mr. Bowles, with an air of submission, "in our eyes the sanctity of the press is at least as great as that of the throne. We desire nothing better than that our wrongs and our glories should be widely known. May I ask, Mr. Pinker, if you have any objection to being presented to the Provost and to General Turnbull?"

"The Provost I have had the honour of meeting," said Auberon, easily. "We old journalists, you know, meet everybody. I should be most delighted to have the same honour again. General Turnbull, also, it would be a gratification to know. The younger men are so interesting. We of the old Fleet Street gang lose touch with them."

"Will you be so good as to step this way?" said the leader of O Company.

"I am always good," said Mr. Pinker. "Lead on."

CHAPTER III

The Great Army of South Kensington

The article from the special correspondent of the *Court Journal* arrived in due course, written on very coarse copy-paper in the King's arabesque of handwriting, in which three words filled a page, and yet were illegible. Moreover, the contribution was the more perplexing at first, as it opened with a succession of erased paragraphs. The writer appeared to have attempted the article once or twice in several journalistic styles. At the side of one experiment was written, "Try American style," and the fragment began—

"The King must go. We want gritty men. Flapdoodle is all very…" and then broke off, followed by the note, "Good sound journalism safer. Try it."

The experiment in good sound journalism appeared to begin—

"The greatest of English poets has said that a rose by any…"

This also stopped abruptly. The next annotation at the side was almost undecipherable, but seemed to be something like—

"How about old Steevens and the *mot juste*? E.g.…"

"Morning winked a little wearily at me over the curt edge of Campden Hill and its houses with their sharp shadows. Under the abrupt black cardboard of the outline, it took some little time to detect colours; but at length I saw a brownish yellow shifting in the obscurity, and I knew that it was the guard of Swindon's West Kensington army. They are being held as a reserve, and lining the whole ridge above the Bayswater Road. Their camp and their main force is under the great Waterworks Tower on Campden Hill. I forgot to say that the Waterworks Tower looked swart.

"As I passed them and came over the curve of Silver Street, I saw the blue cloudy masses of Barker's men blocking the entrance to the high-road like a sapphire smoke (good). The disposition of the allied troops, under the general management of Mr. Wilson, appears to be as follows: The Yellow army (if I may so describe the West Kensingtonians) lies, as I have said, in a strip along the ridge, its furthest point westward being the west side of Campden Hill Road, its furthest point eastward the beginning of Kensington Gardens. The Green army of Wilson lines the Notting Hill High Road itself from Queen's Road to the corner of Pembridge Road, curving round the latter, and extending some three hundred yards up towards Westbourne Grove. Westbourne Grove itself is occupied by Barker of South Kensington. The fourth side of this rough square, the Queen's Road side, is held by some of Buck's Purple warriors.

"The whole resembles some ancient and dainty Dutch flower-bed. Along the crest of Campden Hill lie the golden crocuses of West Kensington. They are, as it were, the first fiery fringe of the whole. Northward lies our hyacinth Barker, with all his blue hyacinths. Round to the south-west run the green rushes of Wilson of Bayswater, and a line of violet irises (aptly symbolised by Mr. Buck) complete the whole. The argent exterior... (I am losing the style. I should have said 'Curving with a whisk' instead of merely 'Curving.' Also I should have called the hyacinths 'sudden.' I cannot keep this up. War is too rapid for this style of writing. Please ask office-boy to insert *mots justes*.)

"The truth is that there is nothing to report. That commonplace element which is always ready to devour all beautiful things (as the Black Pig in the Irish Mythology will finally devour the stars and gods); that commonplace element, as I say, has in its Black Piggish way devoured finally the chances of any romance in this affair; that which once consisted of absurd but thrilling combats in the streets, has degenerated into something which is the very prose of warfare—it has degenerated into a siege. A siege may be defined as a peace plus the inconvenience of war. Of course Wayne cannot hold out. There is no more chance of help from anywhere else than of ships from the moon. And if old Wayne had stocked his street with tinned meats till all his garrison had to sit on them, he couldn't hold out for more than a month or two. As a matter of melancholy fact, he has done something rather like this. He has stocked his street with food until there must be uncommonly little room to turn round. But what is the good? To hold out for all that time and then to give in of necessity, what does it mean? It means waiting until your victories are forgotten, and then taking the trouble to be defeated. I cannot understand how Wayne can be so inartistic.

"And how odd it is that one views a thing quite differently when one knows it is defeated! I always thought Wayne was rather fine. But now, when I know that he is done for, there seem to be nothing else but Wayne. All the streets seem to point at him, all the chimneys seem to lean towards him. I suppose it is a morbid feeling; but Pump Street seems to be the only part of London that I feel physically. I suppose, I say, that it is morbid. I suppose it is exactly how a man feels about his heart when his heart is weak. 'Pump Street'—the heart is a pump. And I am drivelling.

"Our finest leader at the front is, beyond all question, General Wilson. He has adopted alone among the other Provosts the uniform of his own halberdiers, although that fine old sixteenth-century garb was not originally intended to go with red side-whiskers. It was he who, against a most admirable and desperate defence, broke last night into Pump Street and held it for at least half an hour. He was afterwards expelled from it by General Turnbull, of Notting Hill, but only after desperate fighting and the sudden descent of that terrible darkness which proved so much more fatal to the forces of General Buck and General Swindon.

"Provost Wayne himself, with whom I had, with great good fortune, a most interesting interview, bore the most eloquent testimony to the conduct of General Wilson and his men. His precise words are as follows: 'I have bought sweets at his funny little shop when I was four years old, and ever since. I never noticed anything, I am ashamed to say, except that he talked through his nose, and didn't wash himself particularly. And he came over our barricade like a devil from hell.' I repeated this speech to General Wilson himself, with some delicate improvements, and he seemed pleased with it. He does not, however, seem pleased with anything so much just now as he is with the wearing of a sword. I have it from the front on the best authority that General Wilson was not completely shaved yesterday. It is believed in military circles that he is growing a moustache....

"As I have said, there is nothing to report. I walk wearily to the pillar-box at the corner of Pembridge Road to post my copy. Nothing whatever has happened, except the preparations for a particularly long and feeble siege, during which I trust I shall not be required to be at the Front. As I glance up Pembridge Road in the growing dusk, the aspect of that road reminds me that there is one note worth adding.

General Buck has suggested, with characteristic acumen, to General Wilson that, in order to obviate the possibility of such a catastrophe as overwhelmed the allied forces in the last advance on Notting Hill (the catastrophe, I mean, of the extinguished lamps), each soldier should have a lighted lantern round his neck. This is one of the things which I really admire about General Buck. He possesses what people used to mean by 'the humility of the man of science,' that is, he learns steadily from his mistakes. Wayne may score off him in some other way, but not in that way. The lanterns look like fairy lights as they curve round the end of Pembridge Road."

"*Later*—I write with some difficulty, because the blood will run down my face and make patterns on the paper. Blood is a very beautiful thing; that is why it is concealed. If you ask why blood runs down my face, I can only reply that I was kicked by a horse. If you ask me what horse, I can reply with some pride that it was a war-horse. If you ask me how a war-horse came on the scene in our simple pedestrian warfare, I am reduced to the necessity, so painful to a special correspondent, of recounting my experiences.

"I was, as I have said, in the very act of posting my copy at the pillar-box, and of glancing as I did so up the glittering curve of Pembridge Road, studded with the lights of Wilson's men. I don't know what made me pause to examine the matter, but I had a fancy that the line of lights, where it melted into the indistinct brown twilight, was more indistinct than usual. I was almost certain that in a certain stretch of the road where there had been five lights there were now only four. I strained my eyes; I counted them again, and there were only three. A moment after there were only two; an instant after only one; and an instant after that the lanterns near to me swung like jangled bells, as if struck suddenly. They flared and fell; and for the moment the fall of them was like the fall of the sun and stars out of heaven. It left everything in a primal blindness. As a matter of fact, the road was not yet legitimately dark. There were still red rays of a sunset in the sky, and the brown gloaming was still warmed, as it were, with a feeling as of firelight. But for three seconds after the lanterns swung and sank, I saw in front of me a blackness blocking the sky. And with the fourth second I knew that this blackness which blocked the sky was a man on a great horse; and I was trampled and tossed aside as a swirl of horsemen swept round the corner. As they turned I saw that they were not black, but scarlet; they were a sortie of the besieged, Wayne riding ahead.

"I lifted myself from the gutter, blinded with blood from a very slight skin-wound, and, queerly enough, not caring either for the blindness or for the slightness of the wound. For one mortal minute after that amazing cavalcade had spun past, there was dead stillness on the empty road. And then came Barker and all his halberdiers running like devils in the track of them. It had been their business to guard the gate by which the sortie had broken out; but they had not reckoned, and small blame to them, on cavalry. As it was, Barker and his men made a perfectly splendid run after them, almost catching Wayne's horses by the tails.

"Nobody can understand the sortie. It consists only of a small number of Wayne's garrison. Turnbull himself, with the vast mass of it, is undoubtedly still barricaded in Pump Street. Sorties of this kind are natural enough in the majority of historical sieges, such as the siege of Paris in 1870, because in such cases the besieged are certain of some support outside. But what can be the object of it in this case? Wayne knows (or if he is too mad to know anything, at least Turnbull knows) that there is not, and never has been, the smallest chance of support for him outside; that the mass of the sane modern inhabitants of London regard his farcical patriotism with as much contempt as they do the original idiocy that gave it birth—the folly of our miserable King. What Wayne and his horsemen are doing nobody can even conjecture. The general theory round here is that he is simply a traitor, and has abandoned the besieged. But all such larger but yet more soluble riddles are as nothing compared to the one small but unanswerable riddle: Where did they get the horses?"

"*Later*—I have heard a most extraordinary account of the origin of the appearance of the horses. It appears that that amazing person, General Turnbull, who is now ruling Pump Street in the absence of Wayne, sent out, on the morning of the declaration of war, a vast number of little boys (or cherubs of the gutter, as we pressmen say), with half-crowns in their pockets, to take cabs all over London. No less than a hundred and sixty cabs met at Pump Street; were commandeered by the garrison. The men were set free, the cabs used to make barricades, and the horses kept in Pump Street, where they were fed and exercised for several days, until they were sufficiently rapid and efficient to be used for this wild ride out of the town. If this is so, and I have it on the best possible authority, the method of the sortie is explained. But we have no explanation of its object. Just as Barker's Blues were swinging round the corner after them, they were stopped, but not by an enemy; only by the voice of one man, and he a friend. Red Wilson of Bayswater ran alone along the main road like a madman, waving them back with a halberd snatched from a sentinel. He was in supreme command, and Barker stopped at the corner, staring and bewildered. We could hear Wilson's voice loud and distinct out of the dusk, so that it seemed strange that the great voice should come out of the little body. 'Halt, South Kensington! Guard this entry, and prevent them returning. I will pursue. Forward, the Green Guards!'

"A wall of dark blue uniforms and a wood of pole-axes was between me and Wilson, for Barker's men blocked the mouth of the road in two rigid lines. But through them and through the dusk I could hear the clear orders and the clank of arms, and see the green army of Wilson marching by towards the west. They were our great fighting-men. Wilson had filled them with his own fire; in a few days they had become veterans. Each of them wore a silver medal of a pump, to boast that they alone of all the allied armies had stood victorious in Pump Street.

"I managed to slip past the detachment of Barker's Blues, who are guarding the end of Pembridge Road, and a sharp spell of running brought me to the tail of Wilson's green army as it swung down the road in pursuit of the flying Wayne. The dusk had deepened into almost total darkness; for some time I only heard the throb of the marching pace. Then suddenly there was a cry, and the tall fighting men were flung back on me, almost crushing me, and again the lanterns swung and jingled, and the cold nozzles of great horses pushed into the press of us. They had turned and charged us.

"'You fools!' came the voice of Wilson, cleaving our panic with a splendid cold anger. 'Don't you see? the horses have no riders!'

"It was true. We were being plunged at by a stampede of horses with empty saddles. What could it mean? Had Wayne met some of our men and been defeated? Or had he flung these horses at us as some kind of ruse or mad new mode of warfare, such as he seemed bent on inventing? Or did he and his men want to get away in disguise? Or did they want to hide in houses somewhere?

"Never did I admire any man's intellect (even my own) so much as I did Wilson's at that moment. Without a word, he simply pointed the halberd (which he still grasped) to the southern side of the road. As you know, the streets running up to the ridge of Campden Hill from the main road are peculiarly steep, they are more like sudden flights of stairs. We were just opposite Aubrey Road, the steepest of all; up that it would have been far more difficult to urge half-trained horses than to run up on one's feet.

"'Left wheel!' hallooed Wilson. 'They have gone up here,' he added to me, who happened to be at his elbow.

"'Why?' I ventured to ask.

"'Can't say for certain,' replied the Bayswater General. 'They've gone up here in a great hurry, anyhow. They've simply turned their horses loose, because they couldn't take them up. I fancy I know. I fancy they're trying to get over the ridge to Kensingston or Hammersmith, or somewhere, and are striking up here because it's just beyond the end of our line. Damned fools, not to have gone further along the road, though. They've only just shaved our last outpost. Lambert is hardly four hundred yards from here. And I've sent him word.'

"'Lambert!' I said. 'Not young Wilfrid Lambert—my old friend.'

"'Wilfrid Lambert's his name,' said the General; 'used to be a "man about town;" silly fellow with a big nose. That kind of man always volunteers for some war or other; and what's funnier, he generally isn't half bad at it. Lambert is distinctly good. The yellow West Kensingtons I always reckoned the weakest part of the army; but he has pulled them together uncommonly well, though he's subordinate to Swindon, who's a donkey. In the attack from Pembridge Road the other night he showed great pluck.'

"'He has shown greater pluck than that,' I said. 'He has criticised my sense of humour. That was his first engagement.'

"'This remark was, I am sorry to say, lost on the admirable commander of the allied forces. We were in the act of climbing the last half of Aubrey Road, which is so abrupt a slope that it looks like an old-fashioned map leaning up against the wall. There are lines of little trees, one above the other, as in the old-fashioned map.

"We reached the top of it, panting somewhat, and were just about to turn the corner by a place called (in chivalrous anticipation of our wars of sword and axe) Tower Crecy, when we were suddenly knocked in the stomach (I can use no other term) by a horde of men hurled back upon us. They wore the red uniform of Wayne; their halberds were broken; their foreheads bleeding; but the mere impetus of their retreat staggered us as we stood at the last ridge of the slope.

"'Good old Lambert!' yelled out suddenly the stolid Mr. Wilson of Bayswater, in an uncontrollable excitement. 'Damned jolly old Lambert! He's got there already! He's driving them back on us! Hurrah! hurrah! Forward, the Green Guards!'

"We swung round the corner eastwards, Wilson running first, brandishing the halberd...

"Will you pardon a little egotism? Every one likes a little egotism, when it takes the form, as mine does in this case, of a disgraceful confession. The thing is really a little interesting, because it shows how the merely artistic habit has bitten into men like me. It was the most intensely exciting occurrence that had ever come to me in my life; and I was really intensely excited about it. And yet, as we turned that corner, the first impression I had was of something that had nothing to do with the fight at all. I was stricken from the sky as by a thunderbolt, by the height of the Waterworks Tower on Campden Hill. I don't know whether Londoners generally realise how high it looks when one comes out, in this way, almost immediately under it. For the second it seemed to me that at the foot of it even human war was a triviality. For the second I felt as if I had been drunk with some trivial orgie, and that I had been sobered by the shock of that shadow. A moment afterwards, I realised that under it was going on something more enduring than stone, and something wilder than the dizziest height—the agony of man. And I knew that, compared to that, this overwhelming tower was itself a triviality; it was a mere stalk of stone which humanity could snap like a stick.

"I don't know why I have talked so much about this silly old Waterworks Tower, which at the very best was only a tremendous background. It was that, certainly, a sombre and awful landscape, against which our figures were relieved. But I think the real reason was, that there was in my own mind so sharp a transition from the tower of stone to the man of flesh. For what I saw first when I had shaken off, as it were, the shadow of the tower, was a man, and a man I knew.

"Lambert stood at the further corner of the street that curved round the tower, his figure outlined in some degree by the beginning of moonrise. He looked magnificent, a hero; but he looked something much more interesting than that. He was, as it happened, in almost precisely the same swaggering attitude in which he had stood nearly fifteen years ago, when he swung his walking-stick and struck it into the ground, and told me that all my subtlety was drivel. And, upon my soul, I think he required more courage to say that than to fight as he does now. For then he was fighting against something that was in the ascendant, fashionable, and victorious. And now he is fighting (at the risk of his life, no doubt) merely against something which is already dead, which is impossible, futile; of which nothing has been more impossible and futile than this very sortie which has brought him into contact with it. People nowadays allow infinitely too little for the psychological sense of victory as a factor in affairs. Then he was attacking the degraded but undoubtedly victorious Quin; now he is attacking the interesting but totally extinguished Wayne.

"His name recalls me to the details of the scene. The facts were these. A line of red halberdiers, headed by Wayne, were marching up the street, close under the northern wall, which is, in fact, the bottom of a sort of dyke or fortification of the Waterworks. Lambert and his yellow West Kensingtons had that instant swept round the corner and had shaken the Waynites heavily, hurling back a few of the more timid, as I have just described, into our very arms. When our force struck the tail of Wayne's, every one knew that all was up with him. His favourite military barber was struck down. His grocer was stunned. He himself was hurt in the thigh, and reeled back against the wall. We had him in a trap with two jaws. 'Is that you?' shouted Lambert, genially, to Wilson, across the hemmed-in host of Notting Hill. 'That's about the ticket,' replied General Wilson; 'keep them under the wall.'

"The men of Notting Hill were falling fast. Adam Wayne threw up his long arms to the wall above him, and with a spring stood upon it; a gigantic figure against the moon. He tore the banner out of the hands of the standard-bearer below him, and shook it out suddenly above our heads, so that it was like thunder in the heavens.

"'Round the Red Lion!' he cried. 'Swords round the Red Lion! Halberds round the Red Lion! They are the thorns round rose.'

"His voice and the crack of the banner made a momentary rally, and Lambert, whose idiotic face was almost beautiful with battle, felt it as by an instinct, and cried—

"'Drop your public-house flag, you footler! Drop it!'

"'The banner of the Red Lion seldom stoops,' said Wayne, proudly, letting it out luxuriantly on the night wind.

"The next moment I knew that poor Adam's sentimental theatricality had cost him much. Lambert was on the wall at a bound, his sword in his teeth, and had slashed at Wayne's head before he had time to draw his sword, his hands being busy with the enormous flag. He stepped back only just in time to avoid the first cut, and let the flag-staff fall, so that the spear-blade at the end of it pointed to Lambert.

"'The banner stoops,' cried Wayne, in a voice that must have startled streets. 'The banner of Notting Hill stoops to a hero.' And with the words he drove the spear-point and half the flag-staff through Lambert's body and dropped him dead upon the road below, a stone upon the stones of the street.

"'Notting Hill! Notting Hill!' cried Wayne, in a sort of divine rage. 'Her banner is all the holier for the blood of a brave enemy! Up on the wall, patriots! Up on the wall! Notting Hill!'

"With his long strong arm he actually dragged a man up on to the wall to be silhouetted against the moon, and more and more men climbed up there, pulled themselves and were pulled, till clusters and crowds of the half-massacred men of Pump Street massed upon the wall above us.

"'Notting Hill! Notting Hill!' cried Wayne, unceasingly.

"'Well, what about Bayswater?' said a worthy working-man in Wilson's army, irritably. 'Bayswater for ever!'

"'We have won!' cried Wayne, striking his flag-staff in the ground. 'Bayswater for ever! We have taught our enemies patriotism!'

"'Oh, cut these fellows up and have done with it!' cried one of Lambert's lieutenants, who was reduced to something bordering on madness by the responsibility of succeeding to the command.

"'Let us by all means try,' said Wilson, grimly; and the two armies closed round the third.

"I simply cannot describe what followed. I am sorry, but there is such a thing as physical fatigue, as physical nausea, and, I may add, as physical terror. Suffice it to say that the above paragraph was written about 11 p.m., and that it is now about 2 A.M., and that the battle is not finished, and is not likely to be. Suffice it further to say that down the steep streets which lead from the Waterworks Tower to the Notting Hill High Road, blood has been running, and is running, in great red serpents, that curl out into the main thoroughfare and shine in the moon.

"*Later*—The final touch has been given to all this terrible futility. Hours have passed; morning has broken; men are still swaying and fighting at the foot of the tower and round the corner of Aubrey Road; the fight has not finished. But I know it is a farce.

"News has just come to show that Wayne's amazing sortie, followed by the amazing resistance through a whole night on the wall of the Waterworks, is as if it had not been. What was the object of that strange exodus we shall probably never know, for the simple reason that every one who knew will probably be cut to pieces in the course of the next two or three hours.

"I have heard, about three minutes ago, that Buck and Buck's methods have won after all. He was perfectly right, of course, when one comes to think of it, in holding that it was physically impossible for a street to defeat a city. While we thought he was patrolling the eastern gates with his Purple army; while we were rushing about the streets and waving halberds and lanterns; while poor old Wilson was scheming like Moltke and fighting like Achilles to entrap the wild Provost of Notting Hill—Mr. Buck, retired draper, has simply driven down in a hansom cab and done something about as plain as butter and about as useful and nasty. He has gone down to South Kensington, Brompton, and Fulham, and by spending about four thousand pounds of his private means, has raised an army of nearly as many men; that is to say, an army big enough to beat, not only Wayne, but Wayne and all his present enemies put together. The army, I understand, is encamped along High Street, Kensington, and fills it from the Church to Addison Road Bridge. It is to advance by ten different roads uphill to the north.

"I cannot endure to remain here. Everything makes it worse than it need be. The dawn, for instance, has broken round Campden Hill; splendid spaces of silver, edged with gold, are torn out of the sky. Worse still, Wayne and his men feel the dawn; their faces, though bloody and pale, are strangely hopeful...insupportably pathetic. Worst of all, for the moment they are winning. If it were not for Buck and the new army they might just, and only just, win.

"I repeat, I cannot stand it. It is like watching that wonderful play of old Maeterlinck's (you know my partiality for the healthy, jolly old authors of the nineteenth century), in which one has to watch the quiet conduct of people inside a parlour, while knowing that the very men are outside the door whose word can blast it all with tragedy. And this is worse, for the men are not talking, but writhing and bleeding and dropping dead for a thing that is already settled—and settled against them. The great grey masses of men still toil and tug and sway hither and thither around the great grey tower; and the tower is still motionless, as it will always be motionless. These men will be crushed before the sun is set; and new men will arise and be crushed, and new wrongs done, and tyranny will always rise again like the sun, and injustice will always be as fresh as the flowers of spring. And the stone tower will always look down on it. Matter, in its brutal beauty, will always look down on those who are mad enough to consent to die, and yet more mad, since they consent to live."

Thus ended abruptly the first and last contribution of the Special Correspondent of the *Court Journal* to that valued periodical.

The Correspondent himself, as has been said, was simply sick and gloomy at the last news of the triumph of Buck. He slouched sadly down the steep Aubrey Road, up which he had the night before run in so unusual an excitement, and strolled out into the empty dawn-lit main road, looking vaguely for a cab. He saw nothing in the vacant space except a blue-and-gold glittering thing, running very fast, which looked at first like a very tall beetle, but turned out, to his great astonishment, to be Barker.

"Have you heard the good news?" asked that gentleman.

"Yes," said Quin, with a measured voice. "I have heard the glad tidings of great joy. Shall we take a hansom down to Kensington? I see one over there."

They took the cab, and were, in four minutes, fronting the ranks of the multitudinous and invincible army. Quin had not spoken a word all the way, and something about him had prevented the essentially impressionable Barker from speaking either.

The great army, as it moved up Kensington High Street, calling many heads to the numberless windows, for it was long indeed— longer than the lives of most of the tolerably young—since such an army had been seen in London. Compared with the vast organisation which was now swallowing up the miles, with Buck at its head as leader, and the King hanging at its tail as journalist, the whole story of our problem was insignificant. In the presence of that army the red Notting Hills and the green Bayswaters were alike tiny and straggling groups. In its presence the whole struggle round Pump Street was like an ant-hill under the hoof of an ox. Every man who felt or looked at that infinity of men knew that it was the triumph of Buck's brutal arithmetic. Whether Wayne was right or wrong, wise or foolish, was quite a fair matter for discussion. But it was a matter of history. At the foot of Church Street, opposite Kensington Church, they paused in their glowing good humour.

"Let us send some kind of messenger or herald up to them," said Buck, turning to Barker and the King. "Let us send and ask them to cave in without more muddle."

"What shall we say to them?" said Barker, doubtfully.

"The facts of the case are quite sufficient," rejoined Buck. "It is the facts of the case that make an army surrender. Let us simply say that our army that is fighting their army, and their army that is fighting our army, amount altogether to about a thousand men. Say that we have four thousand. It is very simple. Of the thousand fighting, they have at the very most, three hundred, so that, with those three hundred, they have now to fight four thousand seven hundred men. Let them do it if it amuses them."

And the Provost of North Kensington laughed.

The herald who was despatched up Church Street in all the pomp of the South Kensington blue and gold, with the Three Birds on his tabard, was attended by two trumpeters.

"What will they do when they consent?" asked Barker, for the sake of saying something in the sudden stillness of that immense army.

"I know my Wayne very well," said Buck, laughing. "When he submits he will send a red herald flaming with the Lion of Notting Hill. Even defeat will be delightful to him, since it is formal and romantic."

The King, who had strolled up to the head of the line, broke silence for the first time.

"I shouldn't wonder," he said, "if he defied you, and didn't send the herald after all. I don't think you do know your Wayne quite so well as you think."

"All right, your Majesty," said Buck, easily; "if it isn't disrespectful, I'll put my political calculations in a very simple form. I'll lay you ten pounds to a shilling the herald comes with the surrender."

"All right," said Auberon. "I may be wrong, but it's my notion of Adam Wayne that he'll die in his city, and that, till he is dead, it will not be a safe property."

"The bet's made, your Majesty," said Buck.

Another long silence ensued, in the course of which Barker alone, amid the motionless army, strolled and stamped in his restless way.

Then Buck suddenly leant forward.

"It's taking your money, your Majesty," he said. "I knew it was. There comes the herald from Adam Wayne."

"It's not," cried the King, peering forward also. "You brute, it's a red omnibus."

"It's not," said Buck, calmly; and the King did not answer, for down the centre of the spacious and silent Church Street was walking, beyond question, the herald of the Red Lion, with two trumpeters.

Buck had something in him which taught him how to be magnanimous. In his hour of success he felt magnanimous towards Wayne, whom he really admired; magnanimous towards the King, off whom he had scored so publicly; and, above all, magnanimous towards Barker, who was the titular leader of this vast South Kensington army, which his own talent had evoked.

"General Barker," he said, bowing, "do you propose now to receive the message from the besieged?"

Barker bowed also, and advanced towards the herald.

"Has your master, Mr. Adam Wayne, received our request for surrender?" he asked.

The herald conveyed a solemn and respectful affirmative.

Barker resumed, coughing slightly, but encouraged.

"What answer does your master send?"

The herald again inclined himself submissively, and answered in a kind of monotone.

"My message is this. Adam Wayne, Lord High Provost of Notting Hill, under the charter of King Auberon and the laws of God and all mankind, free and of a free city, greets James Barker, Lord High Provost of South Kensington, by the same rights free and honourable, leader of the army of the South. With all friendly reverence, and with all constitutional consideration, he desires James Barker to lay down his arms, and the whole army under his command to lay down their arms also."

Before the words were ended the King had run forward into the open space with shining eyes. The rest of the staff and the forefront of the army were literally struck breathless. When they recovered they began to laugh beyond restraint; the revulsion was too sudden.

"The Lord High Provost of Notting Hill," continued the herald, "does not propose, in the event of your surrender, to use his victory for any of those repressive purposes which others have entertained against him. He will leave you your free laws and your free cities, your flags and your governments. He will not destroy the religion of South Kensington, or crush the old customs of Bayswater."

An irrepressible explosion of laughter went up from the forefront of the great army.

"The King must have had something to do with this humour," said Buck, slapping his thigh. "It's too deliciously insolent. Barker, have a glass of wine."

And in his conviviality he actually sent a soldier across to the restaurant opposite the church and brought out two glasses for a toast.

When the laughter had died down, the herald continued quite monotonously—

"In the event of your surrendering your arms and dispersing under the superintendence of our forces, these local rights of yours shall be carefully observed. In the event of your not doing so, the Lord High Provost of Notting Hill desires to announce that he has just captured the Waterworks Tower, just above you, on Campden Hill, and that within ten minutes from now, that is, on the reception through me of your refusal, he will open the great reservoir and flood the whole valley where you stand in thirty feet of water. God save King Auberon!"

Buck had dropped his glass and sent a great splash of wine over the road.

"But—but—" he said; and then by a last and splendid effort of his great sanity, looked the facts in the face.

"We must surrender," he said. "You could do nothing against fifty thousand tons of water coming down a steep hill, ten minutes hence. We must surrender. Our four thousand men might as well be four. *Vicisti Galilae!* Perkins, you may as well get me another glass of wine."

In this way the vast army of South Kensington surrendered and the Empire of Notting Hill began. One further fact in this connection is perhaps worth mentioning—the fact that, after his victory, Adam Wayne caused the great tower on Campden Hill to be plated with gold and inscribed with a great epitaph, saying that it was the monument of Wilfrid Lambert, the heroic defender of the place, and surmounted with a statue, in which his large nose was done something less than justice to.

Book V

CHAPTER I

The Empire of Notting Hill

On the evening of the third of October, twenty years after the great victory of Notting Hill, which gave it the dominion of London, King Auberon came, as of old, out of Kensington Palace.

He had changed little, save for a streak or two of grey in his hair, for his face had always been old, and his step slow, and, as it were, decrepit.

If he looked old, it was not because of anything physical or mental. It was because he still wore, with a quaint conservatism, the frock-coat and high hat of the days before the great war. "I have survived the Deluge," he said. "I am a pyramid, and must behave as such."

As he passed up the street the Kensingtonians, in their picturesque blue smocks, saluted him as a King, and then looked after him as a curiosity. It seemed odd to them that men had once worn so elvish an attire.

The King, cultivating the walk attributed to the oldest inhabitant ("Gaffer Auberon" his friends were now confidentially desired to call him), went toddling northward. He paused, with reminiscence in his eye, at the Southern Gate of Notting Hill, one of those nine great gates of bronze and steel, wrought with reliefs of the old battles, by the hand of Chiffy himself.

"Ah!" he said, shaking his head and assuming an unnecessary air of age, and a provincialism of accent—"Ah! I mind when there warn't none of this here."

He passed through the Ossington Gate, surmounted by a great lion, wrought in red copper on yellow brass, with the motto, "Nothing Ill." The guard in red and gold saluted him with his halberd.

It was about sunset, and the lamps were being lit. Auberon paused to look at them, for they were Chiffy's finest work, and his artistic eye never failed to feast on them. In memory of the Great Battle of the Lamps, each great iron lamp was surmounted by a veiled figure, sword in hand, holding over the flame an iron hood or extinguisher, as if ready to let it fall if the armies of the South and West should again show their flags in the city. Thus no child in Notting Hill could play about the streets without the very lamp-posts reminding him of the salvation of his country in the dreadful year.

"Old Wayne was right in a way," commented the King. "The sword does make things beautiful. It has made the whole world romantic by now. And to think people once thought me a buffoon for suggesting a romantic Notting Hill. Deary me, deary me! (I think that is the expression)—it seems like a previous existence."

Turning a corner, he found himself in Pump Street, opposite the four shops which Adam Wayne had studied twenty years before. He entered idly the shop of Mr. Mead, the grocer. Mr. Mead was somewhat older, like the rest of the world, and his red beard, which he now wore with a moustache, and long and full, was partly blanched and discoloured. He was dressed in a long and richly embroidered robe of blue, brown, and crimson, interwoven with an Eastern complexity of pattern, and covered with obscure symbols and pictures, representing his wares passing from hand to hand and from nation to nation. Round his neck was the chain with the Blue Argosy cut in turquoise, which he wore as Grand Master of the Grocers. The whole shop had the sombre and sumptuous look of its owner. The wares were displayed as prominently as in the old days, but they were now blended and arranged with a sense of tint and grouping, too often neglected by the dim grocers of those forgotten days. The wares were shown plainly, but shown not so much as an old grocer would have shown his stock, but rather as an educated virtuoso would have shown his treasures. The tea was stored in great blue and green vases, inscribed with the nine indispensable sayings of the wise men of China. Other vases of a confused orange and purple, less rigid and dominant, more humble and dreamy, stored symbolically the tea of India. A row of caskets of a simple silvery metal contained tinned meats. Each was wrought with some rude but rhythmic form, as a shell, a horn, a fish, or an apple, to indicate what material had been canned in it.

"Your Majesty," said Mr. Mead, sweeping an Oriental reverence. "This is an honour to me, but yet more an honour to the city."

Auberon took off his hat.

"Mr. Mead," he said, "Notting Hill, whether in giving or taking, can deal in nothing but honour. Do you happen to sell liquorice?"

"Liquorice, sire," said Mr. Mead, "is not the least important of our benefits out of the dark heart of Arabia."

And going reverently towards a green and silver canister, made in the form of an Arabian mosque, he proceeded to serve his customer.

"I was just thinking, Mr. Mead," said the King, reflectively, "I don't know why I should think about it just now, but I was just thinking of twenty years ago. Do you remember the times before the war?"

The grocer, having wrapped up the liquorice sticks in a piece of paper (inscribed with some appropriate sentiment), lifted his large grey eyes dreamily, and looked at the darkening sky outside.

"Oh yes, your Majesty," he said. "I remember these streets before the Lord Provost began to rule us. I can't remember how we felt very well. All the great songs and the fighting change one so; and I don't think we can really estimate all we owe to the Provost; but I can remember his coming into this very shop twenty-two years ago, and I remember the things he said. The singular thing is that, as far as I remember, I thought the things he said odd at that time. Now it's the things that I said, as far as I can recall them, that seem to me odd—as odd as a madman's antics."

"Ah!" said the King; and looked at him with an unfathomable quietness.

"I thought nothing of being a grocer then," he said. "Isn't that odd enough for anybody? I thought nothing of all the wonderful places that my goods come from, and wonderful ways that they are made. I did not know that I was for all practical purposes a king with slaves spearing fishes near the secret pool, and gathering fruits in the islands under the world. My mind was a blank on the thing. I was as mad as a hatter."

The King turned also, and stared out into the dark, where the great lamps that commemorated the battle were already flaming.

"And is this the end of poor old Wayne?" he said, half to himself. "To inflame every one so much that he is lost himself in the blaze. Is this his victory that he, my incomparable Wayne, is now only one in a world of Waynes? Has he conquered and become by conquest commonplace? Must Mr. Mead, the grocer, talk as high as he? Lord! what a strange world in which a man cannot remain unique even by taking the trouble to go mad!"

And he went dreamily out of the shop. He paused outside the next one almost precisely as the Provost had done two decades before.

"How uncommonly creepy this shop looks!" he said. "But yet somehow encouragingly creepy, invitingly creepy. It looks like something in a jolly old nursery story in which you are frightened out of your skin, and yet know that things always end well. The way those low sharp gables are carved like great black bat's wings folded down, and the way those queer-coloured bowls underneath are made to shine like giants' eye-balls. It looks like a benevolent warlock's hut. It is apparently a chemist's."

Almost as he spoke, Mr. Bowles, the chemist, came to his shop door in a long black velvet gown and hood, monastic as it were, but yet with a touch of the diabolic. His hair was still quite black, and his face even paler than of old. The only spot of colour he carried was a red star cut in some precious stone of strong tint, hung on his breast. He belonged to the Society of the Red Star of Charity, founded on the lamps displayed by doctors and chemists.

"A fine evening, sir," said the chemist. "Why, I can scarcely be mistaken in supposing it to be your Majesty. Pray step inside and share a bottle of sal volatile, or anything that may take your fancy. As it happens, there is an old acquaintance of your Majesty's in my shop carousing (if I may be permitted the term) upon that beverage at this moment."

The King entered the shop, which was an Aladdin's garden of shades and hues, for as the chemist's scheme of colour was more brilliant than the grocer's scheme, so it was arranged with even more delicacy and fancy. Never, if the phrase may be employed, had such a nosegay of medicines been presented to the artistic eye.

But even the solemn rainbow of that evening interior was rivalled or even eclipsed by the figure standing in the centre of the shop. His form, which was a large and stately one, was clad in a brilliant blue velvet, cut in the richest Renaissance fashion, and slashed so as to show gleams and gaps of a wonderful lemon or pale yellow. He had several chains round his neck, and his plumes, which were of several tints of bronze and gold, hung down to the great gold hilt of his long sword. He was drinking a dose of sal volatile, and admiring its opal tint. The King advanced with a slight mystification towards the tall figure, whose face was in shadow; then he said—

"By the Great Lord of Luck, Barker!"

The figure removed his plumed cap, showing the same dark head and long, almost equine face which the King had so often seen rising out of the high collar of Bond Street. Except for a grey patch on each temple, it was totally unchanged.

"Your Majesty," said Barker, "this is a meeting nobly retrospective, a meeting that has about it a certain October gold. I drink to old days," and he finished his sal volatile with simple feeling.

"I am delighted to see you again, Barker," said the King. "It is indeed long since we met. What with my travels in Asia Minor, and my book having to be written (you have read my *Life of Prince Albert for Children*, of course?), we have scarcely met twice since the Great War. That is twenty years ago."

"I wonder," said Barker, thoughtfully, "if I might speak freely to your Majesty?"

"Well," said Auberon, "it's rather late in the day to start speaking respectfully. Flap away, my bird of freedom."

"Well, your Majesty," replied Barker, lowering his voice, "I don't think it will be so long to the next war."

"What do you mean?" asked Auberon.

"We will stand this insolence no longer," burst out Barker, fiercely. "We are not slaves because Adam Wayne twenty years ago cheated us with a water-pipe. Notting Hill is Notting Hill; it is not the world. We in South Kensington, we also have memories— ay, and hopes. If they fought for these trumpery shops and a few lamp-posts, shall we not fight for the great High Street and the sacred Natural History Museum?"

"Great Heavens!" said the astounded Auberon. "Will wonders never cease? Have the two greatest marvels been achieved? Have you turned altruistic, and has Wayne turned selfish? Are you the patriot, and he the tyrant?"

"It is not from Wayne himself altogether that the evil comes," answered Barker. "He, indeed, is now mostly wrapped in dreams, and sits with his old sword beside the fire. But Notting Hill is the tyrant, your Majesty. Its Council and its crowds have been so intoxicated by the spreading over the whole city of Wayne's old ways and visions, that they try to meddle with every one, and rule every one, and civilise every one, and tell every one what is good for him. I do not deny the great impulse which his old war, wild as it seemed, gave to the civic life of our time. It came when I was still a young man, and I admit it enlarged my career. But we are not going to see our own cities flouted and thwarted from day to day because of something Wayne did for us all nearly a quarter of a century ago. I am just waiting here for news upon this very matter. It is rumoured that Notting Hill has vetoed the statue of General Wilson they are putting up opposite Chepstow Place. If that is so, it is a black and white shameless breach of the terms on which we surrendered to Turnbull after the battle of the Tower.

We were to keep our own customs and self-government. If that is so—"

"It is so," said a deep voice; and both men turned round.

A burly figure in purple robes, with a silver eagle hung round his neck and moustaches almost as florid as his plumes, stood in the doorway.

"Yes," he said, acknowledging the King's start, "I am Provost Buck, and the news is true. These men of the Hill have forgotten that we fought round the Tower as well as they, and that it is sometimes foolish, as well as base, to despise the conquered."

"Let us step outside," said Barker, with a grim composure.

Buck did so, and stood rolling his eyes up and down the lamp-lit street.

"I would like to have a go at smashing all this," he muttered, "though I am over sixty. I would like—"

His voice ended in a cry, and he reeled back a step, with his hands to his eyes, as he had done in those streets twenty years before.

"Darkness!" he cried—"darkness again! What does it mean?"

For in truth every lamp in the street had gone out, so that they could not see even each other's outline, except faintly. The voice of the chemist came with startling cheerfulness out of the density.

"Oh, don't you know?" he said. "Did they never tell you this is the Feast of the Lamps, the anniversary of the great battle that almost lost and just saved Notting Hill? Don't you know, your Majesty, that on this night twenty-one years ago we saw Wilson's green uniforms charging down this street, and driving Wayne and Turnbull back upon the gas-works, fighting with their handful like fiends from hell? And that then, in that great hour, Wayne sprang through a window of the gas-works, with one blow of his hand brought darkness on the whole city, and then with a cry like a lion's, that was heard through four streets, flew at Wilson's men, sword in hand, and swept them, bewildered as they were, and ignorant of the map, clear out of the sacred street again? And don't you know that upon that night every year all lights are turned out for half an hour while we sing the Notting Hill anthem in the darkness? Hark! there it begins."

Through the night came a crash of drums, and then a strong swell of human voices—

> *"When the world was in the balance, there was night on Notting Hill,*
> *(There was night on Notting Hill): it was nobler than the day;*
> *On the cities where the lights are and the firesides glow,*
> *From the seas and from the deserts came the thing we did not know,*
> *Came the darkness, came the darkness, came the darkness on the foe,*
> *And the old guard of God turned to bay.*
> *For the old guard of God turns to bay, turns to bay,*
> *And the stars fall down before it ere its banners fall today:*
> *For when armies were around us as a howling and a horde,*
> *When falling was the citadel and broken was the sword,*
> *The darkness came upon them like the Dragon of the Lord,*
> *When the old guard of God turned to bay."*

The voices were just uplifting themselves in a second verse when they were stopped by a scurry and a yell. Barker had bounded into the street with a cry of "South Kensington!" and a drawn dagger. In less time than a man could blink, the whole packed street was full of curses and struggling. Barker was flung back against the shop-front, but used the second only to draw his sword as well as his dagger, and calling out, "This is not the first time I've come through the thick of you," flung himself again into the press. It was evident that he had drawn blood at last, for a more violent outcry arose, and many other knives and swords were discernible in the faint light. Barker, after having wounded more than one man, seemed on the point of being flung back again, when Buck suddenly stepped out into the street. He had no weapon, for he affected rather the peaceful magnificence of the great burgher, than the pugnacious dandyism which had replaced the old sombre dandyism in Barker. But with a blow of his clenched fist he broke the pane of the next shop, which was the old curiosity shop, and, plunging in his hand, snatched a kind of Japanese scimitar, and calling out, "Kensington! Kensington!" rushed to Barker's assistance.

Barker's sword was broken, but he was laying about him with his dagger. Just as Buck ran up, a man of Notting Hill struck Barker down, but Buck struck the man down on top of him, and Barker sprang up again, the blood running down his face.

Suddenly all these cries were cloven by a great voice, that seemed to fall out of heaven. It was terrible to Buck and Barker and the King, from its seeming to come out the empty skies; but it was more terrible because it was a familiar voice, and one which at the same time they had not heard for so long.

"Turn up the lights," said the voice from above them, and for a moment there was no reply, but only a tumult.

"In the name of Notting Hill and of the great Council of the City, turn up the lights."

There was again a tumult and a vagueness for a moment, then the whole street and every object in it sprang suddenly out of the darkness, as every lamp sprang into life. And looking up they saw, standing upon a balcony near the roof of one of the highest houses, the figure and the face of Adam Wayne, his red hair blowing behind him, a little streaked with grey.

"What is this, my people?" he said. "Is it altogether impossible to make a thing good without it immediately insisting on being wicked? The glory of Notting Hill in having achieved its independence, has been enough for me to dream of for many years, as I sat beside the fire. Is it really not enough for you, who have had so many other affairs to excite and distract you? Notting Hill is a nation. Why should it condescend to be a mere Empire? You wish to pull down the statue of General Wilson, which the men of Bayswater have so rightly erected in Westbourne Grove. Fools! Who erected that statue? Did Bayswater erect it? No. Notting Hill erected it. Do you not see that it is the glory of our achievement that we have infected the other cities with the idealism of Notting Hill? It is we who have created not only our own side, but both sides of this controversy. O too humble fools, why should you wish to destroy your enemies? You have done something more to them. You have created your enemies. You wish to pull down that gigantic silver hammer, which stands, like an obelisk, in the centre of the Broadway of Hammersmith. Fools! Before Notting Hill arose, did any person passing through Hammersmith Broadway expect to see there a gigantic silver hammer? You wish to abolish the great bronze figure of a knight standing upon the artificial bridge at Knightsbridge. Fools! Who would have thought of it before Notting Hill arose? I have even heard, and with deep pain I have heard it, that the evil eye of our imperial envy has been cast towards the remote horizon of the west, and that we have objected to the great black monument of a crowned raven, which commemorates the skirmish of Ravenscourt Park. Who created all these things? Were they there before we came? Cannot you be content with that destiny which was enough for Athens, which was enough for Nazareth? The destiny, the humble purpose, of creating a new world. Is Athens angry because Romans and Florentines have adopted her phraseology for expressing their own patriotism? Is Nazareth angry because as a little village it has become the type of all little villages out of which, as the Snobs say, no good can come? Has Athens asked every one to wear the chlamys? Are all followers of the Nazarene compelled to wear turbans. No! But the soul of Athens went forth and made men drink hemlock, and the soul of Nazareth went forth and made men consent to be crucified. So has the soul of Notting Hill gone forth and made men realise what it is to live in a city. Just as we inaugurated our symbols and ceremonies, so they have inaugurated theirs; and are you so mad as to contend against them? Notting Hill is right; it has always been right. It has moulded itself on its own necessities, its own *sine qua non*; it has accepted its own ultimatum. Because it is a nation it has created itself; and because it is a nation it can destroy itself. Notting Hill shall always be the judge. If it is your will because of this matter of General Wilson's statue to make war upon Bayswater—"

A roar of cheers broke in upon his words, and further speech was impossible. Pale to the lips, the great patriot tried again and again to speak; but even his authority could not keep down the dark and roaring masses in the street below him. He said something further, but it was not audible. He descended at last sadly from the garret in which he lived, and mingled with the crowd at the foot of the houses.

Finding General Turnbull, he put his hand on his shoulder with a queer affection and gravity, and said—

"Tomorrow, old man, we shall have a new experience, as fresh as the flowers of spring. We shall be defeated. You and I have been through three battles together, and have somehow or other missed this peculiar delight. It is unfortunate that we shall not probably be able to exchange our experiences, because, as it most annoyingly happens, we shall probably both be dead."

Turnbull looked dimly surprised.

"I don't mind so much about being dead," he said, "but why should you say that we shall be defeated?"

"The answer is very simple," replied Wayne, calmly. "It is because we ought to be defeated. We have been in the most horrible holes before now; but in all those I was perfectly certain that the stars were on our side, and that we ought to get out. Now I know that we ought not to get out; and that takes away from me everything with which I won."

As Wayne spoke he started a little, for both men became aware that a third figure was listening to them—a small figure with wondering eyes.

"Is it really true, my dear Wayne," said the King, interrupting, "that you think you will be beaten tomorrow?"

"There can be no doubt about it whatever," replied Adam Wayne; "the real reason is the one of which I have just spoken. But as a concession to your materialism, I will add that they have an organised army of a hundred allied cities against our one. That in itself, however, would be unimportant."

Quin, with his round eyes, seemed strangely insistent.

"You are quite sure," he said, "that you must be beaten?"

"I am afraid," said Turnbull, gloomily, "that there can be no doubt about it."

"Then," cried the King, flinging out his arms, "give me a halberd! Give me a halberd, somebody! I desire all men to witness that I, Auberon, King of England, do here and now abdicate, and implore the Provost of Notting Hill to permit me to enlist in his army. Give me a halberd!"

He seized one from some passing guard, and, shouldering it, stamped solemnly after the shouting columns of halberdiers which were, by this time, parading the streets. He had, however, nothing to do with the wrecking of the statue of General Wilson, which took place before morning.

CHAPTER II

The Last Battle

The day was cloudy when Wayne went down to die with all his army in Kensington Gardens; it was cloudy again when that army had been swallowed up by the vast armies of a new world. There had been an almost uncanny interval of sunshine, in which the Provost of Notting Hill, with all the placidity of an onlooker, had gazed across to the hostile armies on the great spaces of verdure opposite; the long strips of green and blue and gold lay across the park in squares and oblongs like a proposition in Euclid wrought in a rich embroidery. But the sunlight was a weak and, as it were, a wet sunlight, and was soon swallowed up. Wayne spoke to the King, with a queer sort of coldness and languor, as to the military operations. It was as he had said the night before—that being deprived of his sense of an impracticable rectitude, he was, in effect, being deprived of everything. He was out of date, and at sea in a mere world of compromise and competition, of Empire against Empire, of the tolerably right and the tolerably wrong.

When his eye fell on the King, however, who was marching very gravely with a top hat and a halberd, it brightened slightly.

"Well, your Majesty," he said, "you at least ought to be proud today. If your children are fighting each other, at least those who win are your children. Other kings have distributed justice, you have distributed life. Other kings have ruled a nation, you have created nations. Others have made kingdoms, you have begotten them. Look at your children, father!" and he stretched his hand out towards the enemy.

Auberon did not raise his eyes.

"See how splendidly," cried Wayne, "the new cities come on—the new cities from across the river. See where Battersea advances over there—under the flag of the Lost Dog; and Putney—don't you see the Man on the White Boar shining on their standard as the sun catches it? It is the coming of a new age, your Majesty. Notting Hill is not a common empire; it is a thing like Athens, the mother of a mode of life, of a manner of living, which shall renew the youth of the world—a thing like Nazareth. When I was young I remember, in the old dreary days, wiseacres used to write books about how trains would get faster, and all the world be one empire, and tram-cars go to the moon. And even as a child I used to say to myself, 'Far more likely that we shall go on the crusades again, or worship the gods of the city.' And so it has been. And I am glad, though this is my last battle."

Even as he spoke there came a crash of steel from the left, and he turned his head.

"Wilson!" he cried, with a kind of joy. "Red Wilson has charged our left. No one can hold him in; he eats swords. He is as keen a soldier as Turnbull, but less patient—less really great. Ha! and Barker is moving. How Barker has improved; how handsome he looks! It is not all having plumes; it is also having a soul in one's daily life. Ha!"

And another crash of steel on the right showed that Barker had closed with Notting Hill on the other side.

"Turnbull is there!" cried Wayne. "See him hurl them back! Barker is checked! Turnbull charges—wins! But our left is broken. Wilson has smashed Bowles and Mead, and may turn our flank. Forward, the Provost's Guard!"

And the whole centre moved forward, Wayne's face and hair and sword flaming in the van.

The King ran suddenly forward.

The next instant a great jar that went through it told that it had met the enemy. And right over against them through the wood of their own weapons Auberon saw the Purple Eagle of Buck of North Kensington.

On the left Red Wilson was storming the broken ranks, his little green figure conspicuous even in the tangle of men and weapons, with the flaming red moustaches and the crown of laurel. Bowles slashed at his head and tore away some of the wreath, leaving the rest bloody, and, with a roar like a bull's, Wilson sprang at him, and, after a rattle of fencing, plunged his point into the chemist, who fell, crying, "Notting Hill!" Then the Notting Hillers wavered, and Bayswater swept them back in confusion. Wilson had carried everything before him.

On the right, however, Turnbull had carried the Red Lion banner with a rush against Barker's men, and the banner of the Golden Birds bore up with difficulty against it. Barker's men fell fast. In the centre Wayne and Buck were engaged, stubborn and confused. So far as the fighting went, it was precisely equal. But the fighting was a farce. For behind the three small armies with which Wayne's small army was engaged lay the great sea of the allied armies, which looked on as yet as scornful spectators, but could have broken all four armies by moving a finger.

Suddenly they did move. Some of the front contingents, the pastoral chiefs from Shepherd's Bush, with their spears and fleeces, were seen advancing, and the rude clans from Paddington Green. They were advancing for a very good reason. Buck, of North Kensington, was signalling wildly; he was surrounded, and totally cut off. His regiments were a struggling mass of people, islanded in a red sea of Notting Hill.

The allies had been too careless and confident. They had allowed Barker's force to be broken to pieces by Turnbull, and the moment that was done, the astute old leader of Notting Hill swung his men round and attacked Buck behind and on both sides. At the same moment Wayne cried, "Charge!" and struck him in front like a thunderbolt.

Two-thirds of Buck's men were cut to pieces before their allies could reach them. Then the sea of cities came on with their banners like breakers, and swallowed Notting Hill for ever. The battle was not over, for not one of Wayne's men would surrender, and it lasted till sundown, and long after. But it was decided; the story of Notting Hill was ended.

When Turnbull saw it, he ceased a moment from fighting, and looked round him. The evening sunlight struck his face; it looked like a child's.

"I have had my youth," he said. Then, snatching an axe from a man, he dashed into the thick of the spears of Shepherd's Bush, and died somewhere far in the depths of their reeling ranks. Then the battle roared on; every man of Notting Hill was slain before night.

Wayne was standing by a tree alone after the battle. Several men approached him with axes. One struck at him. His foot seemed partly to slip; but he flung his hand out, and steadied himself against the tree.

Barker sprang after him, sword in hand, and shaking with excitement.

"How large now, my lord," he cried, "is the Empire of Notting Hill?"

Wayne smiled in the gathering dark.

"Always as large as this," he said, and swept his sword round in a semicircle of silver.

Barker dropped, wounded in the neck; and Wilson sprang over his body like a tiger-cat, rushing at Wayne. At the same moment there came behind the Lord of the Red Lion a cry and a flare of yellow, and a mass of the West Kensington halberdiers ploughed up the slope, knee-deep in grass, bearing the yellow banner of the city before them, and shouting aloud.

At the same second Wilson went down under Wayne's sword, seemingly smashed like a fly. The great sword rose again like a bird, but Wilson seemed to rise with it, and, his sword being broken, sprang at Wayne's throat like a dog. The foremost of the yellow halberdiers had reached the tree and swung his axe above the struggling Wayne. With a curse the King whirled up his own halberd, and dashed the blade in the man's face. He reeled and rolled down the slope, just as the furious Wilson was flung on his back again. And again he was on his feet, and again at Wayne's throat. Then he was flung again, but this time laughing triumphantly. Grasped in his hand was the red and yellow favour that Wayne wore as Provost of Notting Hill. He had torn it from the place where it had been carried for twenty-five years.

With a shout the West Kensington men closed round Wayne, the great yellow banner flapping over his head.

"Where is your favour now, Provost?" cried the West Kensington leader.

And a laugh went up.

Adam struck at the standard-bearer and brought him reeling forward. As the banner stooped, he grasped the yellow folds and tore off a shred.

A halberdier struck him on the shoulder, wounding bloodily.

"Here is one colour!" he cried, pushing the yellow into his belt. "And here!" he cried, pointing to his own blood—"Here is the other."

At the same instant the shock of a sudden and heavy halberd laid the King stunned or dead. In the wild visions of vanishing consciousness, he saw again something that belonged to an utterly forgotten time, something that he had seen somewhere long ago in a restaurant. He saw, with his swimming eyes, red and yellow, the colours of Nicaragua.

Quin did not see the end. Wilson, wild with joy, sprang again at Adam Wayne, and the great sword of Notting Hill was whirled above once more. Then men ducked instinctively at the rushing noise of the sword coming down out of the sky, and Wilson of Bayswater was smashed and wiped down upon the floor like a fly. Nothing was left of him but a wreck; but the blade that had broken him was broken. In dying he had snapped the great sword and the spell of it; the sword of Wayne was broken at the hilt. One rush of the enemy carried Wayne by force against the tree. They were too close to use halberd or even sword; they were breast to breast, even nostrils to nostrils. But Buck got his dagger free.

"Kill him!" he cried, in a strange stifled voice. "Kill him! Good or bad, he is none of us! Do not be blinded by the face!... God! Have we not been blinded all along!" and he drew his arm back for a stab, and seemed to close his eyes.

Wayne did not drop the hand that hung on to the tree-branch. But a mighty heave went over his breast and his whole huge figure, like an earthquake over great hills. And with that convulsion of effort he rent the branch out of the tree, with tongues of torn wood; and, swaying it once only, he let the splintered club fall on Buck, breaking his neck. The planner of the Great Road fell face foremost dead, with his dagger in a grip of steel.

"For you and me, and for all brave men, my brother," said Wayne, in his strange chant, "there is good wine poured in the inn at the end of the world."

The packed men made another lurch or heave towards him; it was almost too dark to fight clearly. He caught hold of the oak again, this time getting his hand into a wide crevice and grasping, as it were, the bowels of the tree. The whole crowd, numbering some thirty men, made a rush to tear him away from it; they hung on with all their weight and numbers, and nothing stirred. A solitude could not have been stiller than that group of straining men. Then there was a faint sound.

"His hand is slipping," cried two men in exultation.

"You don't know much of him," said another, grimly (a man of the old war). "More likely his bone cracks."

"It is neither—by God, it is neither!" said one of the first two.

"What is it, then?" asked the second.

"The tree is falling," he replied.

"As the tree falleth, so shall it lie," said Wayne's voice out of the darkness, and it had the same sweet and yet horrible air that it had had throughout, of coming from a great distance, from before or after the event. Even when he was struggling like an eel or battering like a madman, he spoke like a spectator. "As the tree falleth, so shall it lie," he said. "Men have called that a gloomy text. It is the essence of all exultation. I am doing now what I have done all my life, what is the only happiness, what is the only universality. I am clinging to something. Let it fall, and there let it lie. Fools, you go about and see the kingdoms of the earth, and are liberal and wise and cosmopolitan, which is all that the devil can give you—all that he could offer to Christ, only to be spurned away. I am doing what the truly wise do. When a child goes out into the garden and takes hold of a tree, saying, 'Let this tree be all I have,' that moment its roots take hold on hell and its branches on the stars. The joy I have is what the lover knows when a woman is everything. It is what a savage knows when his idol is everything. It is what I know when Notting Hill is everything. I have a city. Let it stand or fall."

As he spoke, the turf lifted itself like a living thing, and out of it rose slowly, like crested serpents, the roots of the oak. Then the great head of the tree, that seemed a green cloud among grey ones, swept the sky suddenly like a broom, and the whole tree heeled over like a ship, smashing every one in its fall.

CHAPTER III

Two Voices

In a place in which there was total darkness for hours, there was also for hours total silence. Then a voice spoke out of the darkness, no one could have told from where, and said aloud—

"So ends the Empire of Notting Hill. As it began in blood, so it ended in blood, and all things are always the same."

And there was silence again, and then again there was a voice, but it had not the same tone; it seemed that it was not the same voice.

"If all things are always the same, it is because they are always heroic. If all things are always the same, it is because they are always new. To each man one soul only is given; to each soul only is given a little power—the power at some moments to outgrow and swallow up the stars. If age after age that power comes upon men, whatever gives it to them is great. Whatever makes men feel old is mean—an empire or a skin-flint shop. Whatever makes men feel young is great—a great war or a love-story. And in the darkest of the books of God there is written a truth that is also a riddle. It is of the new things that men tire—of fashions and proposals and improvements and change. It is the old things that startle and intoxicate. It is the old things that are young. There is no sceptic who does not feel that many have doubted before. There is no rich and fickle man who does not feel that all his novelties are ancient. There is no worshipper of change who does not feel upon his neck the vast weight of the weariness of the universe. But we who do the old things are fed by nature with a perpetual infancy. No man who is in love thinks that any one has been in love before. No woman who has a child thinks that there have been such things as children. No people that fight for their own city are haunted with the burden of the broken empires. Yes, O dark voice, the world is always the same, for it is always unexpected."

A little gust of wind blew through the night, and then the first voice answered—

"But in this world there are some, be they wise or foolish, whom nothing intoxicates. There are some who see all your disturbances like a cloud of flies. They know that while men will laugh at your Notting Hill, and will study and rehearse and sing of Athens and Jerusalem, Athens and Jerusalem were silly suburbs like your Notting Hill. They know that the earth itself is a suburb, and can feel only drearily and respectably amused as they move upon it."

"They are philosophers or they are fools," said the other voice. "They are not men. Men live, as I say, rejoicing from age to age in something fresher than progress—in the fact that with every baby a new sun and a new moon are made. If our ancient humanity were a single man, it might perhaps be that he would break down under the memory of so many loyalties, under the burden of so many diverse heroisms, under the load and terror of all the goodness of men. But it has pleased God so to isolate the individual soul that it can only learn of all other souls by hearsay, and to each one goodness and happiness come with the youth and violence of lightning, as momentary and as pure. And the doom of failure that lies on all human systems does not in real fact affect them any more than the worms of the inevitable grave affect a children's game in a meadow. Notting Hill has fallen; Notting Hill has died. But that is not the tremendous issue. Notting Hill has lived."

"But if," answered the other voice, "if what is achieved by all these efforts be only the common contentment of humanity, why do men so extravagantly toil and die in them? Has nothing been done by Notting Hill than any chance clump of farmers or clan of savages would not have done without it? What might have been done to Notting Hill if the world had been different may be a deep question; but there is a deeper. What could have happened to the world if Notting Hill had never been?"

The other voice replied—

"The same that would have happened to the world and all the starry systems if an apple-tree grew six apples instead of seven; something would have been eternally lost. There has never been anything in the world absolutely like Notting Hill. There will never be anything quite like it to the crack of doom. I cannot believe anything but that God loved it as He must surely love anything that is itself and unreplaceable. But even for that I do not care. If God, with all His thunders, hated it, I loved it."

And with the voice a tall, strange figure lifted itself out of the debris in the half-darkness.

The other voice came after a long pause, and as it were hoarsely.

"But suppose the whole matter were really a hocus-pocus. Suppose that whatever meaning you may choose in your fancy to give to it, the real meaning of the whole was mockery. Suppose it was all folly. Suppose—"

"I have been in it," answered the voice from the tall and strange figure, "and I know it was not."

A smaller figure seemed half to rise in the dark.

"Suppose I am God," said the voice, "and suppose I made the world in idleness. Suppose the stars, that you think eternal, are only the idiot fireworks of an everlasting schoolboy. Suppose the sun and the moon, to which you sing alternately, are only the two eyes of one vast and sneering giant, opened alternately in a never-ending wink. Suppose the trees, in my eyes, are as foolish as enormous toad-stools. Suppose Socrates and Charlemagne are to me only beasts, made funnier by walking on their hind legs. Suppose I am God, and having made things, laugh at them."

"And suppose I am man," answered the other. "And suppose that I give the answer that shatters even a laugh. Suppose I do not laugh back at you, do not blaspheme you, do not curse you. But suppose, standing up straight under the sky, with every power of my being, I thank you for the fools' paradise you have made. Suppose I praise you, with a literal pain of ecstasy, for the jest that has brought me so terrible a joy. If we have taken the child's games, and given them the seriousness of a Crusade, if we have drenched your grotesque Dutch garden with the blood of martyrs, we have turned a nursery into a temple. I ask you, in the name of Heaven, who wins?"

The sky close about the crests of the hills and trees was beginning to turn from black to grey, with a random suggestion of the morning. The slight figure seemed to crawl towards the larger one, and the voice was more human.

"But suppose, friend," it said, "suppose that, in a bitterer and more real sense, it was all a mockery. Suppose that there had been, from the beginning of these great wars, one who watched them with a sense that is beyond expression, a sense of detachment, of responsibility, of irony, of agony. Suppose that there were one who knew it was all a joke."

The tall figure answered—

"He could not know it. For it was not all a joke."

And a gust of wind blew away some clouds that sealed the skyline, and showed a strip of silver behind his great dark legs. Then the other voice came, having crept nearer still.

"Adam Wayne," it said, "there are men who confess only in *articulo mortis*; there are people who blame themselves only when they can no longer help others. I am one of them. Here, upon the field of the bloody end of it all, I come to tell you plainly what you would never understand before. Do you know who I am?"

"I know you, Auberon Quin," answered the tall figure, "and I shall be glad to unburden your spirit of anything that lies upon it."

"Adam Wayne," said the other voice, "of what I have to say you cannot in common reason be glad to unburden me. Wayne, it was all a joke. When I made these cities, I cared no more for them than I care for a centaur, or a merman, or a fish with legs, or a pig with feathers, or any other absurdity. When I spoke to you solemnly and encouragingly about the flag of your freedom and the peace of your city, I was playing a vulgar practical joke on an honest gentleman, a vulgar practical joke that has lasted for twenty years. Though no one could believe it of me, perhaps, it is the truth that I am a man both timid and tender-hearted. I never dared in the early days of your hope, or the central days of your supremacy, to tell you this; I never dared to break the colossal calm of your face. God knows why I should do it now, when my farce has ended in tragedy and the ruin of all your people! But I say it now. Wayne, it was done as a joke."

There was silence, and the freshening breeze blew the sky clearer and clearer, leaving great spaces of the white dawn.

At last Wayne said, very slowly—

"You did it all only as a joke?"

"Yes," said Quin, briefly.

"When you conceived the idea," went on Wayne, dreamily, "of an army for Bayswater and a flag for Notting Hill, there was no gleam, no suggestion in your mind that such things might be real and passionate?"

"No," answered Auberon, turning his round white face to the morning with a dull and splendid sincerity; "I had none at all."

Wayne sprang down from the height above him and held out his hand.

"I will not stop to thank you," he said, with a curious joy in his voice, "for the great good for the world you have actually wrought. All that I think of that I have said to you a moment ago, even when I thought that your voice was the voice of a derisive omnipotence, its laughter older than the winds of heaven. But let me say what is immediate and true. You and I, Auberon Quin, have both of us throughout our lives been again and again called mad. And we are mad. We are mad, because we are not two men, but one man. We are mad, because we are two lobes of the same brain, and that brain has been cloven in two. And if you ask for the proof of it, it is not hard to find. It is not merely that you, the humorist, have been in these dark days stripped of the joy of gravity. It is not merely that I, the fanatic, have had to grope without humour. It is that, though we seem to be opposite in everything, we have been opposite like man and woman, aiming at the same moment at the same practical thing. We are the father and the mother of the Charter of the Cities."

Quin looked down at the debris of leaves and timber, the relics of the battle and stampede, now glistening in the growing daylight, and finally said—

"Yet nothing can alter the antagonism—the fact that I laughed at these things and you adored them."

Wayne's wild face flamed with something god-like, as he turned it to be struck by the sunrise.

"I know of something that will alter that antagonism, something that is outside us, something that you and I have all our lives perhaps taken too little account of. The equal and eternal human being will alter that antagonism, for the human being sees no real antagonism between laughter and respect, the human being, the common man, whom mere geniuses like you and me can only worship like a god. When dark and dreary days come, you and I are necessary, the pure fanatic, the pure satirist. We have between us remedied a great wrong. We have lifted the modern cities into that poetry which every one who knows mankind knows to be immeasurably more common than the commonplace. But in healthy people there is no war between us. We are but the two lobes of the brain of a ploughman. Laughter and love are everywhere. The cathedrals, built in the ages that loved God, are full of blasphemous grotesques. The mother laughs continually at the child, the lover laughs continually at the lover, the wife at the husband, the friend at the friend. Auberon Quin, we have been too long separated; let us go out together. You have a halberd and I a sword, let us start our wanderings over the world. For we are its two essentials. Come, it is already day."

In the blank white light Auberon hesitated a moment. Then he made the formal salute with his halberd, and they went away together into the unknown world.

THE END

THE MAN WHO WAS THURSDAY

A NIGHTMARE

To EDMUND CLERIHEW BENTLEY

A cloud was on the mind of men, and wailing went the weather,
Yea, a sick cloud upon the soul when we were boys together.
Science announced nonentity and art admired decay;
The world was old and ended: but you and I were gay;
Round us in antic order their crippled vices came—
Lust that had lost its laughter, fear that had lost its shame.
Like the white lock of Whistler, that lit our aimless gloom,
Men showed their own white feather as proudly as a plume.
Life was a fly that faded, and death a drone that stung;
The world was very old indeed when you and I were young.
They twisted even decent sin to shapes not to be named:
Men were ashamed of honour; but we were not ashamed.
Weak if we were and foolish, not thus we failed, not thus;
When that black Baal blocked the heavens he had no hymns from us
Children we were—our forts of sand were even as weak as we,
High as they went we piled them up to break that bitter sea.
Fools as we were in motley, all jangling and absurd,
When all church bells were silent our cap and bells were heard.

Not all unhelped we held the fort, our tiny flags unfurled;
Some giants laboured in that cloud to lift it from the world.
I find again the book we found, I feel the hour that flings
Far out of fish-shaped Paumanok some cry of cleaner things;
And the Green Carnation withered, as in forest fires that pass,
Roared in the wind of all the world ten million leaves of grass;
Or sane and sweet and sudden as a bird sings in the rain—

Truth out of Tusitala spoke and pleasure out of pain.
Yea, cool and clear and sudden as a bird sings in the grey,
Dunedin to Samoa spoke, and darkness unto day.
But we were young; we lived to see God break their bitter charms.
God and the good Republic come riding back in arms:
We have seen the City of Mansoul, even as it rocked, relieved—
Blessed are they who did not see, but being blind, believed.

This is a tale of those old fears, even of those emptied hells,
And none but you shall understand the true thing that it tells—
Of what colossal gods of shame could cow men and yet crash,
Of what huge devils hid the stars, yet fell at a pistol flash.
The doubts that were so plain to chase, so dreadful to withstand—
Oh, who shall understand but you; yea, who shall understand?
The doubts that drove us through the night as we two talked amain,
And day had broken on the streets e'er it broke upon the brain.
Between us, by the peace of God, such truth can now be told;
Yea, there is strength in striking root and good in growing old.
We have found common things at last and marriage and a creed,
And I may safely write it now, and you may safely read.

G. K. C.

CHAPTER I

The Two Poets of Saffron Park

The suburb of Saffron Park lay on the sunset side of London, as red and ragged as a cloud of sunset. It was built of a bright brick throughout; its sky-line was fantastic, and even its ground plan was wild. It had been the outburst of a speculative builder, faintly tinged with art, who called its architecture sometimes Elizabethan and sometimes Queen Anne, apparently under the impression that the two sovereigns were identical. It was described with some justice as an artistic colony, though it never in any definable way produced any art. But although its pretensions to be an intellectual centre were a little vague, its pretensions to be a pleasant place were quite indisputable. The stranger who looked for the first time at the quaint red houses could only think how very oddly shaped the people must be who could fit in to them. Nor when he met the people was he disappointed in this respect. The place was not only pleasant, but perfect, if once he could regard it not as a deception but rather as a dream. Even if the people were not "artists," the whole was nevertheless artistic. That young man with the long, auburn hair and the impudent face—that young man was not really a poet; but surely he was a poem. That old gentleman with the wild, white beard and the wild, white hat—that venerable humbug was not really a philosopher; but at least he was the cause of philosophy in others. That scientific gentleman with the bald, egg-like head and the bare, bird-like neck had no real right to the airs of science that he assumed. He had not discovered anything new in biology; but what biological creature could he have discovered more singular than himself? Thus, and thus only, the whole place had properly to be regarded; it had to be considered not so much as a workshop for artists, but as a frail but finished work of art. A man who stepped into its social atmosphere felt as if he had stepped into a written comedy.

More especially this attractive unreality fell upon it about nightfall, when the extravagant roofs were dark against the afterglow and the whole insane village seemed as separate as a drifting cloud. This again was more strongly true of the many nights of local festivity, when the little gardens were often illuminated, and the big Chinese lanterns glowed in the dwarfish trees like some fierce and monstrous fruit. And this was strongest of all on one particular evening, still vaguely remembered in the locality, of which the auburn-haired poet was the hero. It was not by any means the only evening of which he was the hero. On many nights those passing by his little back garden might hear his high, didactic voice laying down the law to men and particularly to women. The attitude of women in such cases was indeed one of the paradoxes of the place. Most of the women were of the kind vaguely called emancipated, and professed some protest against male supremacy. Yet these new women would always pay to a man the extravagant compliment which no ordinary woman ever pays to him, that of listening while he is talking. And Mr. Lucian Gregory, the red-haired poet, was really (in some sense) a man worth listening to, even if one only laughed at the end of it. He put the old cant of the lawlessness of art and the art of lawlessness with a certain impudent freshness which gave at least a momentary pleasure. He was helped in some degree by the arresting oddity of his appearance, which he worked, as the phrase goes, for all it was worth. His dark red hair parted in the middle was literally like a woman's, and curved into the slow curls of a virgin in a pre-Raphaelite picture. From within this almost saintly oval, however, his face projected suddenly broad and brutal, the chin carried forward with a look of cockney contempt. This combination at once tickled and terrified the nerves of a neurotic population. He seemed like a walking blasphemy, a blend of the angel and the ape.

This particular evening, if it is remembered for nothing else, will be remembered in that place for its strange sunset. It looked like the end of the world. All the heaven seemed covered with a quite vivid and palpable plumage; you could only say that the sky was full of feathers, and of feathers that almost brushed the face. Across the great part of the dome they were grey, with the strangest tints of violet and mauve and an unnatural pink or pale green; but towards the west the whole grew past description, transparent and passionate, and the last red-hot plumes of it covered up the sun like something too good to be seen. The whole was so close about the earth, as to express nothing but a violent secrecy. The very empyrean seemed to be a secret. It expressed that splendid smallness which is the soul of local patriotism. The very sky seemed small.

I say that there are some inhabitants who may remember the evening if only by that oppressive sky. There are others who may remember it because it marked the first appearance in the place of the second poet of Saffron Park. For a long time the red-haired revolutionary had reigned without a rival; it was upon the night of the sunset that his solitude suddenly ended. The new poet, who introduced himself by the name of Gabriel Syme was a very mild-looking mortal, with a fair, pointed beard and faint, yellow hair. But an impression grew that he was less meek than he looked. He signalised his entrance by differing with the established poet, Gregory, upon the whole nature of poetry. He said that he (Syme) was poet of law, a poet of order; nay, he said he was a poet of respectability. So all the Saffron Parkers looked at him as if he had that moment fallen out of that impossible sky.

In fact, Mr. Lucian Gregory, the anarchic poet, connected the two events.

"It may well be," he said, in his sudden lyrical manner, "it may well be on such a night of clouds and cruel colours that there is brought forth upon the earth such a portent as a respectable poet. You say you are a poet of law; I say you are a contradiction in terms.

I only wonder there were not comets and earthquakes on the night you appeared in this garden."

The man with the meek blue eyes and the pale, pointed beard endured these thunders with a certain submissive solemnity. The third party of the group, Gregory's sister Rosamond, who had her brother's braids of red hair, but a kindlier face underneath them, laughed with such mixture of admiration and disapproval as she gave commonly to the family oracle.

Gregory resumed in high oratorical good humour.

"An artist is identical with an anarchist," he cried. "You might transpose the words anywhere. An anarchist is an artist. The man who throws a bomb is an artist, because he prefers a great moment to everything. He sees how much more valuable is one burst of blazing light, one peal of perfect thunder, than the mere common bodies of a few shapeless policemen. An artist disregards all governments, abolishes all conventions. The poet delights in disorder only. If it were not so, the most poetical thing in the world would be the Underground Railway."

"So it is," said Mr. Syme.

"Nonsense!" said Gregory, who was very rational when anyone else attempted paradox. "Why do all the clerks and navvies in the railway trains look so sad and tired, so very sad and tired? I will tell you. It is because they know that the train is going right. It is because they know that whatever place they have taken a ticket for that place they will reach. It is because after they have passed Sloane Square they know that the next station must be Victoria, and nothing but Victoria. Oh, their wild rapture! oh, their eyes like stars and their souls again in Eden, if the next station were unaccountably Baker Street!"

"It is you who are unpoetical," replied the poet Syme. "If what you say of clerks is true, they can only be as prosaic as your poetry. The rare, strange thing is to hit the mark; the gross, obvious thing is to miss it. We feel it is epical when man with one wild arrow strikes a distant bird. Is it not also epical when man with one wild engine strikes a distant station? Chaos is dull; because in chaos the train might indeed go anywhere, to Baker Street or to Bagdad. But man is a magician, and his whole magic is in this, that he does say Victoria, and lo! it is Victoria. No, take your books of mere poetry and prose; let me read a time table, with tears of pride. Take your Byron, who commemorates the defeats of man; give me Bradshaw, who commemorates his victories. Give me Bradshaw, I say!"

"Must you go?" inquired Gregory sarcastically.

"I tell you," went on Syme with passion, "that every time a train comes in I feel that it has broken past batteries of besiegers, and that man has won a battle against chaos. You say contemptuously that when one has left Sloane Square one must come to Victoria. I say that one might do a thousand things instead, and that whenever I really come there I have the sense of hairbreadth escape. And when I hear the guard shout out the word 'Victoria,' it is not an unmeaning word. It is to me the cry of a herald announcing conquest. It is to me indeed 'Victoria'; it is the victory of Adam."

Gregory wagged his heavy, red head with a slow and sad smile.

"And even then," he said, "we poets always ask the question, 'And what is Victoria now that you have got there?' You think Victoria is like the New Jerusalem. We know that the New Jerusalem will only be like Victoria. Yes, the poet will be discontented even in the streets of heaven. The poet is always in revolt."

"There again," said Syme irritably, "what is there poetical about being in revolt? You might as well say that it is poetical to be seasick. Being sick is a revolt. Both being sick and being rebellious may be the wholesome thing on certain desperate occasions; but I'm hanged if I can see why they are poetical. Revolt in the abstract is—revolting. It's mere vomiting."

The girl winced for a flash at the unpleasant word, but Syme was too hot to heed her.

"It is things going right," he cried, "that is poetical! Our digestions, for instance, going sacredly and silently right, that is the foundation of all poetry. Yes, the most poetical thing, more poetical than the flowers, more poetical than the stars—the most poetical thing in the world is not being sick."

"Really," said Gregory superciliously, "the examples you choose—"

"I beg your pardon," said Syme grimly, "I forgot we had abolished all conventions."

For the first time a red patch appeared on Gregory's forehead.

"You don't expect me," he said, "to revolutionise society on this lawn?"

Syme looked straight into his eyes and smiled sweetly.

"No, I don't," he said; "but I suppose that if you were serious about your anarchism, that is exactly what you would do."

Gregory's big bull's eyes blinked suddenly like those of an angry lion, and one could almost fancy that his red mane rose.

"Don't you think, then," he said in a dangerous voice, "that I am serious about my anarchism?"

"I beg your pardon?" said Syme.

"Am I not serious about my anarchism?" cried Gregory, with knotted fists.

"My dear fellow!" said Syme, and strolled away.

With surprise, but with a curious pleasure, he found Rosamond Gregory still in his company.

"Mr. Syme," she said, "do the people who talk like you and my brother often mean what they say? Do you mean what you say now?"

Syme smiled.

"Do you?" he asked.

"What do you mean?" asked the girl, with grave eyes.

"My dear Miss Gregory," said Syme gently, "there are many kinds of sincerity and insincerity. When you say 'thank you' for the salt, do you mean what you say? No. When you say 'the world is round,' do you mean what you say? No. It is true, but you don't mean it. Now, sometimes a man like your brother really finds a thing he does mean. It may be only a half-truth, quarter-truth, tenth-truth; but then he says more than he means—from sheer force of meaning it."

She was looking at him from under level brows; her face was grave and open, and there had fallen upon it the shadow of that unreasoning responsibility which is at the bottom of the most frivolous woman, the maternal watch which is as old as the world.

"Is he really an anarchist, then?" she asked.

"Only in that sense I speak of," replied Syme; "or if you prefer it, in that nonsense."

She drew her broad brows together and said abruptly—

"He wouldn't really use—bombs or that sort of thing?"

Syme broke into a great laugh, that seemed too large for his slight and somewhat dandified figure.

"Good Lord, no!" he said, "that has to be done anonymously."

And at that the corners of her own mouth broke into a smile, and she thought with a simultaneous pleasure of Gregory's absurdity and of his safety.

Syme strolled with her to a seat in the corner of the garden, and continued to pour out his opinions. For he was a sincere man, and in spite of his superficial airs and graces, at root a humble one. And it is always the humble man who talks too much; the proud man watches himself too closely. He defended respectability with violence and exaggeration. He grew passionate in his praise of tidiness and propriety. All the time there was a smell of lilac all round him. Once he heard very faintly in some distant street a barrel-organ begin to play, and it seemed to him that his heroic words were moving to a tiny tune from under or beyond the world.

He stared and talked at the girl's red hair and amused face for what seemed to be a few minutes; and then, feeling that the groups in such a place should mix, rose to his feet. To his astonishment, he discovered the whole garden empty. Everyone had gone long ago, and he went himself with a rather hurried apology. He left with a sense of champagne in his head, which he could not afterwards explain. In the wild events which were to follow this girl had no part at all; he never saw her again until all his tale was over. And yet, in some indescribable way, she kept recurring like a motive in music through all his mad adventures afterwards, and the glory of her strange hair ran like a red thread through those dark and ill-drawn tapestries of the night. For what followed was so improbable, that it might well have been a dream.

When Syme went out into the starlit street, he found it for the moment empty. Then he realised (in some odd way) that the silence was rather a living silence than a dead one. Directly outside the door stood a street lamp, whose gleam gilded the leaves of the tree that bent out over the fence behind him. About a foot from the lamp-post stood a figure almost as rigid and motionless as the lamp-post itself. The tall hat and long frock coat were black; the face, in an abrupt shadow, was almost as dark. Only a fringe of fiery hair against the light, and also something aggressive in the attitude, proclaimed that it was the poet Gregory. He had something of the look of a masked bravo waiting sword in hand for his foe.

He made a sort of doubtful salute, which Syme somewhat more formally returned.

"I was waiting for you," said Gregory. "Might I have a moment's conversation?"

"Certainly. About what?" asked Syme in a sort of weak wonder.

Gregory struck out with his stick at the lamp-post, and then at the tree. "About *this* and *this*," he cried; "about order and anarchy. There is your precious order, that lean, iron lamp, ugly and barren; and there is anarchy, rich, living, reproducing itself—there is anarchy, splendid in green and gold."

"All the same," replied Syme patiently, "just at present you only see the tree by the light of the lamp. I wonder when you would ever see the lamp by the light of the tree." Then after a pause he said, "But may I ask if you have been standing out here in the dark only to resume our little argument?"

"No," cried out Gregory, in a voice that rang down the street, "I did not stand here to resume our argument, but to end it for ever."

The silence fell again, and Syme, though he understood nothing, listened instinctively for something serious. Gregory began in a smooth voice and with a rather bewildering smile.

"Mr. Syme," he said, "this evening you succeeded in doing something rather remarkable. You did something to me that no man born of woman has ever succeeded in doing before."

"Indeed!"

"Now I remember," resumed Gregory reflectively, "one other person succeeded in doing it. The captain of a penny steamer (if I remember correctly) at Southend. You have irritated me."

"I am very sorry," replied Syme with gravity.

"I am afraid my fury and your insult are too shocking to be wiped out even with an apology," said Gregory very calmly. "No duel could wipe it out. If I struck you dead I could not wipe it out. There is only one way by which that insult can be erased, and that way I choose. I am going, at the possible sacrifice of my life and honour, to prove to you that you were wrong in what you said."

"In what I said?"

"You said I was not serious about being an anarchist."

"There are degrees of seriousness," replied Syme. "I have never doubted that you were perfectly sincere in this sense, that you thought what you said well worth saying, that you thought a paradox might wake men up to a neglected truth."

Gregory stared at him steadily and painfully.

"And in no other sense," he asked, "you think me serious? You think me a *flâneur* who lets fall occasional truths. You do not think that in a deeper, a more deadly sense, I am serious."

Syme struck his stick violently on the stones of the road.

"Serious!" he cried. "Good Lord! Is this street serious? Are these damned Chinese lanterns serious? Is the whole caboodle serious? One comes here and talks a pack of bosh, and perhaps some sense as well, but I should think very little of a man who didn't keep something in the background of his life that was more serious than all this talking—something more serious, whether it was religion or only drink."

"Very well," said Gregory, his face darkening, "you shall see something more serious than either drink or religion."

Syme stood waiting with his usual air of mildness until Gregory again opened his lips.

"You spoke just now of having a religion. Is it really true that you have one?"

"Oh," said Syme with a beaming smile, "we are all Catholics now."

"Then may I ask you to swear by whatever gods or saints your religion involves that you will not reveal what I am now going to tell you to any son of Adam, and especially not to the police? Will you swear that! If you will take upon yourself this awful abnegation if you will consent to burden your soul with a vow that you should never make and a knowledge you should never dream about, I will promise you in return—"

"You will promise me in return?" inquired Syme, as the other paused.

"I will promise you a very entertaining evening." Syme suddenly took off his hat.

"Your offer," he said, "is far too idiotic to be declined. You say that a poet is always an anarchist. I disagree; but I hope at least that he is always a sportsman. Permit me, here and now, to swear as a Christian, and promise as a good comrade and a fellow-artist, that I will not report anything of this, whatever it is, to the police. And now, in the name of Colney Hatch, what is it?"

"I think," said Gregory, with placid irrelevancy, "that we will call a cab."

He gave two long whistles, and a hansom came rattling down the road. The two got into it in silence. Gregory gave through the trap the address of an obscure public-house on the Chiswick bank of the river. The cab whisked itself away again, and in it these two fantastics quitted their fantastic town.

CHAPTER II

The Secret of Gabriel Syme

The cab pulled up before a particularly dreary and greasy beer-shop, into which Gregory rapidly conducted his companion. They seated themselves in a close and dim sort of bar-parlour, at a stained wooden table with one wooden leg. The room was so small and dark, that very little could be seen of the attendant who was summoned, beyond a vague and dark impression of something bulky and bearded.

"Will you take a little supper?" asked Gregory politely. "The *pâte de foie gras* is not good here, but I can recommend the game."

Syme received the remark with stolidity, imagining it to be a joke. Accepting the vein of humour, he said, with a well-bred indifference—

"Oh, bring me some lobster mayonnaise."

To his indescribable astonishment, the man only said "Certainly, sir!" and went away apparently to get it.

"What will you drink?" resumed Gregory, with the same careless yet apologetic air. "I shall only have a *crême de menthe* myself; I have dined. But the champagne can really be trusted. Do let me start you with a half-bottle of Pommery at least?"

"Thank you!" said the motionless Syme. "You are very good."

His further attempts at conversation, somewhat disorganised in themselves, were cut short finally as by a thunderbolt by the actual appearance of the lobster. Syme tasted it, and found it particularly good. Then he suddenly began to eat with great rapidity and appetite.

"Excuse me if I enjoy myself rather obviously!" he said to Gregory, smiling. "I don't often have the luck to have a dream like this. It is new to me for a nightmare to lead to a lobster. It is commonly the other way."

"You are not asleep, I assure you," said Gregory. "You are, on the contrary, close to the most actual and rousing moment of your existence. Ah, here comes your champagne! I admit that there may be a slight disproportion, let us say, between the inner arrangements of this excellent hotel and its simple and unpretentious exterior. But that is all our modesty. We are the most modest men that ever lived on earth."

"And who are *we?*" asked Syme, emptying his champagne glass.

"It is quite simple," replied Gregory. "We are the serious anarchists, in whom you do not believe."

"Oh!" said Syme shortly. "You do yourselves well in drinks."

"Yes, we are serious about everything," answered Gregory.

Then after a pause he added—

"If in a few moments this table begins to turn round a little, don't put it down to your inroads into the champagne. I don't wish you to do yourself an injustice."

"Well, if I am not drunk, I am mad," replied Syme with perfect calm; "but I trust I can behave like a gentleman in either condition. May I smoke?"

"Certainly!" said Gregory, producing a cigar-case. "Try one of mine."

Syme took the cigar, clipped the end off with a cigar-cutter out of his waistcoat pocket, put it in his mouth, lit it slowly, and let out a long cloud of smoke. It is not a little to his credit that he performed these rites with so much composure, for almost before he had begun them the table at which he sat had begun to revolve, first slowly, and then rapidly, as if at an insane séance.

"You must not mind it," said Gregory; "it's a kind of screw."

"Quite so," said Syme placidly, "a kind of screw. How simple that is!"

The next moment the smoke of his cigar, which had been wavering across the room in snaky twists, went straight up as if from a factory chimney, and the two, with their chairs and table, shot down through the floor as if the earth had swallowed them. They went rattling down a kind of roaring chimney as rapidly as a lift cut loose, and they came with an abrupt bump to the bottom. But when Gregory threw open a pair of doors and let in a red subterranean light, Syme was still smoking with one leg thrown over the other, and had not turned a yellow hair.

Gregory led him down a low, vaulted passage, at the end of which was the red light. It was an enormous crimson lantern, nearly as big as a fireplace, fixed over a small but heavy iron door. In the door there was a sort of hatchway or grating, and on this Gregory struck five times. A heavy voice with a foreign accent asked him who he was. To this he gave the more or less unexpected reply, "Mr. Joseph Chamberlain." The heavy hinges began to move; it was obviously some kind of password.

Inside the doorway the passage gleamed as if it were lined with a network of steel. On a second glance, Syme saw that the glittering pattern was really made up of ranks and ranks of rifles and revolvers, closely packed or interlocked.

"I must ask you to forgive me all these formalities," said Gregory; "we have to be very strict here."

"Oh, don't apologise," said Syme. "I know your passion for law and order," and he stepped into the passage lined with the steel weapons. With his long, fair hair and rather foppish frock-coat, he looked a singularly frail and fanciful figure as he walked down that shining avenue of death.

They passed through several such passages, and came out at last into a queer steel chamber with curved walls, almost spherical in shape, but presenting, with its tiers of benches, something of the appearance of a scientific lecture-theatre. There were no rifles or pistols in this apartment, but round the walls of it were hung more dubious and dreadful shapes, things that looked like the bulbs of iron plants, or the eggs of iron birds. They were bombs, and the very room itself seemed like the inside of a bomb. Syme knocked his cigar ash off against the wall, and went in.

"And now, my dear Mr. Syme," said Gregory, throwing himself in an expansive manner on the bench under the largest bomb, "now we are quite cosy, so let us talk properly. Now no human words can give you any notion of why I brought you here. It was one of those quite arbitrary emotions, like jumping off a cliff or falling in love. Suffice it to say that you were an inexpressibly irritating fellow, and, to do you justice, you are still. I would break twenty oaths of secrecy for the pleasure of taking you down a peg. That way you have of lighting a cigar would make a priest break the seal of confession. Well, you said that you were quite certain I was not a serious anarchist. Does this place strike you as being serious?"

"It does seem to have a moral under all its gaiety," assented Syme; "but may I ask you two questions? You need not fear to give me information, because, as you remember, you very wisely extorted from me a promise not to tell the police, a promise I shall certainly keep. So it is in mere curiosity that I make my queries. First of all, what is it really all about? What is it you object to? You want to abolish Government?"

"To abolish God!" said Gregory, opening the eyes of a fanatic. "We do not only want to upset a few despotisms and police regulations; that sort of anarchism does exist, but it is a mere branch of the Nonconformists. We dig deeper and we blow you higher. We wish to deny all those arbitrary distinctions of vice and virtue, honour and treachery, upon which mere rebels base themselves. The silly sentimentalists of the French Revolution talked of the Rights of Man! We hate Rights as we hate Wrongs. We have abolished Right and Wrong."

"And Right and Left," said Syme with a simple eagerness, "I hope you will abolish them too. They are much more troublesome to me."

"You spoke of a second question," snapped Gregory.

"With pleasure," resumed Syme. "In all your present acts and surroundings there is a scientific attempt at secrecy. I have an aunt who lived over a shop, but this is the first time I have found people living from preference under a public-house. You have a heavy iron door. You cannot pass it without submitting to the humiliation of calling yourself Mr. Chamberlain. You surround yourself with steel instruments which make the place, if I may say so, more impressive than homelike. May I ask why, after taking all this trouble to barricade yourselves in the bowels of the earth, you then parade your whole secret by talking about anarchism to every silly woman in Saffron Park?"

Gregory smiled.

"The answer is simple," he said. "I told you I was a serious anarchist, and you did not believe me. Nor do they believe me. Unless I took them into this infernal room they would not believe me."

Syme smoked thoughtfully, and looked at him with interest. Gregory went on.

"The history of the thing might amuse you," he said. "When first I became one of the New Anarchists I tried all kinds of respectable disguises. I dressed up as a bishop. I read up all about bishops in our anarchist pamphlets, in *Superstition the Vampire* and *Priests of Prey*. I certainly understood from them that bishops are strange and terrible old men keeping a cruel secret from mankind. I was misinformed. When on my first appearing in episcopal gaiters in a drawing-room I cried out in a voice of thunder, 'Down! down! presumptuous human reason!' they found out in some way that I was not a bishop at all. I was nabbed at once. Then I made up as a millionaire; but I defended Capital with so much intelligence that a fool could see that I was quite poor. Then I tried being a major. Now I am a humanitarian myself, but I have, I hope, enough intellectual breadth to understand the position of those who, like Nietzsche, admire violence—the proud, mad war of Nature and all that, you know. I threw myself into the major. I drew my sword and waved it constantly. I called out 'Blood!' abstractedly, like a man calling for wine. I often said, 'Let the weak perish; it is the Law.' Well, well, it seems majors don't do this. I was nabbed again. At last I went in despair to the President of the Central Anarchist Council, who is the greatest man in Europe."

"What is his name?" asked Syme.

"You would not know it," answered Gregory. "That is his greatness. Caesar and Napoleon put all their genius into being heard of, and they were heard of. He puts all his genius into not being heard of, and he is not heard of. But you cannot be for five minutes in the room with him without feeling that Caesar and Napoleon would have been children in his hands."

He was silent and even pale for a moment, and then resumed—

"But whenever he gives advice it is always something as startling as an epigram, and yet as practical as the Bank of England. I said to him, 'What disguise will hide me from the world? What can I find more respectable than bishops and majors?' He looked at me with his large but indecipherable face. 'You want a safe disguise, do you? You want a dress which will guarantee you harmless; a dress in which no one would ever look for a bomb?' I nodded. He suddenly lifted his lion's voice. 'Why, then, dress up as an *anarchist*, you fool!' he roared so that the room shook. 'Nobody will ever expect you to do anything dangerous then.' And he turned his broad back on me without another word. I took his advice, and have never regretted it. I preached blood and murder to those women day and night, and—by God!—they would let me wheel their perambulators."

Syme sat watching him with some respect in his large, blue eyes.

"You took me in," he said. "It is really a smart dodge."

Then after a pause he added—

"What do you call this tremendous President of yours?"

"We generally call him Sunday," replied Gregory with simplicity. "You see, there are seven members of the Central Anarchist Council, and they are named after days of the week. He is called Sunday, by some of his admirers Bloody Sunday. It is curious you should mention the matter, because the very night you have dropped in (if I may so express it) is the night on which our London branch, which assembles in this room, has to elect its own deputy to fill a vacancy in the Council. The gentleman who has for some time past played, with propriety and general applause, the difficult part of Thursday, has died quite suddenly. Consequently, we have called a meeting this very evening to elect a successor."

He got to his feet and strolled across the room with a sort of smiling embarrassment.

"I feel somehow as if you were my mother, Syme," he continued casually. "I feel that I can confide anything to you, as you have promised to tell nobody. In fact, I will confide to you something that I would not say in so many words to the anarchists who will be coming to the room in about ten minutes. We shall, of course, go through a form of election; but I don't mind telling you that it is practically certain what the result will be." He looked down for a moment modestly. "It is almost a settled thing that I am to be Thursday."

"My dear fellow." said Syme heartily, "I congratulate you. A great career!"

Gregory smiled in deprecation, and walked across the room, talking rapidly.

"As a matter of fact, everything is ready for me on this table," he said, "and the ceremony will probably be the shortest possible."

Syme also strolled across to the table, and found lying across it a walking-stick, which turned out on examination to be a sword-stick, a large Colt's revolver, a sandwich case, and a formidable flask of brandy. Over the chair, beside the table, was thrown a heavy-looking cape or cloak.

"I have only to get the form of election finished," continued Gregory with animation, "then I snatch up this cloak and stick, stuff these other things into my pocket, step out of a door in this cavern, which opens on the river, where there is a steam-tug already waiting for me, and then—then—oh, the wild joy of being Thursday!" And he clasped his hands.

Syme, who had sat down once more with his usual insolent languor, got to his feet with an unusual air of hesitation.

"Why is it," he asked vaguely, "that I think you are quite a decent fellow? Why do I positively like you, Gregory?" He paused a moment, and then added with a sort of fresh curiosity, "Is it because you are such an ass?"

There was a thoughtful silence again, and then he cried out—

"Well, damn it all! this is the funniest situation I have ever been in in my life, and I am going to act accordingly. Gregory, I gave you a promise before I came into this place. That promise I would keep under red-hot pincers. Would you give me, for my own safety, a little promise of the same kind?"

"A promise?" asked Gregory, wondering.

"Yes," said Syme very seriously, "a promise. I swore before God that I would not tell your secret to the police. Will you swear by Humanity, or whatever beastly thing you believe in, that you will not tell my secret to the anarchists?"

"Your secret?" asked the staring Gregory. "Have you got a secret?"

"Yes," said Syme, "I have a secret." Then after a pause, "Will you swear?"

Gregory glared at him gravely for a few moments, and then said abruptly—

"You must have bewitched me, but I feel a furious curiosity about you. Yes, I will swear not to tell the anarchists anything you tell me. But look sharp, for they will be here in a couple of minutes."

Syme rose slowly to his feet and thrust his long, white hands into his long, grey trousers' pockets. Almost as he did so there came five knocks on the outer grating, proclaiming the arrival of the first of the conspirators.

"Well," said Syme slowly, "I don't know how to tell you the truth more shortly than by saying that your expedient of dressing up as an aimless poet is not confined to you or your President. We have known the dodge for some time at Scotland Yard."

Gregory tried to spring up straight, but he swayed thrice.

"What do you say?" he asked in an inhuman voice.

"Yes," said Syme simply, "I am a police detective. But I think I hear your friends coming."

From the doorway there came a murmur of "Mr. Joseph Chamberlain." It was repeated twice and thrice, and then thirty times, and the crowd of Joseph Chamberlains (a solemn thought) could be heard trampling down the corridor.

CHAPTER III

The Man Who Was Thursday

Before one of the fresh faces could appear at the doorway, Gregory's stunned surprise had fallen from him. He was beside the table with a bound, and a noise in his throat like a wild beast. He caught up the Colt's revolver and took aim at Syme. Syme did not flinch, but he put up a pale and polite hand.

"Don't be such a silly man," he said, with the effeminate dignity of a curate. "Don't you see it's not necessary? Don't you see that we're both in the same boat? Yes, and jolly sea-sick."

Gregory could not speak, but he could not fire either, and he looked his question.

"Don't you see we've checkmated each other?" cried Syme. "I can't tell the police you are an anarchist. You can't tell the anarchists I'm a policeman. I can only watch you, knowing what you are; you can only watch me, knowing what I am. In short, it's a lonely, intellectual duel, my head against yours. I'm a policeman deprived of the help of the police. You, my poor fellow, are an anarchist deprived of the help of that law and organisation which is so essential to anarchy. The one solitary difference is in your favour. You are not surrounded by inquisitive policemen; I am surrounded by inquisitive anarchists. I cannot betray you, but I might betray myself. Come, come! wait and see me betray myself. I shall do it so nicely."

Gregory put the pistol slowly down, still staring at Syme as if he were a sea-monster.

"I don't believe in immortality," he said at last, "but if, after all this, you were to break your word, God would make a hell only for you, to howl in for ever."

"I shall not break my word," said Syme sternly, "nor will you break yours. Here are your friends."

The mass of the anarchists entered the room heavily, with a slouching and somewhat weary gait; but one little man, with a black beard and glasses—a man somewhat of the type of Mr. Tim Healy—detached himself, and bustled forward with some papers in his hand.

"Comrade Gregory," he said, "I suppose this man is a delegate?"

Gregory, taken by surprise, looked down and muttered the name of Syme; but Syme replied almost pertly—

"I am glad to see that your gate is well enough guarded to make it hard for anyone to be here who was not a delegate."

The brow of the little man with the black beard was, however, still contracted with something like suspicion.

"What branch do you represent?" he asked sharply.

"I should hardly call it a branch," said Syme, laughing; "I should call it at the very least a root."

"What do you mean?"

"The fact is," said Syme serenely, "the truth is I am a Sabbatarian. I have been specially sent here to see that you show a due observance of Sunday."

The little man dropped one of his papers, and a flicker of fear went over all the faces of the group. Evidently the awful President, whose name was Sunday, did sometimes send down such irregular ambassadors to such branch meetings.

"Well, comrade," said the man with the papers after a pause, "I suppose we'd better give you a seat in the meeting?"

"If you ask my advice as a friend," said Syme with severe benevolence, "I think you'd better."

When Gregory heard the dangerous dialogue end, with a sudden safety for his rival, he rose abruptly and paced the floor in painful thought. He was, indeed, in an agony of diplomacy. It was clear that Syme's inspired impudence was likely to bring him out of all merely accidental dilemmas. Little was to be hoped from them. He could not himself betray Syme, partly from honour, but partly also because, if he betrayed him and for some reason failed to destroy him, the Syme who escaped would be a Syme freed from all obligation of secrecy, a Syme who would simply walk to the nearest police station. After all, it was only one night's discussion, and only one detective who would know of it. He would let out as little as possible of their plans that night, and then let Syme go, and chance it.

He strode across to the group of anarchists, which was already distributing itself along the benches.

"I think it is time we began," he said; "the steam-tug is waiting on the river already. I move that Comrade Buttons takes the chair."

This being approved by a show of hands, the little man with the papers slipped into the presidential seat.

"Comrades," he began, as sharp as a pistol-shot, "our meeting tonight is important, though it need not be long. This branch has always had the honour of electing Thursdays for the Central European Council. We have elected many and splendid Thursdays. We all lament the sad decease of the heroic worker who occupied the post until last week. As you know, his services to the cause were considerable. He organised the great dynamite coup of Brighton which, under happier circumstances, ought to have killed everybody on the pier. As you also know, his death was as self-denying as his life, for he died through his faith in a hygienic mixture of chalk and water as a substitute for milk, which beverage he regarded as barbaric, and as involving cruelty to the cow. Cruelty, or anything approaching to cruelty, revolted him always. But it is not to acclaim his virtues that we are met, but for a harder task. It is difficult properly to praise his qualities, but it is more difficult to replace them. Upon you, comrades, it devolves this evening to choose out of the company present the man who shall be Thursday. If any comrade suggests a name I will put it to the vote. If no comrade suggests a name, I can only tell myself that that dear dynamiter, who is gone from us, has carried into the unknowable abysses the last secret of his virtue and his innocence."

There was a stir of almost inaudible applause, such as is sometimes heard in church. Then a large old man, with a long and venerable white beard, perhaps the only real working-man present, rose lumberingly and said—

"I move that Comrade Gregory be elected Thursday," and sat lumberingly down again.

"Does anyone second?" asked the chairman.

A little man with a velvet coat and pointed beard seconded.

"Before I put the matter to the vote," said the chairman, "I will call on Comrade Gregory to make a statement."

Gregory rose amid a great rumble of applause. His face was deadly pale, so that by contrast his queer red hair looked almost scarlet. But he was smiling and altogether at ease. He had made up his mind, and he saw his best policy quite plain in front of him like a white road. His best chance was to make a softened and ambiguous speech, such as would leave on the detective's mind the impression that the anarchist brotherhood was a very mild affair after all. He believed in his own literary power, his capacity for suggesting fine shades and picking perfect words. He thought that with care he could succeed, in spite of all the people around him, in conveying an impression of the institution, subtly and delicately false. Syme had once thought that anarchists, under all their bravado, were only playing the fool. Could he not now, in the hour of peril, make Syme think so again?

"Comrades," began Gregory, in a low but penetrating voice, "it is not necessary for me to tell you what is my policy, for it is your policy also. Our belief has been slandered, it has been disfigured, it has been utterly confused and concealed, but it has never been altered. Those who talk about anarchism and its dangers go everywhere and anywhere to get their information, except to us, except to the fountain head. They learn about anarchists from sixpenny novels; they learn about anarchists from tradesmen's newspapers;

they learn about anarchists from *Ally Sloper's Half-Holiday* and the *Sporting Times*. They never learn about anarchists from anarchists. We have no chance of denying the mountainous slanders which are heaped upon our heads from one end of Europe to another. The man who has always heard that we are walking plagues has never heard our reply. I know that he will not hear it tonight, though my passion were to rend the roof. For it is deep, deep under the earth that the persecuted are permitted to assemble, as the Christians assembled in the Catacombs. But if, by some incredible accident, there were here tonight a man who all his life had thus immensely misunderstood us, I would put this question to him: 'When those Christians met in those Catacombs, what sort of moral reputation had they in the streets above? What tales were told of their atrocities by one educated Roman to another? Suppose' (I would say to him), 'suppose that we are only repeating that still mysterious paradox of history. Suppose we seem as shocking as the Christians because we are really as harmless as the Christians. Suppose we seem as mad as the Christians because we are really as meek.'"

The applause that had greeted the opening sentences had been gradually growing fainter, and at the last word it stopped suddenly. In the abrupt silence, the man with the velvet jacket said, in a high, squeaky voice—

"I'm not meek!"

"Comrade Witherspoon tells us," resumed Gregory, "that he is not meek. Ah, how little he knows himself! His words are, indeed, extravagant; his appearance is ferocious, and even (to an ordinary taste) unattractive. But only the eye of a friendship as deep and delicate as mine can perceive the deep foundation of solid meekness which lies at the base of him, too deep even for himself to see. I repeat, we are the true early Christians, only that we come too late. We are simple, as they revere simple—look at Comrade Witherspoon. We are modest, as they were modest—look at me. We are merciful—"

"No, no!" called out Mr. Witherspoon with the velvet jacket.

"I say we are merciful," repeated Gregory furiously, "as the early Christians were merciful. Yet this did not prevent their being accused of eating human flesh. We do not eat human flesh—"

"Shame!" cried Witherspoon. "Why not?"

"Comrade Witherspoon," said Gregory, with a feverish gaiety, "is anxious to know why nobody eats him (laughter). In our society, at any rate, which loves him sincerely, which is founded upon love—"

"No, no!" said Witherspoon, "down with love."

"Which is founded upon love," repeated Gregory, grinding his teeth, "there will be no difficulty about the aims which we shall pursue as a body, or which I should pursue were I chosen as the representative of that body. Superbly careless of the slanders that represent us as assassins and enemies of human society, we shall pursue with moral courage and quiet intellectual pressure, the permanent ideals of brotherhood and simplicity."

Gregory resumed his seat and passed his hand across his forehead. The silence was sudden and awkward, but the chairman rose like an automaton, and said in a colourless voice—

"Does anyone oppose the election of Comrade Gregory?"

The assembly seemed vague and sub-consciously disappointed, and Comrade Witherspoon moved restlessly on his seat and muttered in his thick beard. By the sheer rush of routine, however, the motion would have been put and carried. But as the chairman was opening his mouth to put it, Syme sprang to his feet and said in a small and quiet voice—

"Yes, Mr. Chairman, I oppose."

The most effective fact in oratory is an unexpected change in the voice. Mr. Gabriel Syme evidently understood oratory. Having said these first formal words in a moderated tone and with a brief simplicity, he made his next word ring and volley in the vault as if one of the guns had gone off.

"Comrades!" he cried, in a voice that made every man jump out of his boots. "Have we come here for this? Do we live underground like rats in order to listen to talk like this? This is talk we might listen to while eating buns at a Sunday School treat. Do we line these walls with weapons and bar that door with death lest anyone should come and hear Comrade Gregory saying to us, 'Be good, and you will be happy,' 'Honesty is the best policy,' and 'Virtue is its own reward'? There was not a word in Comrade Gregory's address to which a curate could not have listened with pleasure (hear, hear). But I am not a curate (loud cheers), and I did not listen to it with pleasure (renewed cheers). The man who is fitted to make a good curate is not fitted to make a resolute, forcible, and efficient Thursday (hear, hear).

"Comrade Gregory has told us, in only too apologetic a tone, that we are not the enemies of society. But I say that we are the enemies of society, and so much the worse for society. We are the enemies of society, for society is the enemy of humanity, its oldest and its most pitiless enemy (hear, hear). Comrade Gregory has told us (apologetically again) that we are not murderers. There I agree. We are not murderers, we are executioners (cheers)."

Ever since Syme had risen Gregory had sat staring at him, his face idiotic with astonishment. Now in the pause his lips of clay parted, and he said, with an automatic and lifeless distinctness—

"You damnable hypocrite!"

Syme looked straight into those frightful eyes with his own pale blue ones, and said with dignity—

"Comrade Gregory accuses me of hypocrisy. He knows as well as I do that I am keeping all my engagements and doing nothing but my duty. I do not mince words. I do not pretend to. I say that Comrade Gregory is unfit to be Thursday for all his amiable qualities. He is unfit to be Thursday because of his amiable qualities. We do not want the Supreme Council of Anarchy infected with a maudlin mercy (hear, hear). This is no time for ceremonial politeness, neither is it a time for ceremonial modesty. I set myself against Comrade Gregory as I would set myself against all the Governments of Europe, because the anarchist who has given himself to anarchy has forgotten modesty as much as he has forgotten pride (cheers). I am not a man at all. I am a cause (renewed cheers). I set myself against Comrade Gregory as impersonally and as calmly as I should choose one pistol rather than another out of that rack upon the wall; and I say that rather than have Gregory and his milk-and-water methods on the Supreme Council, I would offer myself for election—"

His sentence was drowned in a deafening cataract of applause. The faces, that had grown fiercer and fiercer with approval as his tirade grew more and more uncompromising, were now distorted with grins of anticipation or cloven with delighted cries. At the moment when he announced himself as ready to stand for the post of Thursday, a roar of excitement and assent broke forth, and became uncontrollable, and at the same moment Gregory sprang to his feet, with foam upon his mouth, and shouted against the shouting.

"Stop, you blasted madmen!" he cried, at the top of a voice that tore his throat. "Stop, you—"

But louder than Gregory's shouting and louder than the roar of the room came the voice of Syme, still speaking in a peal of pitiless thunder—

"I do not go to the Council to rebut that slander that calls us murderers; I go to earn it (loud and prolonged cheering). To the priest who says these men are the enemies of religion, to the judge who says these men are the enemies of law, to the fat parliamentarian who says these men are the enemies of order and public decency, to all these I will reply, 'You are false kings, but you are true prophets. I am come to destroy you, and to fulfil your prophecies.'"

The heavy clamour gradually died away, but before it had ceased Witherspoon had jumped to his feet, his hair and beard all on end, and had said—

"I move, as an amendment, that Comrade Syme be appointed to the post."

"Stop all this, I tell you!" cried Gregory, with frantic face and hands. "Stop it, it is all—"

The voice of the chairman clove his speech with a cold accent.

"Does anyone second this amendment?" he said. A tall, tired man, with melancholy eyes and an American chin beard, was observed on the back bench to be slowly rising to his feet. Gregory had been screaming for some time past; now there was a change in his accent, more shocking than any scream. "I end all this!" he said, in a voice as heavy as stone.

"This man cannot be elected. He is a—"

"Yes," said Syme, quite motionless, "what is he?" Gregory's mouth worked twice without sound; then slowly the blood began to crawl back into his dead face. "He is a man quite inexperienced in our work," he said, and sat down abruptly.

Before he had done so, the long, lean man with the American beard was again upon his feet, and was repeating in a high American monotone—

"I beg to second the election of Comrade Syme."

"The amendment will, as usual, be put first," said Mr. Buttons, the chairman, with mechanical rapidity.

"The question is that Comrade Syme—"

Gregory had again sprung to his feet, panting and passionate.

"Comrades," he cried out, "I am not a madman."

"Oh, oh!" said Mr. Witherspoon.

"I am not a madman," reiterated Gregory, with a frightful sincerity which for a moment staggered the room, "but I give you a counsel which you can call mad if you like. No, I will not call it a counsel, for I can give you no reason for it. I will call it a command. Call it a mad command, but act upon it. Strike, but hear me! Kill me, but obey me! Do not elect this man." Truth is so terrible, even in fetters, that for a moment Syme's slender and insane victory swayed like a reed. But you could not have guessed it from Syme's bleak blue eyes. He merely began—

"Comrade Gregory commands—"

Then the spell was snapped, and one anarchist called out to Gregory—

"Who are you? You are not Sunday;" and another anarchist added in a heavier voice, "And you are not Thursday."

"Comrades," cried Gregory, in a voice like that of a martyr who in an ecstacy of pain has passed beyond pain, "it is nothing to me whether you detest me as a tyrant or detest me as a slave. If you will not take my command, accept my degradation. I kneel to you. I throw myself at your feet. I implore you. Do not elect this man."

"Comrade Gregory," said the chairman after a painful pause, "this is really not quite dignified."

For the first time in the proceedings there was for a few seconds a real silence. Then Gregory fell back in his seat, a pale wreck of a man, and the chairman repeated, like a piece of clock-work suddenly started again—

"The question is that Comrade Syme be elected to the post of Thursday on the General Council."

The roar rose like the sea, the hands rose like a forest, and three minutes afterwards Mr. Gabriel Syme, of the Secret Police Service, was elected to the post of Thursday on the General Council of the Anarchists of Europe.

Everyone in the room seemed to feel the tug waiting on the river, the sword-stick and the revolver, waiting on the table. The instant the election was ended and irrevocable, and Syme had received the paper proving his election, they all sprang to their feet, and the fiery groups moved and mixed in the room. Syme found himself, somehow or other, face to face with Gregory, who still regarded him with a stare of stunned hatred. They were silent for many minutes.

"You are a devil!" said Gregory at last.

"And you are a gentleman," said Syme with gravity.

"It was you that entrapped me," began Gregory, shaking from head to foot, "entrapped me into—"

"Talk sense," said Syme shortly. "Into what sort of devils' parliament have you entrapped me, if it comes to that? You made me swear before I made you. Perhaps we are both doing what we think right. But what we think right is so damned different that there can be nothing between us in the way of concession. There is nothing possible between us but honour and death," and he pulled the great cloak about his shoulders and picked up the flask from the table.

"The boat is quite ready," said Mr. Buttons, bustling up. "Be good enough to step this way."

With a gesture that revealed the shop-walker, he led Syme down a short, iron-bound passage, the still agonised Gregory following feverishly at their heels. At the end of the passage was a door, which Buttons opened sharply, showing a sudden blue and silver picture of the moonlit river, that looked like a scene in a theatre. Close to the opening lay a dark, dwarfish steam-launch, like a baby dragon with one red eye.

Almost in the act of stepping on board, Gabriel Syme turned to the gaping Gregory.

"You have kept your word," he said gently, with his face in shadow. "You are a man of honour, and I thank you. You have kept it even down to a small particular. There was one special thing you promised me at the beginning of the affair, and which you have certainly given me by the end of it."

"What do you mean?" cried the chaotic Gregory. "What did I promise you?"

"A very entertaining evening," said Syme, and he made a military salute with the sword-stick as the steamboat slid away.

CHAPTER IV

The Tale of a Detective

Gabriel Syme was not merely a detective who pretended to be a poet; he was really a poet who had become a detective. Nor was his hatred of anarchy hypocritical. He was one of those who are driven early in life into too conservative an attitude by the bewildering folly of most revolutionists. He had not attained it by any tame tradition. His respectability was spontaneous and sudden, a rebellion against rebellion. He came of a family of cranks, in which all the oldest people had all the newest notions. One of his uncles always walked about without a hat, and another had made an unsuccessful attempt to walk about with a hat and nothing else. His father cultivated art and self-realisation; his mother went in for simplicity and hygiene. Hence the child, during his tenderer years, was wholly unacquainted with any drink between the extremes of absinth and cocoa, of both of which he had a healthy dislike. The more his mother preached a more than Puritan abstinence the more did his father expand into a more than pagan latitude; and by the time the former had come to enforcing vegetarianism, the latter had pretty well reached the point of defending cannibalism.

Being surrounded with every conceivable kind of revolt from infancy, Gabriel had to revolt into something, so he revolted into the only thing left—sanity. But there was just enough in him of the blood of these fanatics to make even his protest for common sense a little too fierce to be sensible. His hatred of modern lawlessness had been crowned also by an accident. It happened that he was walking in a side street at the instant of a dynamite outrage. He had been blind and deaf for a moment, and then seen, the smoke clearing, the broken windows and the bleeding faces. After that he went about as usual—quiet, courteous, rather gentle; but there was a spot on his mind that was not sane. He did not regard anarchists, as most of us do, as a handful of morbid men, combining ignorance with intellectualism. He regarded them as a huge and pitiless peril, like a Chinese invasion.

He poured perpetually into newspapers and their waste-paper baskets a torrent of tales, verses and violent articles, warning men of this deluge of barbaric denial. But he seemed to be getting no nearer his enemy, and, what was worse, no nearer a living. As he paced the Thames embankment, bitterly biting a cheap cigar and brooding on the advance of Anarchy, there was no anarchist with a bomb in his pocket so savage or so solitary as he. Indeed, he always felt that Government stood alone and desperate, with its back to the wall. He was too quixotic to have cared for it otherwise.

He walked on the Embankment once under a dark red sunset. The red river reflected the red sky, and they both reflected his anger. The sky, indeed, was so swarthy, and the light on the river relatively so lurid, that the water almost seemed of fiercer flame than the sunset it mirrored. It looked like a stream of literal fire winding under the vast caverns of a subterranean country.

Syme was shabby in those days. He wore an old-fashioned black chimney-pot hat; he was wrapped in a yet more old-fashioned cloak, black and ragged; and the combination gave him the look of the early villains in Dickens and Bulwer Lytton. Also his yellow beard and hair were more unkempt and leonine than when they appeared long afterwards, cut and pointed, on the lawns of Saffron Park. A long, lean, black cigar, bought in Soho for twopence, stood out from between his tightened teeth, and altogether he looked a very satisfactory specimen of the anarchists upon whom he had vowed a holy war. Perhaps this was why a policeman on the Embankment spoke to him, and said "Good evening."

Syme, at a crisis of his morbid fears for humanity, seemed stung by the mere stolidity of the automatic official, a mere bulk of blue in the twilight.

"A good evening is it?" he said sharply. "You fellows would call the end of the world a good evening. Look at that bloody red sun and that bloody river! I tell you that if that were literally human blood, spilt and shining, you would still be standing here as solid as ever, looking out for some poor harmless tramp whom you could move on. You policemen are cruel to the poor, but I could forgive you even your cruelty if it were not for your calm."

"If we are calm," replied the policeman, "it is the calm of organised resistance."

"Eh?" said Syme, staring.

"The soldier must be calm in the thick of the battle," pursued the policeman. "The composure of an army is the anger of a nation."

"Good God, the Board Schools!" said Syme. "Is this undenominational education?"

"No," said the policeman sadly, "I never had any of those advantages. The Board Schools came after my time. What education I had was very rough and old-fashioned, I am afraid."

"Where did you have it?" asked Syme, wondering.

"Oh, at Harrow," said the policeman

The class sympathies which, false as they are, are the truest things in so many men, broke out of Syme before he could control them.

"But, good Lord, man," he said, "you oughtn't to be a policeman!"

The policeman sighed and shook his head.

"I know," he said solemnly, "I know I am not worthy."

"But why did you join the police?" asked Syme with rude curiosity.

"For much the same reason that you abused the police," replied the other. "I found that there was a special opening in the service for those whose fears for humanity were concerned rather with the aberrations of the scientific intellect than with the normal and excusable, though excessive, outbreaks of the human will. I trust I make myself clear."

"If you mean that you make your opinion clear," said Syme, "I suppose you do. But as for making yourself clear, it is the last thing you do. How comes a man like you to be talking philosophy in a blue helmet on the Thames embankment?"

"You have evidently not heard of the latest development in our police system," replied the other. "I am not surprised at it. We are keeping it rather dark from the educated class, because that class contains most of our enemies. But you seem to be exactly in the right frame of mind. I think you might almost join us."

"Join you in what?" asked Syme.

"I will tell you," said the policeman slowly. "This is the situation: The head of one of our departments, one of the most celebrated detectives in Europe, has long been of opinion that a purely intellectual conspiracy would soon threaten the very existence of civilisation. He is certain that the scientific and artistic worlds are silently bound in a crusade against the Family and the State. He has, therefore, formed a special corps of policemen, policemen who are also philosophers. It is their business to watch the beginnings of this conspiracy, not merely in a criminal but in a controversial sense. I am a democrat myself, and I am fully aware of the value of the ordinary man in matters of ordinary valour or virtue. But it would obviously be undesirable to employ the common policeman in an investigation which is also a heresy hunt."

Syme's eyes were bright with a sympathetic curiosity.

"What do you do, then?" he said.

"The work of the philosophical policeman," replied the man in blue, "is at once bolder and more subtle than that of the ordinary detective. The ordinary detective goes to pot-houses to arrest thieves; we go to artistic tea-parties to detect pessimists. The ordinary detective discovers from a ledger or a diary that a crime has been committed. We discover from a book of sonnets that a crime will be committed. We have to trace the origin of those dreadful thoughts that drive men on at last to intellectual fanaticism and intellectual crime. We were only just in time to prevent the assassination at Hartlepool, and that was entirely due to the fact that our Mr. Wilks (a smart young fellow) thoroughly understood a triolet."

"Do you mean," asked Syme, "that there is really as much connection between crime and the modern intellect as all that?"

"You are not sufficiently democratic," answered the policeman, "but you were right when you said just now that our ordinary treatment of the poor criminal was a pretty brutal business. I tell you I am sometimes sick of my trade when I see how perpetually it means merely a war upon the ignorant and the desperate. But this new movement of ours is a very different affair. We deny the snobbish English assumption that the uneducated are the dangerous criminals. We remember the Roman Emperors. We remember the great poisoning princes of the Renaissance. We say that the dangerous criminal is the educated criminal. We say that the most dangerous criminal now is the entirely lawless modern philosopher. Compared to him, burglars and bigamists are essentially moral men; my heart goes out to them. They accept the essential ideal of man; they merely seek it wrongly. Thieves respect property. They merely wish the property to become their property that they may more perfectly respect it. But philosophers dislike property as property; they wish to destroy the very idea of personal possession. Bigamists respect marriage, or they would not go through the highly ceremonial and even ritualistic formality of bigamy. But philosophers despise marriage as marriage. Murderers respect human life; they merely wish to attain a greater fulness of human life in themselves by the sacrifice of what seems to them to be lesser lives. But philosophers hate life itself, their own as much as other people's."

Syme struck his hands together.

"How true that is," he cried. "I have felt it from my boyhood, but never could state the verbal antithesis. The common criminal is a bad man, but at least he is, as it were, a conditional good man. He says that if only a certain obstacle be removed—say a wealthy uncle—he is then prepared to accept the universe and to praise God. He is a reformer, but not an anarchist. He wishes to cleanse

the edifice, but not to destroy it. But the evil philosopher is not trying to alter things, but to annihilate them. Yes, the modern world
has retained all those parts of police work which are really oppressive and ignominious, the harrying of the poor, the spying upon
the unfortunate. It has given up its more dignified work, the punishment of powerful traitors in the State and powerful heresiarchs
in the Church. The moderns say we must not punish heretics. My
only doubt is whether we have a right to punish anybody else."

"But this is absurd!" cried the policeman, clasping his hands
with an excitement uncommon in persons of his figure and costume, "but it is intolerable! I don't know what you're doing, but
you're wasting your life. You must, you shall, join our special army
against anarchy. Their armies are on our frontiers. Their bolt is
ready to fall. A moment more, and you may lose the glory of working with us, perhaps the glory of dying with the last heroes of the
world."

"It is a chance not to be missed, certainly," assented Syme, "but
still I do not quite understand. I know as well as anybody that the
modern world is full of lawless little men and mad little movements. But, beastly as they are, they generally have the one merit of
disagreeing with each other. How can you talk of their leading one
army or hurling one bolt. What is this anarchy?"

"Do not confuse it," replied the constable, "with those chance
dynamite outbreaks from Russia or from Ireland, which are really
the outbreaks of oppressed, if mistaken, men. This is a vast philo-
sophic movement, consisting of an outer and an inner ring. You
might even call the outer ring the laity and the inner ring the
priesthood. I prefer to call the outer ring the innocent section, the
inner ring the supremely guilty section. The outer ring—the main
mass of their supporters—are merely anarchists; that is, men who
believe that rules and formulas have destroyed human happiness.
They believe that all the evil results of human crime are the results
of the system that has called it crime. They do not believe that the
crime creates the punishment. They believe that the punishment
has created the crime. They believe that if a man seduced seven

women he would naturally walk away as blameless as the flowers of spring. They believe that if a man picked a pocket he would naturally feel exquisitely good. These I call the innocent section."

"Oh!" said Syme.

"Naturally, therefore, these people talk about 'a happy time coming'; 'the paradise of the future'; 'mankind freed from the bondage of vice and the bondage of virtue'; and so on. And so also the men of the inner circle speak—the sacred priesthood. They also speak to applauding crowds of the happiness of the future, and of mankind freed at last. But in their mouths"—and the policeman lowered his voice—"in their mouths these happy phrases have a horrible meaning. They are under no illusions; they are too intellectual to think that man upon this earth can ever be quite free of original sin and the struggle. And they mean death. When they say that mankind shall be free at last, they mean that mankind shall commit suicide. When they talk of a paradise without right or wrong, they mean the grave.

"They have but two objects, to destroy first humanity and then themselves. That is why they throw bombs instead of firing pistols. The innocent rank and file are disappointed because the bomb has not killed the king; but the high-priesthood are happy because it has killed somebody."

"How can I join you?" asked Syme, with a sort of passion.

"I know for a fact that there is a vacancy at the moment," said the policeman, "as I have the honour to be somewhat in the confidence of the chief of whom I have spoken. You should really come and see him. Or rather, I should not say see him, nobody ever sees him; but you can talk to him if you like."

"Telephone?" inquired Syme, with interest.

"No," said the policeman placidly, "he has a fancy for always sitting in a pitch-dark room. He says it makes his thoughts brighter. Do come along."

Somewhat dazed and considerably excited, Syme allowed himself to be led to a side-door in the long row of buildings of Scotland Yard. Almost before he knew what he was doing, he had been passed through the hands of about four intermediate officials, and was suddenly shown into a room, the abrupt blackness of which startled him like a blaze of light. It was not the ordinary darkness, in which forms can be faintly traced; it was like going suddenly stone-blind.

"Are you the new recruit?" asked a heavy voice.

And in some strange way, though there was not the shadow of a shape in the gloom, Syme knew two things: first, that it came from a man of massive stature; and second, that the man had his back to him.

"Are you the new recruit?" said the invisible chief, who seemed to have heard all about it. "All right. You are engaged."

Syme, quite swept off his feet, made a feeble fight against this irrevocable phrase.

"I really have no experience," he began.

"No one has any experience," said the other, "of the Battle of Armageddon."

"But I am really unfit—"

"You are willing, that is enough," said the unknown.

"Well, really," said Syme, "I don't know any profession of which mere willingness is the final test."

"I do," said the other—"martyrs. I am condemning you to death. Good day."

Thus it was that when Gabriel Syme came out again into the crimson light of evening, in his shabby black hat and shabby, lawless cloak, he came out a member of the New Detective Corps for the frustration of the great conspiracy. Acting under the advice of his friend the policeman (who was professionally inclined to neatness), he trimmed his hair and beard, bought a good hat, clad himself in an exquisite summer suit of light blue-grey, with a pale yellow flower in the button-hole, and, in short, became that elegant and rather insupportable person whom Gregory had first encountered in the little garden of Saffron Park. Before he finally left the police premises his friend provided him with a small blue card, on which was written, "The Last Crusade," and a number, the sign of his official authority. He put this carefully in his upper waistcoat pocket, lit a cigarette, and went forth to track and fight the enemy in all the drawing-rooms of London. Where his adventure ultimately led him we have already seen. At about half-past one on a February night he found himself steaming in a small tug up the silent Thames, armed with swordstick and revolver, the duly elected Thursday of the Central Council of Anarchists.

When Syme stepped out on to the steam-tug he had a singular sensation of stepping out into something entirely new; not merely into the landscape of a new land, but even into the landscape of a new planet. This was mainly due to the insane yet solid decision of that evening, though partly also to an entire change in the weather and the sky since he entered the little tavern some two hours before. Every trace of the passionate plumage of the cloudy sunset had been swept away, and a naked moon stood in a naked sky. The moon was so strong and full that (by a paradox often to be noticed) it seemed like a weaker sun. It gave, not the sense of bright moonshine, but rather of a dead daylight.

Over the whole landscape lay a luminous and unnatural discoloration, as of that disastrous twilight which Milton spoke of as shed by the sun in eclipse; so that Syme fell easily into his first thought, that he was actually on some other and emptier planet, which circled round some sadder star. But the more he felt this glittering desolation in the moonlit land, the more his own chivalric folly glowed in the night like a great fire. Even the common things he carried with him—the food and the brandy and the loaded pistol—took on exactly that concrete and material poetry which a child feels when he takes a gun upon a journey or a bun with him to bed. The sword-stick and the brandy-flask, though in themselves only the tools of morbid conspirators, became the expressions of his own more healthy romance. The sword-stick became almost the sword of chivalry, and the brandy the wine of the stirrup-cup. For even the most dehumanised modern fantasies depend on some older and simpler figure; the adventures may be mad, but the adventurer must be sane. The dragon without St.

George would not even be grotesque. So this inhuman landscape was only imaginative by the presence of a man really human. To Syme's exaggerative mind the bright, bleak houses and terraces by the Thames looked as empty as the mountains of the moon. But even the moon is only poetical because there is a man in the moon.

The tug was worked by two men, and with much toil went comparatively slowly. The clear moon that had lit up Chiswick had gone down by the time that they passed Battersea, and when they came under the enormous bulk of Westminster day had already begun to break. It broke like the splitting of great bars of lead, showing bars of silver; and these had brightened like white fire when the tug, changing its onward course, turned inward to a large landing stage rather beyond Charing Cross.

The great stones of the Embankment seemed equally dark and gigantic as Syme looked up at them. They were big and black against the huge white dawn. They made him feel that he was landing on the colossal steps of some Egyptian palace; and, indeed, the thing suited his mood, for he was, in his own mind, mounting to attack the solid thrones of horrible and heathen kings. He leapt out of the boat on to one slimy step, and stood, a dark and slender figure, amid the enormous masonry. The two men in the tug put her off again and turned up stream. They had never spoken a word.

CHAPTER V

The Feast of Fear

At first the large stone stair seemed to Syme as deserted as a pyramid; but before he reached the top he had realised that there was a man leaning over the parapet of the Embankment and looking out across the river. As a figure he was quite conventional, clad in a silk hat and frock-coat of the more formal type of fashion; he had a red flower in his buttonhole. As Syme drew nearer to him step by step, he did not even move a hair; and Syme could come close enough to notice even in the dim, pale morning light that his face was long, pale and intellectual, and ended in a small triangular tuft of dark beard at the very point of the chin, all else being clean-shaven. This scrap of hair almost seemed a mere oversight; the rest of the face was of the type that is best shaven—clear-cut, ascetic, and in its way noble. Syme drew closer and closer, noting all this, and still the figure did not stir.

At first an instinct had told Syme that this was the man whom he was meant to meet. Then, seeing that the man made no sign, he had concluded that he was not. And now again he had come back to a certainty that the man had something to do with his mad adventure. For the man remained more still than would have been natural if a stranger had come so close. He was as motionless as a wax-work, and got on the nerves somewhat in the same way. Syme looked again and again at the pale, dignified and delicate face, and the face still looked blankly across the river. Then he took out of his pocket the note from Buttons proving his election, and put it before that sad and beautiful face. Then the man smiled, and his smile was a shock, for it was all on one side, going up in the right cheek and down in the left.

There was nothing, rationally speaking, to scare anyone about this. Many people have this nervous trick of a crooked smile, and in many it is even attractive. But in all Syme's circumstances, with the dark dawn and the deadly errand and the loneliness on the great dripping stones, there was something unnerving in it.

There was the silent river and the silent man, a man of even classic face. And there was the last nightmare touch that his smile suddenly went wrong.

The spasm of smile was instantaneous, and the man's face dropped at once into its harmonious melancholy. He spoke without further explanation or inquiry, like a man speaking to an old colleague.

"If we walk up towards Leicester Square," he said, "we shall just be in time for breakfast. Sunday always insists on an early breakfast. Have you had any sleep?"

"No," said Syme.

"Nor have I," answered the man in an ordinary tone. "I shall try to get to bed after breakfast."

He spoke with casual civility, but in an utterly dead voice that contradicted the fanaticism of his face. It seemed almost as if all friendly words were to him lifeless conveniences, and that his only life was hate. After a pause the man spoke again.

"Of course, the Secretary of the branch told you everything that can be told. But the one thing that can never be told is the last notion of the President, for his notions grow like a tropical forest. So in case you don't know, I'd better tell you that he is carrying out his notion of concealing ourselves by not concealing ourselves to the most extraordinary lengths just now. Originally, of course, we met in a cell underground, just as your branch does. Then Sunday made us take a private room at an ordinary restaurant. He said that if you didn't seem to be hiding nobody hunted you out. Well, he is the only man on earth, I know; but sometimes

I really think that his huge brain is going a little mad in its old age. For now we flaunt ourselves before the public. We have our breakfast on a balcony—on a balcony, if you please—overlooking Leicester Square."

"And what do the people say?" asked Syme.

"It's quite simple what they say," answered his guide. "They say we are a lot of jolly gentlemen who pretend they are anarchists."

"It seems to me a very clever idea," said Syme.

"Clever! God blast your impudence! Clever!" cried out the other in a sudden, shrill voice which was as startling and discordant as his crooked smile. "When you've seen Sunday for a split second you'll leave off calling him clever."

With this they emerged out of a narrow street, and saw the early sunlight filling Leicester Square. It will never be known, I suppose, why this square itself should look so alien and in some ways so continental. It will never be known whether it was the foreign look that attracted the foreigners or the foreigners who gave it the foreign look. But on this particular morning the effect seemed singularly bright and clear. Between the open square and the sunlit leaves and the statue and the Saracenic outlines of the Alhambra, it looked the replica of some French or even Spanish public place. And this effect increased in Syme the sensation, which in many shapes he had had through the whole adventure, the eerie sensation of having strayed into a new world. As a fact, he had bought bad cigars round Leicester Square ever since he was a boy. But as he turned that corner, and saw the trees and the Moorish cupolas, he could have sworn that he was turning into an unknown Place de something or other in some foreign town.

At one corner of the square there projected a kind of angle of a prosperous but quiet hotel, the bulk of which belonged to a street behind. In the wall there was one large French window, probably the window of a large coffee-room; and outside this window, almost literally overhanging the square, was a formidably buttressed balcony, big enough to contain a dining-table. In fact, it did contain a dining-table, or more strictly a breakfast-table; and round the breakfast-table, glowing in the sunlight and evident to the street, were a group of noisy and talkative men, all dressed in the insolence of fashion, with white waistcoats and expensive button-holes. Some of their jokes could almost be heard across the square. Then the grave Secretary gave his unnatural smile, and Syme knew that this boisterous breakfast party was the secret conclave of the European Dynamiters.

Then, as Syme continued to stare at them, he saw something that he had not seen before. He had not seen it literally because it was too large to see. At the nearest end of the balcony, blocking up a great part of the perspective, was the back of a great mountain of a man. When Syme had seen him, his first thought was that the weight of him must break down the balcony of stone. His vastness did not lie only in the fact that he was abnormally tall and quite incredibly fat. This man was planned enormously in his original proportions, like a statue carved deliberately as colossal. His head, crowned with white hair, as seen from behind looked bigger than a head ought to be. The ears that stood out from it looked larger than human ears. He was enlarged terribly to scale; and this sense of size was so staggering, that when Syme saw him all the other figures seemed quite suddenly to dwindle and become dwarfish. They were still sitting there as before with their flowers and frock-coats, but now it looked as if the big man was entertaining five children to tea.

As Syme and the guide approached the side door of the hotel, a waiter came out smiling with every tooth in his head.

"The gentlemen are up there, sare," he said. "They do talk and they do laugh at what they talk. They do say they will throw bombs at ze king."

And the waiter hurried away with a napkin over his arm, much pleased with the singular frivolity of the gentlemen upstairs.

The two men mounted the stairs in silence.

Syme had never thought of asking whether the monstrous man who almost filled and broke the balcony was the great President of whom the others stood in awe. He knew it was so, with an unaccountable but instantaneous certainty. Syme, indeed, was one of those men who are open to all the more nameless psychological influences in a degree a little dangerous to mental health. Utterly devoid of fear in physical dangers, he was a great deal too sensitive to the smell of spiritual evil. Twice already that night little unmeaning things had peeped out at him almost pruriently, and given him a sense of drawing nearer and nearer to the head-quarters of hell. And this sense became overpowering as he drew nearer to the great President.

The form it took was a childish and yet hateful fancy. As he walked across the inner room towards the balcony, the large face of Sunday grew larger and larger; and Syme was gripped with a fear that when he was quite close the face would be too big to be possible, and that he would scream aloud. He remembered that as a child he would not look at the mask of Memnon in the British Museum, because it was a face, and so large.

By an effort, braver than that of leaping over a cliff, he went to an empty seat at the breakfast-table and sat down. The men greeted him with good-humoured raillery as if they had always known him. He sobered himself a little by looking at their conventional coats and solid, shining coffee-pot; then he looked again at Sunday. His face was very large, but it was still possible to humanity.

In the presence of the President the whole company looked sufficiently commonplace; nothing about them caught the eye at first, except that by the President's caprice they had been dressed up with a festive respectability, which gave the meal the look of a wedding breakfast. One man indeed stood out at even a superficial glance. He at least was the common or garden Dynamiter. He wore, indeed, the high white collar and satin tie that were the uniform of the occasion; but out of this collar there sprang a head quite unmanageable and quite unmistakable, a bewildering bush of brown hair and beard that almost obscured the eyes like those of a Skye terrier. But the eyes did look out of the tangle, and they were the sad eyes of some Russian serf. The effect of this figure was not terrible like that of the President, but it had every diablerie that can come from the utterly grotesque. If out of that stiff tie and collar there had come abruptly the head of a cat or a dog, it could not have been a more idiotic contrast.

The man's name, it seemed, was Gogol; he was a Pole, and in this circle of days he was called Tuesday. His soul and speech were incurably tragic; he could not force himself to play the prosperous and frivolous part demanded of him by President Sunday. And, indeed, when Syme came in the President, with that daring disregard of public suspicion which was his policy, was actually chaffing Gogol upon his inability to assume conventional graces.

"Our friend Tuesday," said the President in a deep voice at once of quietude and volume, "our friend Tuesday doesn't seem to grasp the idea. He dresses up like a gentleman, but he seems to be too great a soul to behave like one. He insists on the ways of the stage conspirator. Now if a gentleman goes about London in a top hat and a frock-coat, no one need know that he is an anarchist. But if a gentleman puts on a top hat and a frock-coat, and then goes about on his hands and knees—well, he may attract attention. That's what Brother Gogol does. He goes about on his hands and knees with such inexhaustible diplomacy, that by this time he finds it quite difficult to walk upright."

"I am not good at concealment," said Gogol sulkily, with a thick foreign accent; "I am not ashamed of the cause."

"Yes you are, my boy, and so is the cause of you," said the President good-naturedly. "You hide as much as anybody; but you can't do it, you see, you're such an ass! You try to combine two inconsistent methods. When a householder finds a man under his bed, he will probably pause to note the circumstance. But if he finds a man under his bed in a top hat, you will agree with me, my dear Tuesday, that he is not likely even to forget it. Now when you were found under Admiral Biffin's bed—"

"I am not good at deception," said Tuesday gloomily, flushing.

"Right, my boy, right," said the President with a ponderous heartiness, "you aren't good at anything."

While this stream of conversation continued, Syme was look-ing more steadily at the men around him. As he did so, he gradually felt all his sense of something spiritually queer return.

He had thought at first that they were all of common stature and costume, with the evident exception of the hairy Gogol. But as he looked at the others, he began to see in each of them exactly what he had seen in the man by the river, a demoniac detail some-where. That lop-sided laugh, which would suddenly disfigure the fine face of his original guide, was typical of all these types. Each man had something about him, perceived perhaps at the tenth or twentieth glance, which was not normal, and which seemed hardly human. The only metaphor he could think of was this, that they all looked as men of fashion and presence would look, with the additional twist given in a false and curved mirror.

Only the individual examples will express this half-concealed eccentricity. Syme's original cicerone bore the title of Monday; he was the Secretary of the Council, and his twisted smile was regarded with more terror than anything, except the President's horrible, happy laughter. But now that Syme had more space and light to observe him, there were other touches. His fine face was so emaciated, that Syme thought it must be wasted with some dis-ease; yet somehow the very distress of his dark eyes denied this. It was no physical ill that troubled him. His eyes were alive with intellectual torture, as if pure thought was pain.

He was typical of each of the tribe; each man was subtly and differently wrong. Next to him sat Tuesday, the tousle-headed Gogol, a man more obviously mad. Next was Wednesday, a certain Marquis de St. Eustache, a sufficiently characteristic figure. The first few glances found nothing unusual about him, except that he was the only man at table who wore the fashionable clothes as if they were really his own. He had a black French beard cut square and a black English frock-coat cut even squarer. But Syme, sensitive to such things, felt somehow that the man carried a rich atmosphere with him, a rich atmosphere that suffocated. It reminded one irra-tionally of drowsy odours and of dying lamps in the darker poems of Byron and Poe. With this went a sense of his being clad, not in lighter colours, but in softer materials; his black seemed richer and warmer than the black shades about him, as if it were compounded of profound colour. His black coat looked as if it were only black by being too dense a purple. His black beard looked as if it were only black by being too deep a blue. And in the gloom and thickness of the beard his dark red mouth showed sensual and scornful. Whatever he was he was not a Frenchman; he might be a Jew; he might be something deeper yet in the dark heart of the East. In the bright coloured Persian tiles and pictures showing tyrants hunting, you may see just those almond eyes, those blue-black beards, those cruel, crimson lips.

Then came Syme, and next a very old man, Professor de Worms, who still kept the chair of Friday, though every day it was expected that his death would leave it empty. Save for his intellect, he was in the last dissolution of senile decay. His face was as grey as his long grey beard, his forehead was lifted and fixed finally in a furrow of mild despair. In no other case, not even that of Gogol, did the bridegroom brilliancy of the morning dress express a more painful contrast. For the red flower in his button-hole showed up against a face that was literally discoloured like lead; the whole hideous effect was as if some drunken dandies had put their clothes upon a corpse. When he rose or sat down, which was with long labour and peril, something worse was expressed than mere weakness, something indefinably connected with the horror of the whole scene. It did not express decrepitude merely, but corruption. Another hateful fancy crossed Syme's quivering mind. He could not help thinking that whenever the man moved a leg or arm might fall off.

Right at the end sat the man called Saturday, the simplest and the most baffling of all. He was a short, square man with a dark, square face clean-shaven, a medical practitioner going by the name of Bull. He had that combination of *savoir-faire* with a sort of well-groomed coarseness which is not uncommon in young doctors. He carried his fine clothes with confidence rather than ease, and he mostly wore a set smile. There was nothing whatever odd about him, except that he wore a pair of dark, almost opaque spectacles. It may have been merely a crescendo of nervous fancy that had gone before, but those black discs were dreadful to Syme; they reminded him of half-remembered ugly tales, of some story about pennies being put on the eyes of the dead. Syme's eye always caught the black glasses and the blind grin. Had the dying Professor worn them, or even the pale Secretary, they would have been appropriate. But on the younger and grosser man they seemed only an enigma. They took away the key of the face. You could not tell what his smile or his gravity meant. Partly from this, and partly because he had a vulgar virility wanting in most of the others it seemed to Syme that he might be the wickedest of all those wicked men. Syme even had the thought that his eyes might be covered up because they were too frightful to see.

CHAPTER VI

The Exposure

S uch were the six men who had sworn to destroy the world.
Again and again Syme strove to pull together his common
sense in their presence. Sometimes he saw for an instant that these
notions were subjective, that he was only looking at ordinary men,
one of whom was old, another nervous, another short-sighted. The
sense of an unnatural symbolism always settled back on him again.
Each figure seemed to be, somehow, on the borderland of things,
just as their theory was on the borderland of thought. He knew
that each one of these men stood at the extreme end, so to speak,
of some wild road of reasoning. He could only fancy, as in some
old-world fable, that if a man went westward to the end of the
world he would find something—say a tree—that was more or less
than a tree, a tree possessed by a spirit; and that if he went east
to the end of the world he would find something else that was
not wholly itself—a tower, perhaps, of which the very shape was
wicked. So these figures seemed to stand up, violent and unaccountable, against an ultimate horizon, visions from the verge. The
ends of the earth were closing in.

Talk had been going on steadily as he took in the scene; and
not the least of the contrasts of that bewildering breakfast-table
was the contrast between the easy and unobtrusive tone of talk and
its terrible purport. They were deep in the discussion of an actual
and immediate plot. The waiter downstairs had spoken quite correctly when he said that they were talking about bombs and kings.

Only three days afterwards the Czar was to meet the President of the French Republic in Paris, and over their bacon and eggs upon their sunny balcony these beaming gentlemen had decided how both should die. Even the instrument was chosen; the black-bearded Marquis, it appeared, was to carry the bomb.

Ordinarily speaking, the proximity of this positive and objective crime would have sobered Syme, and cured him of all his merely mystical tremors. He would have thought of nothing but the need of saving at least two human bodies from being ripped in pieces with iron and roaring gas. But the truth was that by this time he had begun to feel a third kind of fear, more piercing and practical than either his moral revulsion or his social responsibility. Very simply, he had no fear to spare for the French President or the Czar; he had begun to fear for himself. Most of the talkers took little heed of him, debating now with their faces closer together, and almost uniformly grave, save when for an instant the smile of the Secretary ran aslant across his face as the jagged lightning runs aslant across the sky. But there was one persistent thing which first troubled Syme and at last terrified him. The President was always looking at him, steadily, and with a great and baffling interest. The enormous man was quite quiet, but his blue eyes stood out of his head. And they were always fixed on Syme.

Syme felt moved to spring up and leap over the balcony. When the President's eyes were on him he felt as if he were made of glass. He had hardly the shred of a doubt that in some silent and extraordinary way Sunday had found out that he was a spy. He looked over the edge of the balcony, and saw a policeman, standing abstractedly just beneath, staring at the bright railings and the sunlit trees.

Then there fell upon him the great temptation that was to torment him for many days. In the presence of these powerful and repulsive men, who were the princes of anarchy, he had almost forgotten the frail and fanciful figure of the poet Gregory, the mere aesthete of anarchism. He even thought of him now with an old kindness, as if they had played together when children. But he remembered that he was still tied to Gregory by a great promise. He had promised never to do the very thing that he now felt himself almost in the act of doing. He had promised not to jump over that balcony and speak to that policeman. He took his cold hand off the cold stone balustrade. His soul swayed in a vertigo of moral indecision. He had only to snap the thread of a rash vow made to a villainous society, and all his life could be as open and sunny as the square beneath him. He had, on the other hand, only to keep his antiquated honour, and be delivered inch by inch into the power of this great enemy of mankind, whose very intellect was a torture-chamber. Whenever he looked down into the square he saw the comfortable policeman, a pillar of common sense and common order. Whenever he looked back at the breakfast-table he saw the President still quietly studying him with big, unbearable eyes.

In all the torrent of his thought there were two thoughts that never crossed his mind. First, it never occurred to him to doubt that the President and his Council could crush him if he continued to stand alone. The place might be public, the project might seem impossible. But Sunday was not the man who would carry himself thus easily without having, somehow or somewhere, set open his iron trap. Either by anonymous poison or sudden street accident, by hypnotism or by fire from hell, Sunday could certainly strike him. If he defied the man he was probably dead, either struck stiff there in his chair or long afterwards as by an innocent ailment. If he called in the police promptly, arrested everyone, told all, and set against them the whole energy of England, he would probably escape; certainly not otherwise. They were a balconyful of gentlemen overlooking a bright and busy square; but he felt no more safe with them than if they had been a boatful of armed pirates overlooking an empty sea.

There was a second thought that never came to him. It never occurred to him to be spiritually won over to the enemy. Many moderns, inured to a weak worship of intellect and force, might have wavered in their allegiance under this oppression of a great personality. They might have called Sunday the super-man. If any such creature be conceivable, he looked, indeed, somewhat like it, with his earth-shaking abstraction, as of a stone statue walking. He might have been called something above man, with his large plans, which were too obvious to be detected, with his large face, which was too frank to be understood. But this was a kind of modern meanness to which Syme could not sink even in his extreme morbidity. Like any man, he was coward enough to fear great force; but he was not quite coward enough to admire it.

The men were eating as they talked, and even in this they were typical. Dr. Bull and the Marquis ate casually and conventionally of the best things on the table—cold pheasant or Strasbourg pie. But the Secretary was a vegetarian, and he spoke earnestly of the projected murder over half a raw tomato and three quarters of a glass of tepid water. The old Professor had such slops as suggested a sickening second childhood. And even in this President Sunday preserved his curious predominance of mere mass. For he ate like twenty men; he ate incredibly, with a frightful freshness of appetite, so that it was like watching a sausage factory. Yet continually, when he had swallowed a dozen crumpets or drunk a quart of coffee, he would be found with his great head on one side staring at Syme.

"I have often wondered," said the Marquis, taking a great bite out of a slice of bread and jam, "whether it wouldn't be better for me to do it with a knife. Most of the best things have been brought off with a knife. And it would be a new emotion to get a knife into a French President and wriggle it round."

"You are wrong," said the Secretary, drawing his black brows together. "The knife was merely the expression of the old personal quarrel with a personal tyrant. Dynamite is not only our best tool, but our best symbol. It is as perfect a symbol of us as is incense of the prayers of the Christians. It expands; it only destroys because it broadens; even so, thought only destroys because it broadens. A man's brain is a bomb," he cried out, loosening suddenly his strange passion and striking his own skull with violence. "My brain feels like a bomb, night and day. It must expand! It must expand! A man's brain must expand, if it breaks up the universe."

"I don't want the universe broken up just yet," drawled the Marquis. "I want to do a lot of beastly things before I die. I thought of one yesterday in bed."

"No, if the only end of the thing is nothing," said Dr. Bull with his sphinx-like smile, "it hardly seems worth doing."

The old Professor was staring at the ceiling with dull eyes.

"Every man knows in his heart," he said, "that nothing is worth doing."

There was a singular silence, and then the Secretary said—

"We are wandering, however, from the point. The only question is how Wednesday is to strike the blow. I take it we should all agree with the original notion of a bomb. As to the actual arrangements, I should suggest that tomorrow morning he should go first of all to—"

The speech was broken off short under a vast shadow. President Sunday had risen to his feet, seeming to fill the sky above them.

"Before we discuss that," he said in a small, quiet voice, "let us go into a private room. I have something very particular to say."

Syme stood up before any of the others. The instant of choice had come at last, the pistol was at his head. On the pavement before he could hear the policeman idly stir and stamp, for the morning, though bright, was cold.

A barrel-organ in the street suddenly sprang with a jerk into a jovial tune. Syme stood up taut, as if it had been a bugle before the battle. He found himself filled with a supernatural courage that came from nowhere. That jingling music seemed full of the vivacity, the vulgarity, and the irrational valour of the poor, who in all those unclean streets were all clinging to the decencies and the charities of Christendom. His youthful prank of being a policeman had faded from his mind; he did not think of himself as the representative of the corps of gentlemen turned into fancy constables, or of the old eccentric who lived in the dark room. But he did feel himself as the ambassador of all these common and kindly people in the street, who every day marched into battle to the music of the barrel-organ.

And this high pride in being human had lifted him unaccountably to an infinite height above the monstrous men around him. For an instant, at least, he looked down upon all their sprawling eccentricities from the starry pinnacle of the commonplace. He felt towards them all that unconscious and elementary superiority that a brave man feels over powerful beasts or a wise man over powerful errors. He knew that he had neither the intellectual nor the physical strength of President Sunday; but in that moment he minded it no more than the fact that he had not the muscles of a tiger or a horn on his nose like a rhinoceros. All was swallowed up in an ultimate certainty that the President was wrong and that the barrel-organ was right. There clanged in his mind that unanswerable and terrible truism in the song of Roland, "*Païens ont tort et Chretiens ont droit*," which in the old nasal French has the clang and groan of great iron. This liberation of his spirit from the load of his weakness went with a quite clear decision to embrace death. If the people of the barrel-organ could keep their old-world obligations, so could he. This very pride in keeping his word was that he was keeping it to miscreants. It was his last triumph over these lunatics to go down into their dark room and die for something that they could not even understand. The barrel-organ seemed to give the marching tune with the energy and the mingled noises of a whole orchestra; and he could hear deep and rolling, under all the trumpets of the pride of life, the drums of the pride of death.

The conspirators were already filing through the open window and into the rooms behind. Syme went last, outwardly calm, but with all his brain and body throbbing with romantic rhythm. The President led them down an irregular side stair, such as might be used by servants, and into a dim, cold, empty room, with a table and benches, like an abandoned boardroom. When they were all in, he closed and locked the door.

The first to speak was Gogol, the irreconcilable, who seemed bursting with inarticulate grievance.

"Zso! Zso!" he cried, with an obscure excitement, his heavy Polish accent becoming almost impenetrable. "You zay you nod 'ide. You zay you show himselves. It is all nuzzinks. Ven you vant talk importance you run yourselves in a dark box!"

The President seemed to take the foreigner's incoherent satire with entire good humour.

"You can't get hold of it yet, Gogol," he said in a fatherly way. "When once they have heard us talking nonsense on that balcony they will not care where we go afterwards. If we had come here first, we should have had the whole staff at the keyhole. You don't seem to know anything about mankind."

"I die for zem," cried the Pole in thick excitement, "and I slay zare oppressors. I care not for these games of gonzealment. I would zmite ze tyrant in ze open square."

"I see, I see," said the President, nodding kindly as he seated himself at the top of a long table. "You die for mankind first, and then you get up and smite their oppressors. So that's all right. And now may I ask you to control your beautiful sentiments, and sit down with the other gentlemen at this table. For the first time this morning something intelligent is going to be said."

Syme, with the perturbed promptitude he had shown since the original summons, sat down first. Gogol sat down last, grumbling in his brown beard about gombromise. No one except Syme seemed to have any notion of the blow that was about to fall. As for him, he had merely the feeling of a man mounting the scaffold with the intention, at any rate, of making a good speech.

"Comrades," said the President, suddenly rising, "we have spun out this farce long enough. I have called you down here to tell you something so simple and shocking that even the waiters upstairs (long inured to our levities) might hear some new seriousness in my voice. Comrades, we were discussing plans and naming places. I propose, before saying anything else, that those plans and places should not be voted by this meeting, but should be left wholly in the control of some one reliable member. I suggest Comrade Saturday, Dr. Bull."

They all stared at him; then they all started in their seats, for the next words, though not loud, had a living and sensational emphasis. Sunday struck the table.

"Not one word more about the plans and places must be said at this meeting. Not one tiny detail more about what we mean to do must be mentioned in this company."

Sunday had spent his life in astonishing his followers; but it seemed as if he had never really astonished them until now. They all moved feverishly in their seats, except Syme. He sat stiff in his, with his hand in his pocket, and on the handle of his loaded revolver. When the attack on him came he would sell his life dear. He would find out at least if the President was mortal.

Sunday went on smoothly—

"You will probably understand that there is only one possible motive for forbidding free speech at this festival of freedom. Strangers overhearing us matters nothing. They assume that we are joking. But what would matter, even unto death, is this, that there should be one actually among us who is not of us, who knows our grave purpose, but does not share it, who—"

The Secretary screamed out suddenly like a woman.

"It can't be!" he cried, leaping. "There can't—"

The President flapped his large flat hand on the table like the fin of some huge fish.

"Yes," he said slowly, "there is a spy in this room. There is a traitor at this table. I will waste no more words. His name—"

Syme half rose from his seat, his finger firm on the trigger.

"His name is Gogol," said the President. "He is that hairy humbug over there who pretends to be a Pole."

Gogol sprang to his feet, a pistol in each hand. With the same flash three men sprang at his throat. Even the Professor made an effort to rise. But Syme saw little of the scene, for he was blinded with a beneficent darkness; he had sunk down into his seat shuddering, in a palsy of passionate relief.

CHAPTER VII

The Unaccountable Conduct of Professor De Worms

" S it down!" said Sunday in a voice that he used once or twice
in his life, a voice that made men drop drawn swords.

The three who had risen fell away from Gogol, and that equiv-
ocal person himself resumed his seat.

"Well, my man," said the President briskly, addressing him as
one addresses a total stranger, "will you oblige me by putting your
hand in your upper waistcoat pocket and showing me what you
have there?"

The alleged Pole was a little pale under his tangle of dark hair,
but he put two fingers into the pocket with apparent coolness and
pulled out a blue strip of card. When Syme saw it lying on the
table, he woke up again to the world outside him. For although
the card lay at the other extreme of the table, and he could read
nothing of the inscription on it, it bore a startling resemblance to
the blue card in his own pocket, the card which had been given to
him when he joined the anti-anarchist constabulary.

"Pathetic Slav," said the President, "tragic child of Poland, are
you prepared in the presence of that card to deny that you are in
this company—shall we say *de trop?*"

"Right oh!" said the late Gogol. It made everyone jump to hear
a clear, commercial and somewhat cockney voice coming out of
that forest of foreign hair. It was irrational, as if a Chinaman had
suddenly spoken with a Scotch accent.

"I gather that you fully understand your position," said Sunday.

"You bet," answered the Pole. "I see it's a fair cop. All I say is, I don't believe any Pole could have imitated my accent like I did his."

"I concede the point," said Sunday. "I believe your own accent to be inimitable, though I shall practise it in my bath. Do you mind leaving your beard with your card?"

"Not a bit," answered Gogol; and with one finger he ripped off the whole of his shaggy head-covering, emerging with thin red hair and a pale, pert face. "It was hot," he added.

"I will do you the justice to say," said Sunday, not without a sort of brutal admiration, "that you seem to have kept pretty cool under it. Now listen to me. I like you. The consequence is that it would annoy me for just about two and a half minutes if I heard that you had died in torments. Well, if you ever tell the police or any human soul about us, I shall have that two and a half minutes of discomfort. On your discomfort I will not dwell. Good day. Mind the step."

The red-haired detective who had masqueraded as Gogol rose to his feet without a word, and walked out of the room with an air of perfect nonchalance. Yet the astonished Syme was able to realise that this ease was suddenly assumed; for there was a slight stumble outside the door, which showed that the departing detective had not minded the step.

"Time is flying," said the President in his gayest manner, after glancing at his watch, which like everything about him seemed bigger than it ought to be. "I must go off at once; I have to take the chair at a Humanitarian meeting."

The Secretary turned to him with working eyebrows.

"Would it not be better," he said a little sharply, "to discuss further the details of our project, now that the spy has left us?"

"No, I think not," said the President with a yawn like an unobtrusive earthquake. "Leave it as it is. Let Saturday settle it. I must be off. Breakfast here next Sunday."

But the late loud scenes had whipped up the almost naked nerves of the Secretary. He was one of those men who are conscientious even in crime.

"I must protest, President, that the thing is irregular," he said. "It is a fundamental rule of our society that all plans shall be debated in full council. Of course, I fully appreciate your forethought when in the actual presence of a traitor—"

"Secretary," said the President seriously, "if you'd take your head home and boil it for a turnip it might be useful. I can't say. But it might."

The Secretary reared back in a kind of equine anger.

"I really fail to understand—" he began in high offense.

"That's it, that's it," said the President, nodding a great many times. "That's where you fail right enough. You fail to understand. Why, you dancing donkey," he roared, rising, "you didn't want to be overheard by a spy, didn't you? How do you know you aren't overheard now?"

And with these words he shouldered his way out of the room, shaking with incomprehensible scorn.

Four of the men left behind gaped after him without any apparent glimmering of his meaning. Syme alone had even a glimmering, and such as it was it froze him to the bone. If the last words of the President meant anything, they meant that he had not after all passed unsuspected. They meant that while Sunday could not denounce him like Gogol, he still could not trust him like the others.

The other four got to their feet grumbling more or less, and betook themselves elsewhere to find lunch, for it was already well past midday. The Professor went last, very slowly and painfully. Syme sat long after the rest had gone, revolving his strange position. He had escaped a thunderbolt, but he was still under a cloud. At last he rose and made his way out of the hotel into Leicester Square. The bright, cold day had grown increasingly colder, and when he came out into the street he was surprised by a few flakes of snow. While he still carried the sword-stick and the rest of Gregory's portable luggage, he had thrown the cloak down and left it somewhere, perhaps on the steam-tug, perhaps on the balcony. Hoping, therefore, that the snow-shower might be slight, he stepped back out of the street for a moment and stood up under the doorway of a small and greasy hair-dresser's shop, the front window of which was empty, except for a sickly wax lady in evening dress.

Snow, however, began to thicken and fall fast; and Syme, having found one glance at the wax lady quite sufficient to depress his spirits, stared out instead into the white and empty street. He was considerably astonished to see, standing quite still outside the shop and staring into the window, a man. His top hat was loaded with snow like the hat of Father Christmas, the white drift was rising round his boots and ankles; but it seemed as if nothing could tear him away from the contemplation of the colourless wax doll in dirty evening dress. That any human being should stand in such weather looking into such a shop was a matter of sufficient wonder to Syme; but his idle wonder turned suddenly into a personal shock; for he realised that the man standing there was the paralytic old Professor de Worms. It scarcely seemed the place for a person of his years and infirmities.

Syme was ready to believe anything about the perversions of this dehumanized brotherhood; but even he could not believe that the Professor had fallen in love with that particular wax lady. He could only suppose that the man's malady (whatever it was) involved some momentary fits of rigidity or trance. He was not inclined, however, to feel in this case any very compassionate concern. On the contrary, he rather congratulated himself that the Professor's stroke and his elaborate and limping walk would make it easy to escape from him and leave him miles behind. For Syme thirsted first and last to get clear of the whole poisonous atmosphere, if only for an hour. Then he could collect his thoughts, formulate his policy, and decide finally whether he should or should not keep faith with Gregory.

He strolled away through the dancing snow, turned up two or three streets, down through two or three others, and entered a small Soho restaurant for lunch. He partook reflectively of four small and quaint courses, drank half a bottle of red wine, and ended up over black coffee and a black cigar, still thinking. He had taken his seat in the upper room of the restaurant, which was full of the chink of knives and the chatter of foreigners. He remembered that in old days he had imagined that all these harmless and kindly aliens were anarchists. He shuddered, remembering the real thing. But even the shudder had the delightful shame of escape. The wine, the common food, the familiar place, the faces of natural and talkative men, made him almost feel as if the Council of the Seven Days had been a bad dream; and although he knew it was nevertheless an objective reality, it was at least a distant one. Tall houses and populous streets lay between him and his last sight of the shameful seven; he was free in free London, and drinking wine among the free. With a somewhat easier action, he took his hat and stick and strolled down the stair into the shop below.

When he entered that lower room he stood stricken and rooted to the spot. At a small table, close up to the blank window and the white street of snow, sat the old anarchist Professor over a glass of milk, with his lifted livid face and pendent eyelids. For an instant Syme stood as rigid as the stick he leant upon. Then with a gesture as of blind hurry, he brushed past the Professor, dashing open the door and slamming it behind him, and stood outside in the snow.

"Can that old corpse be following me?" he asked himself, biting his yellow moustache. "I stopped too long up in that room, so that even such leaden feet could catch me up. One comfort is, with a little brisk walking I can put a man like that as far away as Timbuctoo. Or am I too fanciful? Was he really following me? Surely Sunday would not be such a fool as to send a lame man?"

He set off at a smart pace, twisting and whirling his stick, in the direction of Covent Garden. As he crossed the great market the snow increased, growing blinding and bewildering as the afternoon began to darken. The snow-flakes tormented him like a swarm of silver bees. Getting into his eyes and beard, they added their unremitting futility to his already irritated nerves; and by the time that he had come at a swinging pace to the beginning of Fleet Street, he lost patience, and finding a Sunday teashop, turned into it to take shelter. He ordered another cup of black coffee as an excuse. Scarcely had he done so, when Professor de Worms hobbled heavily into the shop, sat down with difficulty and ordered a glass of milk.

Syme's walking-stick had fallen from his hand with a great clang, which confessed the concealed steel. But the Professor did not look round. Syme, who was commonly a cool character, was literally gaping as a rustic gapes at a conjuring trick. He had seen no cab following; he had heard no wheels outside the shop; to all mortal appearances the man had come on foot. But the old man could only walk like a snail, and Syme had walked like the wind. He started up and snatched his stick, half crazy with the contradiction in mere arithmetic, and swung out of the swinging doors, leaving his coffee untasted. An omnibus going to the Bank went rattling by with an unusual rapidity. He had a violent run of a hundred yards to reach it; but he managed to spring, swaying upon the splash-board and, pausing for an instant to pant, he climbed on to the top. When he had been seated for about half a minute, he heard behind him a sort of heavy and asthmatic breathing.

Turning sharply, he saw rising gradually higher and higher up the omnibus steps a top hat soiled and dripping with snow, and under the shadow of its brim the short-sighted face and shaky shoulders of Professor de Worms. He let himself into a seat with characteristic care, and wrapped himself up to the chin in the mackintosh rug.

Every movement of the old man's tottering figure and vague hands, every uncertain gesture and panic-stricken pause, seemed to put it beyond question that he was helpless, that he was in the last imbecility of the body. He moved by inches, he let himself down with little gasps of caution. And yet, unless the philosophical entities called time and space have no vestige even of a practical existence, it appeared quite unquestionable that he had run after the omnibus.

Syme sprang erect upon the rocking car, and after staring wildly at the wintry sky, that grew gloomier every moment, he ran down the steps. He had repressed an elemental impulse to leap over the side.

Too bewildered to look back or to reason, he rushed into one of the little courts at the side of Fleet Street as a rabbit rushes into a hole. He had a vague idea, if this incomprehensible old Jack-in-the-box was really pursuing him, that in that labyrinth of little streets he could soon throw him off the scent. He dived in and out of those crooked lanes, which were more like cracks than thoroughfares; and by the time that he had completed about twenty alternate angles and described an unthinkable polygon, he paused to listen for any sound of pursuit. There was none; there could not in any case have been much, for the little streets were thick with the soundless snow. Somewhere behind Red Lion Court, however, he noticed a place where some energetic citizen had cleared away the snow for a space of about twenty yards, leaving the wet, glistening cobble-stones. He thought little of this as he passed it, only plunging into yet another arm of the maze. But when a few hundred yards farther on he stood still again to listen, his heart stood still also, for he heard from that space of rugged stones the clinking crutch and labouring feet of the infernal cripple.

The sky above was loaded with the clouds of snow, leaving London in a darkness and oppression premature for that hour of the evening. On each side of Syme the walls of the alley were blind and featureless; there was no little window or any kind of eve. He felt a new impulse to break out of this hive of houses, and to get once more into the open and lamp-lit street. Yet he rambled and dodged for a long time before he struck the main thoroughfare. When he did so, he struck it much farther up than he had fancied. He came out into what seemed the vast and void of Ludgate Circus, and saw St. Paul's Cathedral sitting in the sky.

At first he was startled to find these great roads so empty, as if a pestilence had swept through the city. Then he told himself that some degree of emptiness was natural; first because the snowstorm was even dangerously deep, and secondly because it was Sunday. And at the very word Sunday he bit his lip; the word was henceforth for hire like some indecent pun. Under the white fog of snow high up in the heaven the whole atmosphere of the city was turned to a very queer kind of green twilight, as of men under the sea. The sealed and sullen sunset behind the dark dome of St. Paul's had in it smoky and sinister colours—colours of sickly green, dead red or decaying bronze, that were just bright enough to emphasise the solid whiteness of the snow. But right up against these dreary colours rose the black bulk of the cathedral; and upon the top of the cathedral was a random splash and great stain of snow, still clinging as to an Alpine peak. It had fallen accidentally, but just so fallen as to half drape the dome from its very topmost point, and to pick out in perfect silver the great orb and the cross. When Syme saw it he suddenly straightened himself, and made with his sword-stick an involuntary salute.

He knew that that evil figure, his shadow, was creeping quickly or slowly behind him, and he did not care.

It seemed a symbol of human faith and valour that while the skies were darkening that high place of the earth was bright. The devils might have captured heaven, but they had not yet captured the cross. He had a new impulse to tear out the secret of this danc-ing, jumping and pursuing paralytic; and at the entrance of the court as it opened upon the Circus he turned, stick in hand, to face his pursuer.

Professor de Worms came slowly round the corner of the irreg-ular alley behind him, his unnatural form outlined against a lonely gas-lamp, irresistibly recalling that very imaginative figure in the nursery rhymes, "the crooked man who went a crooked mile." He really looked as if he had been twisted out of shape by the tortu-ous streets he had been threading. He came nearer and nearer, the lamplight shining on his lifted spectacles, his lifted, patient face. Syme waited for him as St. George waited for the dragon, as a man waits for a final explanation or for death. And the old Professor came right up to him and passed him like a total stranger, without even a blink of his mournful eyelids.

There was something in this silent and unexpected innocence that left Syme in a final fury. The man's colourless face and manner seemed to assert that the whole following had been an accident.

Syme was galvanised with an energy that was something between bitterness and a burst of boyish derision. He made a wild gesture as if to knock the old man's hat off, called out something like "Catch me if you can," and went racing away across the white, open Circus. Concealment was impossible now; and looking back over his shoulder, he could see the black figure of the old gentleman coming after him with long, swinging strides like a man winning a mile race. But the head upon that bounding body was still pale, grave and professional, like the head of a lecturer upon the body of a harlequin.

This outrageous chase sped across Ludgate Circus, up Ludgate Hill, round St. Paul's Cathedral, along Cheapside, Syme remembering all the nightmares he had ever known. Then Syme broke away towards the river, and ended almost down by the docks. He saw the yellow panes of a low, lighted public-house, flung himself into it and ordered beer. It was a foul tavern, sprinkled with foreign sailors, a place where opium might be smoked or knives drawn.

A moment later Professor de Worms entered the place, sat down carefully, and asked for a glass of milk.

CHAPTER VIII

The Professor Explains

W hen Gabriel Syme found himself finally established in a chair, and opposite to him, fixed and final also, the lifted eyebrows and leaden eyelids of the Professor, his fears fully returned. This incomprehensible man from the fierce council, after all, had certainly pursued him. If the man had one character as a paralytic and another character as a pursuer, the antithesis might make him more interesting, but scarcely more soothing. It would be a very small comfort that he could not find the Professor out, if by some serious accident the Professor should find him out. He emptied a whole pewter pot of ale before the professor had touched his milk.

One possibility, however, kept him hopeful and yet helpless. It was just possible that this escapade signified something other than even a slight suspicion of him. Perhaps it was some regular form or sign. Perhaps the foolish scamper was some sort of friendly signal that he ought to have understood. Perhaps it was a ritual. Perhaps the new Thursday was always chased along Cheapside, as the new Lord Mayor is always escorted along it. He was just selecting a tentative inquiry, when the old Professor opposite suddenly and simply cut him short. Before Syme could ask the first diplomatic question, the old anarchist had asked suddenly, without any sort of preparation—

"Are you a policeman?"

Whatever else Syme had expected, he had never expected anything so brutal and actual as this. Even his great presence of mind could only manage a reply with an air of rather blundering jocularity.

"A policeman?" he said, laughing vaguely. "Whatever made you think of a policeman in connection with me?"

"The process was simple enough," answered the Professor patiently. "I thought you looked like a policeman. I think so now."

"Did I take a policeman's hat by mistake out of the restaurant?" asked Syme, smiling wildly. "Have I by any chance got a number stuck on to me somewhere? Have my boots got that watchful look? Why must I be a policeman? Do, do let me be a postman."

The old Professor shook his head with a gravity that gave no hope, but Syme ran on with a feverish irony.

"But perhaps I misunderstood the delicacies of your German philosophy. Perhaps policeman is a relative term. In an evolutionary sense, sir, the ape fades so gradually into the policeman, that I myself can never detect the shade. The monkey is only the policeman that may be. Perhaps a maiden lady on Clapham Common is only the policeman that might have been. I don't mind being the policeman that might have been. I don't mind being anything in German thought."

"Are you in the police service?" said the old man, ignoring all Syme's improvised and desperate raillery. "Are you a detective?"

Syme's heart turned to stone, but his face never changed.

"Your suggestion is ridiculous," he began. "Why on earth—"

The old man struck his palsied hand passionately on the rickety table, nearly breaking it.

"Did you hear me ask a plain question, you pattering spy?" he shrieked in a high, crazy voice. "Are you, or are you not, a police detective?"

"No!" answered Syme, like a man standing on the hangman's drop.

"You swear it," said the old man, leaning across to him, his dead face becoming as it were loathsomely alive. "You swear it! You swear it! If you swear falsely, will you be damned? Will you be sure that the devil dances at your funeral? Will you see that the nightmare sits on your grave? Will there really be no mistake? You are an anarchist, you are a dynamiter! Above all, you are not in any sense a detective? You are not in the British police?"

He leant his angular elbow far across the table, and put up his large loose hand like a flap to his ear.

"I am not in the British police," said Syme with insane calm.

Professor de Worms fell back in his chair with a curious air of kindly collapse.

"That's a pity," he said, "because I am."

Syme sprang up straight, sending back the bench behind him with a crash.

"Because you are what?" he said thickly. "You are what?"

"I am a policeman," said the Professor with his first broad smile, and beaming through his spectacles. "But as you think policeman only a relative term, of course I have nothing to do with you. I am in the British police force; but as you tell me you are not in the British police force, I can only say that I met you in a dynamiters' club. I suppose I ought to arrest you." And with these words he laid on the table before Syme an exact facsimile of the blue card which Syme had in his own waistcoat pocket, the symbol of his power from the police.

Syme had for a flash the sensation that the cosmos had turned exactly upside down, that all trees were growing downwards and that all stars were under his feet. Then came slowly the opposite conviction. For the last twenty-four hours the cosmos had really been upside down, but now the capsized universe had come right side up again. This devil from whom he had been fleeing all day was only an elder brother of his own house, who on the other side of the table lay back and laughed at him. He did not for the moment ask any questions of detail; he only knew the happy and silly fact that this shadow, which had pursued him with an intolerable oppression of peril, was only the shadow of a friend trying to catch him up. He knew simultaneously that he was a fool and a free man. For with any recovery from morbidity there must go a certain healthy humiliation. There comes a certain point in such conditions when only three things are possible: first a perpetuation of Satanic pride, secondly tears, and third laughter. Syme's egotism held hard to the first course for a few seconds, and then suddenly adopted the third. Taking his own blue police ticket from his own waist coat pocket, he tossed it on to the table; then he flung his head back until his spike of yellow beard almost pointed at the ceiling, and shouted with a barbaric laughter.

Even in that close den, perpetually filled with the din of knives, plates, cans, clamorous voices, sudden struggles and stampedes, there was something Homeric in Syme's mirth which made many half-drunken men look round.

"What yer laughing at, guv'nor?" asked one wondering labourer from the docks.

"At myself," answered Syme, and went off again into the agony of his ecstatic reaction.

"Pull yourself together," said the Professor, "or you'll get hysterical. Have some more beer. I'll join you."

"You haven't drunk your milk," said Syme.

"My milk!" said the other, in tones of withering and unfathomable contempt, "my milk! Do you think I'd look at the beastly stuff when I'm out of sight of the bloody anarchists? We're all Christians in this room, though perhaps," he added, glancing around at the reeling crowd, "not strict ones. Finish my milk? Great blazes! yes, I'll finish it right enough!" and he knocked the tumbler off the table, making a crash of glass and a splash of silver fluid.

Syme was staring at him with a happy curiosity.

"I understand now," he cried; "of course, you're not an old man at all."

"I can't take my face off here," replied Professor de Worms. "It's rather an elaborate make-up. As to whether I'm an old man, that's not for me to say. I was thirty-eight last birthday."

"Yes, but I mean," said Syme impatiently, "there's nothing the matter with you."

"Yes," answered the other dispassionately. "I am subject to colds."

Syme's laughter at all this had about it a wild weakness of relief. He laughed at the idea of the paralytic Professor being really a young actor dressed up as if for the foot-lights. But he felt that he would have laughed as loudly if a pepperpot had fallen over.

The false Professor drank and wiped his false beard.

"Did you know," he asked, "that that man Gogol was one of us?"

"I? No, I didn't know it," answered Syme in some surprise. "But didn't you?"

"I knew no more than the dead," replied the man who called himself de Worms. "I thought the President was talking about me, and I rattled in my boots."

"And I thought he was talking about me," said Syme, with his rather reckless laughter. "I had my hand on my revolver all the time."

"So had I," said the Professor grimly; "so had Gogol evidently."

Syme struck the table with an exclamation.

"Why, there were three of us there!" he cried. "Three out of seven is a fighting number. If we had only known that we were three!"

The face of Professor de Worms darkened, and he did not look up.

"We were three," he said. "If we had been three hundred we could still have done nothing."

"Not if we were three hundred against four?" asked Syme, jeering rather boisterously.

"No," said the Professor with sobriety, "not if we were three hundred against Sunday."

And the mere name struck Syme cold and serious; his laughter had died in his heart before it could die on his lips. The face of the unforgettable President sprang into his mind as startling as a coloured photograph, and he remarked this difference between Sunday and all his satellites, that their faces, however fierce or sinister, became gradually blurred by memory like other human faces, whereas Sunday's seemed almost to grow more actual during absence, as if a man's painted portrait should slowly come alive.

They were both silent for a measure of moments, and then Syme's speech came with a rush, like the sudden foaming of champagne.

"Professor," he cried, "it is intolerable. Are you afraid of this man?"

The Professor lifted his heavy lids, and gazed at Syme with large, wide-open, blue eyes of an almost ethereal honesty.

"Yes, I am," he said mildly. "So are you."

Syme was dumb for an instant. Then he rose to his feet erect, like an insulted man, and thrust the chair away from him.

"Yes," he said in a voice indescribable, "you are right. I am afraid of him. Therefore I swear by God that I will seek out this man whom I fear until I find him, and strike him on the mouth. If heaven were his throne and the earth his footstool, I swear that I would pull him down."

"How?" asked the staring Professor. "Why?"

"Because I am afraid of him," said Syme; "and no man should leave in the universe anything of which he is afraid."

De Worms blinked at him with a sort of blind wonder. He made an effort to speak, but Syme went on in a low voice, but with an undercurrent of inhuman exaltation—

"Who would condescend to strike down the mere things that he does not fear? Who would debase himself to be merely brave, like any common prizefighter? Who would stoop to be fearless— like a tree? Fight the thing that you fear. You remember the old tale of the English clergyman who gave the last rites to the brigand of Sicily, and how on his death-bed the great robber said, 'I can give you no money, but I can give you advice for a lifetime: your thumb on the blade, and strike upwards.' So I say to you, strike upwards, if you strike at the stars."

The other looked at the ceiling, one of the tricks of his pose.

"Sunday is a fixed star," he said.

"You shall see him a falling star," said Syme, and put on his hat.

The decision of his gesture drew the Professor vaguely to his feet.

"Have you any idea," he asked, with a sort of benevolent bewilderment, "exactly where you are going?"

"Yes," replied Syme shortly, "I am going to prevent this bomb being thrown in Paris."

"Have you any conception how?" inquired the other.

"No," said Syme with equal decision.

"You remember, of course," resumed the soi-disant de Worms, pulling his beard and looking out of the window, "that when we broke up rather hurriedly the whole arrangements for the atrocity were left in the private hands of the Marquis and Dr. Bull. The Marquis is by this time probably crossing the Channel. But where he will go and what he will do it is doubtful whether even the President knows; certainly we don't know. The only man who does know is Dr. Bull."

"Confound it!" cried Syme. "And we don't know where he is."

"Yes," said the other in his curious, absent-minded way, "I know where he is myself."

"Will you tell me?" asked Syme with eager eyes.

"I will take you there," said the Professor, and took down his own hat from a peg.

Syme stood looking at him with a sort of rigid excitement.

"What do you mean?" he asked sharply. "Will you join me? Will you take the risk?"

"Young man," said the Professor pleasantly, "I am amused to observe that you think I am a coward. As to that I will say only one word, and that shall be entirely in the manner of your own philosophical rhetoric. You think that it is possible to pull down the President. I know that it is impossible, and I am going to try it," and opening the tavern door, which let in a blast of bitter air, they went out together into the dark streets by the docks.

Most of the snow was melted or trampled to mud, but here and there a clot of it still showed grey rather than white in the gloom. The small streets were sloppy and full of pools, which reflected the flaming lamps irregularly, and by accident, like fragments of some other and fallen world. Syme felt almost dazed as he stepped through this growing confusion of lights and shadows; but his companion walked on with a certain briskness, towards where, at the end of the street, an inch or two of the lamplit river looked like a bar of flame.

"Where are you going?" Syme inquired.

"Just now," answered the Professor, "I am going just round the corner to see whether Dr. Bull has gone to bed. He is hygienic, and retires early."

"Dr. Bull!" exclaimed Syme. "Does he live round the corner?"

"No," answered his friend. "As a matter of fact he lives some way off, on the other side of the river, but we can tell from here whether he has gone to bed."

Turning the corner as he spoke, and facing the dim river, flecked with flame, he pointed with his stick to the other bank. On the Surrey side at this point there ran out into the Thames, seeming almost to overhang it, a bulk and cluster of those tall tenements, dotted with lighted windows, and rising like factory chimneys to an almost insane height. Their special poise and position made one block of buildings especially look like a Tower of Babel with a hundred eyes. Syme had never seen any of the sky-scraping buildings in America, so he could only think of the buildings in a dream.

Even as he stared, the highest light in this innumerably lighted turret abruptly went out, as if this black Argus had winked at him with one of his innumerable eyes.

Professor de Worms swung round on his heel, and struck his stick against his boot.

"We are too late," he said, "the hygienic Doctor has gone to bed."

"What do you mean?" asked Syme. "Does he live over there, then?"

"Yes," said de Worms, "behind that particular window which you can't see. Come along and get some dinner. We must call on him tomorrow morning."

Without further parley, he led the way through several by-ways until they came out into the flare and clamour of the East India Dock Road. The Professor, who seemed to know his way about the neighbourhood, proceeded to a place where the line of lighted shops fell back into a sort of abrupt twilight and quiet, in which an old white inn, all out of repair, stood back some twenty feet from the road.

"You can find good English inns left by accident everywhere, like fossils," explained the Professor. "I once found a decent place in the West End."

"I suppose," said Syme, smiling, "that this is the corresponding decent place in the East End?"

"It is," said the Professor reverently, and went in.

In that place they dined and slept, both very thoroughly. The beans and bacon, which these unaccountable people cooked well, the astonishing emergence of Burgundy from their cellars, crowned Syme's sense of a new comradeship and comfort. Through all this ordeal his root horror had been isolation, and there are no words to express the abyss between isolation and having one ally. It may be conceded to the mathematicians that four is twice two. But two is not twice one; two is two thousand times one. That is why, in spite of a hundred disadvantages, the world will always return to monogamy.

Syme was able to pour out for the first time the whole of his outrageous tale, from the time when Gregory had taken him to the little tavern by the river. He did it idly and amply, in a luxuriant monologue, as a man speaks with very old friends. On his side, also, the man who had impersonated Professor de Worms was not less communicative. His own story was almost as silly as Syme's.

"That's a good get-up of yours," said Syme, draining a glass of Mâcon; "a lot better than old Gogol's. Even at the start I thought he was a bit too hairy."

"A difference of artistic theory," replied the Professor pensively. "Gogol was an idealist. He made up as the abstract or platonic ideal of an anarchist. But I am a realist. I am a portrait painter. But, indeed, to say that I am a portrait painter is an inadequate expression. I am a portrait."

"I don't understand you," said Syme.

"I am a portrait," repeated the Professor. "I am a portrait of the celebrated Professor de Worms, who is, I believe, in Naples."

"You mean you are made up like him," said Syme. "But doesn't he know that you are taking his nose in vain?"

"He knows it right enough," replied his friend cheerfully.

"Then why doesn't he denounce you?"

"I have denounced him," answered the Professor.

"Do explain yourself," said Syme.

"With pleasure, if you don't mind hearing my story," replied the eminent foreign philosopher. "I am by profession an actor, and my name is Wilks. When I was on the stage I mixed with all sorts of Bohemian and blackguard company. Sometimes I touched the edge of the turf, sometimes the riff-raff of the arts, and occasionally the political refugee. In some den of exiled dreamers I was introduced to the great German Nihilist philosopher, Professor de Worms. I did not gather much about him beyond his appearance, which was very disgusting, and which I studied carefully. I understood that he had proved that the destructive principle in the universe was God; hence he insisted on the need for a furious and incessant energy, rending all things in pieces. Energy, he said, was the All. He was lame, shortsighted, and partially paralytic. When I met him I was in a frivolous mood, and I disliked him so much that I resolved to imitate him. If I had been a draughtsman I would have drawn a caricature. I was only an actor, I could only act a caricature. I made myself up into what was meant for a wild exaggeration of the old Professor's dirty old self. When I went into the room full of his supporters I expected to be received with a roar of laughter, or (if they were too far gone) with a roar of indignation at the insult. I cannot describe the surprise I felt when my entrance was received with a respectful silence, followed (when I had first opened my lips) with a murmur of admiration. The curse of the perfect artist had fallen upon me. I had been too subtle, I had been too true. They thought I really was the great Nihilist Professor. I was a healthy-minded young man at the time, and I confess that it was a blow. Before I could fully recover, however, two or three of these admirers ran up to me radiating indignation, and told me that a public insult had been put upon me in the next room. I inquired its nature. It seemed that an impertinent fellow had dressed himself up as a preposterous parody of myself. I had drunk more champagne than was good for me, and in a flash of folly I decided to see the situation through. Consequently it was to meet the glare of the company and my own lifted eyebrows and freezing eyes that the real Professor came into the room.

"I need hardly say there was a collision. The pessimists all round me looked anxiously from one Professor to the other Professor to see which was really the more feeble. But I won. An old man in poor health, like my rival, could not be expected to be so impressively feeble as a young actor in the prime of life. You see, he really had paralysis, and working within this definite limitation, he couldn't be so jolly paralytic as I was. Then he tried to blast my claims intellectually. I countered that by a very simple dodge. Whenever he said something that nobody but he could understand, I replied with something which I could not even understand myself. 'I don't fancy,' he said, 'that you could have worked out the principle that evolution is only negation, since there inheres in it the introduction of lacuna, which are an essential of differentiation.' I replied quite scornfully, 'You read all that up in Pinckwerts; the notion that involution functioned eugenically was exposed long ago by Glumpe.' It is unnecessary for me to say that there never were such people as Pinckwerts and Glumpe. But the people all round (rather to my surprise) seemed to remember them quite well, and the Professor, finding that the learned and mysterious method left him rather at the mercy of an enemy slightly deficient in scruples, fell back upon a more popular form of wit. 'I see,' he sneered, 'you prevail like the false pig in Aesop.' 'And you fail,' I answered, smiling, 'like the hedgehog in Montaigne.' Need I say that there is no hedgehog in Montaigne? 'Your claptrap comes off,' he said; 'so would your beard.' I had no intelligent answer to this, which was quite true and rather witty. But I laughed heartily, answered, 'Like the Pantheist's boots,' at random, and turned on my heel with all the honours of victory. The real Professor was thrown out, but not with violence, though one man tried very patiently to pull off his nose. He is now, I believe, received everywhere in Europe as a delightful impostor. His apparent earnestness and anger, you see, make him all the more entertaining."

"Well," said Syme, "I can understand your putting on his dirty old beard for a night's practical joke, but I don't understand your never taking it off again."

"That is the rest of the story," said the impersonator. "When I myself left the company, followed by reverent applause, I went limping down the dark street, hoping that I should soon be far enough away to be able to walk like a human being. To my astonishment, as I was turning the corner, I felt a touch on the shoulder, and turning, found myself under the shadow of an enormous policeman. He told me I was wanted. I struck a sort of paralytic attitude, and cried in a high German accent, 'Yes, I am wanted—by the oppressed of the world. You are arresting me on the charge of being the great anarchist, Professor de Worms.' The policeman impassively consulted a paper in his hand, 'No, sir,' he said civilly, 'at least, not exactly, sir. I am arresting you on the charge of not being the celebrated anarchist, Professor de Worms.' This charge, if it was criminal at all, was certainly the lighter of the two, and I went along with the man, doubtful, but not greatly dismayed. I was shown into a number of rooms, and eventually into the presence of a police officer, who explained that a serious campaign had been opened against the centres of anarchy, and that this, my successful masquerade, might be of considerable value to the public safety. He offered me a good salary and this little blue card. Though our conversation was short, he struck me as a man of very massive common sense and humour; but I cannot tell you much about him personally, because—"

Syme laid down his knife and fork.

"I know," he said, "because you talked to him in a dark room."

Professor de Worms nodded and drained his glass.

CHAPTER IX

The Man in Spectacles

"Burgundy is a jolly thing," said the Professor sadly, as he set his glass down.

"You don't look as if it were," said Syme; "you drink it as if it were medicine."

"You must excuse my manner," said the Professor dismally, "my position is rather a curious one. Inside I am really bursting with boyish merriment; but I acted the paralytic Professor so well, that now I can't leave off. So that when I am among friends, and have no need at all to disguise myself, I still can't help speaking slow and wrinkling my forehead—just as if it were my forehead. I can be quite happy, you understand, but only in a paralytic sort of way. The most buoyant exclamations leap up in my heart, but they come out of my mouth quite different. You should hear me say, 'Buck up, old cock!' It would bring tears to your eyes."

"It does," said Syme; "but I cannot help thinking that apart from all that you are really a bit worried."

The Professor started a little and looked at him steadily.

"You are a very clever fellow," he said, "it is a pleasure to work with you. Yes, I have rather a heavy cloud in my head. There is a great problem to face," and he sank his bald brow in his two hands.

Then he said in a low voice—

"Can you play the piano?"

"Yes," said Syme in simple wonder, "I'm supposed to have a good touch."

Then, as the other did not speak, he added—

"I trust the great cloud is lifted."

After a long silence, the Professor said out of the cavernous shadow of his hands—

"It would have done just as well if you could work a typewriter."

"Thank you," said Syme, "you flatter me."

"Listen to me," said the other, "and remember whom we have to see tomorrow. You and I are going tomorrow to attempt something which is very much more dangerous than trying to steal the Crown Jewels out of the Tower. We are trying to steal a secret from a very sharp, very strong, and very wicked man. I believe there is no man, except the President, of course, who is so seriously startling and formidable as that little grinning fellow in goggles. He has not perhaps the white-hot enthusiasm unto death, the mad martyrdom for anarchy, which marks the Secretary. But then that very fanaticism in the Secretary has a human pathos, and is almost a redeeming trait. But the little Doctor has a brutal sanity that is more shocking than the Secretary's disease. Don't you notice his detestable virility and vitality. He bounces like an india-rubber ball. Depend on it, Sunday was not asleep (I wonder if he ever sleeps?) when he locked up all the plans of this outrage in the round, black head of Dr. Bull."

"And you think," said Syme, "that this unique monster will be soothed if I play the piano to him?"

"Don't be an ass," said his mentor. "I mentioned the piano because it gives one quick and independent fingers. Syme, if we are to go through this interview and come out sane or alive, we must have some code of signals between us that this brute will not see. I have made a rough alphabetical cypher corresponding to the five fingers—like this, see," and he rippled with his fingers on the wooden table—"B-A-D, bad, a word we may frequently require."

Syme poured himself out another glass of wine, and began to study the scheme. He was abnormally quick with his brains at puzzles, and with his hands at conjuring, and it did not take him long to learn how he might convey simple messages by what would seem to be idle taps upon a table or knee. But wine and companionship had always the effect of inspiring him to a farcical ingenuity, and the Professor soon found himself struggling with the too vast energy of the new language, as it passed through the heated brain of Syme.

"We must have several word-signs," said Syme serious-ly—"words that we are likely to want, fine shades of meaning. My favourite word is 'coeval.' What's yours?"

"Do stop playing the goat," said the Professor plaintively. "You don't know how serious this is."

"'Lush' too," said Syme, shaking his head sagaciously, "we must have 'lush'—word applied to grass, don't you know?"

"Do you imagine," asked the Professor furiously, "that we are going to talk to Dr. Bull about grass?"

"There are several ways in which the subject could be approached," said Syme reflectively, "and the word introduced without appearing forced. We might say, 'Dr. Bull, as a revolution-ist, you remember that a tyrant once advised us to eat grass; and indeed many of us, looking on the fresh lush grass of summer...'"

"Do you understand," said the other, "that this is a tragedy?"

"Perfectly," replied Syme; "always be comic in a tragedy. What the deuce else can you do? I wish this language of yours had a wider scope. I suppose we could not extend it from the fingers to the toes? That would involve pulling off our boots and socks during the conversation, which however unobtrusively performed—"

"Syme," said his friend with a stern simplicity, "go to bed!"

Syme, however, sat up in bed for a considerable time mastering the new code. He was awakened next morning while the east was still sealed with darkness, and found his grey-bearded ally standing like a ghost beside his bed.

Syme sat up in bed blinking; then slowly collected his thoughts, threw off the bed-clothes, and stood up. It seemed to him in some curious way that all the safety and sociability of the night before fell with the bedclothes off him, and he stood up in an air of cold danger. He still felt an entire trust and loyalty towards his companion; but it was the trust between two men going to the scaffold.

"Well," said Syme with a forced cheerfulness as he pulled on his trousers, "I dreamt of that alphabet of yours. Did it take you long to make it up?"

The Professor made no answer, but gazed in front of him with eyes the colour of a wintry sea; so Syme repeated his question.

"I say, did it take you long to invent all this? I'm considered good at these things, and it was a good hour's grind. Did you learn it all on the spot?"

The Professor was silent; his eyes were wide open, and he wore a fixed but very small smile.

"How long did it take you?"

The Professor did not move.

"Confound you, can't you answer?" called out Syme, in a sudden anger that had something like fear underneath. Whether or no the Professor could answer, he did not.

Syme stood staring back at the stiff face like parchment and the blank, blue eyes. His first thought was that the Professor had gone mad, but his second thought was more frightful. After all, what did he know about this queer creature whom he had heedlessly accepted as a friend? What did he know, except that the man had been at the anarchist breakfast and had told him a ridiculous tale? How improbable it was that there should be another friend there beside Gogol! Was this man's silence a sensational way of declaring war? Was this adamantine stare after all only the awful sneer of some threefold traitor, who had turned for the last time? He stood and strained his ears in this heartless silence. He almost fancied he could hear dynamiters come to capture him shifting softly in the corridor outside.

Then his eye strayed downwards, and he burst out laughing. Though the Professor himself stood there as voiceless as a statue, his five dumb fingers were dancing alive upon the dead table. Syme watched the twinkling movements of the talking hand, and read clearly the message—

"I will only talk like this. We must get used to it."

He rapped out the answer with the impatience of relief—

"All right. Let's get out to breakfast."

They took their hats and sticks in silence; but as Syme took his sword-stick, he held it hard.

They paused for a few minutes only to stuff down coffee and coarse thick sandwiches at a coffee stall, and then made their way across the river, which under the grey and growing light looked as desolate as Acheron. They reached the bottom of the huge block of buildings which they had seen from across the river, and began in silence to mount the naked and numberless stone steps, only pausing now and then to make short remarks on the rail of the banisters. At about every other flight they passed a window; each window showed them a pale and tragic dawn lifting itself laboriously over London. From each the innumerable roofs of slate looked like the leaden surges of a grey, troubled sea after rain. Syme was increasingly conscious that his new adventure had somehow a quality of cold sanity worse than the wild adventures of the past. Last night, for instance, the tall tenements had seemed to him like a tower in a dream. As he now went up the weary and perpetual steps, he was daunted and bewildered by their almost infinite series. But it was not the hot horror of a dream or of anything that might be exaggeration or delusion. Their infinity was more like the empty infinity of arithmetic, something unthinkable, yet necessary to thought. Or it was like the stunning statements of astronomy about the distance of the fixed stars. He was ascending the house of reason, a thing more hideous than unreason itself.

By the time they reached Dr. Bull's landing, a last window showed them a harsh, white dawn edged with banks of a kind of coarse red, more like red clay than red cloud. And when they entered Dr. Bull's bare garret it was full of light.

Syme had been haunted by a half historic memory in connection with these empty rooms and that austere daybreak. The moment he saw the garret and Dr. Bull sitting writing at a table, he remembered what the memory was—the French Revolution.

There should have been the black outline of a guillotine against that heavy red and white of the morning. Dr. Bull was in his white shirt and black breeches only; his cropped, dark head might well have just come out of its wig; he might have been Marat or a more slipshod Robespierre.

Yet when he was seen properly, the French fancy fell away. The Jacobins were idealists; there was about this man a murderous materialism. His position gave him a somewhat new appearance. The strong, white light of morning coming from one side creating sharp shadows, made him seem both more pale and more angular than he had looked at the breakfast on the balcony. Thus the two black glasses that encased his eyes might really have been black cavities in his skull, making him look like a death's-head. And, indeed, if ever Death himself sat writing at a wooden table, it might have been he.

He looked up and smiled brightly enough as the men came in, and rose with the resilient rapidity of which the Professor had spoken. He set chairs for both of them, and going to a peg behind the door, proceeded to put on a coat and waistcoat of rough, dark tweed; he buttoned it up neatly, and came back to sit down at his table.

The quiet good humour of his manner left his two opponents helpless. It was with some momentary difficulty that the Professor broke silence and began, "I'm sorry to disturb you so early, comrade," said he, with a careful resumption of the slow de Worms manner. "You have no doubt made all the arrangements for the Paris affair?" Then he added with infinite slowness, "We have information which renders intolerable anything in the nature of a moment's delay."

Dr. Bull smiled again, but continued to gaze on them without speaking. The Professor resumed, a pause before each weary word—

"Please do not think me excessively abrupt; but I advise you to alter those plans, or if it is too late for that, to follow your agent with all the support you can get for him. Comrade Syme and I have had an experience which it would take more time to recount than we can afford, if we are to act on it. I will, however, relate the occurrence in detail, even at the risk of losing time, if you really feel that it is essential to the understanding of the problem we have to discuss."

He was spinning out his sentences, making them intolerably long and lingering, in the hope of maddening the practical little Doctor into an explosion of impatience which might show his hand. But the little Doctor continued only to stare and smile, and the monologue was uphill work. Syme began to feel a new sickness and despair. The Doctor's smile and silence were not at all like the cataleptic stare and horrible silence which he had confronted in the Professor half an hour before. About the Professor's makeup and all his antics there was always something merely grotesque, like a gollywog. Syme remembered those wild woes of yesterday as one remembers being afraid of Bogy in childhood. But here was daylight; here was a healthy, square-shouldered man in tweeds, not odd save for the accident of his ugly spectacles, not glaring or grinning at all, but smiling steadily and not saying a word. The whole had a sense of unbearable reality. Under the increasing sunlight the colours of the Doctor's complexion, the pattern of his tweeds, grew and expanded outrageously, as such things grow too important in a realistic novel. But his smile was quite slight, the pose of his head polite; the only uncanny thing was his silence.

"As I say," resumed the Professor, like a man toiling through heavy sand, "the incident that has occurred to us and has led us to ask for information about the Marquis, is one which you may think it better to have narrated; but as it came in the way of Comrade Syme rather than me—"

His words he seemed to be dragging out like words in an anthem; but Syme, who was watching, saw his long fingers rattle quickly on the edge of the crazy table. He read the message, "You must go on. This devil has sucked me dry!"

Syme plunged into the breach with that bravado of improvisation which always came to him when he was alarmed.

"Yes, the thing really happened to me," he said hastily. "I had the good fortune to fall into conversation with a detective who took me, thanks to my hat, for a respectable person. Wishing to clinch my reputation for respectability, I took him and made him very drunk at the Savoy. Under this influence he became friendly, and told me in so many words that within a day or two they hope to arrest the Marquis in France.

"So unless you or I can get on his track—"

The Doctor was still smiling in the most friendly way, and his protected eyes were still impenetrable. The Professor signalled to Syme that he would resume his explanation, and he began again with the same elaborate calm.

"Syme immediately brought this information to me, and we came here together to see what use you would be inclined to make of it. It seems to me unquestionably urgent that—"

All this time Syme had been staring at the Doctor almost as steadily as the Doctor stared at the Professor, but quite without the smile. The nerves of both comrades-in-arms were near snapping under that strain of motionless amiability, when Syme suddenly leant forward and idly tapped the edge of the table. His message to his ally ran, "I have an intuition."

The Professor, with scarcely a pause in his monologue, signalled back, "Then sit on it."

Syme telegraphed, "It is quite extraordinary."

The other answered, "Extraordinary rot!"

Syme said, "I am a poet."

The other retorted, "You are a dead man."

Syme had gone quite red up to his yellow hair, and his eyes were burning feverishly. As he said he had an intuition, and it had risen to a sort of lightheaded certainty. Resuming his symbolic taps, he signalled to his friend, "You scarcely realise how poetic my intuition is. It has that sudden quality we sometimes feel in the coming of spring."

He then studied the answer on his friend's fingers. The answer was, "Go to hell!"

The Professor then resumed his merely verbal monologue addressed to the Doctor.

"Perhaps I should rather say," said Syme on his fingers, "that it resembles that sudden smell of the sea which may be found in the heart of lush woods."

His companion disdained to reply.

"Or yet again," tapped Syme, "it is positive, as is the passionate red hair of a beautiful woman."

The Professor was continuing his speech, but in the middle of it Syme decided to act. He leant across the table, and said in a voice that could not be neglected—

"Dr. Bull!"

The Doctor's sleek and smiling head did not move, but they could have sworn that under his dark glasses his eyes darted towards Syme.

"Dr. Bull," said Syme, in a voice peculiarly precise and courteous, "would you do me a small favour? Would you be so kind as to take off your spectacles?"

The Professor swung round on his seat, and stared at Syme with a sort of frozen fury of astonishment. Syme, like a man who has thrown his life and fortune on the table, leaned forward with a fiery face. The Doctor did not move.

For a few seconds there was a silence in which one could hear a pin drop, split once by the single hoot of a distant steamer on the Thames. Then Dr. Bull rose slowly, still smiling, and took off his spectacles.

Syme sprang to his feet, stepping backwards a little, like a chemical lecturer from a successful explosion. His eyes were like stars, and for an instant he could only point without speaking.

The Professor had also started to his feet, forgetful of his supposed paralysis. He leant on the back of the chair and stared doubtfully at Dr. Bull, as if the Doctor had been turned into a toad before his eyes. And indeed it was almost as great a transformation scene.

The two detectives saw sitting in the chair before them a very boyish-looking young man, with very frank and happy hazel eyes, an open expression, cockney clothes like those of a city clerk, and an unquestionable breath about him of being very good and rather commonplace. The smile was still there, but it might have been the first smile of a baby.

"I knew I was a poet," cried Syme in a sort of ecstasy. "I knew my intuition was as infallible as the Pope. It was the spectacles that did it! It was all the spectacles. Given those beastly black eyes, and all the rest of him his health and his jolly looks, made him a live devil among dead ones."

"It certainly does make a queer difference," said the Professor shakily. "But as regards the project of Dr. Bull—"

"Project be damned!" roared Syme, beside himself. "Look at him! Look at his face, look at his collar, look at his blessed boots! You don't suppose, do you, that that thing's an anarchist?"

"Syme!" cried the other in an apprehensive agony.

"Why, by God," said Syme, "I'll take the risk of that myself! Dr. Bull, I am a police officer. There's my card," and he flung down the blue card upon the table.

The Professor still feared that all was lost; but he was loyal. He pulled out his own official card and put it beside his friend's. Then the third man burst out laughing, and for the first time that morning they heard his voice.

"I'm awfully glad you chaps have come so early," he said, with a sort of schoolboy flippancy, "for we can all start for France together. Yes, I'm in the force right enough," and he flicked a blue card towards them lightly as a matter of form.

Clapping a brisk bowler on his head and resuming his goblin glasses, the Doctor moved so quickly towards the door, that the others instinctively followed him.

Syme seemed a little distrait, and as he passed under the doorway he suddenly struck his stick on the stone passage so that it rang.

"But Lord God Almighty," he cried out, "if this is all right, there were more damned detectives than there were damned dynamiters at the damned Council!"

"We might have fought easily," said Bull; "we were four against three."

The Professor was descending the stairs, but his voice came up from below.

"No," said the voice, "we were not four against three—we were not so lucky. We were four against One."

The others went down the stairs in silence.

The young man called Bull, with an innocent courtesy characteristic of him, insisted on going last until they reached the street; but there his own robust rapidity asserted itself unconsciously, and he walked quickly on ahead towards a railway inquiry office, talking to the others over his shoulder.

"It is jolly to get some pals," he said. "I've been half dead with the jumps, being quite alone. I nearly flung my arms round Gogol and embraced him, which would have been imprudent. I hope you won't despise me for having been in a blue funk."

"All the blue devils in blue hell," said Syme, "contributed to my blue funk! But the worst devil was you and your infernal goggles."

The young man laughed delightedly.

"Wasn't it a rag?" he said. "Such a simple idea—not my own. I haven't got the brains. You see, I wanted to go into the detective service, especially the anti-dynamite business. But for that purpose they wanted someone to dress up as a dynamiter; and they all swore by blazes that I could never look like a dynamiter. They said my very walk was respectable, and that seen from behind I looked like the British Constitution. They said I looked too healthy and too optimistic, and too reliable and benevolent; they called me all sorts of names at Scotland Yard. They said that if I had been a criminal, I might have made my fortune by looking so like an honest man; but as I had the misfortune to be an honest man, there was not even the remotest chance of my assisting them by ever looking like a criminal. But at last I was brought before some old josser who was high up in the force, and who seemed to have no end of a head on his shoulders. And there the others all talked hopelessly. One asked whether a bushy beard would hide my nice smile; another said that if they blacked my face I might look like a negro anarchist; but this old chap chipped in with a most extraordinary remark. 'A pair of smoked spectacles will do it,' he said positively. 'Look at him now; he looks like an angelic office boy. Put him on a pair of smoked spectacles, and children will scream at the sight of him.' And so it was, by George! When once my eyes were covered, all the rest, smile and big shoulders and short hair, made me look a perfect little devil. As I say, it was simple enough when it was done, like miracles; but that wasn't the really miraculous part of it. There was one really staggering thing about the business, and my head still turns at it."

"What was that?" asked Syme.

"I'll tell you," answered the man in spectacles. "This big pot in the police who sized me up so that he knew how the goggles would go with my hair and socks—by God, he never saw me at all!"

Syme's eyes suddenly flashed on him.

"How was that?" he asked. "I thought you talked to him."

"So I did," said Bull brightly; "but we talked in a pitch-dark room like a coalcellar. There, you would never have guessed that."

"I could not have conceived it," said Syme gravely.

"It is indeed a new idea," said the Professor.

Their new ally was in practical matters a whirlwind. At the inquiry office he asked with businesslike brevity about the trains for Dover. Having got his information, he bundled the company into a cab, and put them and himself inside a railway carriage before they had properly realised the breathless process. They were already on the Calais boat before conversation flowed freely.

"I had already arranged," he explained, "to go to France for my lunch; but I am delighted to have someone to lunch with me. You see, I had to send that beast, the Marquis, over with his bomb, because the President had his eye on me, though God knows how. I'll tell you the story some day. It was perfectly choking. Whenever I tried to slip out of it I saw the President somewhere, smiling out of the bow-window of a club, or taking off his hat to me from the top of an omnibus. I tell you, you can say what you like, that fellow sold himself to the devil; he can be in six places at once."

"So you sent the Marquis off, I understand," asked the Professor. "Was it long ago? Shall we be in time to catch him?"

"Yes," answered the new guide, "I've timed it all. He'll still be at Calais when we arrive."

"But when we do catch him at Calais," said the Professor, "what are we going to do?"

At this question the countenance of Dr. Bull fell for the first time. He reflected a little, and then said—

"Theoretically, I suppose, we ought to call the police."

"Not I," said Syme. "Theoretically I ought to drown myself first. I promised a poor fellow, who was a real modern pessimist, on my word of honour not to tell the police. I'm no hand at casuistry, but I can't break my word to a modern pessimist. It's like breaking one's word to a child."

"I'm in the same boat," said the Professor. "I tried to tell the police and I couldn't, because of some silly oath I took. You see, when I was an actor I was a sort of all-round beast. Perjury or treason is the only crime I haven't committed. If I did that I shouldn't know the difference between right and wrong."

"I've been through all that," said Dr. Bull, "and I've made up my mind. I gave my promise to the Secretary—you know him, man who smiles upside down. My friends, that man is the most utterly unhappy man that was ever human. It may be his digestion, or his conscience, or his nerves, or his philosophy of the universe, but he's damned, he's in hell! Well, I can't turn on a man like that, and hunt him down. It's like whipping a leper. I may be mad, but that's how I feel; and there's jolly well the end of it."

"I don't think you're mad," said Syme. "I knew you would decide like that when first you—"

"Eh?" said Dr. Bull.

"When first you took off your spectacles."

Dr. Bull smiled a little, and strolled across the deck to look at the sunlit sea. Then he strolled back again, kicking his heels care-lessly, and a companionable silence fell between the three men.

"Well," said Syme, "it seems that we have all the same kind of morality or immorality, so we had better face the fact that comes of it."

"Yes," assented the Professor, "you're quite right; and we must hurry up, for I can see the Grey Nose standing out from France."

"The fact that comes of it," said Syme seriously, "is this, that we three are alone on this planet. Gogol has gone, God knows where; perhaps the President has smashed him like a fly. On the Council we are three men against three, like the Romans who held the bridge. But we are worse off than that, first because they can appeal to their organization and we cannot appeal to ours, and second because—"

"Because one of those other three men," said the Professor, "is not a man."

Syme nodded and was silent for a second or two, then he said—

"My idea is this. We must do something to keep the Marquis in Calais till tomorrow midday. I have turned over twenty schemes in my head. We cannot denounce him as a dynamiter; that is agreed. We cannot get him detained on some trivial charge, for we should have to appear; he knows us, and he would smell a rat. We cannot pretend to keep him on anarchist business; he might swallow much in that way, but not the notion of stopping in Calais while the Czar went safely through Paris. We might try to kidnap him, and lock him up ourselves; but he is a well-known man here. He has a whole bodyguard of friends; he is very strong and brave, and the event is doubtful. The only thing I can see to do is actu-ally to take advantage of the very things that are in the Marquis's favour. I am going to profit by the fact that he is a highly respected nobleman. I am going to profit by the fact that he has many friends and moves in the best society."

"What the devil are you talking about?" asked the Professor.

"The Symes are first mentioned in the fourteenth century," said Syme; "but there is a tradition that one of them rode behind Bruce at Bannockburn. Since 1350 the tree is quite clear."

"He's gone off his head," said the little Doctor, staring.

"Our bearings," continued Syme calmly, "are 'argent a chevron gules charged with three cross crosslets of the field.' The motto varies."

The Professor seized Syme roughly by the waistcoat.

"We are just inshore," he said. "Are you seasick or joking in the wrong place?"

"My remarks are almost painfully practical," answered Syme, in an unhurried manner. "The house of St. Eustache also is very ancient. The Marquis cannot deny that he is a gentleman. He cannot deny that I am a gentleman. And in order to put the matter of my social position quite beyond a doubt, I propose at the earliest opportunity to knock his hat off. But here we are in the harbour."

They went on shore under the strong sun in a sort of daze. Syme, who had now taken the lead as Bull had taken it in London, led them along a kind of marine parade until he came to some cafés, embowered in a bulk of greenery and overlooking the sea. As he went before them his step was slightly swaggering, and he swung his stick like a sword. He was making apparently for the extreme end of the line of cafés, but he stopped abruptly. With a sharp gesture he motioned them to silence, but he pointed with one gloved finger to a café table under a bank of flowering foliage at which sat the Marquis de St. Eustache, his teeth shining in his thick, black beard, and his bold, brown face shadowed by a light yellow straw hat and outlined against the violet sea.

CHAPTER X

The Duel

Syme sat down at a café table with his companions, his blue eyes sparkling like the bright sea below, and ordered a bottle of Saumur with a pleased impatience. He was for some reason in a condition of curious hilarity. His spirits were already unnaturally high; they rose as the Saumur sank, and in half an hour his talk was a torrent of nonsense. He professed to be making out a plan of the conversation which was going to ensue between himself and the deadly Marquis. He jotted it down wildly with a pencil. It was arranged like a printed catechism, with questions and answers, and was delivered with an extraordinary rapidity of utterance.

"I shall approach. Before taking off his hat, I shall take off my own. I shall say, 'The Marquis de Saint Eustache, I believe.' He will say, 'The celebrated Mr. Syme, I presume.' He will say in the most exquisite French, 'How are you?' I shall reply in the most exquisite Cockney, 'Oh, just the Syme—'"

"Oh, shut it," said the man in spectacles. "Pull yourself together, and chuck away that bit of paper. What are you really going to do?"

"But it was a lovely catechism," said Syme pathetically. "Do let me read it you. It has only forty-three questions and answers, and some of the Marquis's answers are wonderfully witty. I like to be just to my enemy."

"But what's the good of it all?" asked Dr. Bull in exasperation.

"It leads up to my challenge, don't you see," said Syme, beaming. "When the Marquis has given the thirty-ninth reply, which runs—"

"Has it by any chance occurred to you," asked the Professor, with a ponderous simplicity, "that the Marquis may not say all the forty-three things you have put down for him? In that case, I understand, your own epigrams may appear somewhat more forced."

Syme struck the table with a radiant face.

"Why, how true that is," he said, "and I never thought of it. Sir, you have an intellect beyond the common. You will make a name."

"Oh, you're as drunk as an owl!" said the Doctor.

"It only remains," continued Syme quite unperturbed, "to adopt some other method of breaking the ice (if I may so express it) between myself and the man I wish to kill. And since the course of a dialogue cannot be predicted by one of its parties alone (as you have pointed out with such recondite acumen), the only thing to be done, I suppose, is for the one party, as far as possible, to do all the dialogue by himself. And so I will, by George!" And he stood up suddenly, his yellow hair blowing in the slight sea breeze.

A band was playing in a *café chantant* hidden somewhere among the trees, and a woman had just stopped singing. On Syme's heated head the bray of the brass band seemed like the jar and jingle of that barrel-organ in Leicester Square, to the tune of which he had once stood up to die. He looked across to the little table where the Marquis sat. The man had two companions now, solemn Frenchmen in frock-coats and silk hats, one of them with the red rosette of the Legion of Honour, evidently people of a solid social position. Besides these black, cylindrical costumes, the Marquis, in his loose straw hat and light spring clothes, looked Bohemian and even barbaric; but he looked the Marquis. Indeed, one might say that he looked the king, with his animal elegance, his scornful eyes, and his proud head lifted against the purple sea. But he was no Christian king, at any rate; he was, rather, some swarthy despot, half Greek, half Asiatic, who in the days when slavery seemed natural looked down on the Mediterranean, on his galley and his groaning slaves. Just so, Syme thought, would the brown-gold face of such a tyrant have shown against the dark green olives and the burning blue.

"Are you going to address the meeting?" asked the Professor peevishly, seeing that Syme still stood up without moving.

Syme drained his last glass of sparkling wine.

"I am," he said, pointing across to the Marquis and his companions, "that meeting. That meeting displeases me. I am going to pull that meeting's great ugly, mahogany-coloured nose."

He stepped across swiftly, if not quite steadily. The Marquis, seeing him, arched his black Assyrian eyebrows in surprise, but smiled politely.

"You are Mr. Syme, I think," he said.

Syme bowed.

"And you are the Marquis de Saint Eustache," he said gracefully. "Permit me to pull your nose."

He leant over to do so, but the Marquis started backwards, upsetting his chair, and the two men in top hats held Syme back by the shoulders.

"This man has insulted me!" said Syme, with gestures of explanation.

"Insulted you?" cried the gentleman with the red rosette, "when?"

"Oh, just now," said Syme recklessly. "He insulted my mother."

"Insulted your mother!" exclaimed the gentleman incredulously.

"Well, anyhow," said Syme, conceding a point, "my aunt."

"But how can the Marquis have insulted your aunt just now?" said the second gentleman with some legitimate wonder. "He has been sitting here all the time."

"Ah, it was what he said!" said Syme darkly.

"I said nothing at all," said the Marquis, "except something about the band. I only said that I liked Wagner played well."

"It was an allusion to my family," said Syme firmly. "My aunt played Wagner badly. It was a painful subject. We are always being insulted about it."

"This seems most extraordinary," said the gentleman who was decore, looking doubtfully at the Marquis.

"Oh, I assure you," said Syme earnestly, "the whole of your conversation was simply packed with sinister allusions to my aunt's weaknesses."

"This is nonsense!" said the second gentleman. "I for one have said nothing for half an hour except that I liked the singing of that girl with black hair."

"Well, there you are again!" said Syme indignantly. "My aunt's was red."

"It seems to me," said the other, "that you are simply seeking a pretext to insult the Marquis."

"By George!" said Syme, facing round and looking at him, "what a clever chap you are!"

The Marquis started up with eyes flaming like a tiger's.

"Seeking a quarrel with me!" he cried. "Seeking a fight with me! By God! there was never a man who had to seek long. These gentlemen will perhaps act for me. There are still four hours of daylight. Let us fight this evening."

Syme bowed with a quite beautiful graciousness.

"Marquis," he said, "your action is worthy of your fame and blood. Permit me to consult for a moment with the gentlemen in whose hands I shall place myself."

In three long strides he rejoined his companions, and they, who had seen his champagne-inspired attack and listened to his idiotic explanations, were quite startled at the look of him. For now that he came back to them he was quite sober, a little pale, and he spoke in a low voice of passionate practicality.

"I have done it," he said hoarsely. "I have fixed a fight on the beast. But look here, and listen carefully. There is no time for talk. You are my seconds, and everything must come from you. Now you must insist, and insist absolutely, on the duel coming off after seven tomorrow, so as to give me the chance of preventing him from catching the 7.45 for Paris. If he misses that he misses his crime. He can't refuse to meet you on such a small point of time and place. But this is what he will do. He will choose a field somewhere near a wayside station, where he can pick up the train. He is a very good swordsman, and he will trust to killing me in time to catch it. But I can fence well too, and I think I can keep him in play, at any rate, until the train is lost. Then perhaps he may kill me to console his feelings. You understand? Very well then, let me introduce you to some charming friends of mine," and leading them quickly across the parade, he presented them to the Marquis's seconds by two very aristocratic names of which they had not previously heard.

Syme was subject to spasms of singular common sense, not otherwise a part of his character. They were (as he said of his impulse about the spectacles) poetic intuitions, and they sometimes rose to the exaltation of prophecy.

He had correctly calculated in this case the policy of his opponent. When the Marquis was informed by his seconds that Syme could only fight in the morning, he must fully have realised that an obstacle had suddenly arisen between him and his bomb-throwing business in the capital. Naturally he could not explain this objection to his friends, so he chose the course which Syme had predicted. He induced his seconds to settle on a small meadow not far from the railway, and he trusted to the fatality of the first engagement.

When he came down very coolly to the field of honour, no one could have guessed that he had any anxiety about a journey; his hands were in his pockets, his straw hat on the back of his head, his handsome face brazen in the sun. But it might have struck a stranger as odd that there appeared in his train, not only his seconds carrying the sword-case, but two of his servants carrying a portmanteau and a luncheon basket.

Early as was the hour, the sun soaked everything in warmth, and Syme was vaguely surprised to see so many spring flowers burning gold and silver in the tall grass in which the whole company stood almost knee-deep.

With the exception of the Marquis, all the men were in sombre and solemn morning-dress, with hats like black chimney-pots; the little Doctor especially, with the addition of his black spectacles, looked like an undertaker in a farce. Syme could not help feeling a comic contrast between this funereal church parade of apparel and the rich and glistening meadow, growing wild flowers everywhere. But, indeed, this comic contrast between the yellow blossoms and the black hats was but a symbol of the tragic contrast between the yellow blossoms and the black business. On his right was a little wood; far away to his left lay the long curve of the railway line, which he was, so to speak, guarding from the Marquis, whose goal and escape it was. In front of him, behind the black group of his opponents, he could see, like a tinted cloud, a small almond bush in flower against the faint line of the sea.

The member of the Legion of Honour, whose name it seemed was Colonel Ducroix, approached the Professor and Dr. Bull with great politeness, and suggested that the play should terminate with the first considerable hurt.

Dr. Bull, however, having been carefully coached by Syme upon this point of policy, insisted, with great dignity and in very bad French, that it should continue until one of the combatants was disabled. Syme had made up his mind that he could avoid disabling the Marquis and prevent the Marquis from disabling him for at least twenty minutes. In twenty minutes the Paris train would have gone by.

"To a man of the well-known skill and valour of Monsieur de St. Eustache," said the Professor solemnly, "it must be a matter of indifference which method is adopted, and our principal has strong reasons for demanding the longer encounter, reasons the delicacy of which prevent me from being explicit, but for the just and honourable nature of which I can—"

"*Peste!*" broke from the Marquis behind, whose face had suddenly darkened, "let us stop talking and begin," and he slashed off the head of a tall flower with his stick.

Syme understood his rude impatience and instinctively looked over his shoulder to see whether the train was coming in sight. But there was no smoke on the horizon.

Colonel Ducroix knelt down and unlocked the case, taking out a pair of twin swords, which took the sunlight and turned to two streaks of white fire. He offered one to the Marquis, who snatched it without ceremony, and another to Syme, who took it, bent it, and poised it with as much delay as was consistent with dignity.

Then the Colonel took out another pair of blades, and taking one himself and giving another to Dr. Bull, proceeded to place the men.

Both combatants had thrown off their coats and waistcoats, and stood sword in hand. The seconds stood on each side of the line of fight with drawn swords also, but still sombre in their dark frock-coats and hats. The principals saluted. The Colonel said quietly, "Engage!" and the two blades touched and tingled.

When the jar of the joined iron ran up Syme's arm, all the fantastic fears that have been the subject of this story fell from him like dreams from a man waking up in bed. He remembered them clearly and in order as mere delusions of the nerves—how the fear of the Professor had been the fear of the tyrannic accidents of nightmare, and how the fear of the Doctor had been the fear of the airless vacuum of science. The first was the old fear that any miracle might happen, the second the more hopeless modern fear that no miracle can ever happen. But he saw that these fears were fancies, for he found himself in the presence of the great fact of the fear of death, with its coarse and pitiless common sense. He felt like a man who had dreamed all night of falling over precipices, and had woke up on the morning when he was to be hanged. For as soon as he had seen the sunlight run down the channel of his foe's foreshortened blade, and as soon as he had felt the two tongues of steel touch, vibrating like two living things, he knew that his enemy was a terrible fighter, and that probably his last hour had come.

He felt a strange and vivid value in all the earth around him, in the grass under his feet; he felt the love of life in all living things. He could almost fancy that he heard the grass growing; he could almost fancy that even as he stood fresh flowers were springing up and breaking into blossom in the meadow—flowers blood red and burning gold and blue, fulfilling the whole pageant of the spring. And whenever his eyes strayed for a flash from the calm, staring, hypnotic eyes of the Marquis, they saw the little tuft of almond tree against the sky-line. He had the feeling that if by some miracle he escaped he would be ready to sit for ever before that almond tree, desiring nothing else in the world.

But while earth and sky and everything had the living beauty of a thing lost, the other half of his head was as clear as glass, and he was parrying his enemy's point with a kind of clockwork skill of which he had hardly supposed himself capable. Once his enemy's point ran along his wrist, leaving a slight streak of blood, but it either was not noticed or was tacitly ignored. Every now and then he *riposted*, and once or twice he could almost fancy that he felt his point go home, but as there was no blood on blade or shirt he supposed he was mistaken. Then came an interruption and a change.

At the risk of losing all, the Marquis, interrupting his quiet stare, flashed one glance over his shoulder at the line of railway on his right. Then he turned on Syme a face transfigured to that of a fiend, and began to fight as if with twenty weapons. The attack came so fast and furious, that the one shining sword seemed a shower of shining arrows. Syme had no chance to look at the railway; but also he had no need. He could guess the reason of the Marquis's sudden madness of battle—the Paris train was in sight.

But the Marquis's morbid energy over-reached itself. Twice Syme, parrying, knocked his opponent's point far out of the fighting circle; and the third time his *riposte* was so rapid, that there was no doubt about the hit this time. Syme's sword actually bent under the weight of the Marquis's body, which it had pierced.

Syme was as certain that he had stuck his blade into his enemy as a gardener that he has stuck his spade into the ground. Yet the Marquis sprang back from the stroke without a stagger, and Syme stood staring at his own sword-point like an idiot. There was no blood on it at all.

There was an instant of rigid silence, and then Syme in his turn fell furiously on the other, filled with a flaming curiosity. The Marquis was probably, in a general sense, a better fencer than he, as he had surmised at the beginning, but at the moment the Marquis seemed distraught and at a disadvantage. He fought wildly and even weakly, and he constantly looked away at the railway line, almost as if he feared the train more than the pointed steel. Syme, on the other hand, fought fiercely but still carefully, in an intellectual fury, eager to solve the riddle of his own bloodless sword. For this purpose, he aimed less at the Marquis's body, and more at his throat and head. A minute and a half afterwards he felt his point enter the man's neck below the jaw. It came out clean. Half mad, he thrust again, and made what should have been a bloody scar on the Marquis's cheek. But there was no scar.

For one moment the heaven of Syme again grew black with supernatural terrors. Surely the man had a charmed life. But this new spiritual dread was a more awful thing than had been the mere spiritual topsy-turvydom symbolised by the paralytic who pursued him. The Professor was only a goblin; this man was a devil—perhaps he was the Devil! Anyhow, this was certain, that three times had a human sword been driven into him and made no mark. When Syme had that thought he drew himself up, and all that was good in him sang high up in the air as a high wind sings in the trees. He thought of all the human things in his story—of the Chinese lanterns in Saffron Park, of the girl's red hair in the garden, of the honest, beer-swilling sailors down by the dock, of his loyal companions standing by. Perhaps he had been chosen as a champion of all these fresh and kindly things to cross swords with the enemy of all creation. "After all," he said to himself, "I am more than a devil; I am a man. I can do the one thing which Satan himself cannot do—I can die," and as the word went through his head, he heard a faint and far-off hoot, which would soon be the roar of the Paris train.

He fell to fighting again with a supernatural levity, like a Mohammedan panting for Paradise. As the train came nearer and nearer he fancied he could see people putting up the floral arches in Paris; he joined in the growing noise and the glory of the great Republic whose gate he was guarding against Hell. His thoughts rose higher and higher with the rising roar of the train, which ended, as if proudly, in a long and piercing whistle. The train stopped.

Suddenly, to the astonishment of everyone the Marquis sprang back quite out of sword reach and threw down his sword. The leap was wonderful, and not the less wonderful because Syme had plunged his sword a moment before into the man's thigh.

"Stop!" said the Marquis in a voice that compelled a momentary obedience. "I want to say something."

"What is the matter?" asked Colonel Ducroix, staring. "Has there been foul play?"

"There has been foul play somewhere," said Dr. Bull, who was a little pale. "Our principal has wounded the Marquis four times at least, and he is none the worse."

The Marquis put up his hand with a curious air of ghastly patience.

"Please let me speak," he said. "It is rather important. Mr. Syme," he continued, turning to his opponent, "we are fighting today, if I remember right, because you expressed a wish (which I thought irrational) to pull my nose. Would you oblige me by pulling my nose now as quickly as possible? I have to catch a train."

"I protest that this is most irregular," said Dr. Bull indignantly.

"It is certainly somewhat opposed to precedent," said Colonel Ducroix, looking wistfully at his principal. "There is, I think, one case on record (Captain Bellegarde and the Baron Zumpt) in which the weapons were changed in the middle of the encounter at the request of one of the combatants. But one can hardly call one's nose a weapon."

"Will you or will you not pull my nose?" said the Marquis in exasperation. "Come, come, Mr. Syme! You wanted to do it, do it! You can have no conception of how important it is to me. Don't be so selfish! Pull my nose at once, when I ask you!" and he bent slightly forward with a fascinating smile. The Paris train, panting and groaning, had grated into a little station behind the neighbouring hill.

Syme had the feeling he had more than once had in these adventures—the sense that a horrible and sublime wave lifted to heaven was just toppling over. Walking in a world he half understood, he took two paces forward and seized the Roman nose of this remarkable nobleman. He pulled it hard, and it came off in his hand.

He stood for some seconds with a foolish solemnity, with the pasteboard proboscis still between his fingers, looking at it, while the sun and the clouds and the wooded hills looked down upon this imbecile scene.

The Marquis broke the silence in a loud and cheerful voice.

"If anyone has any use for my left eyebrow," he said, "he can have it. Colonel Ducroix, do accept my left eyebrow! It's the kind of thing that might come in useful any day," and he gravely tore off one of his swarthy Assyrian brows, bringing about half his brown forehead with it, and politely offered it to the Colonel, who stood crimson and speechless with rage.

"If I had known," he spluttered, "that I was acting for a poltroon who pads himself to fight—"

"Oh, I know, I know!" said the Marquis, recklessly throwing various parts of himself right and left about the field. "You are making a mistake; but it can't be explained just now. I tell you the train has come into the station!"

"Yes," said Dr. Bull fiercely, "and the train shall go out of the station. It shall go out without you. We know well enough for what devil's work—"

The mysterious Marquis lifted his hands with a desperate gesture. He was a strange scarecrow standing there in the sun with half his old face peeled off, and half another face glaring and grinning from underneath.

"Will you drive me mad?" he cried. "The train—"

"You shall not go by the train," said Syme firmly, and grasped his sword.

The wild figure turned towards Syme, and seemed to be gathering itself for a sublime effort before speaking.

"You great fat, blasted, blear-eyed, blundering, thundering, brainless, Godforsaken, doddering, damned fool!" he said without taking breath. "You great silly, pink-faced, towheaded turnip! You—"

"You shall not go by this train," repeated Syme.

"And why the infernal blazes," roared the other, "should I want to go by the train?"

"We know all," said the Professor sternly. "You are going to Paris to throw a bomb!"

"Going to Jericho to throw a Jabberwock!" cried the other, tearing his hair, which came off easily.

"Have you all got softening of the brain, that you don't real-ise what I am? Did you really think I wanted to catch that train? Twenty Paris trains might go by for me. Damn Paris trains!"

"Then what did you care about?" began the Professor.

"What did I care about? I didn't care about catching the train; I cared about whether the train caught me, and now, by God! it has caught me."

"I regret to inform you," said Syme with restraint, "that your remarks convey no impression to my mind. Perhaps if you were to remove the remains of your original forehead and some portion of what was once your chin, your meaning would become clearer. Mental lucidity fulfils itself in many ways. What do you mean by saying that the train has caught you? It may be my literary fancy, but somehow I feel that it ought to mean something."

"It means everything," said the other, "and the end of every-thing. Sunday has us now in the hollow of his hand."

"Us!" repeated the Professor, as if stupefied. "What do you mean by 'us'?"

"The police, of course!" said the Marquis, and tore off his scalp and half his face.

The head which emerged was the blonde, well brushed, smooth-haired head which is common in the English constabu-lary, but the face was terribly pale.

"I am Inspector Ratcliffe," he said, with a sort of haste that verged on harshness. "My name is pretty well known to the police, and I can see well enough that you belong to them. But if there is any doubt about my position, I have a card," and he began to pull a blue card from his pocket.

The Professor gave a tired gesture.

"Oh, don't show it us," he said wearily; "we've got enough of them to equip a paper-chase."

The little man named Bull, had, like many men who seem to be of a mere vivacious vulgarity, sudden movements of good taste. Here he certainly saved the situation. In the midst of this staggering transformation scene he stepped forward with all the gravity and responsibility of a second, and addressed the two seconds of the Marquis.

"Gentlemen," he said, "we all owe you a serious apology; but I assure you that you have not been made the victims of such a low joke as you imagine, or indeed of anything undignified in a man of honour. You have not wasted your time; you have helped to save the world. We are not buffoons, but very desperate men at war with a vast conspiracy. A secret society of anarchists is hunting us like hares; not such unfortunate madmen as may here or there throw a bomb through starvation or German philosophy, but a rich and powerful and fanatical church, a church of eastern pessimism, which holds it holy to destroy mankind like vermin. How hard they hunt us you can gather from the fact that we are driven to such disguises as those for which I apologise, and to such pranks as this one by which you suffer."

The younger second of the Marquis, a short man with a black moustache, bowed politely, and said—

"Of course, I accept the apology; but you will in your turn forgive me if I decline to follow you further into your difficulties, and permit myself to say good morning! The sight of an acquaintance and distinguished fellow-townsman coming to pieces in the open air is unusual, and, upon the whole, sufficient for one day. Colonel Ducroix, I would in no way influence your actions, but if you feel with me that our present society is a little abnormal, I am now going to walk back to the town."

Colonel Ducroix moved mechanically, but then tugged abruptly at his white moustache and broke out—

"No, by George! I won't. If these gentlemen are really in a mess with a lot of low wreckers like that, I'll see them through it. I have fought for France, and it is hard if I can't fight for civilization."

Dr. Bull took off his hat and waved it, cheering as at a public meeting.

"Don't make too much noise," said Inspector Ratcliffe, "Sunday may hear you."

"Sunday!" cried Bull, and dropped his hat.

"Yes," retorted Ratcliffe, "he may be with them."

"With whom?" asked Syme.

"With the people out of that train," said the other.

"What you say seems utterly wild," began Syme. "Why, as a matter of fact—But, my God," he cried out suddenly, like a man who sees an explosion a long way off, "by God! if this is true the whole bally lot of us on the Anarchist Council were against anarchy! Every born man was a detective except the President and his personal secretary. What can it mean?"

"Mean!" said the new policeman with incredible violence. "It means that we are struck dead! Don't you know Sunday? Don't you know that his jokes are always so big and simple that one has never thought of them? Can you think of anything more like Sunday than this, that he should put all his powerful enemies on the Supreme Council, and then take care that it was not supreme? I tell you he has bought every trust, he has captured every cable, he has control of every railway line—especially of *that* railway line!" and he pointed a shaking finger towards the small wayside station. "The whole movement was controlled by him; half the world was ready to rise for him. But there were just five people, perhaps, who would have resisted him... and the old devil put them on the Supreme Council, to waste their time in watching each other. Idiots that we are, he planned the whole of our idiocies! Sunday knew that the Professor would chase Syme through London, and that Syme would fight me in France. And he was combining great masses of capital, and seizing great lines of telegraphy, while we five idiots were running after each other like a lot of confounded babies playing blind man's buff."

"Well?" asked Syme with a sort of steadiness.

"Well," replied the other with sudden serenity, "he has found us playing blind man's buff today in a field of great rustic beauty and extreme solitude. He has probably captured the world; it only remains to him to capture this field and all the fools in it. And since you really want to know what was my objection to the arrival of that train, I will tell you. My objection was that Sunday or his Secretary has just this moment got out of it."

Syme uttered an involuntary cry, and they all turned their eyes towards the far-off station. It was quite true that a considerable bulk of people seemed to be moving in their direction. But they were too distant to be distinguished in any way.

"It was a habit of the late Marquis de St. Eustache," said the new policeman, producing a leather case, "always to carry a pair of opera glasses. Either the President or the Secretary is coming after us with that mob. They have caught us in a nice quiet place where we are under no temptations to break our oaths by calling the police. Dr. Bull, I have a suspicion that you will see better through these than through your own highly decorative spectacles."

He handed the field-glasses to the Doctor, who immediately took off his spectacles and put the apparatus to his eyes.

"It cannot be as bad as you say," said the Professor, somewhat shaken. "There are a good number of them certainly, but they may easily be ordinary tourists."

"Do ordinary tourists," asked Bull, with the fieldglasses to his eyes, "wear black masks half-way down the face?"

Syme almost tore the glasses out of his hand, and looked through them. Most men in the advancing mob really looked ordinary enough; but it was quite true that two or three of the leaders in front wore black half-masks almost down to their mouths. This disguise is very complete, especially at such a distance, and Syme found it impossible to conclude anything from the clean-shaven jaws and chins of the men talking in the front. But presently as they talked they all smiled and one of them smiled on one side.

CHAPTER XI

The Criminals Chase the Police

S yme put the field-glasses from his eyes with an almost ghastly
relief.

"The President is not with them, anyhow," he said, and wiped
his forehead.

"But surely they are right away on the horizon," said the bewildered Colonel, blinking and but half recovered from Bull's hasty
though polite explanation. "Could you possibly know your President among all those people?"

"Could I know a white elephant among all those people!"
answered Syme somewhat irritably. "As you very truly say, they are
on the horizon; but if he were walking with them... by God! I
believe this ground would shake."

After an instant's pause the new man called Ratcliffe said with
gloomy decision—

"Of course the President isn't with them. I wish to Gemini he
were. Much more likely the President is riding in triumph through
Paris, or sitting on the ruins of St. Paul's Cathedral."

"This is absurd!" said Syme. "Something may have happened in
our absence; but he cannot have carried the world with a rush like
that. It is quite true," he added, frowning dubiously at the distant
fields that lay towards the little station, "it is certainly true that
there seems to be a crowd coming this way; but they are not all the
army that you make out."

"Oh, they," said the new detective contemptuously; "no they

are not a very valuable force. But let me tell you frankly that they are precisely calculated to our value—we are not much, my boy, in Sunday's universe. He has got hold of all the cables and telegraphs himself. But to kill the Supreme Council he regards as a trivial matter, like a post card; it may be left to his private secretary," and he spat on the grass.

Then he turned to the others and said somewhat austerely—

"There is a great deal to be said for death; but if anyone has any preference for the other alternative, I strongly advise him to walk after me."

With these words, he turned his broad back and strode with silent energy towards the wood. The others gave one glance over their shoulders, and saw that the dark cloud of men had detached itself from the station and was moving with a mysterious discipline across the plain. They saw already, even with the naked eye, black blots on the foremost faces, which marked the masks they wore. They turned and followed their leader, who had already struck the wood, and disappeared among the twinkling trees.

The sun on the grass was dry and hot. So in plunging into the wood they had a cool shock of shadow, as of divers who plunge into a dim pool. The inside of the wood was full of shattered sunlight and shaken shadows. They made a sort of shuddering veil, almost recalling the dizziness of a cinematograph. Even the solid figures walking with him Syme could hardly see for the patterns of sun and shade that danced upon them. Now a man's head was lit as with a light of Rembrandt, leaving all else obliterated; now again he had strong and staring white hands with the face of a negro. The ex-Marquis had pulled the old straw hat over his eyes, and the black shade of the brim cut his face so squarely in two that it seemed to be wearing one of the black half-masks of their pursuers. The fancy tinted Syme's overwhelming sense of wonder. Was he wearing a mask? Was anyone wearing a mask? Was anyone anything? This wood of witchery, in which men's faces turned black and white by turns, in which their figures first swelled into sunlight and then faded into formless night, this mere chaos of chiaroscuro (after the clear daylight outside), seemed to Syme a perfect symbol of the world in which he had been moving for three days, this world where men took off their beards and their spectacles and their noses, and turned into other people. That tragic self-confidence which he had felt when he believed that the Marquis was a devil had strangely disappeared now that he knew that the Marquis was a friend. He felt almost inclined to ask after all these bewilderments what was a friend and what an enemy. Was there anything that was apart from what it seemed? The Marquis had taken off his nose and turned out to be a detective. Might he not just as well take off his head and turn out to be a hobgoblin? Was not everything, after all, like this bewildering woodland, this dance of dark and light? Everything only a glimpse, the glimpse always unforeseen, and always forgotten. For Gabriel Syme had found in the heart of that sun-splashed wood what many modern painters had found there. He had found the thing which the modern people call Impressionism, which is another name for that final scepticism which can find no floor to the universe.

As a man in an evil dream strains himself to scream and wake, Syme strove with a sudden effort to fling off this last and worst of his fancies. With two impatient strides he overtook the man in the Marquis's straw hat, the man whom he had come to address as Ratcliffe. In a voice exaggeratively loud and cheerful, he broke the bottomless silence and made conversation.

"May I ask," he said, "where on earth we are all going to?"

So genuine had been the doubts of his soul, that he was quite glad to hear his companion speak in an easy, human voice.

"We must get down through the town of Lancy to the sea," he said. "I think that part of the country is least likely to be with them."

"What can you mean by all this?" cried Syme. "They can't be running the real world in that way. Surely not many working men are anarchists, and surely if they were, mere mobs could not beat modern armies and police."

"Mere mobs!" repeated his new friend with a snort of scorn. "So you talk about mobs and the working classes as if they were the question. You've got that eternal idiotic idea that if anarchy came it would come from the poor. Why should it? The poor have been rebels, but they have never been anarchists; they have more interest than anyone else in there being some decent government. The poor man really has a stake in the country. The rich man hasn't; he can go away to New Guinea in a yacht. The poor have sometimes objected to being governed badly; the rich have always objected to being governed at all. Aristocrats were always anarchists, as you can see from the barons' wars."

"As a lecture on English history for the little ones," said Syme, "this is all very nice; but I have not yet grasped its application."

"Its application is," said his informant, "that most of old Sunday's right-hand men are South African and American millionaires. That is why he has got hold of all the communications; and that is why the last four champions of the anti-anarchist police force are running through a wood like rabbits."

"Millionaires I can understand," said Syme thoughtfully, "they are nearly all mad. But getting hold of a few wicked old gentlemen with hobbies is one thing; getting hold of great Christian nations is another. I would bet the nose off my face (forgive the allusion) that Sunday would stand perfectly helpless before the task of converting any ordinary healthy person anywhere."

"Well," said the other, "it rather depends what sort of person you mean."

"Well, for instance," said Syme, "he could never convert that person," and he pointed straight in front of him.

They had come to an open space of sunlight, which seemed to express to Syme the final return of his own good sense; and in the middle of this forest clearing was a figure that might well stand for that common sense in an almost awful actuality. Burnt by the sun and stained with perspiration, and grave with the bottomless gravity of small necessary toils, a heavy French peasant was cutting wood with a hatchet. His cart stood a few yards off, already half full of timber; and the horse that cropped the grass was, like his master, valorous but not desperate; like his master, he was even prosperous, but yet was almost sad. The man was a Norman, taller than the average of the French and very angular; and his swarthy figure stood dark against a square of sunlight, almost like some allegoric figure of labour frescoed on a ground of gold.

"Mr. Syme is saying," called out Ratcliffe to the French Colonel, "that this man, at least, will never be an anarchist."

"Mr. Syme is right enough there," answered Colonel Ducroix, laughing, "if only for the reason that he has plenty of property to defend. But I forgot that in your country you are not used to peasants being wealthy."

"He looks poor," said Dr. Bull doubtfully.

"Quite so," said the Colonel; "that is why he is rich."

"I have an idea," called out Dr. Bull suddenly; "how much would he take to give us a lift in his cart? Those dogs are all on foot, and we could soon leave them behind."

"Oh, give him anything!" said Syme eagerly. "I have piles of money on me."

"That will never do," said the Colonel; "he will never have any respect for you unless you drive a bargain."

"Oh, if he haggles!" began Bull impatiently.

"He haggles because he is a free man," said the other. "You do not understand; he would not see the meaning of generosity. He is not being tipped."

And even while they seemed to hear the heavy feet of their strange pursuers behind them, they had to stand and stamp while the French Colonel talked to the French wood-cutter with all the leisurely badinage and bickering of market-day. At the end of the four minutes, however, they saw that the Colonel was right, for the wood-cutter entered into their plans, not with the vague servility of a tout too-well paid, but with the seriousness of a solicitor who had been paid the proper fee. He told them that the best thing they could do was to make their way down to the little inn on the hills above Lancy, where the innkeeper, an old soldier who had become devout in his latter years, would be certain to sympathise with them, and even to take risks in their support. The whole company, therefore, piled themselves on top of the stacks of wood, and went rocking in the rude cart down the other and steeper side of the woodland. Heavy and ramshackle as was the vehicle, it was driven quickly enough, and they soon had the exhilarating impression of distancing altogether those, whoever they were, who were hunting them. For, after all, the riddle as to where the anarchists had got all these followers was still unsolved. One man's presence had sufficed for them; they had fled at the first sight of the deformed smile of the Secretary. Syme every now and then looked back over his shoulder at the army on their track.

As the wood grew first thinner and then smaller with distance, he could see the sunlit slopes beyond it and above it; and across these was still moving the square black mob like one monstrous beetle. In the very strong sunlight and with his own very strong eyes, which were almost telescopic, Syme could see this mass of men quite plainly. He could see them as separate human figures; but he was increasingly surprised by the way in which they moved as one man. They seemed to be dressed in dark clothes and plain hats, like any common crowd out of the streets; but they did not spread and sprawl and trail by various lines to the attack, as would be natural in an ordinary mob. They moved with a sort of dreadful and wicked woodenness, like a staring army of automatons.

Syme pointed this out to Ratcliffe.

"Yes," replied the policeman, "that's discipline. That's Sunday. He is perhaps five hundred miles off, but the fear of him is on all of them, like the finger of God. Yes, they are walking regularly; and you bet your boots that they are talking regularly, yes, and thinking regularly. But the one important thing for us is that they are disappearing regularly."

Syme nodded. It was true that the black patch of the pursuing men was growing smaller and smaller as the peasant belaboured his horse.

The level of the sunlit landscape, though flat as a whole, fell away on the farther side of the wood in billows of heavy slope towards the sea, in a way not unlike the lower slopes of the Sussex downs. The only difference was that in Sussex the road would have been broken and angular like a little brook, but here the white French road fell sheer in front of them like a waterfall. Down this direct descent the cart clattered at a considerable angle, and in a few minutes, the road growing yet steeper, they saw below them the little harbour of Lancy and a great blue arc of the sea. The travelling cloud of their enemies had wholly disappeared from the horizon.

The horse and cart took a sharp turn round a clump of elms, and the horse's nose nearly struck the face of an old gentleman who was sitting on the benches outside the little café of "Le Soleil d'Or." The peasant grunted an apology, and got down from his seat. The others also descended one by one, and spoke to the old gentleman with fragmentary phrases of courtesy, for it was quite evident from his expansive manner that he was the owner of the little tavern.

He was a white-haired, apple-faced old boy, with sleepy eyes and a grey moustache; stout, sedentary, and very innocent, of a type that may often be found in France, but is still commoner in Catholic Germany. Everything about him, his pipe, his pot of beer, his flowers, and his beehive, suggested an ancestral peace; only when his visitors looked up as they entered the inn-parlour, they saw the sword upon the wall.

The Colonel, who greeted the innkeeper as an old friend, passed rapidly into the inn-parlour, and sat down ordering some ritual refreshment. The military decision of his action interested Syme, who sat next to him, and he took the opportunity when the old innkeeper had gone out of satisfying his curiosity.

"May I ask you, Colonel," he said in a low voice, "why we have come here?"

Colonel Ducroix smiled behind his bristly white moustache.

"For two reasons, sir," he said; "and I will give first, not the most important, but the most utilitarian. We came here because this is the only place within twenty miles in which we can get horses."

"Horses!" repeated Syme, looking up quickly.

"Yes," replied the other; "if you people are really to distance your enemies it is horses or nothing for you, unless of course you have bicycles and motor-cars in your pocket."

"And where do you advise us to make for?" asked Syme doubtfully.

"Beyond question," replied the Colonel, "you had better make all haste to the police station beyond the town. My friend, whom I seconded under somewhat deceptive circumstances, seems to me to exaggerate very much the possibilities of a general rising; but even he would hardly maintain, I suppose, that you were not safe with the gendarmes."

Syme nodded gravely; then he said abruptly—

"And your other reason for coming here?"

"My other reason for coming here," said Ducroix soberly, "is that it is just as well to see a good man or two when one is possibly near to death."

Syme looked up at the wall, and saw a crudely-painted and pathetic religious picture. Then he said—

"You are right," and then almost immediately afterwards, "Has anyone seen about the horses?"

"Yes," answered Ducroix, "you may be quite certain that I gave orders the moment I came in. Those enemies of yours gave no impression of hurry, but they were really moving wonderfully fast, like a well-trained army. I had no idea that the anarchists had so much discipline. You have not a moment to waste."

Almost as he spoke, the old innkeeper with the blue eyes and white hair came ambling into the room, and announced that six horses were saddled outside.

By Ducroix's advice the five others equipped themselves with some portable form of food and wine, and keeping their duelling swords as the only weapons available, they clattered away down the steep, white road. The two servants, who had carried the Marquis's luggage when he was a marquis, were left behind to drink at the café by common consent, and not at all against their own inclination.

By this time the afternoon sun was slanting westward, and by its rays Syme could see the sturdy figure of the old innkeeper growing smaller and smaller, but still standing and looking after them quite silently, the sunshine in his silver hair. Syme had a fixed, superstitious fancy, left in his mind by the chance phrase of the Colonel, that this was indeed, perhaps, the last honest stranger whom he should ever see upon the earth.

He was still looking at this dwindling figure, which stood as a mere grey blot touched with a white flame against the great green wall of the steep down behind him. And as he stared over the top of the down behind the innkeeper, there appeared an army of black-clad and marching men. They seemed to hang above the good man and his house like a black cloud of locusts. The horses had been saddled none too soon.

CHAPTER XII

The Earth in Anarchy

U rging the horses to a gallop, without respect to the rather rugged descent of the road, the horsemen soon regained their advantage over the men on the march, and at last the bulk of the first buildings of Lancy cut off the sight of their pursuers. Nevertheless, the ride had been a long one, and by the time they reached the real town the west was warming with the colour and quality of sunset. The Colonel suggested that, before making finally for the police station, they should make the effort, in passing, to attach to themselves one more individual who might be useful.

"Four out of the five rich men in this town," he said, "are common swindlers. I suppose the proportion is pretty equal all over the world. The fifth is a friend of mine, and a very fine fellow; and what is even more important from our point of view, he owns a motor-car."

"I am afraid," said the Professor in his mirthful way, looking back along the white road on which the black, crawling patch might appear at any moment, "I am afraid we have hardly time for afternoon calls."

"Doctor Renard's house is only three minutes off," said the Colonel.

"Our danger," said Dr. Bull, "is not two minutes off."

"Yes," said Syme, "if we ride on fast we must leave them behind, for they are on foot."

"He has a motor-car," said the Colonel.

"But we may not get it," said Bull.

"Yes, he is quite on your side."

"But he might be out."

"Hold your tongue," said Syme suddenly. "What is that noise?"

For a second they all sat as still as equestrian statues, and for a second—for two or three or four seconds—heaven and earth seemed equally still. Then all their ears, in an agony of attention, heard along the road that indescribable thrill and throb that means only one thing—horses!

The Colonel's face had an instantaneous change, as if lightning had struck it, and yet left it scatheless.

"They have done us," he said, with brief military irony. "Prepare to receive cavalry!"

"Where can they have got the horses?" asked Syme, as he mechanically urged his steed to a canter.

The Colonel was silent for a little, then he said in a strained voice—

"I was speaking with strict accuracy when I said that the 'Soleil d'Or' was the only place where one can get horses within twenty miles."

"No!" said Syme violently, "I don't believe he'd do it. Not with all that white hair."

"He may have been forced," said the Colonel gently. "They must be at least a hundred strong, for which reason we are all going to see my friend Renard, who has a motor-car."

With these words he swung his horse suddenly round a street corner, and went down the street with such thundering speed, that the others, though already well at the gallop, had difficulty in following the flying tail of his horse.

Dr. Renard inhabited a high and comfortable house at the top of a steep street, so that when the riders alighted at his door they could once more see the solid green ridge of the hill, with the white road across it, standing up above all the roofs of the town. They breathed again to see that the road as yet was clear, and they rang the bell.

Dr. Renard was a beaming, brown-bearded man, a good example of that silent but very busy professional class which France has preserved even more perfectly than England. When the matter was explained to him he pooh-poohed the panic of the ex-Marquis altogether; he said, with the solid French scepticism, that there was no conceivable probability of a general anarchist rising. "Anarchy," he said, shrugging his shoulders, "it is childishness!"

"*Et ça*," cried out the Colonel suddenly, pointing over the other's shoulder, "and that is childishness, isn't it?"

They all looked round, and saw a curve of black cavalry come sweeping over the top of the hill with all the energy of Attila. Swiftly as they rode, however, the whole rank still kept well together, and they could see the black vizards of the first line as level as a line of uniforms. But although the main black square was the same, though travelling faster, there was now one sensational difference which they could see clearly upon the slope of the hill, as if upon a slanted map. The bulk of the riders were in one block; but one rider flew far ahead of the column, and with frantic movements of hand and heel urged his horse faster and faster, so that one might have fancied that he was not the pursuer but the pursued. But even at that great distance they could see something so fanatical, so unquestionable in his figure, that they knew it was the Secretary himself. "I am sorry to cut short a cultured discussion," said the Colonel, "but can you lend me your motor-car now, in two minutes?"

"I have a suspicion that you are all mad," said Dr. Renard, smiling sociably; "but God forbid that madness should in any way interrupt friendship. Let us go round to the garage."

Dr. Renard was a mild man with monstrous wealth; his rooms were like the Musee de Cluny, and he had three motor-cars. These, however, he seemed to use very sparingly, having the simple tastes of the French middle class, and when his impatient friends came to examine them, it took them some time to assure themselves that one of them even could be made to work. This with some difficulty they brought round into the street before the Doctor's house.

When they came out of the dim garage they were startled to find that twilight had already fallen with the abruptness of night in the tropics. Either they had been longer in the place than they imagined, or some unusual canopy of cloud had gathered over the town. They looked down the steep streets, and seemed to see a slight mist coming up from the sea.

"It is now or never," said Dr. Bull. "I hear horses."

"No," corrected the Professor, "a horse."

And as they listened, it was evident that the noise, rapidly coming nearer on the rattling stones, was not the noise of the whole cavalcade but that of the one horseman, who had left it far behind—the insane Secretary.

Syme's family, like most of those who end in the simple life, had once owned a motor, and he knew all about them. He had leapt at once into the chauffeur's seat, and with flushed face was wrenching and tugging at the disused machinery. He bent his strength upon one handle, and then said quite quietly—

"I am afraid it's no go."

As he spoke, there swept round the corner a man rigid on his rushing horse, with the rush and rigidity of an arrow. He had a smile that thrust out his chin as if it were dislocated. He swept alongside of the stationary car, into which its company had crowded, and laid his hand on the front. It was the Secretary, and his mouth went quite straight in the solemnity of triumph.

Syme was leaning hard upon the steering wheel, and there was no sound but the rumble of the other pursuers riding into the town. Then there came quite suddenly a scream of scraping iron, and the car leapt forward. It plucked the Secretary clean out of his saddle, as a knife is whipped out of its sheath, trailed him kicking terribly for twenty yards, and left him flung flat upon the road far in front of his frightened horse. As the car took the corner of the street with a splendid curve, they could just see the other anarchists filling the street and raising their fallen leader.

"I can't understand why it has grown so dark," said the Professor at last in a low voice.

"Going to be a storm, I think," said Dr. Bull. "I say, it's a pity we haven't got a light on this car, if only to see by."

"We have," said the Colonel, and from the floor of the car he fished up a heavy, old-fashioned, carved iron lantern with a light inside it. It was obviously an antique, and it would seem as if its original use had been in some way semi-religious, for there was a rude moulding of a cross upon one of its sides.

"Where on earth did you get that?" asked the Professor.

"I got it where I got the car," answered the Colonel, chuckling, "from my best friend. While our friend here was fighting with the steering wheel, I ran up the front steps of the house and spoke to Renard, who was standing in his own porch, you will remember. 'I suppose,' I said, 'there's no time to get a lamp.' He looked up, blinking amiably at the beautiful arched ceiling of his own front hall. From this was suspended, by chains of exquisite ironwork, this lantern, one of the hundred treasures of his treasure house. By sheer force he tore the lamp out of his own ceiling, shattering the painted panels, and bringing down two blue vases with his violence. Then he handed me the iron lantern, and I put it in the car. Was I not right when I said that Dr. Renard was worth knowing?"

"You were," said Syme seriously, and hung the heavy lantern over the front. There was a certain allegory of their whole position in the contrast between the modern automobile and its strange ecclesiastical lamp. Hitherto they had passed through the quietest part of the town, meeting at most one or two pedestrians, who could give them no hint of the peace or the hostility of the place. Now, however, the windows in the houses began one by one to be lit up, giving a greater sense of habitation and humanity. Dr. Bull turned to the new detective who had led their flight, and permitted himself one of his natural and friendly smiles.

"These lights make one feel more cheerful."

Inspector Ratcliffe drew his brows together.

"There is only one set of lights that make me more cheerful," he said, "and they are those lights of the police station which I can see beyond the town. Please God we may be there in ten minutes."

Then all Bull's boiling good sense and optimism broke suddenly out of him.

"Oh, this is all raving nonsense!" he cried. "If you really think that ordinary people in ordinary houses are anarchists, you must be madder than an anarchist yourself. If we turned and fought these fellows, the whole town would fight for us."

"No," said the other with an immovable simplicity, "the whole town would fight for them. We shall see."

While they were speaking the Professor had leant forward with sudden excitement.

"What is that noise?" he said.

"Oh, the horses behind us, I suppose," said the Colonel. "I thought we had got clear of them."

"The horses behind us! No," said the Professor, "it is not horses, and it is not behind us."

Almost as he spoke, across the end of the street before them two shining and rattling shapes shot past. They were gone almost in a flash, but everyone could see that they were motor-cars, and the Professor stood up with a pale face and swore that they were the other two motor-cars from Dr. Renard's garage.

"I tell you they were his," he repeated, with wild eyes, "and they were full of men in masks!"

"Absurd!" said the Colonel angrily. "Dr. Renard would never give them his cars."

"He may have been forced," said Ratcliffe quietly. "The whole town is on their side."

"You still believe that," asked the Colonel incredulously.

"You will all believe it soon," said the other with a hopeless calm.

There was a puzzled pause for some little time, and then the Colonel began again abruptly—

"No, I can't believe it. The thing is nonsense. The plain people of a peaceable French town—"

He was cut short by a bang and a blaze of light, which seemed close to his eyes. As the car sped on it left a floating patch of white smoke behind it, and Syme had heard a shot shriek past his ear.

"My God!" said the Colonel, "someone has shot at us."

"It need not interrupt conversation," said the gloomy Ratcliffe. "Pray resume your remarks, Colonel. You were talking, I think, about the plain people of a peaceable French town."

The staring Colonel was long past minding satire. He rolled his eyes all round the street.

"It is extraordinary," he said, "most extraordinary."

"A fastidious person," said Syme, "might even call it unpleasant. However, I suppose those lights out in the field beyond this street are the Gendarmerie. We shall soon get there."

"No," said Inspector Ratcliffe, "we shall never get there."

He had been standing up and looking keenly ahead of him. Now he sat down and smoothed his sleek hair with a weary gesture.

"What do you mean?" asked Bull sharply.

"I mean that we shall never get there," said the pessimist placidly. "They have two rows of armed men across the road already; I can see them from here. The town is in arms, as I said it was. I can only wallow in the exquisite comfort of my own exactitude."

And Ratcliffe sat down comfortably in the car and lit a cigarette, but the others rose excitedly and stared down the road. Syme had slowed down the car as their plans became doubtful, and he brought it finally to a standstill just at the corner of a side street that ran down very steeply to the sea.

The town was mostly in shadow, but the sun had not sunk; wherever its level light could break through, it painted everything a burning gold. Up this side street the last sunset light shone as sharp and narrow as the shaft of artificial light at the theatre. It struck the car of the five friends, and lit it like a burning chariot. But the rest of the street, especially the two ends of it, was in the deepest twilight, and for some seconds they could see nothing. Then Syme, whose eyes were the keenest, broke into a little bitter whistle, and said,

"It is quite true. There is a crowd or an army or some such thing across the end of that street."

"Well, if there is," said Bull impatiently, "it must be something else—a sham fight or the mayor's birthday or something. I cannot and will not believe that plain, jolly people in a place like this walk about with dynamite in their pockets. Get on a bit, Syme, and let us look at them."

The car crawled about a hundred yards farther, and then they were all startled by Dr. Bull breaking into a high crow of laughter.

"Why, you silly mugs!" he cried, "what did I tell you. That crowd's as law-abiding as a cow, and if it weren't, it's on our side."

"How do you know?" asked the professor, staring.

"You blind bat," cried Bull, "don't you see who is leading them?"

They peered again, and then the Colonel, with a catch in his voice, cried out—

"Why, it's Renard!"

There was, indeed, a rank of dim figures running across the road, and they could not be clearly seen; but far enough in front to catch the accident of the evening light was stalking up and down the unmistakable Dr. Renard, in a white hat, stroking his long brown beard, and holding a revolver in his left hand.

"What a fool I've been!" exclaimed the Colonel. "Of course, the dear old boy has turned out to help us."

Dr. Bull was bubbling over with laughter, swinging the sword in his hand as carelessly as a cane. He jumped out of the car and ran across the intervening space, calling out—

"Dr. Renard! Dr. Renard!"

An instant after Syme thought his own eyes had gone mad in his head. For the philanthropic Dr. Renard had deliberately raised his revolver and fired twice at Bull, so that the shots rang down the road.

Almost at the same second as the puff of white cloud went up from this atrocious explosion a long puff of white cloud went up also from the cigarette of the cynical Ratcliffe. Like all the rest he turned a little pale, but he smiled. Dr. Bull, at whom the bullets had been fired, just missing his scalp, stood quite still in the middle of the road without a sign of fear, and then turned very slowly and crawled back to the car, and climbed in with two holes through his hat.

"Well," said the cigarette smoker slowly, "what do you think now?"

"I think," said Dr. Bull with precision, "that I am lying in bed at No. 217 Peabody Buildings, and that I shall soon wake up with a jump; or, if that's not it, I think that I am sitting in a small cushioned cell in Hanwell, and that the doctor can't make much of my case. But if you want to know what I don't think, I'll tell you. I don't think what you think. I don't think, and I never shall think, that the mass of ordinary men are a pack of dirty modern thinkers. No, sir, I'm a democrat, and I still don't believe that Sunday could convert one average navvy or counter-jumper. No, I may be mad, but humanity isn't."

Syme turned his bright blue eyes on Bull with an earnestness which he did not commonly make clear.

"You are a very fine fellow," he said. "You can believe in a sanity which is not merely your sanity. And you're right enough about humanity, about peasants and people like that jolly old innkeeper. But you're not right about Renard. I suspected him from the first. He's rationalistic, and, what's worse, he's rich. When duty and religion are really destroyed, it will be by the rich."

"They are really destroyed now," said the man with a cigarette, and rose with his hands in his pockets. "The devils are coming on!"

The men in the motor-car looked anxiously in the direction of his dreamy gaze, and they saw that the whole regiment at the end of the road was advancing upon them, Dr. Renard marching furiously in front, his beard flying in the breeze.

The Colonel sprang out of the car with an intolerant exclamation.

"Gentlemen," he cried, "the thing is incredible. It must be a practical joke. If you knew Renard as I do—it's like calling Queen Victoria a dynamiter. If you had got the man's character into your head—"

"Dr. Bull," said Syme sardonically, "has at least got it into his hat."

"I tell you it can't be!" cried the Colonel, stamping.

"Renard shall explain it. He shall explain it to me," and he strode forward.

"Don't be in such a hurry," drawled the smoker. "He will very soon explain it to all of us."

But the impatient Colonel was already out of earshot, advancing towards the advancing enemy. The excited Dr. Renard lifted his pistol again, but perceiving his opponent, hesitated, and the Colonel came face to face with him with frantic gestures of remonstrance.

"It is no good," said Syme. "He will never get anything out of that old heathen. I vote we drive bang through the thick of them, bang as the bullets went through Bull's hat. We may all be killed, but we must kill a tidy number of them."

"I won't 'ave it," said Dr. Bull, growing more vulgar in the sincerity of his virtue. "The poor chaps may be making a mistake. Give the Colonel a chance."

"Shall we go back, then?" asked the Professor.

"No," said Ratcliffe in a cold voice, "the street behind us is held too. In fact, I seem to see there another friend of yours, Syme."

Syme spun round smartly, and stared backwards at the track which they had travelled. He saw an irregular body of horsemen gathering and galloping towards them in the gloom. He saw above the foremost saddle the silver gleam of a sword, and then as it grew nearer the silver gleam of an old man's hair. The next moment, with shattering violence, he had swung the motor round and sent it dashing down the steep side street to the sea, like a man that desired only to die.

"What the devil is up?" cried the Professor, seizing his arm.

"The morning star has fallen!" said Syme, as his own car went down the darkness like a falling star.

The others did not understand his words, but when they looked back at the street above they saw the hostile cavalry coming round the corner and down the slopes after them; and foremost of all rode the good innkeeper, flushed with the fiery innocence of the evening light.

"The world is insane!" said the Professor, and buried his face in his hands.

"No," said Dr. Bull in adamantine humility, "it is I."

"What are we going to do?" asked the Professor.

"At this moment," said Syme, with a scientific detachment, "I think we are going to smash into a lamppost."

The next instant the automobile had come with a catastrophic jar against an iron object. The instant after that four men had crawled out from under a chaos of metal, and a tall lean lamp-post that had stood up straight on the edge of the marine parade stood out, bent and twisted, like the branch of a broken tree.

"Well, we smashed something," said the Professor, with a faint smile. "That's some comfort."

"You're becoming an anarchist," said Syme, dusting his clothes with his instinct of daintiness.

"Everyone is," said Ratcliffe.

As they spoke, the white-haired horseman and his followers came thundering from above, and almost at the same moment a dark string of men ran shouting along the sea-front. Syme snatched a sword, and took it in his teeth; he stuck two others under his arm-pits, took a fourth in his left hand and the lantern in his right, and leapt off the high parade on to the beach below.

The others leapt after him, with a common acceptance of such decisive action, leaving the debris and the gathering mob above them.

"We have one more chance," said Syme, taking the steel out of his mouth. "Whatever all this pandemonium means, I suppose the police station will help us. We can't get there, for they hold the way. But there's a pier or breakwater runs out into the sea just here, which we could defend longer than anything else, like Horatius and his bridge. We must defend it till the Gendarmerie turn out. Keep after me."

They followed him as he went crunching down the beach, and in a second or two their boots broke not on the sea gravel, but on broad, flat stones. They marched down a long, low jetty, running out in one arm into the dim, boiling sea, and when they came to the end of it they felt that they had come to the end of their story. They turned and faced the town.

That town was transfigured with uproar. All along the high parade from which they had just descended was a dark and roaring stream of humanity, with tossing arms and fiery faces, groping and glaring towards them. The long dark line was dotted with torches and lanterns; but even where no flame lit up a furious face, they could see in the farthest figure, in the most shadowy gesture, an organised hate. It was clear that they were the accursed of all men, and they knew not why.

Two or three men, looking little and black like monkeys, leapt over the edge as they had done and dropped on to the beach. These came ploughing down the deep sand, shouting horribly, and strove to wade into the sea at random. The example was followed, and the whole black mass of men began to run and drip over the edge like black treacle.

Foremost among the men on the beach Syme saw the peasant who had driven their cart. He splashed into the surf on a huge cart-horse, and shook his axe at them.

"The peasant!" cried Syme. "They have not risen since the Middle Ages."

"Even if the police do come now," said the Professor mournfully, "they can do nothing with this mob."

"Nonsense!" said Bull desperately; "there must be some people left in the town who are human."

"No," said the hopeless Inspector, "the human being will soon be extinct. We are the last of mankind."

"It may be," said the Professor absently. Then he added in his dreamy voice—

"What is all that at the end of the 'Dunciad'?

> *Nor public flame; nor private, dares to shine;*
> *Nor human light is left, nor glimpse divine!*
> *Lo! thy dread Empire, Chaos, is restored;*

> Light dies before thine uncreating word:
> Thy hand, great Anarch, lets the curtain fall;
> And universal darkness buries all."

"Stop!" cried Bull suddenly, "the gendarmes are out."

The low lights of the police station were indeed blotted and broken with hurrying figures, and they heard through the darkness the clash and jingle of a disciplined cavalry.

"They are charging the mob!" cried Bull in ecstacy or alarm.

"No," said Syme, "they are formed along the parade."

"They have unslung their carbines," cried Bull dancing with excitement.

"Yes," said Ratcliffe, "and they are going to fire on us."

As he spoke there came a long crackle of musketry, and bullets seemed to hop like hailstones on the stones in front of them.

"The gendarmes have joined them!" cried the Professor, and struck his forehead.

"I am in the padded cell," said Bull solidly.

There was a long silence, and then Ratcliffe said, looking out over the swollen sea, all a sort of grey purple—

"What does it matter who is mad or who is sane? We shall all be dead soon."

Syme turned to him and said—

"You are quite hopeless, then?"

Mr. Ratcliffe kept a stony silence; then at last he said quietly—

"No; oddly enough I am not quite hopeless. There is one insane little hope that I cannot get out of my mind. The power of this whole planet is against us, yet I cannot help wondering whether this one silly little hope is hopeless yet."

"In what or whom is your hope?" asked Syme with curiosity.

"In a man I never saw," said the other, looking at the leaden sea.

"I know what you mean," said Syme in a low voice, "the man in the dark room. But Sunday must have killed him by now."

"Perhaps," said the other steadily; "but if so, he was the only man whom Sunday found it hard to kill."

"I heard what you said," said the Professor, with his back turned. "I also am holding hard on to the thing I never saw."

All of a sudden Syme, who was standing as if blind with introspective thought, swung round and cried out, like a man waking from sleep—

"Where is the Colonel? I thought he was with us!"

"The Colonel! Yes," cried Bull, "where on earth is the Colonel?"

"He went to speak to Renard," said the Professor.

"We cannot leave him among all those beasts," cried Syme. "Let us die like gentlemen if—"

"Do not pity the Colonel," said Ratcliffe, with a pale sneer. "He is extremely comfortable. He is—"

"No! no! no!" cried Syme in a kind of frenzy, "not the Colonel too! I will never believe it!"

"Will you believe your eyes?" asked the other, and pointed to the beach.

Many of their pursuers had waded into the water shaking their fists, but the sea was rough, and they could not reach the pier. Two or three figures, however, stood on the beginning of the stone footway, and seemed to be cautiously advancing down it. The glare of a chance lantern lit up the faces of the two foremost. One face wore a black half-mask, and under it the mouth was twisting about in such a madness of nerves that the black tuft of beard wriggled round and round like a restless, living thing. The other was the red face and white moustache of Colonel Ducroix. They were in earnest consultation.

"Yes, he is gone too," said the Professor, and sat down on a stone. "Everything's gone. I'm gone! I can't trust my own bodily machinery. I feel as if my own hand might fly up and strike me."

"When my hand flies up," said Syme, "it will strike somebody else," and he strode along the pier towards the Colonel, the sword in one hand and the lantern in the other.

As if to destroy the last hope or doubt, the Colonel, who saw him coming, pointed his revolver at him and fired. The shot missed Syme, but struck his sword, breaking it short at the hilt. Syme rushed on, and swung the iron lantern above his head.

"Judas before Herod!" he said, and struck the Colonel down upon the stones. Then he turned to the Secretary, whose frightful mouth was almost foaming now, and held the lamp high with so rigid and arresting a gesture, that the man was, as it were, frozen for a moment, and forced to hear.

"Do you see this lantern?" cried Syme in a terrible voice. "Do you see the cross carved on it, and the flame inside? You did not make it. You did not light it. Better men than you, men who could believe and obey, twisted the entrails of iron and preserved the legend of fire. There is not a street you walk on, there is not a thread you wear, that was not made as this lantern was, by denying your philosophy of dirt and rats. You can make nothing. You can only destroy. You will destroy mankind; you will destroy the world. Let that suffice you. Yet this one old Christian lantern you shall not destroy. It shall go where your empire of apes will never have the wit to find it."

He struck the Secretary once with the lantern so that he staggered; and then, whirling it twice round his head, sent it flying far out to sea, where it flared like a roaring rocket and fell.

"Swords!" shouted Syme, turning his flaming face to the three behind him. "Let us charge these dogs, for our time has come to die."

His three companions came after him sword in hand. Syme's sword was broken, but he rent a bludgeon from the fist of a fisherman, flinging him down. In a moment they would have flung themselves upon the face of the mob and perished, when an interruption came. The Secretary, ever since Syme's speech, had stood with his hand to his stricken head as if dazed; now he suddenly pulled off his black mask.

The pale face thus peeled in the lamplight revealed not so much rage as astonishment. He put up his hand with an anxious authority.

"There is some mistake," he said. "Mr. Syme, I hardly think you understand your position. I arrest you in the name of the law."

"Of the law?" said Syme, and dropped his stick.

"Certainly!" said the Secretary. "I am a detective from Scotland Yard," and he took a small blue card from his pocket.

"And what do you suppose we are?" asked the Professor, and threw up his arms.

"You," said the Secretary stiffly, "are, as I know for a fact, members of the Supreme Anarchist Council. Disguised as one of you, I—"

Dr. Bull tossed his sword into the sea.

"There never was any Supreme Anarchist Council," he said. "We were all a lot of silly policemen looking at each other. And all these nice people who have been peppering us with shot thought we were the dynamiters. I knew I couldn't be wrong about the mob," he said, beaming over the enormous multitude, which stretched away to the distance on both sides. "Vulgar people are never mad. I'm vulgar myself, and I know. I am now going on shore to stand a drink to everybody here."

CHAPTER XIII

The Pursuit of the President

Next morning five bewildered but hilarious people took the boat for Dover. The poor old Colonel might have had some cause to complain, having been first forced to fight for two factions that didn't exist, and then knocked down with an iron lantern. But he was a magnanimous old gentleman, and being much relieved that neither party had anything to do with dynamite, he saw them off on the pier with great geniality.

The five reconciled detectives had a hundred details to explain to each other. The Secretary had to tell Syme how they had come to wear masks originally in order to approach the supposed enemy as fellow-conspirators.

Syme had to explain how they had fled with such swiftness through a civilised country. But above all these matters of detail which could be explained, rose the central mountain of the matter that they could not explain. What did it all mean? If they were all harmless officers, what was Sunday? If he had not seized the world, what on earth had he been up to? Inspector Ratcliffe was still gloomy about this.

"I can't make head or tail of old Sunday's little game any more than you can," he said. "But whatever else Sunday is, he isn't a blameless citizen. Damn it! do you remember his face?"

"I grant you," answered Syme, "that I have never been able to forget it."

"Well," said the Secretary, "I suppose we can find out soon, for tomorrow we have our next general meeting. You will excuse me," he said, with a rather ghastly smile, "for being well acquainted with my secretarial duties."

"I suppose you are right," said the Professor reflectively. "I suppose we might find it out from him; but I confess that I should feel a bit afraid of asking Sunday who he really is."

"Why," asked the Secretary, "for fear of bombs?"

"No," said the Professor, "for fear he might tell me."

"Let us have some drinks," said Dr. Bull, after a silence.

Throughout their whole journey by boat and train they were highly convivial, but they instinctively kept together. Dr. Bull, who had always been the optimist of the party, endeavoured to persuade the other four that the whole company could take the same hansom cab from Victoria; but this was over-ruled, and they went in a four-wheeler, with Dr. Bull on the box, singing. They finished their journey at an hotel in Piccadilly Circus, so as to be close to the early breakfast next morning in Leicester Square. Yet even then the adventures of the day were not entirely over. Dr. Bull, discontented with the general proposal to go to bed, had strolled out of the hotel at about eleven to see and taste some of the beauties of London. Twenty minutes afterwards, however, he came back and made quite a clamour in the hall. Syme, who tried at first to soothe him, was forced at last to listen to his communication with quite new attention.

"I tell you I've seen him!" said Dr. Bull, with thick emphasis.

"Whom?" asked Syme quickly. "Not the President?"

"Not so bad as that," said Dr. Bull, with unnecessary laughter, "not so bad as that. I've got him here."

"Got whom here?" asked Syme impatiently.

"Hairy man," said the other lucidly, "man that used to be hairy man—Gogol. Here he is," and he pulled forward by a reluctant elbow the identical young man who five days before had marched out of the Council with thin red hair and a pale face, the first of all the sham anarchists who had been exposed.

"Why do you worry with me?" he cried. "You have expelled me as a spy."

"We are all spies!" whispered Syme.

"We're all spies!" shouted Dr. Bull. "Come and have a drink."

Next morning the battalion of the reunited six marched stolidly towards the hotel in Leicester Square.

"This is more cheerful," said Dr. Bull; "we are six men going to ask one man what he means."

"I think it is a bit queerer than that," said Syme. "I think it is six men going to ask one man what they mean."

They turned in silence into the Square, and though the hotel was in the opposite corner, they saw at once the little balcony and a figure that looked too big for it. He was sitting alone with bent head, poring over a newspaper. But all his councillors, who had come to vote him down, crossed that Square as if they were watched out of heaven by a hundred eyes.

They had disputed much upon their policy, about whether they should leave the unmasked Gogol without and begin diplomatically, or whether they should bring him in and blow up the gunpowder at once. The influence of Syme and Bull prevailed for the latter course, though the Secretary to the last asked them why they attacked Sunday so rashly.

"My reason is quite simple," said Syme. "I attack him rashly because I am afraid of him."

They followed Syme up the dark stair in silence, and they all came out simultaneously into the broad sunlight of the morning and the broad sunlight of Sunday's smile.

"Delightful!" he said. "So pleased to see you all. What an exquisite day it is. Is the Czar dead?"

The Secretary, who happened to be foremost, drew himself together for a dignified outburst.

"No, sir," he said sternly "there has been no massacre. I bring you news of no such disgusting spectacles."

"Disgusting spectacles?" repeated the President, with a bright, inquiring smile. "You mean Dr. Bull's spectacles?"

The Secretary choked for a moment, and the President went on with a sort of smooth appeal—

"Of course, we all have our opinions and even our eyes, but really to call them disgusting before the man himself—"

Dr. Bull tore off his spectacles and broke them on the table.

"My spectacles are blackguardly," he said, "but I'm not. Look at my face."

"I dare say it's the sort of face that grows on one," said the President, "in fact, it grows on you; and who am I to quarrel with the wild fruits upon the Tree of Life? I dare say it will grow on me some day."

"We have no time for tomfoolery," said the Secretary, breaking in savagely. "We have come to know what all this means. Who are you? What are you? Why did you get us all here? Do you know who and what we are? Are you a half-witted man playing the conspirator, or are you a clever man playing the fool? Answer me, I tell you."

"Candidates," murmured Sunday, "are only required to answer eight out of the seventeen questions on the paper. As far as I can make out, you want me to tell you what I am, and what you are, and what this table is, and what this Council is, and what this world is for all I know. Well, I will go so far as to rend the veil of one mystery. If you want to know what you are, you are a set of highly well-intentioned young jackasses."

"And you," said Syme, leaning forward, "what are you?"

"I? What am I?" roared the President, and he rose slowly to an incredible height, like some enormous wave about to arch above them and break. "You want to know what I am, do you? Bull, you are a man of science. Grub in the roots of those trees and find out the truth about them. Syme, you are a poet. Stare at those morning clouds. But I tell you this, that you will have found out the truth of the last tree and the top-most cloud before the truth about me. You will understand the sea, and I shall be still a riddle; you shall know what the stars are, and not know what I am. Since the beginning of the world all men have hunted me like a wolf—kings and sages, and poets and lawgivers, all the churches, and all the philosophies. But I have never been caught yet, and the skies will fall in the time

I turn to bay. I have given them a good run for their money, and I will now."

Before one of them could move, the monstrous man had swung himself like some huge ourang-outang over the balustrade of the balcony. Yet before he dropped he pulled himself up again as on a horizontal bar, and thrusting his great chin over the edge of the balcony, said solemnly—

"There's one thing I'll tell you though about who I am. I am the man in the dark room, who made you all policemen."

With that he fell from the balcony, bouncing on the stones below like a great ball of india-rubber, and went bounding off towards the corner of the Alhambra, where he hailed a hansom-cab and sprang inside it. The six detectives had been standing thunderstruck and livid in the light of his last assertion; but when he disappeared into the cab, Syme's practical senses returned to him, and leaping over the balcony so recklessly as almost to break his legs, he called another cab.

He and Bull sprang into the cab together, the Professor and the Inspector into another, while the Secretary and the late Gogol scrambled into a third just in time to pursue the flying Syme, who was pursuing the flying President. Sunday led them a wild chase towards the north-west, his cabman, evidently under the influence of more than common inducements, urging the horse at breakneck speed. But Syme was in no mood for delicacies, and he stood up in his own cab shouting, "Stop thief!" until crowds ran along beside his cab, and policemen began to stop and ask questions. All this had its influence upon the President's cabman, who began to look dubious, and to slow down to a trot. He opened the trap to talk reasonably to his fare, and in so doing let the long whip droop over the front of the cab. Sunday leant forward, seized it, and jerked it violently out of the man's hand. Then standing up in front of the cab himself, he lashed the horse and roared aloud, so that they went down the streets like a flying storm. Through street after street and square after square went whirling this preposterous vehicle, in which the fare was urging the horse and the driver trying desperately to stop it. The other three cabs came after it (if the phrase be permissible of a cab) like panting hounds. Shops and streets shot by like rattling arrows.

At the highest ecstacy of speed, Sunday turned round on the splashboard where he stood, and sticking his great grinning head out of the cab, with white hair whistling in the wind, he made a horrible face at his pursuers, like some colossal urchin. Then raising his right hand swiftly, he flung a ball of paper in Syme's face and vanished. Syme caught the thing while instinctively warding it off, and discovered that it consisted of two crumpled papers. One was addressed to himself, and the other to Dr. Bull, with a very long, and it is to be feared partly ironical, string of letters after his name. Dr. Bull's address was, at any rate, considerably longer than his communication, for the communication consisted entirely of the words—

What about Martin Tupper NOW?

"What does the old maniac mean?" asked Bull, staring at the words. "What does yours say, Syme?"

Syme's message was, at any rate, longer, and ran as follows—

"No one would regret anything in the nature of an interference by the Archdeacon more than I. I trust it will not come to that. But, for the last time, where are your goloshes? The thing is too bad, especially after what uncle said."

The President's cabman seemed to be regaining some control over his horse, and the pursuers gained a little as they swept round into the Edgware Road. And here there occurred what seemed to the allies a providential stoppage. Traffic of every kind was swerving to right or left or stopping, for down the long road was coming the unmistakable roar announcing the fire-engine, which in a few seconds went by like a brazen thunderbolt. But quick as it went by, Sunday had bounded out of his cab, sprung at the fire-engine, caught it, slung himself on to it, and was seen as he disappeared in the noisy distance talking to the astonished fireman with explanatory gestures.

"After him!" howled Syme. "He can't go astray now. There's no mistaking a fire-engine."

The three cabmen, who had been stunned for a moment, whipped up their horses and slightly decreased the distance between themselves and their disappearing prey. The President acknowledged this proximity by coming to the back of the car, bowing repeatedly, kissing his hand, and finally flinging a neatly-folded note into the bosom of Inspector Ratcliffe. When that gentleman opened it, not without impatience, he found it contained the words—

> *Fly at once. The truth about your trouser-stretchers*
> *is known.* —A FRIEND.

The fire-engine had struck still farther to the north, into a region that they did not recognise; and as it ran by a line of high railings shadowed with trees, the six friends were startled, but somewhat relieved, to see the President leap from the fire-engine, though whether through another whim or the increasing protest of his entertainers they could not see. Before the three cabs, however, could reach up to the spot, he had gone up the high railings like a huge grey cat, tossed himself over, and vanished in a darkness of leaves.

Syme with a furious gesture stopped his cab, jumped out, and sprang also to the escalade. When he had one leg over the fence and his friends were following, he turned a face on them which shone quite pale in the shadow.

"What place can this be?" he asked. "Can it be the old devil's house? I've heard he has a house in North London."

"All the better," said the Secretary grimly, planting a foot in a foothold, "we shall find him at home."

"No, but it isn't that," said Syme, knitting his brows. "I hear the most horrible noises, like devils laughing and sneezing and blowing their devilish noses!"

"His dogs barking, of course," said the Secretary.

"Why not say his black-beetles barking!" said Syme furiously, "snails barking! geraniums barking! Did you ever hear a dog bark like that?"

He held up his hand, and out of the thicket came a long growling roar that seemed to get under the skin and freeze the flesh—a low thrilling roar that made a throbbing in the air all about them.

"The dogs of Sunday would be no ordinary dogs," said Gogol, and shuddered.

Syme had jumped down on the other side, but he still stood listening impatiently.

"Well, listen to that," he said, "is that a dog—anybody's dog?"

There broke upon their ear a hoarse screaming as of things protesting and clamouring in sudden pain; and then, far off like an echo, what sounded like a long nasal trumpet.

"Well, his house ought to be hell!" said the Secretary; "and if it is hell, I'm going in!" and he sprang over the tall railings almost with one swing.

The others followed. They broke through a tangle of plants and shrubs, and came out on an open path. Nothing was in sight, but Dr. Bull suddenly struck his hands together.

"Why, you asses," he cried, "it's the Zoo!"

As they were looking round wildly for any trace of their wild quarry, a keeper in uniform came running along the path with a man in plain clothes.

"Has it come this way?" gasped the keeper.

"Has what?" asked Syme.

"The elephant!" cried the keeper. "An elephant has gone mad and run away!"

"He has run away with an old gentleman," said the other stranger breathlessly, "a poor old gentleman with white hair!"

"What sort of old gentleman?" asked Syme, with great curiosity.

"A very large and fat old gentleman in light grey clothes," said the keeper eagerly.

"Well," said Syme, "if he's that particular kind of old gentleman, if you're quite sure that he's a large and fat old gentleman in grey clothes, you may take my word for it that the elephant has not run away with him. He has run away with the elephant. The elephant is not made by God that could run away with him if he did not consent to the elopement. And, by thunder, there he is!"

There was no doubt about it this time. Clean across the space of grass, about two hundred yards away, with a crowd screaming and scampering vainly at his heels, went a huge grey elephant at an awful stride, with his trunk thrown out as rigid as a ship's bowsprit, and trumpeting like the trumpet of doom. On the back of the bellowing and plunging animal sat President Sunday with all the placidity of a sultan, but goading the animal to a furious speed with some sharp object in his hand.

"Stop him!" screamed the populace. "He'll be out of the gate!"

"Stop a landslide!" said the keeper. "He is out of the gate!"

And even as he spoke, a final crash and roar of terror announced that the great grey elephant had broken out of the gates of the Zoological Gardens, and was careening down Albany Street like a new and swift sort of omnibus.

"Great Lord!" cried Bull, "I never knew an elephant could go so fast. Well, it must be hansom-cabs again if we are to keep him in sight."

As they raced along to the gate out of which the elephant had vanished, Syme felt a glaring panorama of the strange animals in the cages which they passed. Afterwards he thought it queer that he should have seen them so clearly. He remembered especially seeing pelicans, with their preposterous, pendant throats. He wondered why the pelican was the symbol of charity, except it was that it wanted a good deal of charity to admire a pelican. He remembered a hornbill, which was simply a huge yellow beak with a small bird tied on behind it. The whole gave him a sensation, the vividness of which he could not explain, that Nature was always making quite mysterious jokes. Sunday had told them that they would understand him when they had understood the stars. He wondered whether even the archangels understood the hornbill.

The six unhappy detectives flung themselves into cabs and followed the elephant sharing the terror which he spread through the long stretch of the streets. This time Sunday did not turn round, but offered them the solid stretch of his unconscious back, which maddened them, if possible, more than his previous mockeries. Just before they came to Baker Street, however, he was seen to throw something far up into the air, as a boy does a ball meaning to catch it again. But at their rate of racing it fell far behind, just by the cab containing Gogol; and in faint hope of a clue or for some impulse unexplainable, he stopped his cab so as to pick it up. It was addressed to himself, and was quite a bulky parcel. On examination, however, its bulk was found to consist of thirty-three pieces of paper of no value wrapped one round the other. When the last covering was torn away it reduced itself to a small slip of paper, on which was written—

The word, I fancy, should be "pink."

The man once known as Gogol said nothing, but the movements of his hands and feet were like those of a man urging a horse to renewed efforts.

Through street after street, through district after district, went the prodigy of the flying elephant, calling crowds to every window, and driving the traffic left and right. And still through all this insane publicity the three cabs toiled after it, until they came to be regarded as part of a procession, and perhaps the advertisement of a circus. They went at such a rate that distances were shortened beyond belief, and Syme saw the Albert Hall in Kensington when he thought that he was still in Paddington. The animal's pace was even more fast and free through the empty, aristocratic streets of South Kensington, and he finally headed towards that part of the sky-line where the enormous Wheel of Earl's Court stood up in the sky. The wheel grew larger and larger, till it filled heaven like the wheel of stars.

The beast outstripped the cabs. They lost him round several corners, and when they came to one of the gates of the Earl's Court

Exhibition they found themselves finally blocked. In front of them was an enormous crowd; in the midst of it was an enormous elephant, heaving and shuddering as such shapeless creatures do. But the President had disappeared.

"Where has he gone to?" asked Syme, slipping to the ground.

"Gentleman rushed into the Exhibition, sir!" said an official in a dazed manner. Then he added in an injured voice: "Funny gentleman, sir. Asked me to hold his horse, and gave me this."

He held out with distaste a piece of folded paper, addressed: "To the Secretary of the Central Anarchist Council."

The Secretary, raging, rent it open, and found written inside it—

> *When the herring runs a mile,*
> *Let the Secretary smile;*
> *When the herring tries to fly,*
> *Let the Secretary die.* (RUSTIC PROVERB)

"Why the eternal crikey," began the Secretary, "did you let the man in? Do people commonly come to your Exhibition riding on mad elephants? Do—"

"Look!" shouted Syme suddenly. "Look over there!"

"Look at what?" asked the Secretary savagely.

"Look at the captive balloon!" said Syme, and pointed in a frenzy.

"Why the blazes should I look at a captive balloon?" demanded the Secretary. "What is there queer about a captive balloon?"

"Nothing," said Syme, "except that it isn't captive!"

They all turned their eyes to where the balloon swung and swelled above the Exhibition on a string, like a child's balloon. A second afterwards the string came in two just under the car, and the balloon, broken loose, floated away with the freedom of a soap bubble.

"Ten thousand devils!" shrieked the Secretary. "He's got into it!" and he shook his fists at the sky.

The balloon, borne by some chance wind, came right above them, and they could see the great white head of the President peering over the side and looking benevolently down on them.

"God bless my soul!" said the Professor with the elderly manner that he could never disconnect from his bleached beard and parchment face. "God bless my soul! I seemed to fancy that something fell on the top of my hat!"

He put up a trembling hand and took from that shelf a piece of twisted paper, which he opened absently only to find it inscribed with a true lover's knot and, the words—

> *Your beauty has not left me*
> *indifferent. —From* LITTLE SNOWDROP.

There was a short silence, and then Syme said, biting his beard—

"I'm not beaten yet. The blasted thing must come down somewhere. Let's follow it!"

CHAPTER XIV

The Six Philosophers

Across green fields, and breaking through blooming hedges, toiled six draggled detectives, about five miles out of London. The optimist of the party had at first proposed that they should follow the balloon across South England in hansom-cabs. But he was ultimately convinced of the persistent refusal of the balloon to follow the roads, and the still more persistent refusal of the cabmen to follow the balloon. Consequently the tireless though exasperated travellers broke through black thickets and ploughed through ploughed fields till each was turned into a figure too outrageous to be mistaken for a tramp. Those green hills of Surrey saw the final collapse and tragedy of the admirable light grey suit in which Syme had set out from Saffron Park. His silk hat was broken over his nose by a swinging bough, his coat-tails were torn to the shoulder by arresting thorns, the clay of England was splashed up to his collar; but he still carried his yellow beard forward with a silent and furious determination, and his eyes were still fixed on that floating ball of gas, which in the full flush of sunset seemed coloured like a sunset cloud.

"After all," he said, "it is very beautiful!"

"It is singularly and strangely beautiful!" said the Professor. "I wish the beastly gas-bag would burst!"

"No," said Dr. Bull, "I hope it won't. It might hurt the old boy."

"Hurt him!" said the vindictive Professor, "hurt him! Not as much as I'd hurt him if I could get up with him. Little Snowdrop!"

"I don't want him hurt, somehow," said Dr. Bull.

"What!" cried the Secretary bitterly. "Do you believe all that tale about his being our man in the dark room? Sunday would say he was anybody."

"I don't know whether I believe it or not," said Dr. Bull. "But it isn't that that I mean. I can't wish old Sunday's balloon to burst because—"

"Well," said Syme impatiently, "because?"

"Well, because he's so jolly like a balloon himself," said Dr. Bull desperately. "I don't understand a word of all that idea of his being the same man who gave us all our blue cards. It seems to make everything nonsense. But I don't care who knows it, I always had a sympathy for old Sunday himself, wicked as he was. Just as if he was a great bouncing baby. How can I explain what my queer sympathy was? It didn't prevent my fighting him like hell! Shall I make it clear if I say that I liked him because he was so fat?"

"You will not," said the Secretary.

"I've got it now," cried Bull, "it was because he was so fat and so light. Just like a balloon. We always think of fat people as heavy, but he could have danced against a sylph. I see now what I mean. Moderate strength is shown in violence, supreme strength is shown in levity. It was like the old speculations—what would happen if an elephant could leap up in the sky like a grasshopper?"

"Our elephant," said Syme, looking upwards, "has leapt into the sky like a grasshopper."

"And somehow," concluded Bull, "that's why I can't help liking old Sunday. No, it's not an admiration of force, or any silly thing like that. There is a kind of gaiety in the thing, as if he were bursting with some good news. Haven't you sometimes felt it on a spring day? You know Nature plays tricks, but somehow that day proves they are good-natured tricks. I never read the Bible myself, but that part they laugh at is literal truth, 'Why leap ye, ye high hills?' The hills do leap—at least, they try to.... Why do I like Sunday?... how can I tell you?... because he's such a Bounder."

There was a long silence, and then the Secretary said in a curious, strained voice—

"You do not know Sunday at all. Perhaps it is because you are better than I, and do not know hell. I was a fierce fellow, and a trifle morbid from the first. The man who sits in darkness, and who chose us all, chose me because I had all the crazy look of a conspirator—because my smile went crooked, and my eyes were gloomy, even when I smiled. But there must have been something in me that answered to the nerves in all these anarchic men. For when I first saw Sunday he expressed to me, not your airy vitality, but something both gross and sad in the Nature of Things. I found him smoking in a twilight room, a room with brown blind down, infinitely more depressing than the genial darkness in which our master lives. He sat there on a bench, a huge heap of a man, dark and out of shape. He listened to all my words without speaking or even stirring. I poured out my most passionate appeals, and asked my most eloquent questions. Then, after a long silence, the Thing began to shake, and I thought it was shaken by some secret malady. It shook like a loathsome and living jelly. It reminded me of everything I had ever read about the base bodies that are the origin of life—the deep sea lumps and protoplasm. It seemed like the final form of matter, the most shapeless and the most shameful. I could only tell myself, from its shudderings, that it was something at least that such a monster could be miserable. And then it broke upon me that the bestial mountain was shaking with a lonely laughter, and the laughter was at me. Do you ask me to forgive him that? It is no small thing to be laughed at by something at once lower and stronger than oneself."

"Surely you fellows are exaggerating wildly," cut in the clear voice of Inspector Ratcliffe. "President Sunday is a terrible fellow for one's intellect, but he is not such a Barnum's freak physically as you make out. He received me in an ordinary office, in a grey check coat, in broad daylight. He talked to me in an ordinary way. But I'll tell you what is a trifle creepy about Sunday. His room is neat, his clothes are neat, everything seems in order; but he's absent-minded. Sometimes his great bright eyes go quite blind. For hours he forgets that you are there. Now absent-mindedness is just a bit too awful in a bad man. We think of a wicked man as vigilant. We can't think of a wicked man who is honestly and sincerely dreamy, because we daren't think of a wicked man alone with himself. An absentminded man means a good-natured man. It means a man who, if he happens to see you, will apologise. But how will you bear an absentminded man who, if he happens to see you, will kill you? That is what tries the nerves, abstraction combined with cruelty. Men have felt it sometimes when they went through wild forests, and felt that the animals there were at once innocent and pitiless. They might ignore or slay. How would you like to pass ten mortal hours in a parlour with an absent-minded tiger?"

"And what do you think of Sunday, Gogol?" asked Syme.

"I don't think of Sunday on principle," said Gogol simply, "any more than I stare at the sun at noonday."

"Well, that is a point of view," said Syme thoughtfully. "What do you say, Professor?"

The Professor was walking with bent head and trailing stick, and he did not answer at all.

"Wake up, Professor!" said Syme genially. "Tell us what you think of Sunday."

The Professor spoke at last very slowly.

"I think something," he said, "that I cannot say clearly. Or, rather, I think something that I cannot even think clearly. But it is something like this. My early life, as you know, was a bit too large and loose.

"Well, when I saw Sunday's face I thought it was too large—everybody does, but I also thought it was too loose. The face was so big, that one couldn't focus it or make it a face at all. The eye was so far away from the nose, that it wasn't an eye. The mouth was so much by itself, that one had to think of it by itself. The whole thing is too hard to explain."

He paused for a little, still trailing his stick, and then went on—

"But put it this way. Walking up a road at night, I have seen a lamp and a lighted window and a cloud make together a most complete and unmistakable face. If anyone in heaven has that face I shall know him again. Yet when I walked a little farther I found that there was no face, that the window was ten yards away, the lamp ten hundred yards, the cloud beyond the world. Well, Sunday's face escaped me; it ran away to right and left, as such chance pictures run away. And so his face has made me, somehow, doubt whether there are any faces. I don't know whether your face, Bull, is a face or a combination in perspective. Perhaps one black disc of your beastly glasses is quite close and another fifty miles away. Oh, the doubts of a materialist are not worth a dump. Sunday has taught me the last and the worst doubts, the doubts of a spiritualist. I am a Buddhist, I suppose; and Buddhism is not a creed, it is a doubt. My poor dear Bull, I do not believe that you really have a face. I have not faith enough to believe in matter."

Syme's eyes were still fixed upon the errant orb, which, reddened in the evening light, looked like some rosier and more innocent world.

"Have you noticed an odd thing," he said, "about all your descriptions? Each man of you finds Sunday quite different, yet each man of you can only find one thing to compare him to— the universe itself. Bull finds him like the earth in spring, Gogol like the sun at noonday. The Secretary is reminded of the shapeless protoplasm, and the Inspector of the carelessness of virgin forests. The Professor says he is like a changing landscape. This is queer, but it is queerer still that I also have had my odd notion about the President, and I also find that I think of Sunday as I think of the whole world."

"Get on a little faster, Syme," said Bull; "never mind the balloon."

"When I first saw Sunday," said Syme slowly, "I only saw his back; and when I saw his back, I knew he was the worst man in the world. His neck and shoulders were brutal, like those of some apish god. His head had a stoop that was hardly human, like the stoop of an ox. In fact, I had at once the revolting fancy that this was not a man at all, but a beast dressed up in men's clothes."

"Get on," said Dr. Bull.

"And then the queer thing happened. I had seen his back from the street, as he sat in the balcony. Then I entered the hotel, and coming round the other side of him, saw his face in the sunlight. His face frightened me, as it did everyone; but not because it was brutal, not because it was evil. On the contrary, it frightened me because it was so beautiful, because it was so good."

"Syme," exclaimed the Secretary, "are you ill?"

"It was like the face of some ancient archangel, judging justly after heroic wars. There was laughter in the eyes, and in the mouth honour and sorrow. There was the same white hair, the same great, grey-clad shoulders that I had seen from behind. But when I saw him from behind I was certain he was an animal, and when I saw him in front I knew he was a god."

"Pan," said the Professor dreamily, "was a god and an animal."

"Then, and again and always," went on Syme like a man talking to himself, "that has been for me the mystery of Sunday, and it is also the mystery of the world. When I see the horrible back, I am sure the noble face is but a mask. When I see the face but for an instant, I know the back is only a jest. Bad is so bad, that we cannot but think good an accident; good is so good, that we feel certain that evil could be explained. But the whole came to a kind of crest yesterday when I raced Sunday for the cab, and was just behind him all the way."

"Had you time for thinking then?" asked Ratcliffe.

"Time," replied Syme, "for one outrageous thought. I was suddenly possessed with the idea that the blind, blank back of his head really was his face—an awful, eyeless face staring at me! And I fancied that the figure running in front of me was really a figure running backwards, and dancing as he ran."

"Horrible!" said Dr. Bull, and shuddered.

"Horrible is not the word," said Syme. "It was exactly the worst instant of my life. And yet ten minutes afterwards, when he put his head out of the cab and made a grimace like a gargoyle, I knew that he was only like a father playing hide-and-seek with his children."

"It is a long game," said the Secretary, and frowned at his broken boots.

"Listen to me," cried Syme with extraordinary emphasis. "Shall I tell you the secret of the whole world? It is that we have only known the back of the world. We see everything from behind, and it looks brutal. That is not a tree, but the back of a tree. That is not a cloud, but the back of a cloud. Cannot you see that everything is stooping and hiding a face? If we could only get round in front—"

"Look!" cried out Bull clamorously, "the balloon is coming down!"

There was no need to cry out to Syme, who had never taken his eyes off it. He saw the great luminous globe suddenly stagger in the sky, right itself, and then sink slowly behind the trees like a setting sun.

The man called Gogol, who had hardly spoken through all their weary travels, suddenly threw up his hands like a lost spirit.

"He is dead!" he cried. "And now I know he was my friend— my friend in the dark!"

"Dead!" snorted the Secretary. "You will not find him dead easily. If he has been tipped out of the car, we shall find him rolling as a colt rolls in a field, kicking his legs for fun."

"Clashing his hoofs," said the Professor. "The colts do, and so did Pan."

"Pan again!" said Dr. Bull irritably. "You seem to think Pan is everything."

"So he is," said the Professor, "in Greek. He means everything."

"Don't forget," said the Secretary, looking down, "that he also means Panic."

Syme had stood without hearing any of the exclamations.

"It fell over there," he said shortly. "Let us follow it!"

Then he added with an indescribable gesture—

"Oh, if he has cheated us all by getting killed! It would be like one of his larks."

He strode off towards the distant trees with a new energy, his rags and ribbons fluttering in the wind. The others followed him in a more footsore and dubious manner. And almost at the same moment all six men realised that they were not alone in the little field.

Across the square of turf a tall man was advancing towards them, leaning on a strange long staff like a sceptre. He was clad in a fine but old-fashioned suit with knee-breeches; its colour was that shade between blue, violet and grey which can be seen in certain shadows of the woodland. His hair was whitish grey, and at the first glance, taken along with his knee-breeches, looked as if it was powdered. His advance was very quiet; but for the silver frost upon his head, he might have been one to the shadows of the wood.

"Gentlemen," he said, "my master has a carriage waiting for you in the road just by."

"Who is your master?" asked Syme, standing quite still.

"I was told you knew his name," said the man respectfully.

There was a silence, and then the Secretary said—

"Where is this carriage?"

"It has been waiting only a few moments," said the stranger. "My master has only just come home."

Syme looked left and right upon the patch of green field in which he found himself. The hedges were ordinary hedges, the trees seemed ordinary trees; yet he felt like a man entrapped in fairyland.

He looked the mysterious ambassador up and down, but he could discover nothing except that the man's coat was the exact colour of the purple shadows, and that the man's face was the exact colour of the red and brown and golden sky.

"Show us the place," Syme said briefly, and without a word the man in the violet coat turned his back and walked towards a gap in the hedge, which let in suddenly the light of a white road.

As the six wanderers broke out upon this thoroughfare, they saw the white road blocked by what looked like a long row of carriages, such a row of carriages as might close the approach to some house in Park Lane. Along the side of these carriages stood a rank of splendid servants, all dressed in the grey-blue uniform, and all having a certain quality of stateliness and freedom which would not commonly belong to the servants of a gentleman, but rather to the officials and ambassadors of a great king. There were no less than six carriages waiting, one for each of the tattered and miserable band. All the attendants (as if in court-dress) wore swords, and as each man crawled into his carriage they drew them, and saluted with a sudden blaze of steel.

"What can it all mean?" asked Bull of Syme as they separated. "Is this another joke of Sunday's?"

"I don't know," said Syme as he sank wearily back in the cushions of his carriage; "but if it is, it's one of the jokes you talk about. It's a good-natured one."

The six adventurers had passed through many adventures, but not one had carried them so utterly off their feet as this last adventure of comfort. They had all become inured to things going roughly; but things suddenly going smoothly swamped them. They could not even feebly imagine what the carriages were; it was enough for them to know that they were carriages, and carriages with cushions. They could not conceive who the old man was who had led them; but it was quite enough that he had certainly led them to the carriages.

Syme drove through a drifting darkness of trees in utter abandonment. It was typical of him that while he had carried his bearded chin forward fiercely so long as anything could be done, when the whole business was taken out of his hands he fell back on the cushions in a frank collapse.

Very gradually and very vaguely he realised into what rich roads the carriage was carrying him. He saw that they passed the stone gates of what might have been a park, that they began gradually to climb a hill which, while wooded on both sides, was somewhat more orderly than a forest. Then there began to grow upon him, as upon a man slowly waking from a healthy sleep, a pleasure in everything. He felt that the hedges were what hedges should be, living walls; that a hedge is like a human army, disciplined, but all the more alive. He saw high elms behind the hedges, and vaguely thought how happy boys would be climbing there. Then his carriage took a turn of the path, and he saw suddenly and quietly, like a long, low, sunset cloud, a long, low house, mellow in the mild light of sunset. All the six friends compared notes afterwards and quarrelled; but they all agreed that in some unaccountable way the place reminded them of their boyhood. It was either this elm-top or that crooked path, it was either this scrap of orchard or that shape of a window; but each man of them declared that he could remember this place before he could remember his mother.

When the carriages eventually rolled up to a large, low, cavernous gateway, another man in the same uniform, but wearing a silver star on the grey breast of his coat, came out to meet them. This impressive person said to the bewildered Syme—

"Refreshments are provided for you in your room."

Syme, under the influence of the same mesmeric sleep of amazement, went up the large oaken stairs after the respectful attendant. He entered a splendid suite of apartments that seemed to be designed specially for him. He walked up to a long mirror with the ordinary instinct of his class, to pull his tie straight or to smooth his hair; and there he saw the frightful figure that he was— blood running down his face from where the bough had struck him, his hair standing out like yellow rags of rank grass, his clothes torn into long, wavering tatters. At once the whole enigma sprang up, simply as the question of how he had got there, and how he was to get out again. Exactly at the same moment a man in blue, who had been appointed as his valet, said very solemnly—

"I have put out your clothes, sir."

"Clothes!" said Syme sardonically. "I have no clothes except these," and he lifted two long strips of his frock-coat in fascinating festoons, and made a movement as if to twirl like a ballet girl.

"My master asks me to say," said the attendant, "that there is a fancy dress ball tonight, and that he desires you to put on the costume that I have laid out. Meanwhile, sir, there is a bottle of

Burgundy and some cold pheasant, which he hopes you will not refuse, as it is some hours before supper."

"Cold pheasant is a good thing," said Syme reflectively, "and Burgundy is a spanking good thing. But really I do not want either of them so much as I want to know what the devil all this means, and what sort of costume you have got laid out for me. Where is it?"

The servant lifted off a kind of ottoman a long peacock-blue drapery, rather of the nature of a domino, on the front of which was emblazoned a large golden sun, and which was splashed here and there with flaming stars and crescents.

"You're to be dressed as Thursday, sir," said the valet somewhat affably.

"Dressed as Thursday!" said Syme in meditation. "It doesn't sound a warm costume."

"Oh, yes, sir," said the other eagerly, "the Thursday costume is quite warm, sir. It fastens up to the chin."

"Well, I don't understand anything," said Syme, sighing. "I have been used so long to uncomfortable adventures that comfortable adventures knock me out. Still, I may be allowed to ask why I should be particularly like Thursday in a green frock spotted all over with the sun and moon. Those orbs, I think, shine on other days. I once saw the moon on Tuesday, I remember."

"Beg pardon, sir," said the valet, "Bible also provided for you," and with a respectful and rigid finger he pointed out a passage in the first chapter of Genesis. Syme read it wondering. It was that in which the fourth day of the week is associated with the creation of the sun and moon. Here, however, they reckoned from a Christian Sunday.

"This is getting wilder and wilder," said Syme, as he sat down in a chair. "Who are these people who provide cold pheasant and Burgundy, and green clothes and Bibles? Do they provide everything?"

"Yes, sir, everything," said the attendant gravely. "Shall I help you on with your costume?"

"Oh, hitch the bally thing on!" said Syme impatiently.

But though he affected to despise the mummery, he felt a curious freedom and naturalness in his movements as the blue and gold garment fell about him; and when he found that he had to wear a sword, it stirred a boyish dream. As he passed out of the room he flung the folds across his shoulder with a gesture, his sword stood out at an angle, and he had all the swagger of a troubadour. For these disguises did not disguise, but reveal.

CHAPTER XV

The Accuser

As Syme strode along the corridor he saw the Secretary standing at the top of a great flight of stairs. The man had never looked so noble. He was draped in a long robe of starless black, down the centre of which fell a band or broad stripe of pure white, like a single shaft of light. The whole looked like some very severe ecclesiastical vestment. There was no need for Syme to search his memory or the Bible in order to remember that the first day of creation marked the mere creation of light out of darkness. The vestment itself would alone have suggested the symbol; and Syme felt also how perfectly this pattern of pure white and black expressed the soul of the pale and austere Secretary, with his inhuman veracity and his cold frenzy, which made him so easily make war on the anarchists, and yet so easily pass for one of them. Syme was scarcely surprised to notice that, amid all the ease and hospitality of their new surroundings, this man's eyes were still stern. No smell of ale or orchards could make the Secretary cease to ask a reasonable question.

If Syme had been able to see himself, he would have realised that he, too, seemed to be for the first time himself and no one else. For if the Secretary stood for that philosopher who loves the original and formless light, Syme was a type of the poet who seeks always to make the light in special shapes, to split it up into sun and star. The philosopher may sometimes love the infinite; the poet always loves the finite. For him the great moment is not the creation of light, but the creation of the sun and moon.

As they descended the broad stairs together they overtook Ratcliffe, who was clad in spring green like a huntsman, and the pattern upon whose garment was a green tangle of trees. For he stood for that third day on which the earth and green things were made, and his square, sensible face, with its not unfriendly cynicism, seemed appropriate enough to it.

They were led out of another broad and low gateway into a very large old English garden, full of torches and bonfires, by the broken light of which a vast carnival of people were dancing in motley dress. Syme seemed to see every shape in Nature imitated in some crazy costume. There was a man dressed as a windmill with enormous sails, a man dressed as an elephant, a man dressed as a balloon; the two last, together, seemed to keep the thread of their farcical adventures. Syme even saw, with a queer thrill, one dancer dressed like an enormous hornbill, with a beak twice as big as himself—the queer bird which had fixed itself on his fancy like a living question while he was rushing down the long road at the Zoological Gardens. There were a thousand other such objects, however. There was a dancing lamp-post, a dancing apple tree, a dancing ship. One would have thought that the untamable tune of some mad musician had set all the common objects of field and street dancing an eternal jig. And long afterwards, when Syme was middle-aged and at rest, he could never see one of those particular objects—a lamppost, or an apple tree, or a windmill—without thinking that it was a strayed reveller from that revel of masquerade.

On one side of this lawn, alive with dancers, was a sort of green bank, like the terrace in such old-fashioned gardens.

Along this, in a kind of crescent, stood seven great chairs, the thrones of the seven days. Gogol and Dr. Bull were already in their seats; the Professor was just mounting to his. Gogol, or Tuesday, had his simplicity well symbolised by a dress designed upon the division of the waters, a dress that separated upon his forehead and fell to his feet, grey and silver, like a sheet of rain. The Professor, whose day was that on which the birds and fishes—the ruder forms of life—were created, had a dress of dim purple, over which sprawled goggle-eyed fishes and outrageous tropical birds, the union in him of unfathomable fancy and of doubt. Dr. Bull, the last day of Creation, wore a coat covered with heraldic animals in red and gold, and on his crest a man rampant. He lay back in his chair with a broad smile, the picture of an optimist in his element.

One by one the wanderers ascended the bank and sat in their strange seats. As each of them sat down a roar of enthusiasm rose from the carnival, such as that with which crowds receive kings. Cups were clashed and torches shaken, and feathered hats flung in the air. The men for whom these thrones were reserved were men crowned with some extraordinary laurels. But the central chair was empty.

Syme was on the left hand of it and the Secretary on the right. The Secretary looked across the empty throne at Syme, and said, compressing his lips—

"We do not know yet that he is not dead in a field."

Almost as Syme heard the words, he saw on the sea of human faces in front of him a frightful and beautiful alteration, as if heaven had opened behind his head. But Sunday had only passed silently along the front like a shadow, and had sat in the central seat. He was draped plainly, in a pure and terrible white, and his hair was like a silver flame on his forehead.

For a long time—it seemed for hours—that huge masquerade of mankind swayed and stamped in front of them to marching and exultant music. Every couple dancing seemed a separate romance; it might be a fairy dancing with a pillar-box, or a peasant girl dancing with the moon; but in each case it was, somehow, as absurd as Alice in Wonderland, yet as grave and kind as a love story. At last, however, the thick crowd began to thin itself. Couples strolled away into the garden-walks, or began to drift towards that end of the building where stood smoking, in huge pots like fish-kettles, some hot and scented mixtures of old ale or wine. Above all these, upon a sort of black framework on the roof of the house, roared in its iron basket a gigantic bonfire, which lit up the land for miles. It flung the homely effect of firelight over the face of vast forests of grey or brown, and it seemed to fill with warmth even the emptiness of upper night. Yet this also, after a time, was allowed to grow fainter; the dim groups gathered more and more round the great cauldrons, or passed, laughing and clattering, into the inner passages of that ancient house. Soon there were only some ten loiterers in the garden; soon only four. Finally the last stray merry-maker ran into the house whooping to his companions. The fire faded, and the slow, strong stars came out. And the seven strange men were left alone, like seven stone statues on their chairs of stone. Not one of them had spoken a word.

They seemed in no haste to do so, but heard in silence the hum of insects and the distant song of one bird. Then Sunday spoke, but so dreamily that he might have been continuing a conversation rather than beginning one.

"We will eat and drink later," he said. "Let us remain together a little, we who have loved each other so sadly, and have fought so long. I seem to remember only centuries of heroic war, in which you were always heroes—epic on epic, iliad on iliad, and you always brothers in arms. Whether it was but recently (for time is nothing), or at the beginning of the world, I sent you out to war. I sat in the darkness, where there is not any created thing, and to you I was only a voice commanding valour and an unnatural virtue. You heard the voice in the dark, and you never heard it again. The sun in heaven denied it, the earth and sky denied it, all human wisdom denied it. And when I met you in the daylight I denied it myself."

Syme stirred sharply in his seat, but otherwise there was silence, and the incomprehensible went on.

"But you were men. You did not forget your secret honour, though the whole cosmos turned an engine of torture to tear it out of you. I knew how near you were to hell. I know how you, Thursday, crossed swords with King Satan, and how you, Wednesday, named me in the hour without hope."

There was complete silence in the starlit garden, and then the black-browed Secretary, implacable, turned in his chair towards Sunday, and said in a harsh voice—

"Who and what are you?"

"I am the Sabbath," said the other without moving. "I am the peace of God."

The Secretary started up, and stood crushing his costly robe in his hand.

"I know what you mean," he cried, "and it is exactly that that I cannot forgive you. I know you are contentment, optimism, what do they call the thing, an ultimate reconciliation. Well, I am not reconciled. If you were the man in the dark room, why were you also Sunday, an offense to the sunlight? If you were from the first our father and our friend, why were you also our greatest enemy? We wept, we fled in terror; the iron entered into our souls—and you are the peace of God! Oh, I can forgive God His anger, though it destroyed nations; but I cannot forgive Him His peace."

Sunday answered not a word, but very slowly he turned his face of stone upon Syme as if asking a question.

"No," said Syme, "I do not feel fierce like that. I am grateful to you, not only for wine and hospitality here, but for many a fine scamper and free fight. But I should like to know. My soul and heart are as happy and quiet here as this old garden, but my reason is still crying out. I should like to know."

Sunday looked at Ratcliffe, whose clear voice said—

"It seems so *silly* that you should have been on both sides and fought yourself."

Bull said—

"I understand nothing, but I am happy. In fact, I am going to sleep."

"I am not happy," said the Professor with his head in his hands, "because I do not understand. You let me stray a little too near to hell."

And then Gogol said, with the absolute simplicity of a child—

"I wish I knew why I was hurt so much."

Still Sunday said nothing, but only sat with his mighty chin upon his hand, and gazed at the distance. Then at last he said—

"I have heard your complaints in order. And here, I think, comes another to complain, and we will hear him also."

The falling fire in the great cresset threw a last long gleam, like a bar of burning gold, across the dim grass. Against this fiery band was outlined in utter black the advancing legs of a black-clad figure. He seemed to have a fine close suit with knee-breeches such as that which was worn by the servants of the house, only that it was not blue, but of this absolute sable. He had, like the servants, a kind of sword by his side. It was only when he had come quite close to the crescent of the seven and flung up his face to look at them, that Syme saw, with thunder-struck clearness, that the face was the broad, almost ape-like face of his old friend Gregory, with its rank red hair and its insulting smile.

"Gregory!" gasped Syme, half-rising from his seat. "Why, this is the real anarchist!"

"Yes," said Gregory, with a great and dangerous restraint, "I am the real anarchist."

"'Now there was a day,'" murmured Bull, who seemed really to have fallen asleep, "'when the sons of God came to present themselves before the Lord, and Satan came also among them.'"

"You are right," said Gregory, and gazed all round. "I am a destroyer. I would destroy the world if I could."

A sense of a pathos far under the earth stirred up in Syme, and he spoke brokenly and without sequence.

"Oh, most unhappy man," he cried, "try to be happy! You have red hair like your sister."

"My red hair, like red flames, shall burn up the world," said Gregory. "I thought I hated everything more than common men can hate anything; but I find that I do not hate everything so much as I hate you!"

"I never hated you," said Syme very sadly.

Then out of this unintelligible creature the last thunders broke.

"You!" he cried. "You never hated because you never lived. I know what you are all of you, from first to last—you are the people in power! You are the police—the great fat, smiling men in blue and buttons! You are the Law, and you have never been broken. But is there a free soul alive that does not long to break you, only because you have never been broken? We in revolt talk all kind of nonsense doubtless about this crime or that crime of the Government. It is all folly! The only crime of the Government is that it governs. The unpardonable sin of the supreme power is that it is supreme. I do not curse you for being cruel. I do not curse you (though I might) for being kind. I curse you for being safe! You sit in your chairs of stone, and have never come down from them. You are the seven angels of heaven, and you have had no troubles. Oh, I could forgive you everything, you that rule all mankind, if I could feel for once that you had suffered for one hour a real agony such as I—"

Syme sprang to his feet, shaking from head to foot.

"I see everything," he cried, "everything that there is. Why does each thing on the earth war against each other thing? Why does each small thing in the world have to fight against the world itself? Why does a fly have to fight the whole universe? Why does a dandelion have to fight the whole universe? For the same reason that I had to be alone in the dreadful Council of the Days. So that each thing that obeys law may have the glory and isolation of the anarchist. So that each man fighting for order may be as brave and good a man as the dynamiter. So that the real lie of Satan may be flung back in the face of this blasphemer, so that by tears and torture we may earn the right to say to this man, 'You lie!' No agonies can be too great to buy the right to say to this accuser, 'We also have suffered.'

"It is not true that we have never been broken. We have been broken upon the wheel. It is not true that we have never descended from these thrones. We have descended into hell. We were complaining of unforgettable miseries even at the very moment when this man entered insolently to accuse us of happiness. I repel the slander; we have not been happy. I can answer for every one of the great guards of Law whom he has accused. At least—"

He had turned his eyes so as to see suddenly the great face of Sunday, which wore a strange smile.

"Have you," he cried in a dreadful voice, "have you ever suffered?"

As he gazed, the great face grew to an awful size, grew larger than the colossal mask of Memnon, which had made him scream as a child. It grew larger and larger, filling the whole sky; then everything went black. Only in the blackness before it entirely destroyed his brain he seemed to hear a distant voice saying a commonplace text that he had heard somewhere, "Can ye drink of the cup that I drink of?"

When men in books awake from a vision, they commonly find themselves in some place in which they might have fallen asleep; they yawn in a chair, or lift themselves with bruised limbs from a field. Syme's experience was something much more psychologically strange if there was indeed anything unreal, in the earthly sense, about the things he had gone through. For while he could always remember afterwards that he had swooned before the face of Sunday, he could not remember having ever come to at all. He could only remember that gradually and naturally he knew that he was and had been walking along a country lane with an easy and conversational companion. That companion had been a part of his recent drama; it was the red-haired poet Gregory. They were walking like old friends, and were in the middle of a conversation about some triviality. But Syme could only feel an unnatural buoyancy in his body and a crystal simplicity in his mind that seemed to be superior to everything that he said or did. He felt he was in possession of some impossible good news, which made every other thing a triviality, but an adorable triviality.

Dawn was breaking over everything in colours at once clear and timid; as if Nature made a first attempt at yellow and a first attempt at rose. A breeze blew so clean and sweet, that one could not think that it blew from the sky; it blew rather through some hole in the sky. Syme felt a simple surprise when he saw rising all round him on both sides of the road the red, irregular buildings of

Saffron Park. He had no idea that he had walked so near London. He walked by instinct along one white road, on which early birds hopped and sang, and found himself outside a fenced garden. There he saw the sister of Gregory, the girl with the gold-red hair, cutting lilac before breakfast, with the great unconscious gravity of a girl.

THE BALLAD OF THE WHITE HORSE

To MY WIFE

*I say, as do all Christian men, that it is a divine purpose
that rules, and not fate."*

King Alfred's addition to *Boethius*

PREFATORY NOTE

This ballad needs no historical notes, for the simple reason that it does not profess to be historical. All of it that is not frankly fictitious, as in any prose romance about the past, is meant to emphasize tradition rather than history. King Alfred is not a legend in the sense that King Arthur may be a legend; that is, in the sense that he may possibly be a lie. But King Alfred is a legend in this broader and more human sense, that the legends are the most important things about him.

The cult of Alfred was a popular cult, from the darkness of the ninth century to the deepening twilight of the twentieth. It is wholly as a popular legend that I deal with him here. I write as one ignorant of everything, except that I have found the legend of a King of Wessex still alive in the land. I will give three curt cases of what I mean. A tradition connects the ultimate victory of Alfred with the valley in Berkshire called the Vale of the White Horse. I have seen doubts of the tradition, which may be valid doubts. I do not know when or where the story started; it is enough that it started somewhere and ended with me; for I only seek to write upon a hearsay, as the old balladists did. For the second case, there is a popular tale that Alfred played the harp and sang in the Danish camp; I select it because it is a popular tale, at whatever time it arose. For the third case, there is a popular tale that Alfred came in contact with a woman and cakes; I select it because it is a popular tale, because it is a vulgar one. It has been disputed by grave historians, who were, I think, a little too grave to be good judges of it. The two chief charges against the story are that it was first recorded long after Alfred's death, and that (as Mr. Oman urges) Alfred never really wandered all alone without any thanes or soldiers. Both these objections might possibly be met. It has taken us nearly as long to learn the whole truth about Byron, and perhaps longer to learn the whole truth about Pepys, than elapsed between Alfred and the first writing of such tales. And as for the other objection, do the historians really think that Alfred after Wilton, or Napoleon after Leipsic, never walked about in a wood by himself for the matter of an hour or two? Ten minutes might be made sufficient for the essence of the story. But I am not concerned to prove the truth of these popular traditions. It is enough for me to maintain two things: that they are popular traditions; and that without these popular traditions we should have bothered about Alfred about as much as we bother about Eadwig.

One other consideration needs a note. Alfred has come down to us in the best way (that is, by national legends) solely for the same reason as Arthur and Roland and the other giants of that darkness, because he fought for the Christian civilization against the heathen nihilism. But since this work was really done by generation after generation, by the Romans before they withdrew, and by the Britons while they remained, I have summarised this first crusade in a triple symbol, and given to a fictitious Roman, Celt, and Saxon, a part in the glory of Ethandune. I fancy that in fact Alfred's Wessex was of very mixed bloods; but in any case, it is the chief value of legend to mix up the centuries while preserving the sentiment; to see all ages in a sort of splendid foreshortening. That is the use of tradition: it telescopes history.

G. K. C.

DEDICATION

Of great limbs gone to chaos,
A great face turned to night—
Why bend above a shapeless shroud
Seeking in such archaic cloud
Sight of strong lords and light?

Where seven sunken Englands
Lie buried one by one,
Why should one idle spade, I wonder,
Shake up the dust of thanes like
  thunder
To smoke and choke the sun?

In cloud of clay so cast to heaven
What shape shall man discern?
These lords may light the mystery
Of mastery or victory,
And these ride high in history,
But these shall not return.

Gored on the Norman gonfalon
The Golden Dragon died:
We shall not wake with ballad strings
The good time of the smaller things,

We shall not see the holy kings
Ride down by Severn side.

Stiff, strange, and quaintly coloured
As the broidery of Bayeux
The England of that dawn remains,
And this of Alfred and the Danes
Seems like the tales a whole tribe feigns
Too English to be true.

Of a good king on an island
That ruled once on a time;
And as he walked by an apple tree
There came green devils out of the sea
With sea-plants trailing heavily
And tracks of opal slime.

Yet Alfred is no fairy tale;
His days as our days ran,
He also looked forth for an hour
On peopled plains and skies that lower,
From those few windows in the
  tower
That is the head of a man.

But who shall look from Alfred's hood
Or breathe his breath alive?
His century like a small dark cloud
Drifts far; it is an eyeless crowd,
Where the tortured trumpets scream
   aloud
And the dense arrows drive.

Lady, by one light only
We look from Alfred's eyes,
We know he saw athwart the wreck
The sign that hangs about your neck,
Where One more than Melchizedek
Is dead and never dies.

Therefore I bring these rhymes to you
Who brought the cross to me,
Since on you flaming without flaw
I saw the sign that Guthrum saw
When he let break his ships of awe,
And laid peace on the sea.

Do you remember when we went
Under a dragon moon,
And 'mid volcanic tints of night
Walked where they fought the un-
   known fight
And saw black trees on the
   battle-height,
Black thorn on Ethandune?

And I thought, "I will go with you,
As man with God has gone,
And wander with a wandering star,
The wandering heart of things that are,

The fiery cross of love and war
That like yourself, goes on."

O go you onward; where you are
Shall honour and laughter be,
Past purpled forest and pearled foam,
God's winged pavilion free to roam,
Your face, that is a wandering home,
A flying home for me.

Ride through the silent earthquake
   lands,
Wide as a waste is wide,
Across these days like deserts, when
Pride and a little scratching pen
Have dried and split the hearts of
   men,
Heart of the heroes, ride.

Up through an empty house of stars,
Being what heart you are,
Up the inhuman steeps of space
As on a staircase go in grace,
Carrying the firelight on your face
Beyond the loneliest star.

Take these; in memory of the hour
We strayed a space from home
And saw the smoke-hued hamlets,
   quaint
With Westland king and Westland
   saint,
And watched the western glory faint
Along the road to Frome.

BOOK I

The Vision of the King

Before the gods that made the gods
Had seen their sunrise pass,
The White Horse of the White Horse
    Vale
Was cut out of the grass.

Before the gods that made the gods
Had drunk at dawn their fill,
The White Horse of the White Horse
    Vale
Was hoary on the hill.

Age beyond age on British land,
Aeons on aeons gone,
Was peace and war in western hills,
And the White Horse looked on.

For the White Horse knew England
When there was none to know;
He saw the first oar break or bend,
He saw heaven fall and the world
    end,
O God, how long ago.

For the end of the world was long ago,
And all we dwell today
As children of some second birth,
Like a strange people left on earth
After a judgment day.

For the end of the world was long
    ago,
When the ends of the world waxed
    free,
When Rome was sunk in a waste of
    slaves,
And the sun drowned in the sea.

When Caesar's sun fell out of the sky
And whoso hearkened right
Could only hear the plunging
Of the nations in the night.

When the ends of the earth came
    marching in
To torch and cresset gleam.
And the roads of the world that lead
    to Rome

Were filled with faces that moved like
  foam,
Like faces in a dream.

And men rode out of the eastern lands,
Broad river and burning plain;
Trees that are Titan flowers to see,
And tiger skies, striped horribly,
With tints of tropic rain.

Where Ind's enamelled peaks arise
Around that inmost one,
Where ancient eagles on its brink,
Vast as archangels, gather and drink
The sacrament of the sun.

And men brake out of the northern
  lands,
Enormous lands alone,
Where a spell is laid upon life and lust
And the rain is changed to a silver
  dust
And the sea to a great green stone.

And a Shape that moveth murkily
In mirrors of ice and night,
Hath blanched with fear all beasts
  and birds,
As death and a shock of evil words
Blast a man's hair with white.

And the cry of the palms and the
  purple moons,
Or the cry of the frost and foam,
Swept ever around an inmost place,

And the din of distant race on race
Cried and replied round Rome.

And there was death on the Emperor
And night upon the Pope:
And Alfred, hiding in deep grass,
Hardened his heart with hope.

A sea-folk blinder than the sea
Broke all about his land,
But Alfred up against them bare
And gripped the ground and grasped
  the air,
Staggered, and strove to stand.

He bent them back with spear and
  spade,
With desperate dyke and wall,
With foemen leaning on his shield
And roaring on him when he reeled;
And no help came at all.

He broke them with a broken sword
A little towards the sea,
And for one hour of panting peace,
Ringed with a roar that would not
  cease,
With golden crown and girded fleece
Made laws under a tree.

The Northmen came about our land
A Christless chivalry:
Who knew not of the arch or pen,
Great, beautiful half-witted men
From the sunrise and the sea.

Misshapen ships stood on the deep
Full of strange gold and fire,
And hairy men, as huge as sin
With horned heads, came wading in
Through the long, low sea-mire.

Our towns were shaken of tall kings
With scarlet beards like blood:
The world turned empty where they
   trod,
They took the kindly cross of God
And cut it up for wood.

Their souls were drifting as the sea,
And all good towns and lands
They only saw with heavy eyes,
And broke with heavy hands,

Their gods were sadder than the sea,
Gods of a wandering will,
Who cried for blood like beasts at
   night,
Sadly, from hill to hill.

They seemed as trees walking the
   earth,
As witless and as tall,
Yet they took hold upon the heavens
And no help came at all.

They bred like birds in English woods,
They rooted like the rose,
When Alfred came to Athelney
To hide him from their bows

There was not English armour left,
Nor any English thing,
When Alfred came to Athelney
To be an English king.

For earthquake swallowing
   earthquake
Uprent the Wessex tree;
The whirlpool of the pagan sway
Had swirled his sires as sticks away
When a flood smites the sea.

And the great kings of Wessex
Wearied and sank in gore,
And even their ghosts in that great
   stress
Grew greyer and greyer, less and less,
With the lords that died in Lyonesse
And the king that comes no more.

And the God of the Golden Dragon
Was dumb upon his throne,
And the lord of the Golden Dragon
Ran in the woods alone.

And if ever he climbed the crest of luck
And set the flag before,
Returning as a wheel returns,
Came ruin and the rain that burns,
And all began once more.

And naught was left King Alfred
But shameful tears of rage,
In the island in the river
In the end of all his age.

In the island in the river
He was broken to his knee:
And he read, writ with an iron pen,
That God had wearied of Wessex men
And given their country, field and
  fen,
To the devils of the sea.

And he saw in a little picture,
Tiny and far away,
His mother sitting in Egbert's hall,
And a book she showed him, very
  small,
Where a sapphire Mary sat in stall
With a golden Christ at play.

It was wrought in the monk's slow
  manner,
From silver and sanguine shell,
Where the scenes are little and
  terrible,
Keyholes of heaven and hell.

In the river island of Athelney,
With the river running past,
In colours of such simple creed
All things sprang at him, sun and
  weed,
Till the grass grew to be grass indeed
And the tree was a tree at last.

Fearfully plain the flowers grew,
Like the child's book to read,
Or like a friend's face seen in a glass;
He looked; and there Our Lady was,

She stood and stroked the tall live
  grass
As a man strokes his steed.

Her face was like an open word
When brave men speak and choose,
The very colours of her coat
Were better than good news.

She spoke not, nor turned not,
Nor any sign she cast,
Only she stood up straight and free,
Between the flowers in Athelney,
And the river running past.

One dim ancestral jewel hung
On his ruined armour grey,
He rent and cast it at her feet:
Where, after centuries, with slow feet,
Men came from hall and school and
  street
And found it where it lay.

"Mother of God," the wanderer said,
"I am but a common king,
Nor will I ask what saints may ask,
To see a secret thing.

"The gates of heaven are fearful gates
Worse than the gates of hell;
Not I would break the splendours
  barred
Or seek to know the thing they guard,
Which is too good to tell.

"But for this earth most pitiful,
This little land I know,
If that which is for ever is,
Or if our hearts shall break with bliss,
Seeing the stranger go?

"When our last bow is broken, Queen,
And our last javelin cast,
Under some sad, green evening sky,
Holding a ruined cross on high,
Under warm westland grass to lie,
Shall we come home at last?"

And a voice came human but high up,
Like a cottage climbed among
The clouds; or a serf of hut and croft
That sits by his hovel fire as oft,
But hears on his old bare roof aloft
A belfry burst in song.

"The gates of heaven are lightly locked,
We do not guard our gain,
The heaviest hind may easily
Come silently and suddenly
Upon me in a lane.

"And any little maid that walks
In good thoughts apart,
May break the guard of the Three Kings
And see the dear and dreadful things
I hid within my heart.

"The meanest man in grey fields gone
Behind the set of sun,
Heareth between star and other star,

Through the door of the darkness
    fallen ajar,
The council, eldest of things that are,
The talk of the Three in One.

"The gates of heaven are lightly
    locked,
We do not guard our gold,
Men may uproot where worlds begin,
Or read the name of the nameless sin;
But if he fail or if he win
To no good man is told.

"The men of the East may spell the
    stars,
And times and triumphs mark,
But the men signed of the cross of
    Christ
Go gaily in the dark.

"The men of the East may search the
    scrolls
For sure fates and fame,
But the men that drink the blood of
    God
Go singing to their shame.

"The wise men know what wicked
    things
Are written on the sky,
They trim sad lamps, they touch sad
    strings,
Hearing the heavy purple wings,
Where the forgotten seraph kings
Still plot how God shall die.

"The wise men know all evil things
Under the twisted trees,
Where the perverse in pleasure pine
And men are weary of green wine
And sick of crimson seas.

"But you and all the kind of Christ
Are ignorant and brave,
And you have wars you hardly win
And souls you hardly save.

"I tell you naught for your comfort,
Yea, naught for your desire,
Save that the sky grows darker yet
And the sea rises higher.

"Night shall be thrice night over you,
And heaven an iron cope.
Do you have joy without a cause,
Yea, faith without a hope?"

Even as she spoke she was not,
Nor any word said he,
He only heard, still as he stood
Under the old night's nodding hood,
The sea-folk breaking down the wood
Like a high tide from sea.

He only heard the heathen men,
Whose eyes are blue and bleak,
Singing about some cruel thing
Done by a great and smiling king
In daylight on a deck.

He only heard the heathen men,
Whose eyes are blue and blind,
Singing what shameful things are
  done
Between the sunlit sea and the sun
When the land is left behind.

BOOK II

The Gathering of the Chiefs

Up across windy wastes and up
Went Alfred over the shaws,
Shaken of the joy of giants,
The joy without a cause.

In the slopes away to the western
    bays,
Where blows not ever a tree,
He washed his soul in the west wind
And his body in the sea.

And he set to rhyme his ale-measures,
And he sang aloud his laws,
Because of the joy of the giants,
The joy without a cause.

The King went gathering Wessex
    men,
As grain out of the chaff
The few that were alive to die,
Laughing, as littered skulls that lie
After lost battles turn to the sky
An everlasting laugh.

The King went gathering Christian
    men,
As wheat out of the husk;
Eldred, the Franklin by the sea,
And Mark, the man from Italy,
And Colan of the Sacred Tree,
From the old tribe on Usk.

The rook croaked homeward heavily,
The west was clear and warm,
The smoke of evening food and ease
Rose like a blue tree in the trees
When he came to Eldred's farm.

But Eldred's farm was fallen awry,
Like an old cripple's bones,
And Eldred's tools were red with rust,
And on his well was a green crust,
And purple thistles upward thrust,
Between the kitchen stones.

But smoke of some good feasting
Went upwards evermore,

And Eldred's doors stood wide apart
For loitering foot or labouring cart,
And Eldred's great and foolish heart
Stood open like his door.

A mighty man was Eldred,
A bulk for casks to fill,
His face a dreaming furnace,
His body a walking hill.

In the old wars of Wessex
His sword had sunken deep,
But all his friends, he signed and
   said,
Were broken about Ethelred;
And between the deep drink and the
   dead
He had fallen upon sleep.

"Come not to me, King Alfred, Save
   always for the ale:
Why should my harmless hinds be
   slain
Because the chiefs cry once again,
As in all fights, that we shall gain,
And in all fights we fail?

"Your scalds still thunder and
   prophesy
That crown that never comes;
Friend, I will watch the certain
   things,
Swine, and slow moons like silver
   rings,
And the ripening of the plums."

And Alfred answered, drinking,
And gravely, without blame,
"Nor bear I boast of scald or king,
The thing I bear is a lesser thing,
But comes in a better name.

"Out of the mouth of the Mother of
   God,
More than the doors of doom,
I call the muster of Wessex men
From grassy hamlet or ditch or den,
To break and be broken, God knows
   when,
But I have seen for whom.

"Out of the mouth of the Mother of
   God
Like a little word come I;
For I go gathering Christian men
From sunken paving and ford and fen,
To die in a battle, God knows when,
By God, but I know why.

"And this is the word of Mary,
The word of the world's desire
'No more of comfort shall ye get,
Save that the sky grows darker yet
And the sea rises higher.'"

Then silence sank. And slowly
Arose the sea-land lord,
Like some vast beast for mystery,
He filled the room and porch and sky,
And from a cobwebbed nail on high
Unhooked his heavy sword.

Up on the shrill sea-downs and up
Went Alfred all alone,
Turning but once e'er the door was
    shut,
Shouting to Eldred over his butt,
That he bring all spears to the wood-
    man's hut
Hewn under Egbert's Stone.

And he turned his back and broke
    the fern,
And fought the moths of dusk,
And went on his way for other
    friends
Friends fallen of all the wide world's
    ends,
From Rome that wrath and pardon
    sends
And the grey tribes on Usk.

He saw gigantic tracks of death
And many a shape of doom,
Good steadings to grey ashes gone
And a monk's house white like a
    skeleton
In the green crypt of the combe.

And in many a Roman villa
Earth and her ivies eat,
Saw coloured pavements sink and fade
In flowers, and the windy colonnade
Like the spectre of a street.

But the cold stars clustered
Among the cold pines

Ere he was half on his pilgrimage
Over the western lines.

And the white dawn widened
Ere he came to the last pine,
Where Mark, the man from Italy,
Still made the Christian sign.

The long farm lay on the large
    hill-side,
Flat like a painted plan,
And by the side the low white house,
Where dwelt the southland man.

A bronzed man, with a bird's bright
    eye,
And a strong bird's beak and brow,
His skin was brown like buried gold,
And of certain of his sires was told
That they came in the shining ship
    of old,
With Caesar in the prow.

His fruit trees stood like soldiers
Drilled in a straight line,
His strange, stiff olives did not fail,
And all the kings of the earth drank
    ale,
But he drank wine.

Wide over wasted British plains
Stood never an arch or dome,
Only the trees to toss and reel,
The tribes to bicker, the beasts to
    squeal;

But the eyes in his head were strong
　like steel,
And his soul remembered Rome.

Then Alfred of the lonely spear
Lifted his lion head;
And fronted with the Italian's eye,
Asking him of his whence and why,
King Alfred stood and said:

"I am that oft-defeated King
Whose failure fills the land,
Who fled before the Danes of old,
Who chaffered with the Danes with
　gold,
Who now upon the Wessex wold
Hardly has feet to stand.

"But out of the mouth of the Mother
　of God
I have seen the truth like fire,
This—that the sky grows darker yet
And the sea rises higher."

Long looked the Roman on the land;
The trees as golden crowns
Blazed, drenched with dawn and
　dew-empearled
While faintlier coloured, freshlier
　curled,
The clouds from underneath the world
Stood up over the downs.

"These vines be ropes that drag me
　hard,"

He said. "I go not far;
Where would you meet? For you must
　hold
Half Wiltshire and the White Horse
　wold,
And the Thames bank to Owsenfold,
If Wessex goes to war.

"Guthrum sits strong on either bank
And you must press his lines
Inwards, and eastward drive him
　down;
I doubt if you shall take the crown
Till you have taken London town.
For me, I have the vines."

"If each man on the Judgment Day
Meet God on a plain alone,"
Said Alfred, "I will speak for you
As for myself, and call it true
That you brought all fighting folk
　you knew
Lined under Egbert's Stone.

"Though I be in the dust ere then,
I know where you will be."
And shouldering suddenly his spear
He faded like some elfin fear,
Where the tall pines ran up, tier on tier
Tree overtoppling tree.

He shouldered his spear at morning
And laughed to lay it on,
But he leaned on his spear as on a
　staff,

With might and little mood to laugh,
Or ever he sighted chick or calf
Of Colan of Caerleon.

For the man dwelt in a lost land
Of boulders and broken men,
In a great grey cave far off to the
 south
Where a thick green forest stopped the
 mouth,
Giving darkness in his den.

And the man was come like a shadow,
From the shadow of Druid trees,
Where Usk, with mighty
 murmurings,
Past Caerleon of the fallen kings,
Goes out to ghostly seas.

Last of a race in ruin—
He spoke the speech of the Gaels;
His kin were in holy Ireland,
Or up in the crags of Wales.

But his soul stood with his mother's
 folk,
That were of the rain-wrapped isle,
Where Patrick and Brandan westerly
Looked out at last on a landless sea
And the sun's last smile.

His harp was carved and cunning,
As the Celtic craftsman makes,
Graven all over with twisting shapes
Like many headless snakes.

His harp was carved and cunning,
His sword prompt and sharp,
And he was gay when he held the
 sword,
Sad when he held the harp.

For the great Gaels of Ireland
Are the men that God made mad,
For all their wars are merry,
And all their songs are sad.

He kept the Roman order,
He made the Christian sign;
But his eyes grew often blind and
 bright,
And the sea that rose in the rocks at
 night
Rose to his head like wine.

He made the sign of the cross of God,
He knew the Roman prayer,
But he had unreason in his heart
Because of the gods that were.

Even they that walked on the high
 cliffs,
High as the clouds were then,
Gods of unbearable beauty,
That broke the hearts of men.

And whether in seat or saddle,
Whether with frown or smile,
Whether at feast or fight was he,
He heard the noise of a nameless sea
On an undiscovered isle.

Lifting the great green ivy
And the great spear lowering,
One said, "I am Alfred of Wessex,
And I am a conquered king."

And the man of the cave made
  answer,
And his eyes were stars of scorn,
"And better kings were conquered
Or ever your sires were born.

"What goddess was your mother,
What fay your breed begot,
That you should not die with Uther
And Arthur and Lancelot?

"But when you win you brag and
  blow,
And when you lose you rail,
Army of eastland yokels
Not strong enough to fail."

"I bring not boast or railing,"
Spake Alfred not in ire,
"I bring of Our Lady a lesson set,
This—that the sky grows darker yet
And the sea rises higher."

Then Colan of the Sacred Tree
Tossed his black mane on high,
And cried, as rigidly he rose,
"And if the sea and sky be foes,
We will tame the sea and sky."

Smiled Alfred, "Seek ye a fable
More dizzy and more dread
Than all your mad barbarian tales
Where the sky stands on its head?

"A tale where a man looks down on
  the sky
That has long looked down on him;
A tale where a man can swallow a
  sea
That might swallow the seraphim.

"Bring to the hut by Egbert's Stone
All bills and bows ye have."
And Alfred strode off rapidly,
And Colan of the Sacred Tree
Went slowly to his cave.

BOOK III

The Harp of Alfred

In a tree that yawned and twisted
The King's few goods were flung,
A mass-book mildewed, line by line,
And weapons and a skin of wine,
And an old harp unstrung.

By the yawning tree in the twilight
The King unbound his sword,
Severed the harp of all his goods,
And there in the cool and soundless
  woods
Sounded a single chord.

Then laughed; and watched the finches
  flash,
The sullen flies in swarm,
And went unarmed over the hills,
With the harp upon his arm,
Until he came to the White Horse Vale
And saw across the plains,
In the twilight high and far and fell,
Like the fiery terraces of hell,
The camp fires of the Danes—

The fires of the Great Army
That was made of iron men,
Whose lights of sacrilege and scorn
Ran around England red as morn,
Fires over Glastonbury Thorn—
Fires out on Ely Fen.

And as he went by White Horse Vale
He saw lie wan and wide
The old horse graven, God knows
  when,
By gods or beasts or what things then
Walked a new world instead of men
And scrawled on the hill-side.

And when he came to White Horse
  Down
The great White Horse was grey,
For it was ill scoured of the weed,
And lichen and thorn could crawl
  and feed,
Since the foes of settled house and
  creed
Had swept old works away.

King Alfred gazed all sorrowful
At thistle and mosses grey,
Till a rally of Danes with shield and
  bill
Rolled drunk over the dome of the
  hill,
And, hearing of his harp and skill,
They dragged him to their play.

And as they went through the high
  green grass
They roared like the great green sea;
But when they came to the red camp
  fire
They were silent suddenly.

And as they went up the wastes away
They went reeling to and fro;
But when they came to the red camp
  fire
They stood all in a row.

For golden in the firelight,
With a smile carved on his lips,
And a beard curled right cunningly,
Was Guthrum of the Northern Sea,
The emperor of the ships—

With three great earls King Guthrum
Went the rounds from fire to fire,
With Harold, nephew of the King,
And Ogier of the Stone and Sling,
And Elf, whose gold lute had a string
That sighed like all desire.

The Earls of the Great Army
That no men born could tire,
Whose flames anear him or aloof
Took hold of towers or walls of proof,
Fire over Glastonbury roof
And out on Ely, fire.

And Guthrum heard the soldiers' tale
And bade the stranger play;
Not harshly, but as one on high,
On a marble pillar in the sky,
Who sees all folk that live and die—
Pigmy and far away.

And Alfred, King of Wessex,
Looked on his conqueror—
And his hands hardened; but he
  played,
And leaving all later hates unsaid,
He sang of some old British raid
On the wild west march of yore.

He sang of war in the warm wet
  shires,
Where rain nor fruitage fails,
Where England of the motley states
Deepens like a garden to the gates
In the purple walls of Wales.

He sang of the seas of savage heads
And the seas and seas of spears,
Boiling all over Offa's Dyke,
What time a Wessex club could strike
The kings of the mountaineers.

Till Harold laughed and snatched
   the harp,
The kinsman of the King,
A big youth, beardless like a child,
Whom the new wine of war sent wild,
Smote, and began to sing—

And he cried of the ships as eagles
That circle fiercely and fly,
And sweep the seas and strike the
   towns
From Cyprus round to Skye.

How swiftly and with peril
They gather all good things,
The high horns of the forest beasts,
Or the secret stones of kings.

"For Rome was given to rule the
   world,
And gat of it little joy—
But we, but we shall enjoy the world,
The whole huge world a toy.

"Great wine like blood from
   Burgundy,
Cloaks like the clouds from Tyre,
And marble like solid moonlight,
And gold like frozen fire.

"Smells that a man might swill in
   a cup,
Stones that a man might eat,
And the great smooth women like ivory
That the Turks sell in the street."

He sang the song of the thief of the
   world,
And the gods that love the thief;
And he yelled aloud at the
   cloister-yards,
Where men go gathering grief.

"Well have you sung, O stranger,
Of death on the dyke in Wales,
Your chief was a bracelet-giver;
But the red unbroken river
Of a race runs not for ever,
But suddenly it fails.

"Doubtless your sires were
   sword-swingers
When they waded fresh from foam,
Before they were turned to women
By the god of the nails from Rome;

"But since you bent to the shaven
   men,
Who neither lust nor smite,
Thunder of Thor, we hunt you
A hare on the mountain height."

King Guthrum smiled a little,
And said, "It is enough,
Nephew, let Elf retune the string;
A boy must needs like bellowing,
But the old ears of a careful king
Are glad of songs less rough."

Blue-eyed was Elf the minstrel,
With womanish hair and ring,

Yet heavy was his hand on sword,
Though light upon the string.

And as he stirred the strings of the
    harp
To notes but four or five,
The heart of each man moved in him
Like a babe buried alive.

And they felt the land of the
    folk-songs
Spread southward of the Dane,
And they heard the good Rhine
    flowing
In the heart of all Allemagne.

They felt the land of the folk-songs,
Where the gifts hang on the tree,
Where the girls give ale at morning
And the tears come easily.

The mighty people, womanlike,
That have pleasure in their pain
As he sang of Balder beautiful,
Whom the heavens loved in vain.

As he sang of Balder beautiful,
Whom the heavens could not save,
Till the world was like a sea of tears
And every soul a wave.

"There is always a thing forgotten
When all the world goes well;
A thing forgotten, as long ago,
When the gods forgot the mistletoe,

And soundless as an arrow of snow
The arrow of anguish fell.

"The thing on the blind side of the
    heart,
On the wrong side of the door,
The green plant groweth, menacing
Almighty lovers in the spring;
There is always a forgotten thing,
And love is not secure."

And all that sat by the fire were sad,
Save Ogier, who was stern,
And his eyes hardened, even to stones,
As he took the harp in turn;

Earl Ogier of the Stone and Sling
Was odd to ear and sight,
Old he was, but his locks were red,
And jests were all the words he said
Yet he was sad at board and bed
And savage in the fight.

"You sing of the young gods easily
In the days when you are young;
But I go smelling yew and sods,
And I know there are gods behind
    the gods,
Gods that are best unsung.

"And a man grows ugly for women,
And a man grows dull with ale,
Well if he find in his soul at last
Fury, that does not fail.

"The wrath of the gods behind the
  gods
Who would rend all gods and men,
Well if the old man's heart hath still
Wheels sped of rage and roaring will,
Like cataracts to break down and kill,
Well for the old man then—

"While there is one tall shrine to
  shake,
Or one live man to rend;
For the wrath of the gods behind the
  gods
Who are weary to make an end.

"There lives one moment for a man
When the door at his shoulder shakes,
When the taut rope parts under the
  pull,
And the barest branch is beautiful
One moment, while it breaks.

"So rides my soul upon the sea
That drinks the howling ships,
Though in black jest it bows and nods
Under the moons with silver rods,
I know it is roaring at the gods,
Waiting the last eclipse.

"And in the last eclipse the sea
Shall stand up like a tower,
Above all moons made dark and
  riven,
Hold up its foaming head in heaven,
And laugh, knowing its hour.

"And the high ones in the happy town
Propped of the planets seven,
Shall know a new light in the mind,
A noise about them and behind,
Shall hear an awful voice, and find
Foam in the courts of heaven.

"And you that sit by the fire are young,
And true love waits for you;
But the king and I grow old, grow
  old,
And hate alone is true."

And Guthrum shook his head but
  smiled,
For he was a mighty clerk,
And had read lines in the Latin books
When all the north was dark.

He said, "I am older than you, Ogier;
Not all things would I rend,
For whether life be bad or good
It is best to abide the end."

He took the great harp wearily,
Even Guthrum of the Danes,
With wide eyes bright as the one long
  day
On the long polar plains.

For he sang of a wheel returning,
And the mire trod back to mire,
And how red hells and golden
  heavens
Are castles in the fire.

"It is good to sit where the good tales
  go,
To sit as our fathers sat;
But the hour shall come after his
  youth,
When a man shall know not tales but
  truth,
And his heart fail thereat.

"When he shall read what is written
So plain in clouds and clods,
When he shall hunger without hope
Even for evil gods.

"For this is a heavy matter,
And the truth is cold to tell;
Do we not know, have we not heard,
The soul is like a lost bird,
The body a broken shell.

"And a man hopes, being ignorant,
Till in white woods apart
He finds at last the lost bird dead:
And a man may still lift up his head
But never more his heart.

"There comes no noise but weeping
Out of the ancient sky,
And a tear is in the tiniest flower
Because the gods must die.

"The little brooks are very sweet,
Like a girl's ribbons curled,
But the great sea is bitter
That washes all the world.

"Strong are the Roman roses,
Or the free flowers of the heath,
But every flower, like a flower of the
  sea,
Smelleth with the salt of death.

"And the heart of the locked battle
Is the happiest place for men;
When shrieking souls as shafts go by
And many have died and all may die;
Though this word be a mystery,
Death is most distant then.

"Death blazes bright above the cup,
And clear above the crown;
But in that dream of battle
We seem to tread it down.

"Wherefore I am a great king,
And waste the world in vain,
Because man hath not other power,
Save that in dealing death for dower,
He may forget it for an hour
To remember it again."

And slowly his hands and thoughtfully
Fell from the lifted lyre,
And the owls moaned from the
  mighty trees
Till Alfred caught it to his knees
And smote it as in ire.

He heaved the head of the harp on
  high
And swept the framework barred,

And his stroke had all the rattle and
    spark
Of horses flying hard.

"When God put man in a garden
He girt him with a sword,
And sent him forth a free knight
That might betray his lord;

"He brake Him and betrayed Him,
And fast and far he fell,
Till you and I may stretch our necks
And burn our beards in hell.

"But though I lie on the floor of the
    world,
With the seven sins for rods,
I would rather fall with Adam
Than rise with all your gods.

"What have the strong gods given?
Where have the glad gods led?
When Guthrum sits on a hero's throne
And asks if he is dead?

"Sirs, I am but a nameless man,
A rhymester without home,
Yet since I come of the Wessex clay
And carry the cross of Rome,

"I will even answer the mighty earl
That asked of Wessex men
Why they be meek and monkish folk,
And bow to the White Lord's broken
    yoke;

What sign have we save blood and
    smoke?
Here is my answer then.

"That on you is fallen the shadow,
And not upon the Name;
That though we scatter and though
    we fly,
And you hang over us like the sky,
You are more tired of victory,
Than we are tired of shame.

"That though you hunt the Christian
    man
Like a hare on the hill-side,
The hare has still more heart to run
Than you have heart to ride.

"That though all lances split on you,
All swords be heaved in vain,
We have more lust again to lose
Than you to win again.

"Your lord sits high in the saddle,
A broken-hearted king,
But our king Alfred, lost from fame,
Fallen among foes or bonds of shame,
In I know not what mean trade or
    name,
Has still some song to sing;

"Our monks go robed in rain and snow,
But the heart of flame therein,
But you go clothed in feasts and flames,
When all is ice within;

"Nor shall all iron dooms make dumb
Men wondering ceaselessly,
If it be not better to fast for joy
Than feast for misery.

"Nor monkish order only
Slides down, as field to fen,
All things achieved and chosen pass,
As the White Horse fades in the grass,
No work of Christian men.

"Ere the sad gods that made your gods
Saw their sad sunrise pass,
The White Horse of the White Horse
   Vale,
That you have left to darken and fail,
Was cut out of the grass.

"Therefore your end is on you,
Is on you and your kings,
Not for a fire in Ely fen,
Not that your gods are nine or ten,
But because it is only Christian men
Guard even heathen things.

"For our God hath blessed creation,
Calling it good. I know
What spirit with whom you blindly
   band
Hath blessed destruction with his
   hand;
Yet by God's death the stars shall
   stand
And the small apples grow."

And the King, with harp on shoulder,
Stood up and ceased his song;
And the owls moaned from the
   mighty trees,
And the Danes laughed loud and
   long.

Book I

BOOK IV

The Woman in the Forest

Thick thunder of the snorting swine,
Enormous in the gloam,
Rending among all roots that cling,
And the wild horses whinnying,
Were the night's noises when the King
Shouldering his harp, went home.

With eyes of owl and feet of fox,
Full of all thoughts he went;
He marked the tilt of the pagan camp,
The paling of pine, the sentries' tramp,
And the one great stolen altar-lamp
Over Guthrum in his tent.

By scrub and thorn in Ethandune
That night the foe had lain;
Whence ran across the heather grey
The old stones of a Roman way;
And in a wood not far away
The pale road split in twain.

He marked the wood and the cloven
  ways
With an old captain's eyes,

And he thought how many a time
  had he
Sought to see Doom he could not see;
How ruin had come and victory,
And both were a surprise.

Even so he had watched and wondered
Under Ashdown from the plains;
With Ethelred praying in his tent,
Till the white hawthorn swung and
  bent,
As Alfred rushed his spears and rent
The shield-wall of the Danes.

Even so he had watched and
  wondered,
Knowing neither less nor more,
Till all his lords lay dying,
And axes on axes plying,
Flung him, and drove him flying
Like a pirate to the shore.

Wise he had been before defeat,
And wise before success;

Wise in both hours and ignorant,
Knowing neither more nor less.

As he went down to the river-hut
He knew a night-shade scent,
Owls did as evil cherubs rise,
With little wings and lantern eyes,
As though he sank through the
*   under-skies;*
But down and down he went.

As he went down to the river-hut
He went as one that fell;
Seeing the high forest domes and
*   spars.*
Dim green or torn with golden scars,
As the proud look up at the evil stars,
In the red heavens of hell.

For he must meet by the river-hut
Them he had bidden to arm,
Mark from the towers of Italy,
And Colan of the Sacred Tree,
And Eldred who beside the sea
Held heavily his farm.

The roof leaned gaping to the grass,
As a monstrous mushroom lies;
Echoing and empty seemed the place;
But opened in a little space
A great grey woman with scarred face
And strong and humbled eyes.

King Alfred was but a meagre man,
Bright eyed, but lean and pale:

And swordless, with his harp and
*   rags,*
He seemed a beggar, such as lags
Looking for crusts and ale.

And the woman, with a woman's eyes
Of pity at once and ire,
Said, when that she had glared a
*   span,*
"There is a cake for any man
If he will watch the fire."

And Alfred, bowing heavily,
Sat down the fire to stir,
And even as the woman pitied him
So did he pity her.

Saying, "O great heart in the night,
O best cast forth for worst,
Twilight shall melt and morning stir,
And no kind thing shall come to her,
Till God shall turn the world over
And all the last are first.

"And well may God with the
*   serving-folk*
Cast in His dreadful lot;
Is not He too a servant,
And is not He forgot?

"For was not God my gardener
And silent like a slave;
That opened oaks on the uplands
Or thicket in graveyard gave?

"And was not God my armourer,
All patient and unpaid,
That sealed my skull as a helmet,
And ribs for hauberk made?

"Did not a great grey servant
Of all my sires and me,
Build this pavilion of the pines,
And herd the fowls and fill the vines,
And labour and pass and leave no
  signs
Save mercy and mystery?

"For God is a great servant,
And rose before the day,
From some primordial slumber torn;
But all we living later born
Sleep on, and rise after the morn,
And the Lord has gone away.

"On things half sprung from sleeping,
All sleepy suns have shone,
They stretch stiff arms, the yawning
  trees,
The beasts blink upon hands and knees,
Man is awake and does and sees—
But Heaven has done and gone.

"For who shall guess the good riddle
Or speak of the Holiest,
Save in faint figures and failing
  words,
Who loves, yet laughs among the
  swords,
Labours, and is at rest?

"But some see God like Guthrum,
Crowned, with a great beard curled,
But I see God like a good giant,
That, labouring, lifts the world.

"Wherefore was God in Golgotha,
Slain as a serf is slain;
And hate He had of prince and peer,
And love He had and made good cheer,
Of them that, like this woman here,
Go powerfully in pain.

"But in this grey morn of man's life,
Cometh sometime to the mind
A little light that leaps and flies,
Like a star blown on the wind.

"A star of nowhere, a nameless star,
A light that spins and swirls,
And cries that even in hedge and hill,
Even on earth, it may go ill
At last with the evil earls.

"A dancing sparkle, a doubtful star,
On the waste wind whirled and
  driven;
But it seems to sing of a wilder
  worth,
A time discrowned of doom and birth,
And the kingdom of the poor on earth
Come, as it is in heaven.

"But even though such days endure,
How shall it profit her?
Who shall go groaning to the grave,

With many a meek and mighty slave,
Field-breaker and fisher on the wave,
And woodman and waggoner.

"Bake ye the big world all again
A cake with kinder leaven;
Yet these are sorry evermore—
Unless there be a little door,
A little door in heaven."

And as he wept for the woman
He let her business be,
And like his royal oath and rash
The good food fell upon the ash
And blackened instantly.

Screaming, the woman caught a cake
Yet burning from the bar,
And struck him suddenly on the face,
Leaving a scarlet scar.

King Alfred stood up wordless,
A man dead with surprise,
And torture stood and the evil things
That are in the childish hearts of kings
An instant in his eyes.

And even as he stood and stared
Drew round him in the dusk
Those friends creeping from far-off
   farms,
Marcus with all his slaves in arms,
And the strange spears hung with
   ancient charms
Of Colan of the Usk.

With one whole farm marching afoot
The trampled road resounds,
Farm-hands and farm-beasts blun-
   dering by
And jars of mead and stores of rye,
Where Eldred strode above his high
And thunder-throated hounds.

And grey cattle and silver lowed
Against the unlifted morn,
And straw clung to the spear-shafts
   tall.
And a boy went before them all
Blowing a ram's horn.

As mocking such rude revelry,
The dim clan of the Gael
Came like a bad king's burial-end,
With dismal robes that drop and rend
And demon pipes that wail—

In long, outlandish garments,
Torn, though of antique worth,
With Druid beards and Druid spears,
As a resurrected race appears
Out of an elder earth.

And though the King had called them
   forth
And knew them for his own,
So still each eye stood like a gem,
So spectral hung each broidered hem,
Grey carven men he fancied them,
Hewn in an age of stone.

And the two wild peoples of the north
Stood fronting in the gloam,
And heard and knew each in its mind
The third great thunder on the wind,
The living walls that hedge mankind,
The walking walls of Rome.

Mark's were the mixed tribes of the
    west,
Of many a hue and strain,
Gurth, with rank hair like yellow
    grass,
And the Cornish fisher, Gorlias,
And Halmer, come from his first mass,
Lately baptized, a Dane.

But like one man in armour
Those hundreds trod the field,
From red Arabia to the Tyne
The earth had heard that
    marching-line,
Since the cry on the hill Capitoline,
And the fall of the golden shield.

And the earth shook and the King
    stood still
Under the greenwood bough,
And the smoking cake lay at his feet
And the blow was on his brow.

Then Alfred laughed out suddenly,
Like thunder in the spring,
Till shook aloud the lintel-beams,
And the squirrels stirred in dusty
    dreams,

And the startled birds went up in
    streams,
For the laughter of the King.

And the beasts of the earth and the
    birds looked down,
In a wild solemnity,
On a stranger sight than a sylph or
    elf,
On one man laughing at himself
Under the greenwood tree—

The giant laughter of Christian men
That roars through a thousand tales,
Where greed is an ape and pride is
    an ass,
And Jack's away with his master's lass,
And the miser is banged with all his
    brass,
The farmer with all his flails;

Tales that tumble and tales that trick,
Yet end not all in scorning—
Of kings and clowns in a merry
    plight,
And the clock gone wrong and the
    world gone right,
That the mummers sing upon
    Christmas night
And Christmas Day in the morning.

"Now here is a good warrant,"
Cried Alfred, "by my sword;
For he that is struck for an ill servant
Should be a kind lord.

"He that has been a servant
Knows more than priests and kings,
But he that has been an ill servant,
He knows all earthly things.

"Pride flings frail palaces at the sky,
As a man flings up sand,
But the firm feet of humility
Take hold of heavy land.

"Pride juggles with her toppling
    towers,
They strike the sun and cease,
But the firm feet of humility
They grip the ground like trees.

"He that hath failed in a little thing
Hath a sign upon the brow;
And the Earls of the Great Army
Have no such seal to show.

"The red print on my forehead,
Small flame for a red star,
In the van of the violent marching,
    then
When the sky is torn of the trumpets
    ten,
And the hands of the happy howling
    men
Fling wide the gates of war.

"This blow that I return not
Ten times will I return
On kings and earls of all degree,
And armies wide as empires be

Shall slide like landslips to the sea
If the red star burn.

"One man shall drive a hundred,
As the dead kings drave;
Before me rocking hosts be riven,
And battering cohorts backwards
    driven,
For I am the first king known of
    Heaven
That has been struck like a slave.

"Up on the old white road, brothers,
Up on the Roman walls!
For this is the night of the drawing
    of swords,
And the tainted tower of the heathen
    hordes
Leans to our hammers, fires and cords,
Leans a little and falls.

"Follow the star that lives and leaps,
Follow the sword that sings,
For we go gathering heathen men,
A terrible harvest, ten by ten,
As the wrath of the last red
    autumn—then
When Christ reaps down the kings.

"Follow a light that leaps and spins,
Follow the fire unfurled!
For riseth up against realm and rod,
A thing forgotten, a thing downtrod,
The last lost giant, even God,
Is risen against the world."

Roaring they went o'er the Roman
  wall,
And roaring up the lane,
Their torches tossed a ladder of fire,
Higher their hymn was heard and
  higher,
More sweet for hate and for heart's
  desire,
And up in the northern scrub and
  brier,
They fell upon the Dane.

BOOK V

Ethandune: The First Stroke

King Guthrum was a dread king,
Like death out of the north;
Shrines without name or number
He rent and rolled as lumber,
From Chester to the Humber
He drove his foemen forth.

The Roman villas heard him
In the valley of the Thames,
Come over the hills roaring
Above their roofs, and pouring
On spire and stair and flooring
Brimstone and pitch and flames.

Sheer o'er the great chalk uplands
And the hill of the Horse went he,
Till high on Hampshire beacons
He saw the southern sea.

High on the heights of Wessex
He saw the southern brine,
And turned him to a conquered land,
And where the northern thornwoods
  stand,
And the road parts on either hand,
There came to him a sign.

King Guthrum was a war-chief,
A wise man in the field,
And though he prospered well, and
  knew
How Alfred's folk were sad and few,
Not less with weighty care he drew
Long lines for pike and shield.

King Guthrum lay on the upper land,
On a single road at gaze,
And his foe must come with lean array,
Up the left arm of the cloven way,
To the meeting of the ways.

And long ere the noise of armour,
An hour ere the break of light,
The woods awoke with crash and cry,
And the birds sprang clamouring
  harsh and high,
And the rabbits ran like an elves' army
Ere Alfred came in sight.

The live wood came at Guthrum,
On foot and claw and wing,
The nests were noisy overhead,
For Alfred and the star of red,
All life went forth, and the
  forest fled
Before the face of the King.

But halted in the woodways
Christ's few were grim and grey,
And each with a small, far, bird-like
  sight
Saw the high folly of the fight;
And though strange joys had grown
  in the night,
Despair grew with the day.

And when white dawn crawled
  through the wood,
Like cold foam of a flood,
Then weakened every warrior's
  mood,
In hope, though not in hardihood;
And each man sorrowed as he stood
In the fashion of his blood.

For the Saxon Franklin sorrowed
For the things that had been fair;
For the dear dead woman,
  crimson-clad,
And the great feasts and the friends
  he had;
But the Celtic prince's soul was sad
For the things that never were.

In the eyes Italian all things
But a black laughter died;
And Alfred flung his shield to earth
And smote his breast and cried—

"I wronged a man to his slaying,
And a woman to her shame,
And once I looked on a sworn maid
That was wed to the Holy Name.

"And once I took my neighbour's wife,
That was bound to an eastland man,
In the starkness of my evil youth,
Before my griefs began.

"People, if you have any prayers,
Say prayers for me:
And lay me under a Christian stone
In that lost land I thought my own,
To wait till the holy horn is blown,
And all poor men are free."

Then Eldred of the idle farm
Leaned on his ancient sword,
As fell his heavy words and few;
And his eyes were of such alien blue
As gleams where the Northman
  saileth new
Into an unknown fiord.

"I was a fool and wasted ale—
My slaves found it sweet;
I was a fool and wasted bread,
And the birds had bread to eat.

"The kings go up and the kings go
    down,
And who knows who shall rule;
Next night a king may starve or sleep,
But men and birds and beasts shall
    weep
At the burial of a fool.

"O, drunkards in my cellar,
Boys in my apple tree,
The world grows stern and strange
    and new,
And wise men shall govern you,
And you shall weep for me.

"But yoke me my own oxen,
Down to my own farm;
My own dog will whine for me,
My own friends will bend the knee,
And the foes I slew openly
Have never wished me harm."

And all were moved a little,
But Colan stood apart,
Having first pity, and after
Hearing, like rat in rafter,
That little worm of laughter
That eats the Irish heart.

And his grey-green eyes were cruel,
And the smile of his mouth waxed
    hard,
And he said, "And when did Britain
Become your burying-yard?

"Before the Romans lit the land,
When schools and monks were
    none,
We reared such stones to the sun-god
As might put out the sun.

"The tall trees of Britain
We worshipped and were wise,
But you shall raid the whole land
    through
And never a tree shall talk to you,
Though every leaf is a tongue
    taught true
And the forest is full of eyes.

"On one round hill to the seaward
The trees grow tall and grey
And the trees talk together
When all men are away.

"O'er a few round hills forgotten
The trees grow tall in rings,
And the trees talk together
Of many pagan things.

"Yet I could lie and listen
With a cross upon my clay,
And hear unhurt for ever
What the trees of Britain say."

A proud man was the Roman,
His speech a single one,
But his eyes were like an eagle's eyes
That is staring at the sun.

"Dig for me where I die," he said,
"If first or last I fall—
Dead on the fell at the first charge,
Or dead by Wantage wall;

"Lift not my head from bloody
    ground,
Bear not my body home,
For all the earth is Roman earth
And I shall die in Rome."

Then Alfred, King of England,
Bade blow the horns of war,
And fling the Golden Dragon out,
With crackle and acclaim and shout,
Scrolled and aflame and far.

And under the Golden Dragon
Went Wessex all along,
Past the sharp point of the cloven
    ways,
Out from the black wood into the
    blaze
Of sun and steel and song.

And when they came to the open land
They wheeled, deployed and stood;
Midmost were Marcus and the King,
And Eldred on the right-hand wing,
And leftwards Colan darkling,
In the last shade of the wood.

But the Earls of the Great Army
Lay like a long half moon,
Ten poles before their palisades,

With wide-winged helms and runic
    blades
Red giants of an age of raids,
In the thornland of Ethandune.

Midmost the saddles rose and swayed,
And a stir of horses' manes,
Where Guthrum and a few rode high
On horses seized in victory;
But Ogier went on foot to die,
In the old way of the Danes.

Far to the King's left Elf the bard
Led on the eastern wing
With songs and spells that change the
    blood;
And on the King's right Harold stood,
The kinsman of the King.

Young Harold, coarse, with colours
    gay,
Smoking with oil and musk,
And the pleasant violence of the
    young,
Pushed through his people, giving
    tongue
Foewards, where, grey as cobwebs
    hung,
The banners of the Usk.

But as he came before his line
A little space along,
His beardless face broke into mirth,
And he cried: "What broken bits of
    earth

Are here? For what their clothes are
   worth
I would sell them for a song."

For Colan was hung with raiment
Tattered like autumn leaves,
And his men were all as thin as saints,
And all as poor as thieves.

No bows nor slings nor bolts they
   bore,
But bills and pikes ill-made;
And none but Colan bore a sword,
And rusty was its blade.

And Colan's eyes with mystery
And iron laughter stirred,
And he spoke aloud, but lightly
Not labouring to be heard.

"Oh, truly we be broken hearts,
For that cause, it is said,
We light our candles to that Lord
That broke Himself for bread.

"But though we hold but bitterly
What land the Saxon leaves,
Though Ireland be but a land of
   saints,
And Wales a land of thieves,

"I say you yet shall weary
Of the working of your word,
That stricken spirits never strike
Nor lean hands hold a sword.

"And if ever ye ride in Ireland,
The jest may yet be said,
There is the land of broken hearts,
And the land of broken heads."

Not less barbarian laughter
Choked Harold like a flood,
"And shall I fight with scarecrows
That am of Guthrum's blood?

"Meeting may be of war-men,
Where the best war-man wins;
But all this carrion a man shoots
Before the fight begins."

And stopping in his onward strides,
He snatched a bow in scorn
From some mean slave, and bent it on
Colan, whose doom grew dark; and
   shone
Stars evil over Caerleon,
In the place where he was born.

For Colan had not bow nor sling,
On a lonely sword leaned he,
Like Arthur on Excalibur
In the battle by the sea.

To his great gold ear-ring Harold
Tugged back the feathered tail,
And swift had sprung the arrow,
But swifter sprang the Gael.

Whirling the one sword round his
   head,

A great wheel in the sun,
He sent it splendid through the sky,
Flying before the shaft could fly—
It smote Earl Harold over the eye,
And blood began to run.

Colan stood bare and weaponless,
Earl Harold, as in pain,
Strove for a smile, put hand to head,
Stumbled and suddenly fell dead;
And the small white daisies all waxed
    red
With blood out of his brain.

And all at that marvel of the sword,
Cast like a stone to slay,
Cried out. Said Alfred: "Who would
    see
Signs, must give all things. Verily
Man shall not taste of victory
Till he throws his sword away."

Then Alfred, prince of England,
And all the Christian earls,
Unhooked their swords and held
    them up,
Each offered to Colan, like a cup
Of chrysolite and pearls.

And the King said, "Do thou take my
    sword
Who have done this deed of fire,
For this is the manner of Christian
    men,
Whether of steel or priestly pen,

That they cast their hearts out of their
    ken
To get their heart's desire.

"And whether ye swear a hive of
    monks,
Or one fair wife to friend,
This is the manner of Christian men,
That their oath endures the end.

"For love, our Lord, at the end of the
    world,
Sits a red horse like a throne,
With a brazen helm and an iron bow,
But one arrow alone.

"Love with the shield of the Broken
    Heart
Ever his bow doth bend,
With a single shaft for a single prize,
And the ultimate bolt that parts and
    flies
Comes with a thunder of split skies,
And a sound of souls that rend.

"So shall you earn a king's sword,
Who cast your sword away."
And the King took, with a random
    eye,
A rude axe from a hind hard by
And turned him to the fray.

For the swords of the Earls of
    Daneland
Flamed round the fallen lord.

The first blood woke the
  trumpet-tune,
As in monk's rhyme or wizard's rune,
Beginneth the battle of Ethandune
With the throwing of the sword.

BOOK VI

Ethandune: The Slaying of the Chiefs

As the sea flooding the flat sands
Flew on the sea-born horde,
The two hosts shocked with dust
 and din,
Left of the Latian paladin,
Clanged all Prince Harold's
 howling kin
On Colan and the sword.

Crashed in the midst on Marcus,
Ogier with Guthrum by,
And eastward of such central
 stir,
Far to the right and faintlier,
The house of Elf the harp-player,
Struck Eldred's with a cry.

The centre swat for weariness,
Stemming the screaming horde,
And wearily went Colan's hands
That swung King Alfred's sword.

But like a cloud of morning
To eastward easily,

Tall Eldred broke the sea of spears
As a tall ship breaks the sea.

His face like a sanguine sunset,
His shoulder a Wessex down,
His hand like a windy
 hammer-stroke;
Men could not count the crests he
 broke,
So fast the crests went down.

As the tall white devil of the Plague
Moves out of Asian skies,
With his foot on a waste of cities
And his head in a cloud of flies;

Or purple and peacock skies grow
 dark
With a moving locust-tower;
Or tawny sand-winds tall and dry,
Like hell's red banners beat and fly,
When death comes out of Araby,
Was Eldred in his hour.

But while he moved like a massacre
He murmured as in sleep,
And his words were all of low hedges
And little fields and sheep.

Even as he strode like a pestilence,
That strides from Rhine to Rome,
He thought how tall his beans might
  be
If ever he went home.

Spoke some stiff piece of childish prayer,
Dull as the distant chimes,
That thanked our God for good eating
And corn and quiet times—

Till on the helm of a high chief
Fell shatteringly his brand,
And the helm broke and the bone broke
And the sword broke in his hand.

Then from the yelling Northmen
Driven splintering on him ran
Full seven spears, and the seventh
Was never made by man.

Seven spears, and the seventh
Was wrought as the faerie blades,
And given to Elf the minstrel
By the monstrous water-maids;

By them that dwell where luridly
Lost waters of the Rhine
Move among roots of nations,
Being sunken for a sign.

Under all graves they murmur,
They murmur and rebel,
Down to the buried kingdoms creep,
And like a lost rain roar and weep
O'er the red heavens of hell.

Thrice drowned was Elf the minstrel,
And washed as dead on sand;
And the third time men found him
The spear was in his hand.

Seven spears went about Eldred,
Like stays about a mast;
But there was sorrow by the sea
For the driving of the last.

Six spears thrust upon Eldred
Were splintered while he laughed;
One spear thrust into Eldred,
Three feet of blade and shaft.

And from the great heart grievously
Came forth the shaft and blade,
And he stood with the face of a dead
  man,
Stood a little, and swayed—

Then fell, as falls a battle-tower,
On smashed and struggling spears.
Cast down from some unconquered
  town
That, rushing earthward, carries down
Loads of live men of all renown—
Archers and engineers.

And a great clamour of Christian
   men
Went up in agony,
Crying, "Fallen is the tower of Wessex
That stood beside the sea."

Centre and right the Wessex guard
Grew pale for doubt and fear,
And the flank failed at the advance,
For the death-light on the wizard
   lance—
The star of the evil spear.

"Stand like an oak," cried Marcus,
"Stand like a Roman wall!
Eldred the Good is fallen—
Are you too good to fall?

"When we were wan and bloodless
He gave you ale enow;
The pirates deal with him as dung,
God! are you bloodless now?"

"Grip, Wulf and Gorlias, grip the ash!
Slaves, and I make you free!
Stamp, Hildred hard in English land,
Stand Gurth, stand Gorlias, Gawen
   stand!
Hold, Halfgar, with the other hand,
Halmer, hold up on knee!

"The lamps are dying in your homes,
The fruits upon your bough;
Even now your old thatch smoulders,
   Gurth,

Now is the judgment of the earth,
Now is the death-grip, now!"

For thunder of the captain,
Not less the Wessex line,
Leaned back and reeled a space to rear
As Elf charged with the Rhine maids'
   spear,
And roaring like the Rhine.

For the men were borne by the wav-
   ing walls
Of woods and clouds that pass,
By dizzy plains and drifting sea,
And they mixed God with glamoury,
God with the gods of the burning tree
And the wizard's tower and glass.

But Mark was come of the glittering
   towns
Where hot white details show,
Where men can number and expound,
And his faith grew in a hard ground
Of doubt and reason and falsehood
   found,
Where no faith else could grow.

Belief that grew of all beliefs
One moment back was blown
And belief that stood on unbelief
Stood up iron and alone.

The Wessex crescent backwards
Crushed, as with bloody spear
Went Elf roaring and routing,

And Mark against Elf yet shouting,
Shocked, in his mid-career.

Right on the Roman shield and sword
Did spear of the Rhine maids run;
But the shield shifted never,
The sword rang down to sever,
The great Rhine sang for ever,
And the songs of Elf were done.

And a great thunder of Christian
    men
Went up against the sky,
Saying, "God hath broken the evil
    spear
Ere the good man's blood was dry."

"Spears at the charge!" yelled Mark
    amain.
"Death on the gods of death!
Over the thrones of doom and blood
Goeth God that is a craftsman good,
And gold and iron, earth and wood,
Loveth and laboureth.

"The fruits leap up in all your farms,
The lamps in each abode;
God of all good things done on earth,
All wheels or webs of any worth,
The God that makes the roof, Gurth,
The God that makes the road.

"The God that heweth kings in oak
Writeth songs on vellum,
God of gold and flaming glass,

Confregit potentias
Acrcuum, scutum, Gorlias,
Gladium et bellum."

Steel and lightning broke about him,
Battle-bays and palm,
All the sea-kings swayed among
Woods of the Wessex arms upflung,
The trumpet of the Roman tongue,
The thunder of the psalm.

And midmost of that rolling field
Ran Ogier ragingly,
Lashing at Mark, who turned his
    blow,
And brake the helm about his brow,
And broke him to his knee.

Then Ogier heaved over his head
His huge round shield of proof;
But Mark set one foot on the shield,
One on some sundered rock upheeled,
And towered above the tossing field,
A statue on a roof.

Dealing far blows about the fight,
Like thunder-bolts a-roam,
Like birds about the battle-field,
While Ogier writhed under his shield
Like a tortoise in his dome.

But hate in the buried Ogier
Was strong as pain in hell,
With bare brute hand from the inside
He burst the shield of brass and hide,

And a death-stroke to the Roman's
  side
Sent suddenly and well.

Then the great statue on the shield
Looked his last look around
With level and imperial eye;
And Mark, the man from Italy,
Fell in the sea of agony,
And died without a sound.

And Ogier, leaping up alive,
Hurled his huge shield away
Flying, as when a juggler flings
A whizzing plate in play.

And held two arms up rigidly,
And roared to all the Danes:
"Fallen is Rome, yea, fallen
The city of the plains!

"Shall no man born remember,
That breaketh wood or weald,
How long she stood on the roof of the
  world
As he stood on my shield.

"The new wild world forgetteth her
As foam fades on the sea,
How long she stood with her foot on
  Man
As he with his foot on me.

"No more shall the brown men of the
  south

Move like the ants in lines,
To quiet men with olives
Or madden men with vines.

"No more shall the white towns of
  the south,
Where Tiber and Nilus run,
Sitting around a secret sea
Worship a secret sun.

"The blind gods roar for Rome fallen,
And forum and garland gone,
For the ice of the north is broken,
And the sea of the north comes on.

"The blind gods roar and rave and
  dream
Of all cities under the sea,
For the heart of the north is broken,
And the blood of the north is free.

"Down from the dome of the world
  we come,
Rivers on rivers down,
Under us swirl the sects and hordes
And the high dooms we drown.

"Down from the dome of the world
  and down,
Struck flying as a skiff
On a river in spate is spun and
  swirled
Until we come to the end of the world
That breaks short, like a cliff.

"And when we come to the end of the
  world
For me, I count it fit
To take the leap like a good river,
Shot shrieking over it.

"But whatso hap at the end of the
  world,
Where Nothing is struck and sounds,
It is not, by Thor, these monkish men
These humbled Wessex hounds—

"Not this pale line of Christian hinds,
This one white string of men,
Shall keep us back from the end of the
  world,
And the things that happen then.

"It is not Alfred's dwarfish sword,
Nor Egbert's pigmy crown,
Shall stay us now that descend in
  thunder,
Rending the realms and the realms
  thereunder,
Down through the world and down."

There was that in the wild men back
  of him,
There was that in his own wild song,
A dizzy throbbing, a drunkard smoke,
That dazed to death all Wessex folk,
And swept their spears along.

Vainly the sword of Colan
And the axe of Alfred plied—

The Danes poured in like a brainless
  plague,
And knew not when they died.

Prince Colan slew a score of them,
And was stricken to his knee;
King Alfred slew a score and seven
And was borne back on a tree.

Back to the black gate of the woods,
Back up the single way,
Back by the place of the parting ways
Christ's knights were whirled away.

And when they came to the parting
  ways
Doom's heaviest hammer fell,
For the King was beaten, blind, at
  bay,
Down the right lane with his array,
But Colan swept the other way,
Where he smote great strokes and fell.

The thorn-woods over Ethandune
Stand sharp and thick as spears,
By night and furze and forest-harms
Far sundered were the friends in
  arms;
The loud lost blows, the last alarms,
Came not to Alfred's ears.

The thorn-woods over Ethandune
Stand stiff as spikes in mail;
As to the Haut King came at morn
Dead Roland on a doubtful horn,

Seemed unto Alfred lightly borne
The last cry of the Gael.

BOOK VII

Ethandune: The Last Charge

Away in the waste of White Horse
 Down
An idle child alone
Played some small game through
 hours that pass,
And patiently would pluck the grass,
Patiently push the stone.

On the lean, green edge for ever,
Where the blank chalk touched the turf,
The child played on, alone, divine,
As a child plays on the last line
That sunders sand and surf.

For he dwelleth in high divisions
Too simple to understand,
Seeing on what morn of mystery
The Uncreated rent the sea
With roarings, from the land.

Through the long infant hours like
 days
He built one tower in vain—
Piled up small stones to make a town,

And evermore the stones fell down,
And he piled them up again.

And crimson kings on battle-towers,
And saints on Gothic spires,
And hermits on their peaks of snow,
And heroes on their pyres,

And patriots riding royally,
That rush the rocking town,
Stretch hands, and hunger and aspire,
Seeking to mount where high and
 higher,
The child whom Time can never tire,
Sings over White Horse Down.

And this was the might of Alfred,
At the ending of the way;
That of such smiters, wise or wild,
He was least distant from the child,
Piling the stones all day.

For Eldred fought like a frank hunter
That killeth and goeth home;

And Mark had fought because all
  arms
Rang like the name of Rome.

And Colan fought with a double
  mind,
Moody and madly gay;
But Alfred fought as gravely
As a good child at play.

He saw wheels break and work run
  back
And all things as they were;
And his heart was orbed like victory
And simple like despair.

Therefore is Mark forgotten,
That was wise with his tongue and
  brave;
And the cairn over Colan crumbled,
And the cross on Eldred's grave.

Their great souls went on a wind
  away,
And they have not tale or tomb;
And Alfred born in Wantage
Rules England till the doom.

Because in the forest of all fears
Like a strange fresh gust from sea,
Struck him that ancient innocence
That is more than mastery.

And as a child whose bricks fall down
Re-piles them o'er and o'er,

Came ruin and the rain that burns,
Returning as a wheel returns,
And crouching in the furze and ferns
He began his life once more.

He took his ivory horn unslung
And smiled, but not in scorn:
"Endeth the Battle of Ethandune
With the blowing of a horn."

On a dark horse at the double way
He saw great Guthrum ride,
Heard roar of brass and ring of steel,
The laughter and the trumpet peal,
The pagan in his pride.

And Ogier's red and hated head
Moved in some talk or task;
But the men seemed scattered in the
  brier,
And some of them had lit a fire,
And one had broached a cask.

And waggons one or two stood up,
Like tall ships in sight,
As if an outpost were encamped
At the cloven ways for night.

And joyous of the sudden stay
Of Alfred's routed few,
Sat one upon a stone to sigh,
And some slipped up the road to fly,
Till Alfred in the fern hard by
Set horn to mouth and blew.

And they all abode like statues—
One sitting on the stone,
One half-way through the thorn
  hedge tall,
One with a leg across a wall,
And one looked backwards, very
  small,
Far up the road, alone.

Grey twilight and a yellow star
Hung over thorn and hill;
Two spears and a cloven war-shield
  lay
Loose on the road as cast away,
The horn died faint in the forest grey,
And the fleeing men stood still.

"Brothers at arms," said Alfred,
"On this side lies the foe;
Are slavery and starvation flowers,
That you should pluck them so?

"For whether is it better
To be prodded with Danish poles,
Having hewn a chamber in a ditch,
And hounded like a howling witch,
Or smoked to death in holes?

"Or that before the red cock crow
All we, a thousand strong,
Go down the dark road to God's house,
Singing a Wessex song?

"To sweat a slave to a race of slaves,
To drink up infamy?

No, brothers, by your leave, I think
Death is a better ale to drink,
And by all the stars of Christ that
  sink,
The Danes shall drink with me.

"To grow old cowed in a conquered
  land,
With the sun itself discrowned,
To see trees crouch and cattle slink—
Death is a better ale to drink,
And by high Death on the fell brink
That flagon shall go round.

"Though dead are all the paladins
Whom glory had in ken,
Though all your thunder-sworded
  thanes
With proud hearts died among the
  Danes,
While a man remains, great war
  remains:
Now is a war of men.

"The men that tear the furrows,
The men that fell the trees,
When all their lords be lost and dead
The bondsmen of the earth shall tread
The tyrants of the seas.

"The wheel of the roaring stillness
Of all labours under the sun,
Speed the wild work as well at least
As the whole world's work is done.

"Let Hildred hack the shield-wall
Clean as he hacks the hedge;
Let Gurth the fowler stand as cool
As he stands on the chasm's edge;

"Let Gorlias ride the sea-kings
As Gorlias rides the sea,
Then let all hell and Denmark drive,
Yelling to all its fiends alive,
And not a rag care we."

When Alfred's word was ended
Stood firm that feeble line,
Each in his place with club or spear,
And fury deeper than deep fear,
And smiles as sour as brine.

And the King held up the horn
  and said,
"See ye my father's horn,
That Egbert blew in his empery,
Once, when he rode out commonly,
Twice when he rode for venery,
And thrice on the battle-morn.

"But heavier fates have fallen
The horn of the Wessex kings,
And I blew once, the riding sign,
To call you to the fighting line
And glory and all good things.

"And now two blasts, the hunting sign,
Because we turn to bay;
But I will not blow the three blasts,
Till we be lost or they.

"And now I blow the hunting sign,
Charge some by rule and rod;
But when I blow the battle sign,
Charge all and go to God."

Wild stared the Danes at the double
  ways
Where they loitered, all at large,
As that dark line for the last time
Doubled the knee to charge—

And caught their weapons clumsily,
And marvelled how and why—
In such degree, by rule and rod,
The people of the peace of God
Went roaring down to die.

And when the last arrow
Was fitted and was flown,
When the broken shield hung on the
  breast,
And the hopeless lance was laid in rest,
And the hopeless horn blown,

The King looked up, and what he saw
Was a great light like death,
For Our Lady stood on the standards
  rent,
As lonely and as innocent
As when between white walls she
  went
And the lilies of Nazareth.

One instant in a still light
He saw Our Lady then,

Her dress was soft as western sky,
And she was a queen most
  womanly—
But she was a queen of men.

Over the iron forest
He saw Our Lady stand,
Her eyes were sad withouten art,
And seven swords were in her
  heart—
But one was in her hand.

Then the last charge went blindly,
And all too lost for fear:
The Danes closed round, a roaring
  ring,
And twenty clubs rose o'er the King,
Four Danes hewed at him, halloing,
And Ogier of the Stone and Sling
Drove at him with a spear.

But the Danes were wild with
  laughter,
And the great spear swung wide,
The point stuck to a straggling tree,
And either host cried suddenly,
As Alfred leapt aside.

Short time had shaggy Ogier
To pull his lance in line—
He knew King Alfred's axe on high,
He heard it rushing through the sky,

He cowered beneath it with a cry—
It split him to the spine:

And Alfred sprang over him dead,
And blew the battle sign.

Then bursting all and blasting
Came Christendom like death,
Kicked of such catapults of will,
The staves shiver, the barrels spill,
The waggons waver and crash and
  kill
The waggoners beneath.

Barriers go backwards, banners rend,
Great shields groan like a gong—
Horses like horns of nightmare
Neigh horribly and long.

Horses ramp high and rock and boil
And break their golden reins,
And slide on carnage clamorously,
Down where the bitter blood doth lie,
Where Ogier went on foot to die,
In the old way of the Danes.

"The high tide!" King Alfred cried.
"The high tide and the turn!
As a tide turns on the tall grey seas,
See how they waver in the trees,
How stray their spears, how knock
  their knees,
How wild their watchfires burn!

"The Mother of God goes over them,
Walking on wind and flame,
And the storm-cloud drifts from city
  and dale,

And the White Horse stamps in the
   White Horse Vale,
And we all shall yet drink Christian
   ale
In the village of our name.

"The Mother of God goes over them,
On dreadful cherubs borne;
And the psalm is roaring above the
   rune,
And the Cross goes over the sun and
   moon,
Endeth the battle of Ethandune
With the blowing of a horn."

For back indeed disorderly
The Danes went clamouring,
Too worn to take anew the tale,
Or dazed with insolence and ale,
Or stunned of heaven, or stricken pale
Before the face of the King.

For dire was Alfred in his hour
The pale scribe witnesseth,
More mighty in defeat was he
Than all men else in victory,
And behind, his men came
   murderously,
Dry-throated, drinking death.

And Edgar of the Golden Ship
He slew with his own hand,
Took Ludwig from his lady's bower,
And smote down Harmar in
   his hour,

And vain and lonely stood the
   tower—
The tower in Guelderland.

And Torr out of his tiny boat,
Whose eyes beheld the Nile,
Wulf with his war-cry on his lips,
And Harco born in the eclipse,
Who blocked the Seine with
   battleships
Round Paris on the Isle.

And Hacon of the Harvest-Song,
And Dirck from the Elbe he slew,
And Cnut that melted Durham bell
And Fulk and fiery Oscar fell,
And Goderic and Sigael,
And Uriel of the Yew.

And highest sang the slaughter,
And fastest fell the slain,
When from the wood-road's blacken-
   ing throat
A crowning and crashing wonder
   smote
The rear-guard of the Dane.

For the dregs of Colan's company—
Lost down the other road—
Had gathered and grown and heard
   the din,
And with wild yells came pouring in,
Naked as their old British kin,
And bright with blood for woad.

And bare and bloody and aloft
They bore before their band
The body of the mighty lord,
Colan of Caerleon and its horde,
That bore King Alfred's battle-sword
Broken in his left hand.

And a strange music went with him,
Loud and yet strangely far;
The wild pipes of the western land,
Too keen for the ear to understand,
Sang high and deathly on each hand
When the dead man went to war.

Blocked between ghost and buccaneer,
Brave men have dropped and died;
And the wild sea-lords well might
   quail
As the ghastly war-pipes of the Gael
Called to the horns of White Horse
   Vale,
And all the horns replied.

And Hildred the poor hedger
Cut down four captains dead,
And Halmar laid three others low,
And the great earls wavered to and
   fro
For the living and the dead.

And Gorlias grasped the great flag,
The Raven of Odin, torn;
And the eyes of Guthrum altered,
For the first time since morn.

As a turn of the wheel of tempest
Tilts up the whole sky tall,
And cliffs of wan cloud luminous
Lean out like great walls over us,
As if the heavens might fall.

As such a tall and tilted sky
Sends certain snow or light,
So did the eyes of Guthrum change,
And the turn was more certain and
   more strange
Than a thousand men in flight.

For not till the floor of the skies is split,
And hell-fire shines through the sea,
Or the stars look up through the rent
   earth's knees,
Cometh such rending of certainties,
As when one wise man truly sees
What is more wise than he.

He set his horse in the battle-breech
Even Guthrum of the Dane,
And as ever had fallen fell his brand,
A falling tower o'er many a land,
But Gurth the fowler laid one hand
Upon this bridle rein.

King Guthrum was a great lord,
And higher than his gods—
He put the popes to laughter,
He chid the saints with rods,

He took this hollow world of ours
For a cup to hold his wine;

In the parting of the woodways
There came to him a sign.

In Wessex in the forest,
In the breaking of the spears,
We set a sign on Guthrum
To blaze a thousand years.

Where the high saddles jostle
And the horse-tails toss,
There rose to the birds flying
A roar of dead and dying;
In deafness and strong crying
We signed him with the cross.

Far out to the winding river
The blood ran down for days,
When we put the cross on Guthrum
In the parting of the ways.

BOOK VIII

The Scouring of the Horse

In the years of the peace of Wessex,
When the good King sat at home;
Years following on that bloody boon
When she that stands above the moon
Stood above death at Ethandune
And saw his kingdom come—

When the pagan people of the sea
Fled to their palisades,
Nailed there with javelins to cling
And wonder smote the pirate king,
And brought him to his christening
And the end of all his raids.

(For not till the night's blue slate is
   wiped
Of its last star utterly,
And fierce new signs writ there to
   read,
Shall eyes with such amazement
   heed,
As when a great man knows indeed
A greater thing than he.)

And there came to his chrism-loosing
Lords of all lands afar,
And a line was drawn north-westerly
That set King Egbert's empire free,
Giving all lands by the northern sea
To the sons of the northern star.

In the days of the rest of Alfred,
When all these things were done,
And Wessex lay in a patch of peace,
Like a dog in a patch of sun—

The King sat in his orchard,
Among apples green and red,
With the little book in his bosom
And the sunshine on his head.

And he gathered the songs of simple
   men
That swing with helm and hod,
And the alms he gave as a Christian
Like a river alive with fishes ran;
And he made gifts to a beggar man
As to a wandering god.

And he gat good laws of the ancient
    kings,
Like treasure out of the tombs;
And many a thief in thorny nook,
Or noble in sea-stained turret shook,
For the opening of his iron book,
And the gathering of the dooms.

Then men would come from the ends
    of the earth,
Whom the King sat welcoming,
And men would go to the ends of the
    earth
Because of the word of the King.

For folk came in to Alfred's face
Whose javelins had been hurled
On monsters that make boil the sea,
Crakens and coils of mystery.
Or thrust in ancient snows that be
The white hair of the world.

And some had knocked at the north-
    ern gates
Of the ultimate icy floor,
Where the fish freeze and the foam
    turns black,
And the wide world narrows to a
    track,
And the other sea at the world's back
Cries through a closed door.

And men went forth from Alfred's
    face,
Even great gift-bearing lords,

Not to Rome only, but more bold,
Out to the high hot courts of old,
Of negroes clad in cloth of gold,
Silence, and crooked swords,

Scrawled screens and secret gardens
And insect-laden skies—
Where fiery plains stretch on and on
To the purple country of Prester John
And the walls of Paradise.

And he knew the might of the Terre
    Majeure,
Where kings began to reign;
Where in a night-rout, without
    name,
Of gloomy Goths and Gauls there
    came
White, above candles all aflame,
Like a vision, Charlemagne.

And men, seeing such embassies,
Spake with the King and said:
"The steel that sang so sweet a tune
On Ashdown and on Ethandune,
Why hangs it scabbarded so soon,
All heavily like lead?

"Why dwell the Danes in North
    England,
And up to the river ride?
Three more such marches like thine
    own
Would end them; and the Pict should
    own

Our sway; and our feet climb the
   throne
In the mountains of Strathclyde."

And Alfred in the orchard,
Among apples green and red,
With the little book in his bosom,
Looked at green leaves and said:

"When all philosophies shall fail,
This word alone shall fit;
That a sage feels too small for life,
And a fool too large for it.

"Asia and all imperial plains
Are too little for a fool;
But for one man whose eyes can see
The little island of Athelney
Is too large a land to rule.

"Haply it had been better
When I built my fortress there,
Out in the reedy waters wide,
I had stood on my mud wall and cried:
'Take England all, from tide to tide—
Be Athelney my share.'

"Those madmen of the
   throne-scramble—
Oppressors and oppressed—
Had lined the banks by Athelney,
And waved and wailed unceasingly,
Where the river turned to the broad
   sea,
By an island of the blest.

"An island like a little book
Full of a hundred tales,
Like the gilt page the good monks pen,
That is all smaller than a wren,
Yet hath high towns, meteors, and
   men,
And suns and spouting whales;

"A land having a light on it
In the river dark and fast,
An isle with utter clearness lit,
Because a saint had stood in it;
Where flowers are flowers indeed
   and fit,
And trees are trees at last.

"So were the island of a saint;
But I am a common king,
And I will make my fences tough
From Wantage Town to Plymouth
   Bluff,
Because I am not wise enough
To rule so small a thing."

And it fell in the days of Alfred,
In the days of his repose,
That as old customs in his sight
Were a straight road and a steady
   light,
He bade them keep the White Horse
   white
As the first plume of the snows.

And right to the red torchlight,
From the trouble of morning grey,

They stripped the White Horse of the
    grass
As they strip it to this day.

And under the red torchlight
He went dreaming as though dull,
Of his old companions slain like
    kings,
And the rich irrevocable things
Of a heart that hath not openings,
But is shut fast, being full.

And the torchlight touched the pale
    hair
Where silver clouded gold,
And the frame of his face was made
    of cords,
And a young lord turned among the
    lords
And said: "The King is old."

And even as he said it
A post ran in amain,
Crying: "Arm, Lord King, the hamlets
    arm,
In the horror and the shade of harm,
They have burnt Brand of Aynger's
    farm—
The Danes are come again!

"Danes drive the white East Angles
In six fights on the plains,
Danes waste the world about the
    Thames,
Danes to the eastward—Danes!"

And as he stumbled on one knee,
The thanes broke out in ire,
Crying: "Ill the watchmen watch,
    and ill
The sheriffs keep the shire."

But the young earl said: "Ill the
    saints,
The saints of England, guard
The land wherein we pledge them
    gold;
The dykes decay, the King grows old,
And surely this is hard,

"That we be never quit of them;
That when his head is hoar
He cannot say to them he smote,
And spared with a hand hard at the
    throat,
'Go, and return no more.'"

Then Alfred smiled. And the smile
    of him
Was like the sun for power.
But he only pointed: bade them heed
Those peasants of the Berkshire breed,
Who plucked the old Horse of the
    weed
As they pluck it to this hour.

"Will ye part with the weeds for ever?
Or show daisies to the door?
Or will you bid the bold grass
Go, and return no more?

"So ceaseless and so secret
Thrive terror and theft set free;
Treason and shame shall come to pass
While one weed flowers in a morass;
And like the stillness of stiff grass
The stillness of tyranny.

"Over our white souls also
Wild heresies and high
Wave prouder than the plumes of
   grass,
And sadder than their sigh.

"And I go riding against the raid,
And ye know not where I am;
But ye shall know in a day or year,
When one green star of grass grows
   here;
Chaos has charged you, charger and
   spear,
Battle-axe and battering-ram.

"And though skies alter and empires
   melt,
This word shall still be true:
If we would have the horse of old,
Scour ye the horse anew.

"One time I followed a dancing star
That seemed to sing and nod,
And ring upon earth all evil's knell;
But now I wot if ye scour not well
Red rust shall grow on God's great
   bell
And grass in the streets of God."

Ceased Alfred; and above his head
The grand green domes, the Downs,
Showed the first legions of the press,
Marching in haste and bitterness
For Christ's sake and the crown's.

Beyond the cavern of Colan,
Past Eldred's by the sea,
Rose men that owned King Alfred's
   rod,
From the windy wastes of Exe
   untrod,
Or where the thorn of the grave of
   God
Burns over Glastonbury.

Far northward and far westward
The distant tribes drew nigh,
Plains beyond plains, fell beyond fell,
That a man at sunset sees so well,
And the tiny coloured towns that
   dwell
In the corners of the sky.

But dark and thick as thronged the
   host,
With drum and torch and blade,
The still-eyed King sat pondering,
As one that watches a live thing,
The scoured chalk; and he said,

"Though I give this land to Our Lady,
That helped me in Athelney,
Though lordlier trees and lustier sod
And happier hills hath no flesh trod

Than the garden of the Mother of God
Between Thames side and the sea,

"*I know that weeds shall grow in it*
Faster than men can burn;
And though they scatter now and go,
In some far century, sad and slow,
I have a vision, and I know
The heathen shall return.

"*They shall not come with warships,*
They shall not waste with brands,
But books be all their eating,
And ink be on their hands.

"*Not with the humour of hunters*
Or savage skill in war,
But ordering all things with dead
  words,
Strings shall they make of beasts and
  birds,
And wheels of wind and star.

"*They shall come mild as monkish*
  clerks,
With many a scroll and pen;
And backward shall ye turn and gaze,
Desiring one of Alfred's days,
When pagans still were men.

"*The dear sun dwarfed of dreadful*
  suns,
Like fiercer flowers on stalk,
Earth lost and little like a pea
In high heaven's towering forestry,

—These be the small weeds ye shall see
Crawl, covering the chalk.

"*But though they bridge St. Mary's*
  sea,
Or steal St. Michael's wing—
Though they rear marvels over us,
Greater than great Vergilius
Wrought for the Roman king;

"*By this sign you shall know them,*
The breaking of the sword,
And man no more a free knight,
That loves or hates his lord.

"*Yea, this shall be the sign of them,*
The sign of the dying fire;
And Man made like a half-wit,
That knows not of his sire.

"*What though they come with scroll*
  and pen,
And grave as a shaven clerk,
By this sign you shall know them,
That they ruin and make dark;

"*By all men bond to Nothing,*
Being slaves without a lord,
By one blind idiot world obeyed,
Too blind to be abhorred;

"*By terror and the cruel tales*
Of curse in bone and kin,
By weird and weakness winning,
Accursed from the beginning,

By detail of the sinning,
And denial of the sin;

"By thought a crawling ruin,
By life a leaping mire,
By a broken heart in the breast of the
 world,
And the end of the world's desire;

"By God and man dishonoured,
By death and life made vain,
Know ye the old barbarian,
The barbarian come again—

"When is great talk of trend and tide,
And wisdom and destiny,
Hail that undying heathen
That is sadder than the sea.

"In what wise men shall smite him,
Or the Cross stand up again,
Or charity or chivalry,
My vision saith not; and I see
No more; but now ride doubtfully
To the battle of the plain."

And the grass-edge of the great down
Was cut clean as a lawn,
While the levies thronged from near
 and far,
From the warm woods of the western
 star,
And the King went out to his last
 war
On a tall grey horse at dawn.

And news of his far-off fighting
Came slowly and brokenly
From the land of the East Saxons,
From the sunrise and the sea.

From the plains of the white sunrise,
And sad St. Edmund's crown,
Where the pools of Essex pale and
 gleam
Out beyond London Town—

In mighty and doubtful fragments,
Like faint or fabled wars,
Climbed the old hills of his renown,
Where the bald brow of White Horse
 Down
Is close to the cold stars.

But away in the eastern places
The wind of death walked high,
And a raid was driven athwart the
 raid,
The sky reddened and the smoke
 swayed,
And the tall grey horse went by.

The gates of the great river
Were breached as with a barge,
The walls sank crowded, say the
 scribes,
And high towers populous with tribes
Seemed leaning from the charge.

Smoke like rebellious heavens rolled
Curled over coloured flames,

Mirrored in monstrous purple dreams
In the mighty pools of Thames.

Loud was the war on London wall,
And loud in London gates,
And loud the sea-kings in the cloud
Broke through their dreaming gods,
    and loud
Cried on their dreadful Fates.

And all the while on White Horse
    Hill
The horse lay long and wan,
The turf crawled and the fungus crept,
And the little sorrel, while all men
    slept,
Unwrought the work of man.

With velvet finger, velvet foot,
The fierce soft mosses then
Crept on the large white commonweal
All folk had striven to strip and peel,
And the grass, like a great green
    witch's wheel,
Unwound the toils of men.

And clover and silent thistle throve,
And buds burst silently,
With little care for the Thames Valley
Or what things there might be—

That away on the widening river,
In the eastern plains for crown
Stood up in the pale purple sky
One turret of smoke like ivory;
And the smoke changed and the wind
    went by,
And the King took London Town.

Made in the USA
Monee, IL
07 May 2020